American War

American War

Omar El Akkad

Alfred A. Knopf
New York
2017

THIS IS A BORZOI BOOK
PUBLISHED BY ALFRED A. KNOPF

www.aaknopf.com

Library of Congress Cataloging-in-Publication Control Number: 2016042308
ISBN 978-0-451-49358-3 (hardcover)
ISBN 978-0-451-49359-0 (ebook)
ISBN 978-1-5247-1118-4 (open market)

Jacket design by Peter Mendelsund
Maps by David Lindroth

Manufactured in the United States of America

Published April 4, 2017

Second Printing, August 2017

To my father

The one you must punish is the one who punishes you.

—*Kitab al-Aghani* (*The Book of Songs*)

Mine heritage is unto me as a speckled bird, the birds round about are against her; come ye, assemble all the beasts of the field, come to devour.

—*Jeremiah* 12:9

American War

The United States, circa 2075

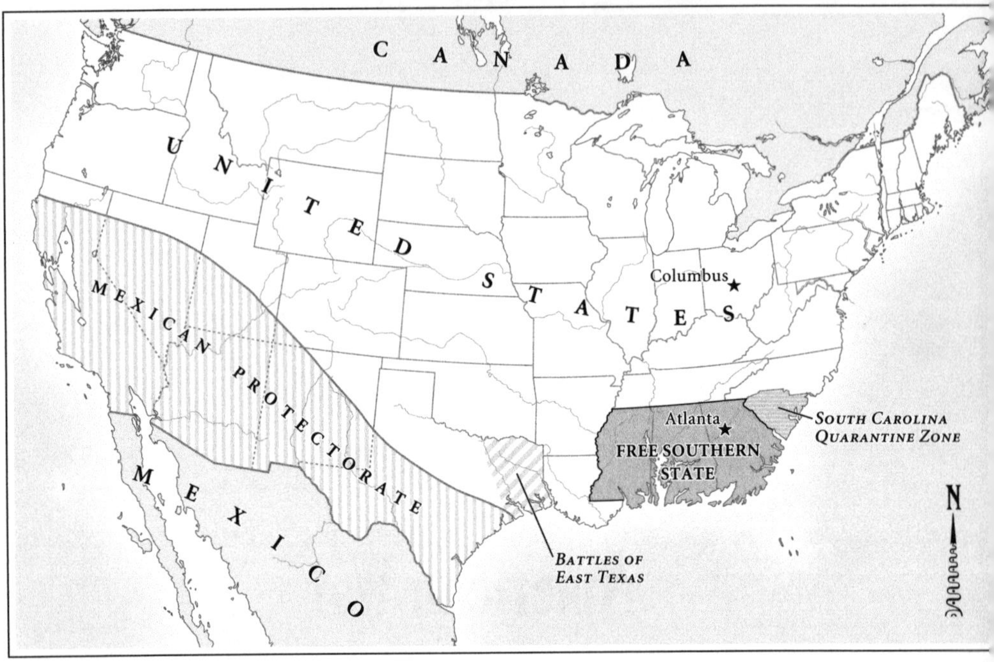

The Free Southern State, circa 2075

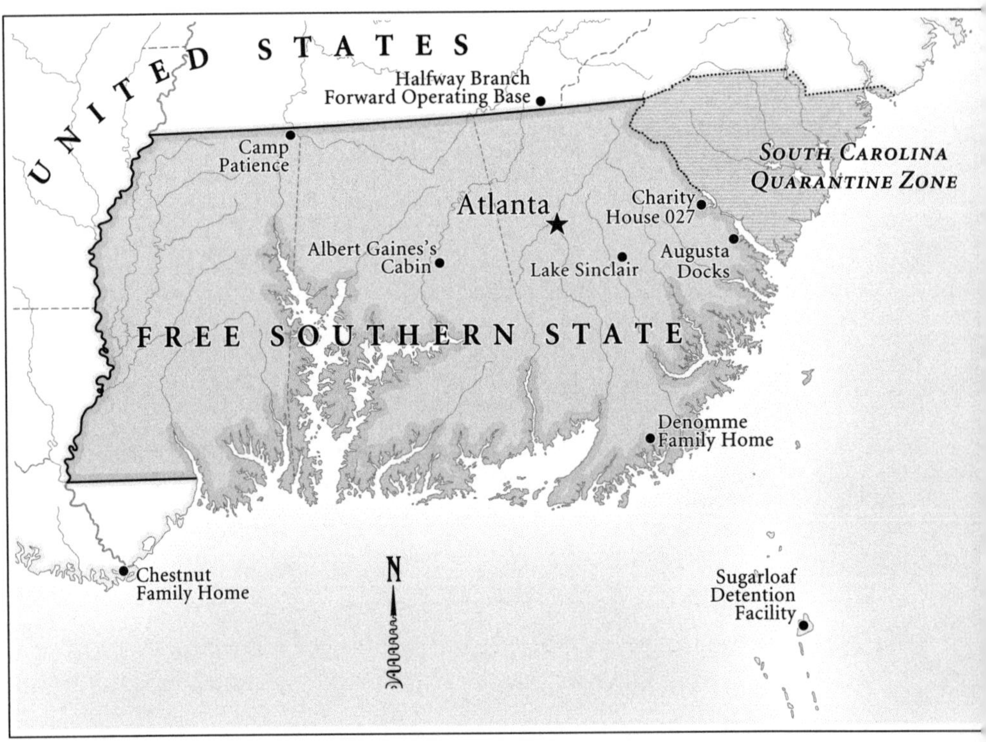

PROLOGUE

When I was young, I collected postcards. I kept them in a shoebox under my bed in the orphanage. Later, when I moved into my first home in New Anchorage, I stored the shoebox at the bottom of an old oil drum in my crumbling toolshed. Having spent most of my life studying the history of war, I found some sense of balance in collecting snapshots of the world that was, idealized and serene.

Sometimes I thought about getting rid of the oil drum. I worried someone, a colleague from the university perhaps, would see it and think it a kind of petulant political statement, like the occasional secessionist flag or gutted muscle car outside houses in the old Red country—impotent trinkets of rebellion, touchstones of a ruined and ruinous past. I am, after all, a Southerner by birth. And even though I arrived in neutral country at the age of six and never spoke to anyone about my life before then, I couldn't rule out the possibility that some of my colleagues secretly believed I still had a little bit of rebel Red in my blood.

My favorite postcards are from the 2030s and 2040s, the last decades before the planet turned on the country and the country turned on itself. They featured pictures of the great ocean beaches before rising waters took them; images of the Southwest before it turned to embers; photographs of the Midwestern plains, endless and empty under bluest sky, before the Inland Exodus filled them with the coastal displaced. A visual reminder of America as it existed in the first half of the twenty-first century: soaring, roaring, oblivious.

I remember the first postcard I bought. It was a photo of old Anchorage. The city's waterfront is thick with fresh snowfall, the water speckled with shelves of ice, the sun low-strung behind the mountains.

I was six years old when I saw my first real Alaskan sunset. I stood on the deck of the smuggler's skiff, a sun-bitten Georgia boy, a refugee. I remember feeling the strange white flakes on my eyelashes, the involuntary rattle of my teeth—feeling, for the first time in my life, cold. I saw near the tops of the mountains that frozen yolk suspended in the sky and thought I had reached the very terminus of the living world. The very end of movement.

☆ ☆ ☆

I BELONG TO WHAT they call the Miraculous Generation: those born in the years between the start of the Second American Civil War in 2074 and its end in 2095. Some extend the definition further, including those born during the decade-long plague that followed the end of the war. This country has a long history of defining its generations by the conflicts that should have killed them, and my generation is no exception. We are the few who escaped the wrath of the homicide bombers and the warring Birds; the few who were spirited into well-stocked cellars or tornado shelters before the Reunification Plague spread across the continent. The few who were just plain lucky.

I've spent my professional career studying this country's bloody war with itself. I've written academic papers and magazine articles, headlined myriad symposiums and workshops. I've studied all the surviving source documents: congressional reports, oral histories, harrowing testimony of the plague's survivors. I've reconstructed the infamous events of Reunification Day, when one of the South's last remaining rebels managed to sneak into the Union capital and unleash the sickness that cast the country into a decade of death. It is estimated that eleven million people died in the war, and almost ten times that number in the plague that followed.

I've received countless letters from readers and critics taking issue with all manner of historical minutiae—whether the rebels were really responsible for a particular homicide bombing; whether the Massacre at Such-and-Such really was as bad as the Southern propagandists claim. My files contain hundreds of such correspondences, all variations on the same theme: that I, a coddled New Anchorage Northerner, a neutral country elite who'd never seen a day of real fighting, don't know the first thing about the war.

But there are things I know that nobody else knows. I know because she told me. And my knowing makes me complicit.

☆ ☆ ☆

5

NOW, AS I NEAR the end of my life, I've been inspecting the accumulated miscellanea of my youth. Recently I found that first postcard I bought. It's been more than a hundred years since its photograph was taken; all but the sea and the mountains are gone. New Anchorage, a sprawl of low buildings and affluent suburbs nestled at the foot of the hills, has moved further inland over the years. The docks where I once arrived as a disoriented war orphan have been raised and reinforced time and time again. And where once there stood wharfs of knotted wood, there are now modular platforms, designed to be dismantled and relocated quickly. Fierce storms come without warning.

Sometimes I stroll along the New Anchorage waterfront, past the wharf and the harbor. It's the closest I can come now to my original arrival point in the neutral country without renting a scavenger's boat. My doctor says it's good to walk regularly and that I should try to keep doing so as long as it doesn't cause me pain. I suspect this is the sort of harmless pabulum he feeds all his terminal patients, those who long ago graduated from "This will help" to "This can't hurt."

It's a strange thing to be dying. For so long I thought the end of my life would come suddenly, when the plague found its way north to the neutral country, or the Red rebelled once more and we were plunged into another bout of fratricide. Instead, I've been sentenced to that most ordinary of deaths, an overabundance of malfunctioning cells. I read once that a moderately ravenous cancer is, in a pragmatic sense, a decent way to die—not so prolonged as to entail years of suffering, but affording enough time that one might have a chance to make the necessary arrangements, to say what needs to be said.

☆ ☆ ☆

IT HASN'T SNOWED in years, but every now and then in late January we'll get a fractal of frost crawling up the windows. On those days I like to go out to the waterfront and watch my breath hang in the air. I feel unburdened. I am no longer afraid.

I stand at the edge of the boardwalk and watch the water. I think of all the things it has taken, and all that was taken from me. Sometimes I stare out at the sea for hours, well past dark, until I am elsewhere in time and elsewhere in place: back in the battered Red country where I was born.

And that's when I see her again, rising out of the water. She is exactly as I remember her, a hulking bronzed body, her back lined with ashen scars, each one a testimony to the torture she was made to endure, the secret crimes committed against her. She rises, a flesh monolith reborn from the severed belly of the Savannah. And I am a child again, yet to be taken from my parents and my home, yet to be betrayed. I am back home by the riverbank and I am happy and I still love her. My secret is I still love her.

This isn't a story about war. It's about ruin.

I

April, 2075
St. James, Louisiana

mydentist, Bath Lane, Mansfield
23 Bath Lane
Mansfield
Nottinghamshire
NG18 2BU
Tel: 01623 626015

Printed on 15/07/2019

RECEIPT OF PAYMENT

Patient Name: Mr P Bradbury
Our Ref: 1030802
Address: 9 Woodlands Park
Rainworth
Notts
NG21 0bt

Amount of: £25.70
Received on: 15/07/2019

For payment to the above account

CHAPTER ONE

I *was happy then.*

☆ ☆ ☆

THE SUN BROKE THROUGH a pilgrimage of clouds and cast its unblinking eye upon the Mississippi Sea.

The coastal waters were brown and still. The sea's mouth opened wide over ruined marshland, and every year grew wider, the water picking away at the silt and sand and clay, until the old riverside plantations and plastics factories and marine railways became unstable. Before the buildings slid into the water for good, they were stripped of their usable parts by the delta's last holdout residents. The water swallowed the land. To the southeast, the once glorious city of New Orleans became a well within the walls of its levees. The baptismal rites of a new America.

A little girl, six years old, sat on the porch of her family's home under a clapboard awning. She held a plastic container of honey, which was made in the shape of a bear. From the top of its head golden liquid slid out onto the cheap pine floorboard.

The girl poured the honey into the wood's deep knots and watched the serpentine manner in which the liquid took to the contours of its new surroundings. This is her earliest memory, the moment she begins.

And this is how, in those moments when the bitterness subsides, I choose to remember her. A child.

I wish I had known her then, in those years when she was still unbroken.

"Sara Chestnut, what do you think you're doing?" said the girl's mother, standing behind her near the door of the shipping container in which the Chestnuts made their home. "What did I tell you about wasting what's not yours to waste?"

"Sorry, Mama."

"Did you work to buy that honey, hmm? No, I didn't think you did.

Go get your sister and get your butt to breakfast before your daddy leaves."

"OK, Mama," the girl said, handing back the half-empty container. She ducked past her mother, who patted dirt from the seat of her fleur-de-lis dress.

Her name was Sara T. Chestnut but she called herself Sarat. The latter was born of a misunderstanding at the schoolhouse earlier that year. The new kindergarten teacher accidentally read the girl's middle initial as the last letter of her first name—*Sarat.* To the little girl's ears, the new name had a bite to it. Sara ended with an impotent exhale, a fading *ahh* that disappeared into the air. *Sarat* snapped shut like a bear trap. A few months later, the school shut down, most of the teachers and students forced northward by the encroaching war. But the name stuck.

Sarat.

A HUNDRED FEET from the western riverbank, the Chestnuts lived in a corrugated steel container salvaged from a nearby shipyard. Wedges of steel plating anchored to cement blocks below the ground held the home in place. At the corners, a brown rust crept slowly outward, incubated in ceaseless humidity.

A lattice of old-fashioned solar panels lined the entirety of the roof, save for one corner occupied by a rainwater tank. A tarp rested near the panels. When storms approached, the tarp was pulled over the roof with ropes tied to its ends and laced through hooks. By guiding the rainfall away from the panels to the tank and, when it overfilled, toward the land and river below, the family was able to collect drinking water and defend their home from rust and decay.

Sometimes, during winter storms, the family took shelter on the porch, where the awning sagged and leaked, but spared them the unbearable acoustics of the shipping container under heavy rain, which sounded like the bowl of a calypso drum.

In the summer, when their house felt like a steel kiln, the family spent much of their time outdoors. It was during this extended season, which burned from March through mid-December, that Sarat, her fraternal twin, Dana, and her older brother, Simon, experienced their purest instances of childhood joy. Under the distant watch of their parents, the children would fill buckets of water from the river and use them to drench the clay embankment until it became a slide. Entire afternoons and evenings were spent this way: the children careening down the greased earth into the river and climbing back up with the aid of a knotted rope; squealing with delight on the way down, their backsides leaving deep grooves in the clay.

In a coop behind the house the family kept an emaciated clutch of chickens. They were loud and moved nervously, their feathers dirty and brown. When they were fed and the weather was not too hot, they produced eggs. In other times, if they were on the edge of revolt or death, they were preemptively slaughtered, their necks pinned down between the nails in a nearby stump.

The shipping container was segmented by standing clapboards. Benjamin and Martina Chestnut lived in the back of the home. Nine-year-old Simon and the six-year-old twins shared the middle third, living in a peace that grew more and more uneasy by the day.

In the final third of the home there was a small kitchen table of sand-colored plywood, smeared and notched from years of heavy use. Near the table a pine pantry and jelly cabinet held sweet potatoes, rice, bags of chips and sugar cereal, pecans, flour, and pebbles of grain milled from the sorghum fields that separated the Chestnuts from their nearest neighbor. In a compact fridge that burdened the solar panels, the family kept milk and butter and cans of old Coke.

By the front door, a statue from the days of Benjamin's childhood kept vigil. It was the Virgin of Guadalupe, cast in ceramic, her hands pressed against each other, her head lowered in prayer. A beaded bouquet of yellow tickseed and white water lilies lay at her feet, alongside a melted, magnolia-scented candle. When the flowers died and hardened the children were sent out to the fields to find more.

Sarat skipped past the statue, looking for her sister. She found her in the back of the house, standing on her parents' bed, inspecting with steel concentration her reflection in the oval vanity mirror. She had taken one of her mother's house dresses, a simple sleeveless tunic whose violet color held despite countless washings. The little girl wore the top half of the dress, which covered the entirety of her frame; the rest of the garment slid limply off the bed and onto the floor. She had applied, far too generously, her mother's cherry red lipstick—the jewel of the simple makeup set her mother owned but rarely used. Despite employing utmost delicacy, Dana could not keep within the lines of her small pink lips, and looked now as though she'd hastily eaten a strawberry pie.

"Come play with me," Sarat said, confounded by what her twin was doing.

Dana turned to her sister, annoyed. "I'm busy," she said.

"But I'm bored."

"I'm being a lady!"

Dana returned to her mirror, trying to wipe some of the lipstick with the back of her hand.

"Mama says we have to go have breakfast with Daddy now."

"OK, oh-*kay,*" Dana said. "Not a moment peace in this house," she added, misquoting a thing she'd heard her mother say on occasion.

Sarat was the second-born girl, five and a half minutes behind her sister. And although she'd been told by her parents that both she and Dana were made of the same flesh, Dana was her father's girl, with his easygoing wit and sincere smile. Sarat was made of her mother: stubborn, hard, undaunted by calamity. They were twins but they were not alike. Sarat often heard her mother use the word *tomboy* to describe her. God gave me two children at once, she said, but only girl enough for one.

☆ ☆ ☆

FOR A FEW MINUTES, after Dana had left, Sarat remained in her parents' room. She observed with some confusion the thing her sister had smeared all over her lips. Unlike the river and the bush and the beasts and birds of the natural world, the lipstick did not interest her; it held no promise of adventure. She knew it only as a prop in her twin sister's ongoing obsession with adulthood. Why Dana wished so desperately to join the ranks of the fully grown, Sarat could not understand.

Dana emerged from the house, still draped in her mother's clothes.

"Didn't I tell you not to go opening my dresser?" Martina said.

"Sorry, Mama."

"Don't sorry me—and pull it up, you're dragging dirt everywhere." Martina pulled the dress off her daughter. "I send your sister in to get you, and now you're out here looking like a mess, and she's inside probably doing the same."

"She can't put makeup on," said Dana. "She's ugly."

Martina knelt down and grabbed her daughter by the shoulders. "Don't ever say that, you hear me? Don't ever call her ugly, don't ever say a bad word about her. She's your sister. She's a beautiful girl."

Dana lowered her head and pouted. Martina cupped her jaw and lifted her head back up.

"Listen to me," she said. "You go back inside and you tell her. You tell her she's a beautiful girl."

Dana stomped back inside the house. She found her sister putting her mother's lipstick back in the makeup box.

"You're a beautiful girl," Dana said, and stormed out of the room.

For a moment, Sarat stood dumbstruck. She was a child still and the purpose of a lie eluded her. She couldn't yet fathom that someone would say something if they didn't believe it. She smiled.

☆ ☆ ☆

OUTSIDE, Martina cooked breakfast on a heavy firewood stove. On the plates and in the bowls there were hard biscuits and sorghum cereal and fried eggs and imitation pepper bacon cooked till crisp in its own fat.

In her slumping cheeks and dark-circled eyes, Martina's thirty-nine years were plainly visible—more so than in the face of her husband, although he was five years her senior and the two of them had lived half their lives together. She was wide around her midsection but not obese, with an organic rural fitness that made her able, when it was necessary, to lift heavy loads and walk long distances. Unlike her husband, who had sneaked into the country from Mexico as a child back when the flow of migrants still moved northward, she was not an immigrant. She was born into the place she lived.

"Breakfast!" Martina shouted, wiping the sweat from her brow with a ragged dish towel. "Get over here now, all of you. I won't say it again."

Benjamin emerged from behind the house, freshly shaven and showered in the family's outdoor stall.

"Hurry up and eat before he gets here," Martina said.

"It's all right, relax," her husband replied. "When's he ever been on time?"

"Where's your good tie?"

"It's not a job interview, just a work permit. I'm only going to a government office; no different than the post office."

"When was the last time people killed one another to get something from a post office?"

Benjamin sat at the table in the yard. He was a lean man with a lean face, his near-touching brows anchoring a smooth, large forehead made larger by setting baldness at the temples. He was at all times clean-shaven, save for a thin black mustache his wife worried made him look unseemly.

He kissed Sarat on the forehead and, when he saw his other daughter, her face smeared with red, kissed her too.

"Your girls been at it again," Martina said. "Won't learn manners, won't do what they're told."

Benjamin shook his head at Dana with mock disapproval, then he leaned close to her ear.

"I think it looks good on you," he whispered.

"Thanks, Daddy," Dana whispered back.

The family assembled around the table. Martina called out for Simon and soon he came around the front porch, carrying in his hands the recently sawed bottom half of the family's ten-rung ladder.

Seeing the look on his mother's face, the eight-year-old blurted, "Dad asked me to do it."

Martina turned to her husband, who bit happily into the bacon and drank the sour, grainy coffee. It was rancid stuff from the ration packs, designed to keep soldiers awake.

"Don't look at me like that. Smith needs a ladder," Benjamin said. "Got new shingles to put up; old ones have all gone to mush."

"So you're going to give him half of ours?"

"It's a fair enough deal, considering he's the one who knows the man at the permit office. Without him, we may as well try to shoot our way across the border."

"He's got enough money to buy himself a million ladders," said Martina. "I thought you said he was doing us a favor."

Benjamin chuckled. "A Northern work permit for half a ladder is still a favor."

Martina poured the last of her coffee in the dirt. "We need to get up and fix our roof just the same as the Smiths," she said.

"We don't need any more than a five-rung ladder to do it," Benjamin replied, "especially now that our own boy's grown tall and strong enough to get himself up there."

It was a point with which Simon vehemently agreed, promising his mother he'd climb up regularly to add chlorine to the tank and clean the bird droppings from the solar panels, just like his father did.

The family ate together. Benjamin, rail-thin his whole life, inhaled the bacon and eggs with shameless appetite. His son looked on, cataloguing his father's every minute ritual into an ironclad manual of what it means to be a man. Soon the boy too had wiped his plate clean.

The twins sipped orange juice from plastic cups and picked at their biscuits until their mother softened the bread with a smear of butter and apricot jam, and then they ate quietly, deep in guarded thought.

Martina watched her husband, her eyes still and silent, a look her children mistook for hardness but her husband knew to be just how she was.

Finally she said, "Don't tell them nothing about doing any work for the Free Southerners."

"It's no secret," Benjamin replied. "They know full well every man around these parts has done some work for the Free Southerners. Doesn't mean I picked up a rifle for them."

"But you don't have to say it. If you say it then they have to check one of the boxes on the form and take you into another room and ask you all kinds of other questions. And then in the end they won't give you a permit on account of security reasons or whatever they call it. Just say you work in the shirt factory. That's not a lie."

"Quit worrying so much," Benjamin said, leaning back in his seat and picking the stray meat from between his teeth. "They'll give us a permit. The North needs workers, we need work."

Simon interjected, "Why do we need to go to the North? We don't know anybody up there."

"They got jobs there," his mother replied. "They got schools there.

You're always complaining about not having enough toys, enough friends, enough everything. Well, up there they have plenty."

"Connor says going to the North is for traitors. Says they should hang."

Sarat listened intently to the conversation, filing the strange new word in her mind. *Traitors.* It sounded exotic. A foreign tribe, perhaps.

"Don't talk like that," Martina said. "You going to listen to your mother or a ten-year-old boy?"

Simon looked down at his plate and mumbled, "Connor's dad told him."

They finished eating and retreated to the porch. Martina sat on the steps and cleaned the lipstick from her daughter's face with a wet dishrag, the girl squirming and whining. Simon smoothed the ends of the half-ladder with a sandpaper block, putting his whole weight into the job, until his father told him he didn't have to work it so hard.

Sarat returned to the scene of her morning experiment, poking at the congealed honey thick in the knots of the wood, enthralled by the amber liquid's viscosity. It fascinated her, how the thing so readily took the shape of its vessel. With her pinky she cracked the crust and tasted a dollop. She expected the honey to taste like wood, but it still tasted like itself.

Benjamin sat on a hickory chair, the weaves of its backrest frayed and peeling. He looked out at the brown, barren river and waited on his patron to arrive.

"Do you know what you're going to say to them, at the permit place?" Martina asked. "Have you thought it through?"

"I'll answer what they ask."

"You got your papers ready?"

"I got my papers ready."

Martina shook her head and cast an eye out for signs of an incoming boat. "Probably there won't even be any permits," she said. "Probably they'll do what they always do and turn us back. That's their way, don't give a damn about nobody south of the Mag line. It's like we aren't human, aren't animal even, like we're something else entirely. They'll just turn you back, I know it."

Benjamin shrugged. "Do you want me to go or not?"

"You know I do."

When she was done wiping the lipstick, Martina set to braiding Dana's hair. It came down in long, smooth strands of the deepest black, unlike Sarat's, which although the same color, was unruly and revolted to fuzz in the humidity.

"You girls know what the best thing about the North is?" she asked.

"What?" Sarat replied.

"Well, you know how at night here it gets so hot you just can't take it, and you wake up with your sheets all damp with sweat?"

"I hate that," Dana said.

"Well when you get far enough north, it never gets hot that way. And in the winter, if you go really far north, they don't even have rain—they have little balls of ice that drop from the sky, and the ground gets all thick with it till you can't see the roads anymore, and the rivers get so cold they turn to solid rock you can walk on."

"That's silly," Dana said. In her mind, these were more of her parents' elaborate fairy tales, the hardening rivers and falling ice no different than the fish with whiskers that her father said once swam in great schools through the lifeless Mississippi back when it was just a river, or the ancient lizards buried in the deserts to the west, whose remains once powered the world. Dana didn't believe any of it.

But Sarat did. Sarat believed every word.

"It's true," Martina said. "Cool in the summer, cool in the winter. *Temperate,* they call it. And safe too. Kids out in the streets playing till late at night; you'll make friends your first day there."

Simon shook his head quietly. He knew that even as she talked to the twins, his mother was really addressing him. With everyone else she spoke directly, with no sentimentality or euphemism. But to her only son, whose inner mental workings she feared she would never learn to decipher, she passed messages through intermediaries in weak, obvious code. Simon hated it. Why couldn't she be like his father? he wondered. Why couldn't she simply say what she meant?

☆ ☆ ☆

BY MID-MORNING, Benjamin's ride had yet to appear. Soon Martina began to believe her husband had been forgotten. Or perhaps Benjamin's acquaintance had finally been caught in that old fossil-powered boat of his and had been arrested. It was true that the states surrounding the rebel Red—a cocoon formed by Louisiana, Arkansas, Tennessee, and North Carolina—were deeply sympathetic to the cause of the Free Southern State. And even though residents of these states still required a permit to move north to the real heart of the Blue country, the states were officially members of the Union nonetheless, and a man caught using fossil fuel in these parts was still an outlaw.

She thought about how much easier it would be for everyone if all these would-be statelets were simply allowed to break free from the Union, to form their own miniature nations along the fault lines of region or creed or race or ideology. Everyone knew there had always been fissures: in the Northwest they were constantly threatening to declare the independence of the proud, pacifist Cascadia; south of Cascadia so much of California, Nevada, Arizona, and West Texas was already under the informal control of the Mexican forces, the map of that corner of the continent slowly reverting to what it was hundreds of years ago. In the Midwest the old-stock nativists harbored a barely restrained animosity toward the millions of coastal refugees who descended onto the middle of the country to escape rising seas and severe storms. And here, in the South, an entire region decided to wage war again, to sever itself from the Union rather than stop using that illicit fuel responsible for so much of the country's misfortune.

Sometimes it seemed to Martina that there had never been a Union at all, that long ago some disinterested or opportunistic party had drawn lines on a map where previously there were none, and in the process created a single country fashioned from many different countries. How bad would it really be, she wondered, if the federal government in Columbus simply stopped wasting so much money and blood trying to hold the fractured continent together? Let the Southerners keep their outdated fuel, she thought, until they've pulled every last drop of it from the beaten ground.

Martina watched the river and waited for the boat to come. She saw Sarat near the water, inspecting a discarded shrimp net that had washed up onshore a few months earlier; the children had made from it a makeshift trap for river debris. The net collected all manner of strange treasure: an iron cross, a neck-rest from a barber's chair, a laminated picture of a long-shuttered leper colony, a small sign that read, "Please No Profanity In The Canteen."

Sarat inspected the soggy pages of a waterlogged book caught in the net. The book's title was *The Changing Earth.* Its cover featured a picture of a huge blue mountain of floating ice. She leafed gingerly through the pages, peeling them from one another. The book was filled with maps of the world, old and new. The new maps looked like the old ones, but with the edges of the land shaved off—whole islands gone, coastlines retreating into their continents. In the old maps America looked bigger.

She saw the shadow of her brother, Simon, standing behind her. "What is it?" he said, snatching at the book.

"None of your business," Sarat replied. "I found it first." She pulled the book away and hopped to her feet, ready to fight him for it if she had to.

"Whatever," Simon said. "I don't even want it, it's just a dumb book." But she could see him inspecting the open page.

"Do you even know what that is?" he asked.

"It's maps," Sarat said. "I know what maps are."

Simon pointed to a corner of the page where the blue of water seemed to overwhelm a few thin shreds of land on the southern edge of the continent.

"That's us, stupid," he said. "That's where we live."

Sarat looked at the place on the map where Simon pointed. It looked wholly abstract, in no way reminiscent of her home.

"You see all that water?" Simon said. "That all used to be land, and now it's gone." He pointed back in the direction of their house. "And one day this'll all be water too. We'll have to get out of here or else we'll drown."

Sarat saw the faint smirk on her brother's face and knew instantly he was trying to scare her. She wondered why he seemed so obsessed with such tricks, why he so often tried to say things in the hopes of making her react in some fearful or foolish way. He was three years older than she was, and a boy—a different species altogether. But still she sensed in her brother a kind of insecurity, as though trying to scare her was not some cruel way to pass the time, but a vital means of proving something to himself. She wondered if all boys were like this, their meanness a self-defense.

And anyway, she knew he was a liar. The water would never eat their home. Maybe the rest of Louisiana, maybe the rest of the world, but never *their* home. Their home would remain on dry land, because that was the way it had always been.

☆ ☆ ☆

LATE IN THE MORNING, Benjamin's acquaintance, Alder Smith, arrived. He was four hours late. His plywood fishing skiff bobbed softly on the parting water, its outboard motor gurgling and coughing fumes. It was an archaic thing, but still faster and nimbler than the Sea-Toks, whose feeble, solar-fed motors barely beat the current.

It said something to own a vehicle that still ran on prohibition fuel; it spoke not only of accumulated wealth, but of connections, of status.

"Mornin'," Smith said as he ushered the boat to the foot of the Chestnuts' landing, throwing a loop of nylon around the docking pole. Like Benjamin, he was tall, but boasted broader shoulders and a full head of brown hair made copper by too much time in the sun. Before the war his father owned a dozen fossil car dealerships between New Orleans and Baton Rouge. Those businesses were now long gone but the wealth they bore still lingered, and Smith lived a comfortable life on the other side of the river. Among the families that still dotted the flooded south of Louisiana and Mississippi, he was known as a facilitator, a man who had plenty of friends. He knew Free Southern State government men in Atlanta and the smugglers who ran the tunnels across the Mississippi-Arkansas line; he knew consuls in the federal offices that dotted the tamed and broken parts of the Union-aligned South. He even claimed to know the right-hand men of senators and congressmen in the federal capital in Columbus.

"Mornin'," Martina replied. "Come on up, we got some sandwiches left, coffee too."

"Thank you kindly, but we're already late. Come on, Ben. Blues don't like waiting."

Benjamin kissed his wife and children goodbye and stepped inside to kiss the feet of the ceramic Virgin. He descended to the river with great care so as to keep from slipping in the clay and dirtying his good pants. He carried with him his old leather briefcase and the half-ladder. His wife watched from the edge of the flat land.

“Dock south and walk into the city,” she told the men. “Don’t let any government people see that boat.”

Smith laughed and started the motor. “Don’t you worry,” he said. “This time next week you’ll be halfway to Chicago.”

“Just be good,” Martina said. “Be careful, I mean.”

The men pushed the skiff from the mud and pointed the hull north in the direction of Baton Rouge. The boat rumbled into the narrowing heart of the great brown river, twin spines of water rising and spreading in its wake.

Excerpted from:

FEDERAL SYLLABUS GUIDELINES— HISTORY, MODULE EIGHT: THE SECOND CIVIL WAR

MODULE SUMMARY:

The Second American Civil War took place between the years of 2074 and 2095. The war was fought between the Union and the secessionist states of Mississippi, Alabama, Georgia, and South Carolina (as well as Texas, prior to the Mexican annexation). The primary cause of the war was Southern resistance to the Sustainable Future Act, a bill prohibiting the use of fossil fuels anywhere in the United States. The bill, championed by President Daniel Ki, was in part a response to decades of adverse climate effects, the waning economic importance of fossil fuels, and a deadly oil train derailment in Williston, North Dakota, in 2069.

The war's key precipitating events include the assassination of President Ki by secessionist suicide bomber Julia Templestowe in Jackson, Mississippi, in December of 2073, and the deaths of Southern protesters in a shooting outside the Fort Jackson, South Carolina, military base in March of 2074.

The secessionist states (unified under the banner of "The Free Southern State") declared independence on October 1, 2074, the date often considered to mark the formal start of the war. Following a series of decisive Union military victories in the first five years of the war—primarily in East Texas and along the northern borders of Mississippi, Alabama, and Georgia ("The Mag")—the fighting largely subsided. However, rebel insurrectionist groups continued to engage in sporadic guerrilla violence for another half decade, aided in part by foreign agents and anti-American saboteurs. After a drawn-out negotiation process that was settled largely in the Union's favor, the war was set to formally conclude with the Reunification Day Ceremony in the federal capital of Columbus, Ohio, on July 3, 2095. On that day, a secessionist terrorist managed to cross the border into Northern territory and release a biological agent ("The Reunification Plague") that resulted in a nationwide epidemic. The effects of the plague, which claimed an estimated 110 million lives, were felt throughout much of the country for the next ten years. The identity of the terrorist responsible remains unknown.

CHAPTER TWO

On the porch railing the Chestnuts kept a bowl lined with oil to trap mosquitoes. Lured by the glistening liquid, the insects landed and became ensnared.

Sarat stood on the porch, the sun hot on her forehead. She watched the mosquitoes squirm. They were heavy black dots, plump as grapes. She picked one between her thumb and forefinger. She held it close to her eye. It showed no signs of what the little girl associated with living things; it said nothing, made no sound, unlike the chirping crickets or the chickens when they were worked into a frenzy. But she knew, nonetheless, that the thing between her fingers was alive.

Sarat pressed her fingers together and the mosquito burst under the pressure, leaving behind a black stain.

"What are you doing?" Dana asked, her approach from within the house unnoticed by her twin.

Sarat startled. "Nothing," she said.

Dana inspected her sister's fingers. "That's gross," she said finally, and walked away.

Sarat wiped her fingers on the rough denim of her overalls. They were hand-me-downs from her brother, their copper buttons turned black with age. She wore them plain with nothing underneath. When the weather was very warm, she undid the straps and tied them around her waist as a kind of belt, where they held at most for a few minutes before coming loose and dragging in the dirt.

She couldn't understand why her sister derived no fascination from exploring the tiny living worlds all around them—worlds whose myriad secrets lay ripe for the taking: the flying balls of blood trapped in the bowl; the eyes of the pine floorboards laced with honey; worms picked by her father's hand and impaled on hooks to teach the children a ritual from the days when the river still carried fish. Dana found such things tedious or repulsive, but to Sarat they were the veins and arteries through which life's magic flowed.

25

☆ ☆ ☆

MARTINA CHESTNUT stood on the grass between her home and the sorghum field. She hung wet clothes on a line drawn between a hook in one of the porch beams and the remains of a beach umbrella wedged into the dirt. Like the tarp that covered the roof panels, the beach umbrella had washed up on the shore a couple of years earlier and was immediately put to use.

Martina folded each garment over the line, pinching the clothes in place with pegs. Droplets fell from the cuffs of the pants and the ends of the shirts; here, under the line, the grass grew a little greener.

The clothes were plain, inoffensive: white and beige of varying shades. After so much use, many of the garments had taken on a ghostly translucence. In some parts of the Mag, where the rebels held most sway, there were families who dyed their denim red to avoid trouble. But to the sleepy Louisiana coast, such concerns had yet to come.

A thousand miles away, out by the eastern seaboard, there were newer clothes to be had, unloaded monthly from the aid ships that arrived from distant empires: cheap robes and polo shirts and track suits and baseball caps, many of them bearing the logos of the Golden Bulls or Al Ahly or the other popular sports clubs. But these were invariably snatched as soon as they reached the Georgia docks—and were, at least on paper, illegal to sell or transfer anywhere outside the three secessionist states of Mississippi, Alabama, and Georgia. Of course this rule was routinely flouted, but by the time the garments made their way as far as Louisiana or Arkansas or west to the Mexican Protectorate, they'd already gone through multiple middlemen and were, for most residents, unaffordable.

Since the earliest days of the civil war, the secessionist states survived on the charity of foreign superpowers. Once, fossil fuels were a worthwhile currency, valuable enough to keep the Louisiana ports and Texas refineries economically viable, even if not flush with cash like in the previous century. But as the rest of the world learned to live off the sun and the wind and the splitting and crashing of atoms, the old fuel became archaic and nearly worthless. The refineries were shuttered and the drills were abandoned, even as the rebel states chose open warfare over prohibition. Now, with the South on the losing end of the conflict and its resources running dry, its people came to rely more and more on the massive ships that arrived every month from the other side of the planet stocked with food, clothing, and other human necessities.

The ships came from the newborn superpowers: China and the Bouazizi Empire, the latter of which, only a few decades earlier, was nothing more than a collection of failed and failing nations spread across the Middle East and North Africa. But that was before the Fifth Spring revolution finally toppled the old regimes. Now in place of those old broken states was a single entity stretching from the Gibraltar Pass in the state of Morocco all the way to the edges of the Black and Caspian Seas.

AT DUSK, when the heat died down, Eliza Polk came over for dinner. She lived a mile north along the riverbank and through the grain field, and was the Chestnuts' closest neighbor. The summer previous she had lost her husband and both teenage sons in one of the battles in East Texas. On account of her fevered, months-long mourning and her refusal to wear anything but plain black dresses every day since, the Chestnut children called her Santa Muerte behind her back. It was a phrase they picked up from their father.

She was forty-eight years old but looked a decade older, made so by her stooped posture and the brittle shiver of her voice. In the year since her family's obliteration in the battlefields of East Texas, she lived simply on a widow's pension from one of the rebel groups. In addition to her pension, she received assistance in other ways. Every few weeks, a Mississippi Sovereigns' boat could be seen coming across the river. Upon arrival, two or three unsmiling young men would go about trimming the yard and cleaning the house and providing the diminutive widow more food and clothing than she could ever eat or wear. Polk handed much of the excess provisions over to the Chestnuts—her part of an unspoken agreement that the family, in return, provide the lonely woman some company to pass the hot, interminable days.

When she arrived Polk hugged her neighbor tightly and asked if she'd heard from her husband. Martina said she had not.

"He's safe, honey, don't you worry," Polk said. "The Lord watches over him, I know it in my heart."

Polk brought with her a mud pie. She set it on the porch railing. She stepped around the house and said hello to Simon, who was perched on the amputated ladder, struggling to hoist himself onto the roof, prohibited by pride from asking his mother for help. She sat down on one of the hickory chairs and wiped the sweat away from her forehead and called for the twins. Dana, who was busy playing house, did not emerge, but Sarat did.

"Well hello, darling, don't you look pretty today," Polk said, kissing Sarat on the cheek and trying, as she often did, to slick back her fuzzy, upturned hair.

"Hi, Santa," Sarat said. As always, the woman assumed she'd earned this nickname as a result of all the gifts she'd given the family.

When she was finished hanging the laundry, Martina walked to the porch and sat beside her guest. The two women sipped on sweet tea and as the daylight faded they watched the children play.

At the riverbank, Simon kept a simple raft tethered to a stump. The raft was made of a plywood sheet on empty oil drums, and in its center stood a crucifix mast of sanded branches on which was draped a bedsheet sail. Even in the best of winds the sail did nothing, but was decorated in black marker with a crude Jolly Roger, and was kept in place to strike fear into the hearts of passing craft, or so Simon hoped.

When the water was calm, Simon was allowed to take the raft on his own as far as the midpoint of the river, rowing madly with a scoop shovel. But if the girls were with him, he had to stay close to the shore. And at all times, he had to keep the boat tethered.

"I'm sure the boys are fine, Martina," Polk said again. "You know how those government offices are, probably told them it'd take a day or two to get the paperwork sorted. They're probably staying overnight so they don't have to go upriver a second time. Probably having the time of their lives at the Home and Away, I bet."

Martina shook her head. "He'd come home. If there were three hours to kill he'd come home."

Polk sipped her tea and retreated into the past, where she spent most of her mind's days. "You know, when the rebels sent news about Henry and the boys, I told them to bury me with them. Bury me in the same grave because I can't go on alone. Life's not worth living alone.

"But you know when I saw them, just before they lay them down in the martyrs' grave out by the Mexican border with the rest of those brave men, they looked as calm and clean as I'd ever seen them. Even the bullet wounds weren't like you see in the pictures, all a mess like that—they were just little holes. You'd see them and think, how could something so little end a life? I was so scared before I saw them, I thought that they'd look bad, ruined. But they didn't, they didn't at all. They looked peaceful. Martina, they looked *happy.*"

"I thought you said my husband's going to be fine," Martina said.

"Of course, honey, of course he will be," Polk said. She paused for a moment and then continued, softly, "But all I'm saying is, if—God forbid—if something were to have happened, if the Blues were to have done something to him, there would be no shame in it. We'd remember him as a proud Southern patriot, no different than my boys."

Martina tossed the last of the sweet tea from her glass on the dirt. "We ain't patriots of the South or anyplace else. We were trying . . . we are trying to get out. We're going to the North. We ain't patriots and we ain't got any martyrs."

Polk touched Martina's shoulder. "Of course, of course, and there's no shame in going, either. I know you want to do what's best for your children, and it's safer up there, no doubt; they don't have to go through what we go through. But you're not *of* them. There's no sin in making a safer life for your children—and maybe when they're old enough to make decisions for themselves they can come back to their own country—but you're not *of* them. You're still Southerners in your bones, you're still Southerners in your blood. That won't ever change."

"We're a family," Martina said, her eyes set on the bend to the north, beyond which it was impossible to see any further upriver. "We're nothing else."

From beyond the bend a sound carried ahead of its source. It was not the gurgling noise of Smith's fossil skiff, but something that cut smoother through the water, a bigger boat. For a moment Martina thought it was one of the rebels' smuggling ships, out earlier in the evening than usual. She yelled for her children to come back to shore, and they did, hustling up the slippery bank with their feet caked in mud. But when the boat came around the bend its spotlights cast sharp circles on the black water; Martina knew rebel ships run dark.

It was a state river monitor, a twenty-foot launch operated out of

Baton Rouge. Nominally, it was supposed to help keep the rebels from running arms across the river to and from the Texas oil fields and the Mexican Protectorate. It moved slow and conspicuous, with glowing solar panels extending out from port and starboard like butterfly wings. The panels were intended to power the boat; only in emergencies was the backup diesel motor to be used. But in practice the officers quickly tired of the panels and their anemic batteries, and out on the water they used, almost exclusively, the fuel whose prohibition they were supposed to enforce.

Martina knew the kind of men who worked on these boats. They were Southerners, all of them, employed by the Mississippi River Protection Agency or the Department of Emergency Security or a dozen other state bureaucracies that were state-run in name only—conceived solely to fulfill Northern wartime objectives. The officers went by the nickname Blue Badges and in rebel parlance these men were said to owe money to the madam. Once or twice a month, a Blue Badge would go missing somewhere along the Mississippi border. His body was usually found a few days later hanging from the twisted branch of a curling catalpa, the lining cut from his pants pockets and stuffed in his mouth. Such were the fortunes of accused traitors—not only in the secessionist country, but in neighboring states whose populace sympathized with the rebels even as their governments sided with the North.

"It's Benjamin," said Martina, watching the boat change its trajectory, shifting in the direction of the Chestnuts' place. "Something's happened to him. Blue Badges don't come out here this late at night if they can help it."

"Just calm down, don't start getting all those ideas," Polk said. "It's probably nothing." But Martina was already out of her chair and headed for the bank. Midway she met her children coming back from the river. They walked with their heads turned back, fixated on the incoming boat.

"Go on inside," Martina said. The girls did as they were told but Simon did not.

"They're going to say something about Dad, aren't they? I'm not a baby, I'm old enough to know."

Without speaking, Martina turned and slapped her son across the face. The boy, stung and reddened, was left speechless. So lengthy were the intervals between those moments when his mother's innate hard strength showed itself that the boy was often lulled into forgetting it existed at all.

"Go inside," Martina repeated to her son, in whose eyes tears of shock and anger had already begun to well. His face hardened with spite, but this time he complied.

The boat docked against the clay bank and two men in drab brown uniforms came ashore. Their clothes resembled sheriff's uniforms; pinned to their breasts were stumpy, plastic-looking badges.

One man was tall and thickset. His hair was buzzed close enough to show the pink of his scalp, and even without seeing, Martina could tell there were small rolls of fat on the back of his neck. The shorter man was of slim build, and appeared to be about ten years older than his partner, who himself could not have been more than twenty-one. The shorter man carried with him a slim paper folder, whose contents he repeatedly consulted by the light of his flashlight.

"Are you Martina Chestnut?" he asked finally.

"What happened to him?" Martina replied.

"Wife of Benjamin Chestnut?"

"Tell me what happened to him."

The officer spoke in a deadened monotone, refusing to look up from the notes in his folder. "Miss Chestnut, at one-seventeen in the afternoon on April first, 2075, an insurrectionist detonated a homicide bomb in the lobby of the Federal Services Building in Baton Rouge . . ."

The rest of the officer's speech floated by Martina, unheard. Her vision darkened and narrowed, such that the men's outline faded into the black river behind them. Vaguely she felt a hot, sharp sickness in the pit of her stomach. Polk's hand was on her shoulder again, and this roused her from her stupor long enough to interrupt the man talking.

"Take me to him," she said. "I want to see my husband."

"Ma'am . . ." the officer started.

"I've got a right to see the body of my husband. I've got a right. You take me to him and then you bring us back home. He don't rest in some morgue, he rests in his own land."

"Ma'am, until the Department of Emergency Security completes its investigation, I'm afraid . . ."

"Goddamn cowards," Martina said. "There's not one real man

among you. You just do whatever they say, don't you? No different than trained dogs. I hope it's your family next, I hope it's your family next."

"Once the investigation is complete you'll be able to claim the remains."

"Get off my land," Martina said. She bent down and dug into the mud and threw it at the officers. It landed in wet splatters on their uniforms and their boots. She bent down again and this time the mud landed on the back of the officers' shirts as they walked to the boat.

As he released the rope from the mooring, the younger of the two men turned briefly to face Martina. "Sorry for your loss," he said.

Martina watched the boat vanish upriver, its outline glistening momentarily as it crossed the rippled crest of the moon's reflection on the water. And then it turned the bend and was gone.

She heard Polk saying, "He's with the Lord now. He's a martyr like mine."

"Go to the children," Martina said. "Make sure they get to bed. I'll be in soon."

"Honey, I won't leave you."

"Go on now, I'll be in soon."

She sent Polk back to the house and for a while she stood alone near the muddy descent to the riverbank.

She watched the black river, endless and endlessly moving. She walked north, the earth cool and damp against her feet. Soon she was among the sorghum, the brown pods of grain bunched around their stalks, hard as ball bearings. When she was far enough from her home that she knew the children would not hear, she fell to her knees and screamed.

AMERICAN WAR

Excerpted from:

THESE THE CALLS OF OUR BLOOD: DISPATCHES FROM THE REBEL SOUTH

The waking hours were the most unkind. She lay still in bed, the mind aflame, the body paralyzed, unable to face the day. She clutched her mother's butterfly brooch in her hand, its faded emerald stones smooth under her fingers. The nurses let her keep it, after they ripped the pin from its back.

This was in the days before—before Julia Templestowe became the rebel South's first martyr, its first killer, the patron saint of its war. It is often forgotten: There's always a before.

The rebels recruited her with the bandages still fresh around her wrists. They found her in a bar on Farish Street across from the abandoned Alamo Theatre, its blue vertical sign missing its first and last letters. She was wearing a stranger's throwaway dress, given to her by one of the nurses. She was drunk and alone once again with the terrible illness in her brain.

They knew how to find the ones who were most likely to do it. They kept watchers in the hospitals, where they looked for suicide attempts, and in the schools, where they looked for outcasts, and in the churches, where they looked for hard-boiled extremists feverish with the spell of the Lord.

From these, they forged weapons.

On the day the President was set to come to Jackson, they drove Julia to an abandoned farmhouse ten miles south of the city, where they outfitted her for death. She was to go in the guise of a pregnant woman. Within the cavity of her false belly they packed a thick paste of fertilizer and diesel fuel, planted with seeds of iron nail. They called it a farmer's suit. A wire ran up along her chest and back down her left arm, covered by the sleeve of her shirt, and ending at a detonator taped to her wrist.

They'll remember you forever, they told her. When this is over they'll build cities in your name.

CHAPTER THREE

Sarat hunched by the front porch, waiting for her mother to return from Eliza Polk's house. She'd gone there to see about a man.

Nearby, Simon struggled to climb onto the roof of the house. Over the last three days, he'd tried a dozen times to hoist his frame over the edge. He knew that the solar panels began to weaken if they weren't wiped down every other day, and that without regular chlorination the water from the rain tank began to smell faintly of eggs. With every passing day his inability to complete these responsibilities gnawed at him.

Once again he set the ladder in the dirt against the side of the shipping container. Here the earth was softened by runoff from the nearby standing shower, and the legs of the ladder sank slightly into the mud.

At Simon's insistence, the twins braced the ladder on both sides, trying to keep it steady. Standing on the top rung, he readied to leap and hike himself onto the roof.

"OK," he said, wiping the midday sweat from his hands. "Ready?"

"Ready," Sarat and Dana replied in unison.

Simon braced his hands against the edge of the container. On his tiptoes he peered over the top.

"Hold it steady," he yelled at his sisters.

"We are," Sarat replied.

"No, hold it so it doesn't move."

"We are!"

Simon screwed up his courage. He thought about the ease with which his father did such labor—how, even when he came home late at night from the shirt factory, his fingers red and raw from stitching, he happily took on the chores of the house: patching a hole in the rain tank, re-boarding the windows after a freak storm, making flour of the sorghum grain with the old hand-crank mill. He recalled the sound of the crank squeaking as it pulverized the grain to fine dust—it was the sound of work.

Simon steadied his feet on the top rung. "One, two, three!" he cried, and jumped as high as he could. With his hands still clamped on the edge of the container he rose, his chest level with the roof. For a moment he was weightless, suspended in air. He tried to pull himself over the top, but like a seesaw unevenly weighted, he leaned a little forward and then tumbled back. He landed with a fat thud, neck-first in the soft earth.

The twins yelped and backed away from the ladder. Sarat watched her brother lie on the ground, mesmerized by the violence of his collision, the way his impact made the earth spit itself up. Dana screamed at the mud stains that suddenly covered her dress.

Simon lay still for the better part of a minute, the wind knocked out of him. Finally he groaned and began to lift himself.

"Never mind," he told his sisters. "You're holding it all wrong."

"Oh my God, just wait for Daddy to come do it," Dana said. "You got mud everywhere." She stormed into the house to change. Simon followed.

Sarat remained outside, looking at the place where Simon had fallen. She knelt to the ground and dug with her hands a small trench in the dirt from the edge of the shower stall to the indentation Simon's fall had made in the earth. Then she turned the tap and let the water flow from the showerhead. Slowly the runoff trickled into the trench. From there it flowed as a miniature river and filled the void of Simon's crater, a newborn sea in the shape of a boy.

"Turn that off," Simon said, reemerging from the house in clean clothes. "You're wasting water."

☆ ☆ ☆

NIGHT FELL. The children ate dinner alone, their mother still at Polk's place across the field. They ate sandwiches of stale bread and preserved pork that came in tin cans labeled in a language they could not understand—an import from the aid ships, given to them by Santa Muerte. In recent days, their neighbor had started coming over more frequently and with more gifts: food of higher quality, better clothes.

The canned meat had the texture of soaked erasers, rubbery against the teeth. When they were finished, the children ate the last of Polk's mud pie, its cream cheese frosting cracked and hard after two days in the refrigerator.

Sarat watched the river. All day she had seen more boats than usual coming across from the eastern banks, and now in the darkness the traffic intensified. She heard the sound of muffled fossil motors about a mile upriver, and occasionally could even make out the voices of unseen men barking commands.

"Is that Daddy?" Dana asked.

"No," Simon replied. "It's the rebels."

"Who are the rebels?"

"Fighters." Simon looked at his sister to see if she comprehended the word. "They're on our side in the war against the North."

"Mama says Daddy's in the North," said Dana. "We're gonna go see him there."

"Mama's lying," Simon said.

Dana turned to her twin, incredulous. "He called Mama a liar!" She turned back to her brother. "I'm telling."

"You think Dad would just take off for the North without us?" Simon said. "He didn't take nothing but a couple of papers with him. Didn't even take a change of clothes. Something bad happened and Mama won't tell us what."

Dana shook her head. "Mama says Daddy's in the North," she repeated. "You don't know what you're talking about."

☆ ☆ ☆

THE BOATS the children heard were rebel ships, moving soldiers and supplies to the oil fields on the western front. They docked near Eliza Polk's house, where they set up a temporary encampment, and where Martina Chestnut came at her neighbor's invitation to talk to a rebel commander about sanctuary.

The Polks' house was made of four trailer homes laid in a square. They were prefabricated blocks with vinyl siding and sloped tin roofing.

Normally quiet, Eliza Polk's land was chaotic with the turbulence of incoming rebels. Martina emerged from the sorghum field to find dozens of men, almost all of them teenagers, moving about the home. In a chain of passing hands they hauled wooden crates and burlap sacks from the unlit boats to the trailers. The rebels carried small portable radios that crackled with orders to prepare for the arrival of more incoming ships. By the riverfront, a boy sat flashing a standing light in sharp bursts to the vessels passing through the dark water.

They wore tattered uniforms of no consistent color or style, composed of whatever was available to them—black jeans, cargo vests, duck hunter's camouflage, fatigues from foreign armies smuggled aboard the aid ships at the request of the rebel leaders. Their weapons were also smuggled in, or else salvaged from the attics and basements of parents and grandparents—the guns often older than the boys who carried them. They were, to a man, untrained and ill-equipped, and ahead of them to the west lay certain death at the hands of a superior army. But behind them, in the dead-end towns where they were born, lay a slower kind of death—death at the hands of poverty and boredom and decay.

Martina stood at the edge of the field, watching them. In the central garden, they had set up a makeshift command table. On the table lay a large contour map of the Louisiana-Texas border. A few of the older men were assembled around the table, marking the map with various pins and highlighters. Occasionally, they looked up to address the younger fighters, who went about hauling crates and erecting tents. One boy, who could not have been more than seventeen, scaled the Polks' river-facing trailer and attempted to fly the rattlesnake flag of the United Rebels from the roof, but was ordered down by an older, more discreet superior.

Near the trailer's front entrance, Martina spotted Eliza Polk. She stood waiting at the front steps as a couple of rebels moved her suitcases from the home to one of the boats docked nearby.

Polk saw Martina and called her over. As she approached the trailer, Martina could feel the eyes of the boys on her, cold and suspicious. But they said nothing.

Polk hugged her neighbor. "Oh, honey, honey," she said. "It all happened so fast."

"I thought you'd said it was just the commander coming."

Polk shook her head. "The Blues are moving east from the Texas oil fields," she said. "Our boys are going out to meet them. They say if they move fast enough they can keep them from getting any further into Louisiana."

Martina looked around her for someone who fit the description of a field commander. "Is he here?" she asked.

"Yes, honey. But he's busy. He won't talk to no one but his men."

"Point him out to me."

"Just wait a while," Polk pleaded. "Won't do no good to try talking to him now."

"Show me where he is."

Reluctantly, Polk guided Martina to a man at the table in the garden. He was tall and skinny, perhaps five or six years younger than Martina. He wore a neatly trimmed beard that narrowed down to the upper tip of his sternum like an arrowhead. He was dressed in black, from his boots to his military cap. Around him, many of the fighters seemed to hover in elongated orbits, rushing to various parts of the temporary encampment to fulfill his orders before returning to be given a new assignment. He spoke softly enough that, until she was standing directly opposite him at the map table, Martina could not make out a word he said.

When he saw her, the field commander said nothing. He looked over at Polk.

"This is my neighbor I told you about," Polk said. "The one whose husband was martyred."

"He wasn't martyred," the man said. "He died."

The field commander was silent once again. The men around him seemed to regard Martina with hostility, but in his eyes there was only stillness.

"I understand you keep a house near Vicksburg for the martyrs' widows," Martina said. "A safe place for the women and the children."

The field commander did not respond.

"I have two little girls and a son, just babies the three of them," Martina continued. "Their father's dead and we got no means to support ourselves." She turned to Polk. "Ms. Polk here's our only neighbor, and her generosity's kept us from starving, but she's leaving now. All I ask is you let us go with her to Vicksburg, where no harm will come to my children. I don't ask anything more."

"Can't be done," the field commander responded.

"Why not? We can be packed in an hour. We can go right now, just the clothes on our back."

"We keep a home for the kin of martyrs," the field commander said. "Unless you got some other man died fighting for the cause, that ain't you."

He turned back to the maps on the table, and quickly around him the fighters resumed their orbit.

"C'mon honey," Polk said, taking Martina by the arm. "Let's leave them be for now. We'll sort something out, I know we can."

Martina pushed Polk's hand away.

"Your men killed my husband," she said to the field commander. "Your men killed one of their own and they have a responsibility to do right by his family."

The field commander walked around the table and over to where Martina stood. Up close she could see he had beautiful green eyes. No movement in them, but beautiful.

"My men kill Northerners and traitors," he said. "Which of those is your husband?"

Polk tugged at the field commander's shirt sleeve, pleading with him to come talk to her alone inside the trailer. The two walked to the home, leaving Martina standing amidst the fighters, many of whom had stopped what they were doing to watch.

"You got some balls talking to him that way," one of them said. "I've seen him shoot men for saying less."

"I don't care what you've seen," Martina replied.

In a while the field commander and Polk emerged from the trailer. The man approached Martina.

"Tomorrow at dawn there's a bus coming up the road along the east bank. It's headed to Mississippi, up to Camp Patience. Because this lady here vouched for you and because of what her men gave to the cause, I'll send word that if you and your children are there tomorrow, they're to make room for you."

"You're telling me to take my kids to a refugee camp?"

"I'm telling you to do what suits you."

The field commander turned back to the maps on the table. "Go on now," he said. "Nothing more for you here."

Martina looked around her at the assembled soldiers.

"Not one of you man enough to speak up? None of you got mothers, none of you got kids?"

The men continued to watch her, some of them cold, others snickering. None spoke.

Martina left them where they stood and marched back the way she came. At the edge of the sorghum field Polk caught up to her.

"Oh, honey, I'm sorry," she said. "I did the best I could."

"So we're not Northerners because we're from the South, and we're not Southerners because we tried to move north," Martina said. "Tell me what we are, then. Tell me what we are."

Polk gave a piece of paper to Martina. On it was scribbled the time and location where the bus would be the following morning. "It's not so bad at the camp, Martina," she said. "They got good food—food straight from the aid ships, and free too. And they got places for the children to play. You'll be safe there."

"We'll be cattle there."

Polk pointed west. "Honey, it's for the good of your children. They say the fighting's closer to us now than ever before, and moving further east every day. The traitors in the Louisiana guard are letting the Blues march right onto our land, and they don't care who they kill. In Patience you'll be among your own. Your children will be safe, Martina. What else matters but that?"

Martina looked into the small steady eyes of her neighbor. "I'm staying in my home," she said. "I'm going to claim my husband's body and I'm going to bury him on his land and I'm going to stay in my home and if the war comes to my door then let it. I'm done waiting on the good favor of little boys with guns."

"I did the best I could," Polk said. "But you shouldn't have said what you did about his people killing one of their own. They're very sensitive to that."

☆ ☆ ☆

WHEN SHE RETURNED HOME Martina found Sarat buried up to her neck in mud by the riverbank. The girl squealed with delight as her brother piled on handfuls of the brown sludge. Dana sat on a nearby stump, watching with vague disapproval.

When he saw his mother Simon sprung to his feet. "She asked me to," he said.

"Dig her out and get cleaned up," Martina said. "And then go to bed."

"Mama, Simon called you a liar," Dana said.

"I did not," Simon replied. He threw a scoop of mud in Dana's direction.

"I won't tell you again," Martina said.

The children marched up the embankment. Sarat skipped ahead of them, slick with mud, the brackish scent of the earth latched on to her skin. She undressed as she walked, dispatching her overalls in the dirt path behind her, and stepped into the shower. Of the three children, she had the darkest skin; Dana and Simon had inherited the brown of their father, Sarat the black of her mother.

Martina brought a change of clothes for her daughter and left them on an upturned water bucket by the stall. Soon the children had all washed and changed. One by one they kissed their mother and retreated into the house.

Martina sat alone on the hickory chair. She ate the sandwich crusts the children had left behind, and the last wet remnants of the canned meat. Still hungry, she stepped quietly into the house and took from the refrigerator a packet of apricot-flavored gel. It was an orange-colored paste of gelatinous texture. It came in a plain silver packet and had once been part of a military ration kit. In the South such kits, sold or discarded or given away, inevitably found their way to the gray market, where they were ripped open and their parts sold off individually. It was highly prized food, not for its taste but because of its utility, the energy it provided.

Instead of returning to the hickory chair, Martina found herself walking—not east to the river or north to the sorghum fields but west, behind the house and along the little-used paths that cut back through the brown-capped weeds to what remained of the inland town.

In the early winter, when the weather cooled and demand for labor grew, this was the route her husband took to the factory in Donaldsonville. There was a shuttle bus that stopped close to the Chestnuts' property, but most days he chose to walk. He followed the footpath through the weeds to where it met a country road. Two miles in, the road crossed a pair of unused railway tracks, thick bushels of grass growing between the crossties.

Martina walked the same road toward the tracks. She moved carefully, cognizant of the deep fissures and cracks in which an ankle could easily turn. Where they still stood and their autonomous solar panels still functioned, a few roadside lights cast white halos on the ground. Otherwise the road was dark.

Just east of where the road met the tracks there stood the ruins of a small farmhouse once owned by friends of Martina's parents. Near the house was a cotton field, long ago gone to seed.

Martina left the road and walked along the dirt driveway. Ahead of her, the simple wooden farmhouse stood frozen in mid-collapse. A cascade of storms coming off the Mississippi Sea had slowly pushed the walls from their moorings, but not enough to bring the structure down. Instead the home leaned visibly to the west, a teetering parallelogram.

Every once in a while, when she needed time alone, Martina came to this place. But for the occasional beer bottle or empty cigarette pack left on the front steps by a drifter, the home never showed signs of life. At the western end of the property there stood a many-limbed pecan tree. Long ago, from its thickest branch, the family hung a tire swing. Since childhood this place was Martina's refuge. Beyond the tree, the land was flat and the view unsoiled for what seemed to be the entirety of western Louisiana.

But in the darkness there was nothing to be seen, the sky a uniform black. Only the Birds flew overhead—soundless warring craft designed to spy and to kill from great distance, their movement and intent once controlled by men in faraway places, who had only the grainy, pixelated footage of vaporized targets to gnaw on their conscience. Early in the war, the Birds were the Union's most effective weapon, until a group of rebels detonated a bomb at the military server farm that kept the drones under the control of their remote pilots. Now the machines, powered by the solar panels that lined their wings, flew rogue, abandoned to the skies, their targets and trajectories random.

She sat on the well-worn swing. The branch gave a little, letting out a faint squeak as Martina's weight pulled the rope tight into the rut in the bark.

She ripped open the gel packet and scooped the orange gunk into her mouth with her finger. Because of its texture the food could not be chewed with any conviction; she mashed it between her tongue and the roof of her mouth, letting it slide down her throat. It tasted not of apricot but of apricot perfume, of apricots as envisioned by engineers unfamiliar with the fruit as it existed in the natural world. In a minute she felt the sugar coursing through her nerve endings.

She heard the sound of shuffling feet. Startled, she began to ask who was there, but stopped, frozen solid. The shuffling came closer, until it was nearly upon her. That was when she finally saw the source of the sound—an emaciated, mangy dog wandering blind through the empty field. It was a foxhound. It moved slow and reticent toward her, probing for any sign of hostility.

Martina squeezed the last of the apricot gel onto her palm and held it out to the dog. It sniffed at the food. Though starved, the dog paused to consider the gel and then turned away.

Martina looked up. A small orange dawn suddenly lit up the sky.

It was a half-dome of bright light on the horizon, visible only for a few seconds. Then it was gone.

In a moment it came again, and this time in its wake a horn of flame shot high into the night sky. It hung in the air for a few seconds, sustained, and then retreated. The sight offered no sound, each wave of illumination as though in a vacuum.

Then came a half-sun to dwarf the previous bursts of light, and a few seconds later a roar unlike anything Martina had ever heard. The sound collided with her chest and sent her tumbling backward off the swing. She fell to the dirt, staring dumbstruck, her ears overwhelmed by a dull ringing. The foxhound yelped and fled. And then Martina too was running, back in the direction of her children and her home.

She sprinted, summoning the legs of her youth. A quarter-mile down the road, her lungs burning, a bang even louder than the one before it shook her off her feet once more. By the time she'd reached her home, winded and bracing against the porch railing for support, two more explosions had shattered the night.

She found her children inside the house, frantic. The twins were huddled together on the floor near their parents' bed, Sarat hugging her wailing sister. Simon was at the front of the house, trying to swing shut the shipping container's hopelessly rusted door, which the family rarely had reason to close in the summertime.

"Where were you?" he asked his mother. "What's happening?"

Martina grabbed her son by the arm and pulled him to the back of her house. "It's all right," she said. "It's just a factory down the way caught fire. It's just a sound, it won't harm us."

She sat on the floor by her children and held them close. She pulled a little-used blanket from the space below her bed and wrapped it around herself and her daughters. "It's just a factory down the way caught fire," she said. "It's just a loud sound, that's all. It'll be over soon." The more she repeated it, the truer it became.

☆ ☆ ☆

THE ERUPTIONS DID NOT RELENT until the early dawn, arriving with unpredictable frequency and severity. By the end of it exhaustion had desensitized the children—the twins curled up against their mother's breast, Simon seated on the floor beside them, unmoving, watching the sunlight seep through the window.

Martina stared ahead at the entrance to her home, waiting. In the wake of the explosions she listened now for small sounds—footsteps, whispered directives, the cocking of a gun. None came. There was only the distressed clucking of the chickens and the audible pulse of the crickets and the sound of her children breathing.

Look what stubbornness took from you already, she thought. Don't let it take any more.

She motioned to her son. "You think you can get us across the river in your boat?"

"Yes," Simon said without hesitation.

"Go on to your room—quiet so you won't wake the girls—and pack as many change of clothes as you can get into your backpack."

"Why?" Simon asked.

"Hurry now. I'm counting on you to get us across the river. Your father's counting on you."

The boy stood up quietly. Martina waited until he was done packing and then she stood up and carried the girls, still groggy and half-asleep, to their beds. She set them down and instantly they dozed off again. While they slept, she pulled the Chestnuts' biggest piece of luggage—an old bronze-detailed suitcase that once belonged to her grandmother—from under the bed. It was deep and wide and brittle at its copper hinges. Stickers covered its sides, each commemorating a visit to some historic site or state park that Martina knew only from the schoolbooks of her youth.

She laid the suitcase open on the bed; the room filled with the smell of mothballs. Inside she found a couple of pens and a cracked frame with no photo inside. She tossed these things on the floor. She opened her dresser drawers and began stuffing the suitcase with clothes and toiletries. Instantly and without thinking, she developed a hierarchy of need, starting closest to the skin and working outward—tampons, underwear, dresses. She packed two towels and two rolls of toilet paper and a packet of wet-naps. When the suitcase was almost full she stopped and went to the kitchen. She took jars and containers of the least perishable foods—jams, peanut butter, all the remaining military rations. She took the large plastic soda containers and emptied their contents outside in the dirt, and then refilled them from the tap connected to the rainwater tank. She packed the suitcase until it threatened not to close. She sat on it to keep it shut but the old clasps would not hold, and so she took two of her husband's belts from the dresser and tied them to each other and looped them around the suitcase to keep it from bursting open. Then she found Sarat's and Dana's matching Minnie Mouse backpacks and filled them with the girls' clothes.

She went outside. Around the south-facing side of the house, near the firewood stove, there was a wide-mouthed drainage pipe that ran from the roof of the home but was connected to nothing. The pipe was sealed shut at its top and bottom. She knelt to the ground and unsealed the bottom cover. A little bit of brown water trickled out of the pipe. She reached inside and felt for a coffee jar. She tugged on it until it came out. She opened the jar and counted its contents: five hundred dollars in American money; another three hundred in Louisiana Assistance Equivalents; three 16-sheets of prewar stamps; two thousand dollars' worth of rebel currency issued by the New Zouaves in the very first days of the war and virtually worthless now as a trade currency, but which Benjamin suspected might one day be valuable as a historical curiosity; and a broken Rolex wristwatch that once belonged to Martina's great-grandfather.

☆ ☆ ☆

WHEN SHE HAD FINISHED PACKING, Martina set the bags out in the front yard and went inside to wake the girls. They gazed at her, glass-eyed, still exhausted and incoherent.

"Girls, we're going to go on a little adventure," she said. "We're going to cross the river together, all right?"

At the mention of adventure, Sarat perked up. "Why are we crossing the river, Mama?"

"Because we have to go live in a new house for a little while, honey."

"Are we going to go see Daddy?"

"Yeah, honey, we're going to see Daddy. Now go on, let's get you dressed. We've got to get moving."

As she and the girls prepared to leave, Martina removed from the bottom of her jewelry box a couple of photos of her and her husband. They were ancient things, taken with her grandfather's camera. She tucked them into her dress.

She walked to the front of the home, where she found Sarat on her tiptoes, struggling to lift the statue of the Virgin of Guadalupe.

"Let that be, honey," Martina said. "We'll come back for it later."

"Daddy will want it," Sarat replied.

"Just leave it for now. We've got to go. Daddy will understand."

"No!" the little girl yelled. With Herculean effort she lifted the statue from the table. It fell into her arms, nearly knocking her over. Sarat hoisted the statue, which was almost as tall as she was, and waddled out the door.

Martina pulled the shipping container's rusted door shut behind her and held it with a flimsy combination lock she knew would not withstand the teeth of even the smallest bolt-cutter. Then she carried her suitcase and led the girls down the embankment to the waterfront, where Simon and the raft were waiting.

They climbed aboard. The raft bobbed and sagged under their weight. Martina had never ridden on it before. She had only crossed the river a handful of times in the last few years, usually on Alder Smith's boat whenever he invited the family into town for one of his cookouts. The raft was a child's thing, unsuited for the crossing, a polyp on the mouth of the Mississippi.

Under the reddening sky the Chestnuts unmoored. Martina took the scoop shovel from her son and began to fight the water. Already she could feel the current pulling them downriver, and she knew by the time they crossed to the eastern bank they'd have to hike a mile or more up the road to reach the place where the bus would be. Wells of sweat formed dark and wide on the arms of her dress; her eyes stung. She continued rowing.

☆ ☆ ☆

MANY YEARS LATER, in the tents of Camp Patience, Martina would silently curse the day she left her home and took her children willingly into the festering heart of the war-torn South.

What she couldn't have known that morning was that the rebels, the federal troops, and the Mexican militias ultimately fought to a standstill; the violence never inched any further into Louisiana than it did on that brittle April day when the Chestnuts left their land.

47

Excerpted from:

**WITNESS TO DISUNION:
EARLY JOURNALISTIC ACCOUNTS OF THE SECOND CIVIL WAR**

"FIRST SHOTS OF CIVIL WAR"

At Least 59 Killed, More Than 200 Injured as Fort Jackson Protests Erupt in Bloodshed

March 15, 2074

Danielle Manak, *The Charleston Feed*

COLUMBIA, S.C.—Federal troops shot at least 59 people dead on Wednesday as the four-day protest at the gates of Fort Jackson turned deadly, marking what many believe is the Columbus government's first assault in an all-out war on the opposition states.

"Let's be clear: this was a massacre of South Carolinians, a massacre of Southerners, and a massacre of all who dare raise their voice in protest," said Governor Davis Brown. "This is a direct statement from the federal government that if you disagree with the Sustainable Future Act, or any decision made in Columbus, you are the enemy and must be destroyed.

"This is a call to war."

A cadre of Marine guards posted at Gate 2 near Strom Thurmond Boulevard—where protesters have amassed by the hundreds in recent days—opened fire on demonstrators at around noon on Wednesday. The guards were stationed in makeshift towers near a hastily constructed fence intended to keep demonstrators from the base entrance.

The first round of rifle fire appeared to hit several of the protesters at the front of the demonstration. What followed was a panicked stampede by those further back, who trampled over one another while attempting to flee the shooting.

"One second the man in front of me was waving his sign, and the next there was this burst of gunfire, and he dropped like a stone," said Elijah Miller, who had joined the demonstration early

Wednesday morning and managed to make his way near the gate before the shooting began.

"I swear to God that man didn't have a gun. He wasn't a threat to anyone, and they shot him dead."

Witnesses described a scene of carnage following the shooting, with several lifeless bodies lining the roadway and pools of blood clearly visible around them.

A soldier inside Fort Jackson, who was not among the guards stationed at Gate 2, said at least one of the protesters near the front of the demonstration fired a pistol at a chain and lock that held part of the temporary fence in place.

"He must have thought it was an action movie, like he could shoot the lock open or something," said the soldier, who spoke on condition of anonymity because the troops stationed at the base have been given instructions not to speak to reporters.

The soldier added that, rather than break the lock, the bullet ricocheted back into the crowd.

"At that point, [the protesters] thought they were under fire, and half of them rushed back while the other half rushed forward against the fence.

"As soon as the Marines saw that fence start to strain, they opened fire."

Many demonstrators dispute that account, saying the Marines were not provoked in any way.

"The cowards on the other side of that fence opened fire for no reason," said Paul Hartig, who had been camped out in front of the gate for the last three days. "They killed all those people for no reason at all, and they should hang for it."

Reaction to the killing came swiftly. In Columbus, the ten senators representing the federal-aligned Southern states of Louisiana, Arkansas, Missouri, Kentucky, and Tennessee issued a joint statement of condemnation, calling the incident "an unnecessary and tragic provocation that only empowers extremists and does nothing to ease the country from the brink of war."

In a statement by the Free Southern State's Council, the governors of Texas, Mississippi, Alabama, Georgia, and South Carolina called the killings "outright cold-blooded murder" and an act of tyranny and treason for which federal president Martin Henley himself should stand trial.

"Every Southern patriot, upon hearing the news of the massacre at Fort Jackson, will know now as a fact that the federal government in Columbus considers Southern lives to be less than worthless," the governors said.

"It is only the willfully blind who can today gaze upon the blood-soaked streets of Columbia and refuse to support the cause of secession."

Throughout South Carolina, where anti-federal sentiment has run higher than perhaps anywhere outside the Texas oil fields, violence quickly erupted as word of the Fort Jackson killings spread. In Columbia, numerous franchises of Northern-headquartered businesses—many already shuttered in the months since federal president Daniel Ki's assassination in Jackson, Mississippi, last December—were torched to the ground. In New Charleston, the bodies of three men, accused by citizen secessionist groups of working as intelligence gatherers for the North, were found bound on the shoreline, their throats slit.

"This isn't only about secession anymore," said a representative of a South Carolina citizens' group. "This is about avenging our dead."

By Wednesday evening, federal president Henley had yet to issue an official statement on the killings. The Department of Defense's official press site, which has not been updated since Monday, continued to feature a terse statement stating that military officials believe the Marines at Fort Jackson are "acting with utmost restraint."

Gov. Brown, who had previously called for all Northern sympathizers in South Carolina to leave the state, repeated that call on Wednesday, and asked for his citizens' help in the cause of resistance.

"The wholesale slaughter of our people is not something to be negotiated. It is not the subject of concessions or compromise," said Gov. Brown.

"From what has been done today in Fort Jackson, there is no going back."

CHAPTER FOUR

Under the fractured shade of palm trees, the Chestnuts waited. In crossing the water, they had been pulled two miles downriver. They walked back along the country road that ran near the river, covering this distance and another mile more. The road was cracked deep in places, as though tilled. The remains of the yellow dividing line were now almost completely gone; there seemed to be no separation between the coming and the going.

They walked until they reached a bend in the road where there was a dirt pull-off and, growing there, a bush of anemic palms. The plants' green, sharp stalks grew and leaned back toward the river, away from the rising sun. At the feet of the trees there were a few variegated yuccas, their machete leaves tinted green and white. This was the place where the man said the bus would be.

"The river's going to take it," Simon complained. He looked smaller under the weight of his backpack, which was full of clothes, comic books, a snorkeling mask, a hand-sharpened stick knife, and boxes of Benjamin Chestnut's unfiltered Yuxis.

The Yuxis, thin and made with weak tobacco, were one of the very few vices the boy's father had maintained. He kept them hidden from his wife behind a loose board in the outhouse. This secrecy was in fact unnecessary, as both son and wife knew of Benjamin's smoking habit. But to maintain an unspoken dignity, they said nothing.

"The river won't take it," Martina said.

"We didn't pull it far enough up the bank. Soon as it rains next, the river's going to rise and it'll float off to sea."

"If it does, I'll make you a new raft."

"You're just saying that because you know we're not coming back."

"Enough."

The family set their belongings down in the clearing and waited for the bus to arrive. Dana, exhausted, fell back asleep on the ground with her backpack for a pillow.

Sarat wandered nearby, foraging around the bushes, inspecting the yuccas. They were resilient-looking things, their leaves flat and rigid. Of the few plants that still grew in the parched Southern earth, the yuccas grew best.

Sarat ran her finger along the leaves. The skin felt dry and its texture resembled that of sandpaper. But it was also rubbery, with some give to its flesh. She pressed her finger against the needle at the end of the leaf, feeling her own skin compress. The needle ends were brown and rigid, immune to sun and storm.

The day grew warmer. The Chestnuts waited but no bus came. Soon, Martina began to wonder if they'd missed it entirely, and if she might soon have to decide whether to take the family eastward by foot.

"What is this, Mama?" Sarat asked, pointing to the yucca.

"It's a plant, honey."

"What kind of plant?"

"A cactus. Don't get too close, you'll hurt yourself."

"Cactus," Sarat repeated, letting her tongue whip every syllable. *"Cac-tus."*

Martina heard the sound of wheels against the road. The bus turned the corner, coming from the south. It was a yellow, prewar school bus, retrofitted with solar panels along the roof. On either side of the bus, where once there would have been stenciled the name of some high school, instead was written, in block letters, CIVILIAN TRANSPORT.

The bus moved slowly, its panels still soaking up sunlight. The driver came to a stop at the clearing. The door folded open.

Martina herded the children to the other side of the road. She peered inside the bus. A driver of about thirty sat at the wheel. He was a chubby man, the sweat beaded on his skin.

Behind the driver sat another man, much taller and broader. He wore a plain white shirt and blue jeans and by his side rested, barrel-up, an old Type-95. It was a cheap and cheaply built rifle, popular with the rebels because it rarely jammed or broke down, and because it could be smuggled with relative ease in the aid ships. The man with the rifle watched Martina, expressionless.

"We're the Chestnuts," Martina told the driver. She realized then that she'd never learned the name of the man who'd promised to grant her passage. "The rebel commander said we'd be allowed to ride to Patience."

The driver chuckled. "The *rebel commander* said that, did he? Well we can't go upsetting him." The smirk disappeared from his lips. "A hundred each."

Martina shook her head. "He said we'd be allowed on. He said—"

"Lady, you speak English? A hundred a head."

Martina shuffled through her baggage for the tin of money. "I've only got three hundred," she said, "in LAEs."

"Did I say LAEs?" the driver replied. "They don't even accept that joke currency in Louisiana no more."

"That's all I got."

The driver shrugged. He pulled a lever by the wheel and the door unfolded shut, knocking Martina back. The bus began to move.

Martina pulled her children from the path of the wheels. She ran alongside the bus and banged on the door with a fistful of dollars. The driver slowed to a stop once more.

"Well won't you look at that?" he said to the man with the rifle. "Guess she just misplaced it is all."

Martina paid the fare and ushered her children onto the bus. Simon hopped on and the twins followed, Sarat still carrying the statue of the Virgin. As he walked, Simon stared at the man with the rifle, hypnotized.

The family shuffled to the back of the bus. An old man, the only other passenger, sat in the second-to-last row. Martina and her children sat behind him on a bench in the very back. They set their bags and belongings on and under the bench, and sat close together on one side, opposite the old man. With a tinny groan, the bus lurched forward once more, its suspension singing to the tune of the cracked country road.

"They sent me all the way down here for this?" the driver asked the guard, who said nothing. "Waste of goddamn time. Why are we even picking up throwaways from outside the Mag? They sided with Columbus, let Columbus deal with them. We got our hands full with our own."

The guard adjusted the banana clip on his rifle. He turned and looked out the window, ignoring the driver.

The driver turned to his passengers. "Well, you best settle the hell in," he said. "Got a full long day ahead of you."

The driver's voice woke the old man, who until then had been asleep, his hat pinned between the window and the side of his head. He wiped a thin line of spittle from his mouth. Martina watched him. He was in his eighties, perhaps even older, a child of the previous millennium. Years of untempered sun had tanned the skin of his face and arms to leather, pocked in places with black spots. He wore a white prewar suit, accented with a red silk handkerchief whose top peered from the breast pocket. The suit jacket and pants were graying in the places where they stretched over the knees and elbows, but elsewhere they retained their whiteness. In its totality the suit gave the man an old-world appearance, an air of dignity. He seemed to Martina a creature not only of a different time but of a divergent one, born to an America that long ago turned along its own dark meridian and left the likes of him behind.

The old man punched the top back into his flattened fedora and set it on his lap. He looked around the bus as though he had no idea how he'd ended up on it. He came to Martina. He stared at her awhile.

Finally, he said, "You from Blind River?"

"No."

"Know anyone from Blind River?"

"Never heard of it," Martina said.

The man quieted and faced forward again.

"My husband's got some cousins out near these parts," Martina said.

He perked up. "Blind River's about thirty miles west of here, give or take. Used to be you'd see signs for it if you were coming up from New Orleans, but that's all gone now."

"Mhmm."

"I lived there fifty-one years," the old man said, a weak pride in his voice. "Lived through Anna in '43 and Michael in '51. Michael spun right through my living room, tore up all the houses for ten blocks every which way, but mine was the only one it couldn't crush. They took a photo of it from the air, ran it on the front page of the *Courier.*"

He stood up and walked over to the Chestnuts' side of the bus. He inspected the children, each in turn—Simon, still transfixed with the rebel and his rifle; the girls, sitting window-side, looking out at the brown remains of farmland and the utility poles, their lines limp and dead.

Sarat sat closest to the window, up on her knees atop the bench, nose pressed close to the glass. Under the warm light of the sun, the land shone clear. Its enormity overwhelmed her.

Dana sat felinelike between her sister and her mother, working tiny braids into Sarat's frazzled hair. When she was done with each braid she set it loose and watched it slowly start to come undone, and then she started braiding another.

"How old are they?" the old man asked.

"Simon's nine, the twins are six," Martina said.

"Twins! They don't look a thing alike."

"Guess they don't."

The old man looked Dana over. "Well aren't you a cute one," he said, and turned back to the mother. "Had a granddaughter just like her. Must be closer to your age now than hers. Her parents took her west to California just before the third Silicon bubble burst in '44. Haven't heard from them since. Probably down in Mexican territory now if they're anywhere."

"You know anything about the camp where they're taking us?" Martina asked. "Is it safe there?"

"They didn't tell me nothing about that," the old man said. "They just showed up and said they needed my land to dock their ships coming in and out of the Mississippi. Gun-runners, all of them, I know it. And there's nobody left there but me, the houses down that way are all at the bottom of the sea now. The boy in charge said if I was younger they'd just toss me in the water. But I guess they got a sense of charity to them, so they gave me ten minutes to pack and they set me off. Ten minutes! To pack up fifty-six years!"

"But at the camp, are they gonna feed us? Are they gonna give us a place to stay? We don't have much money . . ."

". . . But you know, before I left, I said to that boy, if I was younger, it'd be you tossed into the water . . ."

Martina let the old man talk. He spoke for the better part of an hour about his old life in Blind River, adrift on the currents of his memory. In the front she could hear the bus driver talking too. He told the man with the rifle about how his uncle had lined up a good job for him in the vertical farms outside Atlanta. He said all a man had to do to make shift supervisor was keep from falling asleep or pissing in the planting stations, and in six months he'd be promoted to a real suit-and-tie job.

"See, most of these boys' problem is they're too dumb to realize you gotta eat a little shit to get ahead," the driver said. "They get it in one hand and spend it with the other. They got no discipline. But I got discipline. Yes sir, I got discipline."

The guard stared out the window.

Slowly the bus moved alongside the river, traversing the last shredded remnants of lower Louisiana.

Here was where the water finally won. For decades, the governments of the state and the country spent billions trying to save lower Louisiana from the encroaching seas—building hundreds of miles of seawalls, levees, raised causeways, and even, toward the end, floating towns. It was still early days then, and the oceans had not yet devoured the optimistic notion that with enough concrete and dirt and pride and money the low country could be saved.

That was then. All that remained now were the entrails of that long-subsumed world and the futile efforts to preserve it: thin strips of asphalt that disappeared at high tide, ghost towns propped on man-made hills, crumbling bridges that nosedived into the water. Scattered among the islands that remained, these things stood as ruins and like all ruins were in their own way grotesque, a transgression against the passage of time.

☆ ☆ ☆

THE BUS LEFT the riverside and turned onto Interstate 55, headed north. In prewar days, the highway ran under the same number all the way to Chicago. Now it ended in a barricade of razor wire and guard towers ten miles south of Memphis—a checkpoint in the new wartime border.

There were blue signs on the side of the road. They listed the amenities available at every exit. The logos of the gas stations had been blacked out, but atop many of these black squares someone had redrawn the logos in crude graffiti. Thin trees lined the highway. They carried no leaves, only barren branches. Everywhere, the roadside architecture showed the telltale signs of plunder: poles stripped of their wires; cars gutted; factory facades of which only cracked concrete and rebar remained.

In the quietude of the long highway drive, Martina thought about all the things she had forgotten to do in her rush to escape the night before. She'd packed canned food but no can opener; she'd held the shipping container doors shut with a lock whose combination she'd forgotten long ago. She hadn't raised the tarp over the solar panels, or drained the rainwater tank. The chickens remained locked in their coop.

☆ ☆ ☆

TWO HOURS LATER, the bus reached the Louisiana-Mississippi border. Here a drab, prefabricated building stood at the center of a network of guard posts and concrete chicanes. All vehicles were slowly ushered through this bottleneck. A smattering of armed guards—some of them Louisiana Reservists, others bearing the red, three-starred insignia of the Free Southern State—milled about on either side of the border.

The bus slowed to a crawl as it slalomed between the chicanes. A white minivan made the same journey a few feet ahead. The minivan's roof was marked up with lines of black electrical tape that spelled out the word PRESS. At every third chicane the path straightened for a few feet and the vehicles crossed a set of tire shredders aligned northward. An FSS soldier looked on from a nearby guard tower, indifferent.

The bus idled, waiting on the guards to inspect the minivan ahead in line. The soldiers ushered a group of four men out of the vehicle and then stepped inside. Two of the soldiers began removing equipment from the back of the minivan—cameras, tripods, satellite phones, bright green flak vests, and helmets. A third guard stood nearby, inspecting a few sheets of paper given to him by one of the minivan's occupants. He flipped through the pages with no discernible interest in their contents or the various notarized seals upon them. Occasionally the man who'd handed the papers over tried to interject, but was told to keep quiet. More soldiers began to congregate around the minivan, gawking at the equipment now strewn on the ground. Eventually the soldier reading the papers folded them up and placed them in his pocket and ordered the vehicle, its passengers, and contents moved to a small building off to the side of the road. The passengers protested, but to no avail.

Another soldier waved the bus forward. The driver inched closer until he was ordered to stop. The driver opened the door and the soldier came inside.

"Good morning, sir," the driver said. "Just making the run up to Patience. Gonna stay north till Grenada then cut northeast to the border towns. Got my permit from Atlanta right here . . ."

The soldier ignored the driver. He nodded in the direction of the rebel fighter.

The soldier inspected the bus and its five occupants. He was just as spindly as the fighters Martina had seen in Eliza Polk's house. His red Mag uniform, with its gaudy overabundance of copper buttons and stars, hung loosely on his frame. He wore a box military cap with a flat visor that shadowed his eyes. He looked like a child.

"Ain't supposed to bring any in from the Purple country," he said.

"They're the only ones, sir," the driver said, fumbling through his stack of permits. "Just a couple folks displaced by the fighting out near the Texas border. We got an approval order right here from the Mag rep in Baton Rouge, if you'll take a look . . ."

The rebel fighter motioned for the driver to stop talking.

"It's all right," he told the soldier. "They're Red."

The soldier nodded. He took the permits from the driver and walked out of the bus. "Go on," he said.

The driver closed the door and the bus crawled forward toward the gatepost. One of the soldiers untied the post from its moor. The concrete counterweight at the other end dipped and the gatepost opened. The bus passed into the clearing and for a moment it transited through the silent gray suture between two worlds.

Soon they were on the other side. Martina saw out the west-facing windows the mass of refugees packed against the southbound crossing, held back by a small army of Louisiana Reservists. The bus moved forward, gaining speed, and soon the border crossing disappeared.

"Welcome to the Mag," the driver said to his passengers. "The last real set of balls in the whole of God's green earth."

☆ ☆ ☆

THEY MOVED NORTHWARD. Sarat looked out the window. The water that inundated so much of southern Louisiana was gone, but in other ways the land looked the same. The fields they passed were empty and browning, the trees limp and bare. Curls of blown-out tires littered the ditches by the side of the road.

But there were different sights too, things she'd never seen before—craters ten feet in diameter splitting the highway open, covered over in places with haste: sometimes with concrete, other times with crude wheel bridges made of wood and steel planks. An old, fossil-powered muscle car screamed past the bus, its hood decorated with a stylized rattlesnake.

There were strange billboards on the side of the road. They bore images of destruction and carnage: city blocks reduced to rubble; the dust-lacquered corpses of children; soldiers from the Free Southern State assisting the destitute families who lived in the border towns. Affixed to all these images were no words except: Nehemiah 4:14.

Near Jackson, the driver steered the bus eastward. Soon they were in Alabama, and once again headed north. When they reached Huntsville, not far from Alabama's wartime border with the Blues, the driver slowed and turned into town.

"This the North, Mama?" Sarat asked.

"Not yet, baby," her mother replied. "Soon."

The driver squinted, looking ahead at the town from the peak of the highway turnoff. "Christ," he said. "I can see them already, crawling all over one another like rats."

The bus stopped near the doors of a proud brown-brick church. A human swarm blanketed the courtyard: women and their children huddled around sacks and suitcases, men hobbled by age or amputation slumped in their wheelchairs. Volunteers tended to them with cling-wrapped sandwiches and fruit juice cups. Some of the volunteers were priests, clad in their clerical blacks, but all wore white vests on which were stamped, large and readily visible, the symbol of the Red Crescent.

Seeing the bus, the crowd began to fidget. A few volunteers held them at bay behind the black iron gate that marked the church grounds. A priest emerged from the horde and came to the bus. The driver opened the door.

"'Afternoon, Father," the driver said. "You look set to be trampled by your own flock, don't you?"

"They shelled Hazel Green Saturday night," the priest said. "God knows who they were after, but it sent the whole town running. You got ninety for me, right?"

"Eighty-five."

The priest looked at a manifest attached to a clipboard in his hand. "Says here ninety. I already told them ninety would get to leave."

"Don't worry, Father. I bet by now these folks are used to being told all kinds of things that turn out not to be true. Eighty-five, no more."

The priest rubbed his temple. "Fine, wait, just wait a while. And keep the doors closed; when I tell them they might come for your throat."

"Whatever you say, Father."

The priest returned to address part of the crowd in the courtyard, and soon the murmur in the crowd rose, and the priest was shouted down from all directions. Martina listened through a sliver of open window.

"It's my turn, you said it yesterday," a woman said. "You swore it."

"I have no say in the matter," the priest replied.

"The hell you don't," a man leaning on crutches said.

"You know I don't."

"Then show us who does have a say. You give us that man to talk to."

"There is no one man, and you know it," the priest said. "There's just the war. The war has say. And the war says five of you have to wait another night."

The priest huddled with the other volunteers to decide which five would stay. Preemptively, people in the crowd began yelling reasons why they should not be made to wait one more day. They shouted of their ailments, of festering wounds that required urgent care; they shouted the number of their dead and the names of their children. The priest and his advisers looked at the manifest and crossed and uncrossed and crossed the names again.

"Goddamn Anglicans," the bus driver said. "Never could make up their minds."

Finally it was agreed that four men and one teenage boy would remain at the church. The other eighty-five refugees, all but two of them women and children, were made to form a line that snaked back and forth from the courtyard to the sidewalk. The bus driver opened the door and, one by one, they boarded.

It was a sullen, dead-eyed procession. The women filled the seats with mechanical indifference, their children ahead of them, their belongings stuffed in backpacks or suitcases or laundry baskets. They wore track pants and T-shirts and tank tops soiled with food stains and emblazoned with the names and logos of restaurants and hotels and companies that no longer existed. More than a few of the women wore the same cheap polyester T-shirts. On the front of these shirts was drawn the undulating flag of the Free Southern State: three hollow black stars, aligned horizontally, upon a white horizontal bar. The white split evenly an otherwise red background. On the back, the shirts were stamped in bold font with the date October 1, 2074—Southern Independence Day.

Martina shifted close to her children, protecting her corner of the bench. Slowly the bus filled to capacity with its human cargo. The bodies brought with them their warmth; the air within the bus began to turn stale and humid with the pickled acidity of sweat and unbathed skin. Three women filled the rest of the available space on the back bench, their children and belongings piled high upon their laps. One woman, who looked to be in her late twenties and dragged behind her a boy not much younger than Simon, approached Martina.

"You're taking up too much room," she said, pointing at the Chestnuts' belongings. "Get rid of all that shit."

"We're taking up as much room as anyone else," Martina replied.

The woman looked with contempt at the statue of the Virgin, which rested on the bench next to Sarat. "They're keeping my husband another day in that hellhole so you can bring a goddamn statue with you? That ain't fair."

"I didn't know it'd be like this."

"I don't give a shit what you know. Throw it out."

A woman occupying the seat next to the old man from Blind River turned around. "Just sit down, Lara," she said. "Stop pestering the poor woman."

"Shut up, Holly. You ain't in charge of nothing."

At the front of the bus, the rebel guard stood. "Shut your mouth and sit down," he said.

"It ain't fair, it ain't fair!" Lara replied. "Why'd they get to bring every damn thing they own when my husband doesn't even get the seat he was promised?"

The guard slung his rifle around his shoulder and walked to the back of the bus.

"All right, all right," Lara said. "Calm down, hold on a second." But quickly the fighter grabbed her by the arm and dragged her forward. She cursed him and grasped at the backs of the seats, but was easily dislodged. When he reached the front of the bus, the guard pulled the door lever with his free hand and then shoved the woman outside. She landed unbalanced and fell on the sidewalk. Then he turned to the young boy, who'd been tugging at his shirt screaming for him to let go of his mother, and threw him out too. Before any of the church volunteers had a chance to object, he'd tossed their rucksacks as well. He closed the doors and turned to the passengers.

"Anyone else got something to say?" he asked. The passengers said nothing. The guard turned to the driver.

"Go," he said. The driver obeyed.

Soon the bus was back on the highway, headed west, back in the direction of Mississippi. A mile after the highway crossed the wash of Little Yellow Creek, the driver turned northward, navigating by memory a labyrinth of one-lane country roads. The roads meandered around dry beds that once bore the offshoots of the Tennessee River.

Holly turned once more to Martina.

"Don't worry 'bout Lara," she said. "She ain't been the same since she lost her youngest boy to the Birds last winter."

"I didn't know," Martina said. "I didn't know about any of this."

Holly raised her hand over the back of her seat and introduced herself and shook Martina's hand. "Where you from, anyway?" she asked.

"St. James."

"Never heard of it."

"South of Baton Rouge, on the Mississippi."

Holly's brows furrowed. "That's Blue country," she said. "Purple, anyway. What did you do to end up here?"

"The fighting moved east from Texas."

"Sweetheart, you think the Texas fighting is bad? You ain't seen the border towns round here. You should have gone up north when you had the chance. They got an office in Baton Rouge where you can get yourself a work permit."

Martina looked over at her children to see if they'd been following the conversation. They appeared otherwise occupied—Dana asleep, Sarat entranced by the strange new country, Simon talking to Holly's boy, who shared with him a plastic toy alligator he'd brought with him.

"Anyway—what am I saying?—you'll be just fine," Holly continued. "They got good people running Patience. The Red Crescent. That's the best one of those aid groups, you know, the one they send to all the biggest wars. Don't get me wrong, it ain't no hotel, but at least it's big enough that the Blues got no excuse to fire on it by accident the way they sometimes do. And anyway, President Kershaw's people in Atlanta say we'll have peace by Christmas and everybody will get on back to their homes, or what's left of them. He says they might even make the Blues pay to rebuild the border towns, but I'll believe that when I see it."

Martina looked out the window. She saw four old fossil trucks parked by the side of the road. A group of about ten Free Southern State soldiers were standing near the trucks. One of them waved the bus down.

"What do they want now?" Martina said.

"Ain't nothing," Holly replied. "They just can't have armed rebels bringing folks in. It makes the Red Crescent people nervous."

The bus stopped. The rebel fighter traded places with one of the soldiers. The soldier wore the same red uniform as the guards who manned the Louisiana border crossing, his cap folded and pinned under his shoulder mark.

"Mornin'," he said to the passengers. A few nodded and returned the greeting.

"Real upbeat crowd you got here," the soldier said to the driver. "Go on, get us to the gate."

The driver pulled forward. A couple of miles up the road, in a burn-cleared woodland not far from where three states met in the Tennessee River, the bus passed a set of speed bumps. A billboard bore the same crescent illustration that had marked the vests of the church volunteers in Huntsville. The sign said: "Camp Patience Refugee Facility—Neutral Ground."

☆ ☆ ☆

THE REFUGEES SHUFFLED OUT into the Mississippi dusk. The Chestnuts, their legs numb from the daylong drive, were the last to exit. They had barely a moment to regard their new surroundings—an endless expanse of thick canvas tents, teeming with displaced life—before they were ushered by a camp worker into the administrative building.

There they waited in a large intake room, seated on plastic schoolroom chairs. Others, tired of sitting, took blankets from their sacks and spread them on the ground and lay on them and closed their eyes. In parts of the room large standing fans whirred. Many of the incoming refugees congregated near these fans. A couple of aid workers walked around the room, handing out bottled water from a cooler.

"Where are we, Mama?" Sarat asked.

"It's just a place to spend the night, baby," her mother replied.

"It smells funny."

"I know, baby. Just wait a little while longer."

A half-hour after she entered the intake room, Martina heard her name called out by one of the aid workers. She and her children once again picked up their belongings and followed the worker to an office where a man sat behind a cluttered schoolteacher's desk, a pile of intake forms before him.

"Chestnut?" he said.

"That's us," Martina replied.

"Four?"

"Yes."

The man looked over the forms on the desk in front of him a while longer. His thin eyes were circled with the dark shadows of insufficient sleep.

"You're not from the Free Southern State territories," he said.

Martina did not respond. The man flipped through the intake form again.

"Do you have . . . any authorization documents from the FSS consulate . . ." the man started, then paused. "Did anyone give you papers? This is a camp for internally displaced persons of the Free Southern State, yes? You understand what I'm saying?"

"I got no papers," Martina said.

The man set the intake forms down on the desk and scratched his scalp. He sighed and retrieved from another drawer a pink form. He began filling it, asking Martina questions without looking up.

"What is your date of birth?"

"March 21, 2036."

"The boy's name and date of birth?"

"Simon Chestnut. January 1, 2066."

"The girls' . . ."

"Sara Chestnut, December 30, 2068. Dana Chestnut. Same."

"Are they immunized?"

"What?"

"Do they have their shots? Measles, mumps rubella, you understand?"

"No."

"Are they sick? Do they have any communicable diseases? Coughing, fever, anything like that?"

"No."

The man shook his head and struck out several lines on the form. He read over the rest of the sheet and then scratched the bottom half of the page out entirely. He stamped the sheet with the Red Crescent seal and placed it together with the other intake forms in a folder.

"You came here on the bus with the Hazel Green refugees, yes?"

"Yeah."

"Then, for administrative purposes, that is where we will say you are from. If anyone asks you—and sometimes we have members of the media in these facilities—this is where you will say you are from. It's very important, you understand?"

"Sure."

The man called in his assistant, who led the Chestnuts out of the administrative building.

"We're filled up in the Alabama slice right now, so you're going to Mississippi. Row thirty-six, tent fourteen," the assistant said. "Remember that—it's your address now."

In the purple light of dusk, the Chestnuts walked into the huge tent favela that would, until the night of the great massacre, serve as their city of refuge.

Excerpted from:

AN ORAL HISTORY OF THE SECOND AMERICAN CIVIL WAR: VOLUME II, 2074–2080

Q: How many men were on your side?

A: About five hundred where I was, north of Kilgore. Maybe three times that number in the places between Longview and Gladewater, and up to East Mountain. There were fighters all over that side of Texas back then. This was right around the time the Southern State declared independence, and everybody was still excited for a fight.

Q: Can you describe some of the men in your regiment at Kilgore? Their background, where they came from.

A: There was no regiment, just a bunch of men with guns who didn't know they were being led to slaughter. They were Texans, most of them. Or at least, they had ancestry in Texas, family from back when it was a real state. Some of them had experience as soldiers in the National Guard or the Blue military back before Southern independence. You could tell from the beginning they looked down on the rest of us. They had themselves real uniforms, fresh from Austin, and new guns same as the Blues had. The rest of us carried Type-95s from the boats, or old hunting rifles or even handguns and such. A couple of boys from Mississippi came lugging these old rusted broadswords, like it was King Arthur's Court or something. Could barely lift them off the ground.

Q: What motivated the men from outside Texas to come to the oil fields?

A: The ones who came from the purple states—Arkansas, Kansas, Tennessee—they were either broke or jobless or on the lam back home, so they were looking for three squares a day and any kind of soldier's wages, or they were genuinely angry that their home states went along with Columbus and the fuel prohibition, so they were looking for a fight.

The ones from the Mag were for the most part members of the rebel groups—the Palmetto Guns, the New Zouaves, the Mississippi Sovereigns, and about a dozen smaller ones with maybe ten members each, maybe even less. Those ones, any chance they got, they'd talk your ear off about the righteousness of the Southern cause. I think some of them really believed they were doing the Lord's work out there in East Texas.

Then you had the South Carolina men, and they were a different bag altogether. This was before Columbus put that whole state to sleep, but even then the Carolina fighters were the meanest sons of bitches on the front. I've been to that state in peacetime, and didn't meet a single inhospitable soul. But from the first day of the war they didn't talk to no one, didn't smile or shake hands or none of that. You got the sense from being around them that no war in the history of South Carolina had ever ended, that they were still fighting all of them at once.

Then there were some men just sort of showed up—no affiliation, no nothing. Hell, I'd bet some of them were Blues by birth, never left New York state till the week before. I guess they just wanted some excitement, to see the fighting up close, to taste rebellion. Most of the Texans and the rebels hated that kind, called them tourists or spies. But once you got over that sort of thing, there was something comforting about having Northerners wanting to fight on your side. It made you feel your cause was just in an absolute kind of way.

Q: Can you describe what you saw when you first reached the front?

A: When we got to the place, it looked just like farmland you'd see anywhere else, but no crops were growing. They had us set up in and around five abandoned farmhouses. There was one, maybe two miles of space between each house, and that land was overgrown with this sharp brown grass. I don't know what it was, but it itched like hell to walk through it, and no matter what you did to it it wouldn't die. I saw a guy out there with a machete trying to clear a path from one of the houses to a shotgun shack not a hundred feet away. He slashed for the better part of an hour and didn't make a dent in it. When he came back he looked like he'd gone swimming in a jellyfish pond.

Good thing about the grass, though, was it was high. You dropped to your knees in that brush and you became invisible.

So the Texans stationed most of us in the fields. We wrapped old towels around our faces to keep from itching.

Q: Can you talk about the night of the attack?

A: In our part of the field they had us lined up every hundred feet or so, two men to a spot. My partner was a guy from Montgomery named . . . hell, I can't remember anymore. The whole night we whispered back and forth—You see anything? No, you? Nothing.

At around three in the morning I heard something like a—like when you turn the numbers on those old combination locks that suitcases used to have. Just a click-click-click. It wasn't too loud but it was out of place. I remember one of the old Texas army veterans once said nature doesn't do straight lines or straight sounds. This was a straight sound. But before I had a chance to say anything, the ranch house down the way had been blown to bits. It was a bright orange burst and this sound like a metal balloon popping, and then there was nothing left but a lick of fire and a big cloud of black smoke.

That's when all hell broke loose. You could hear men in the fields cursing and giving out commands to fire, but none of them knew what they were firing at. A couple of the fighters had these night vision rigs with them, and everyone around them kept asking what they saw, but they didn't see nothing either. Then there was another click-click-click, and everyone knew now to duck and cover their ears like we'd been taught, and then the ranch house to our left was gone.

I felt the blast like a punch in the gut. When I got the air back in my lungs I called out to my partner to see if he was all right, but he didn't answer. It wasn't till morning that I saw how he was killed. Those bombs they dropped on us had all these tiny darts in them, and his entire left side was torn to shreds. If it'd been me to his left instead of him to mine, he'd have lived and I'd have died. But it didn't happen that way.

When they were done with the houses they bombed the fields. After a while I just lay facedown in the dirt and I said a prayer and I waited.

After the bombs stopped I heard the sound of helicopters overhead. There were still a few men who'd survived the shelling and now they were being mowed down from the air. By then everything sounded distant. I had this awful ringing in my ears. But I could feel the earth shaking all around me.

Then the helicopters flew low, and after a few passes some of them landed. I could feel the soldiers near me but I couldn't see or hear them. They walked in lines up and down the fields. I lay as still as if I was dead. Once they came as close to me as I am to you right now. I don't know if they took me for dead already or if they didn't care or if they wanted me to live and tell, but they just kept walking. An hour later they were gone, but I didn't move till the sun came up.

Q: What did you see in the morning?

A: I saw the dead in the fields, and the houses turned to dust.

Q: Did you see any federal troops, or the bodies of any federal troops?

A: It was like they were never there.

Q: Were you injured?

A: I didn't feel a thing.

Q: What did you do then?

A: First I thought I'd go south back to Kilgore. I thought that's where the others would have gone. I didn't know then that there were no others. Then I thought better of it. I figured next thing the Blues would do is go into Kilgore and all the nearby towns and kill all the enemy that didn't fight.

Q: There were fighters who deserted?

A: No.

Q: They just didn't go in the first place?

A: No, they were never fighters in the first place, but they were the enemy to the Blues. More of an enemy than any of us who had guns.

I don't expect you to understand it. Your side fought the war, but the war never happened to you. In the Red country the war happened.

If you lived in the South during that war, maybe you were never forced from your home at gunpoint, but you knew someone who was. Maybe you didn't lose a loved one when the Birds came and rained down death with no rhyme or reason, but you knew someone who had.

Now for most of people, just knowing wasn't enough to make them take up arms—not everyone can face the thought of getting shot or torn to bits by shrapnel or, even worse, getting captured and sent to rot in Sugarloaf or some other detention camp. But damned if it didn't make you want to do something.

So you gave alms to certain churches, knowing where that money would end up. Or when the Blues raided your town looking for those insurrectionists they were always talking about, even if you knew exactly where they was hiding, you kept your mouth shut and let the Marines tear your home apart until they got frustrated and left. And whenever news came of some—What do you call it up there? Incendiary homicide attack?—that left a few dead anywhere north of the Tennessee line, you didn't say nothing, but inside you were pleased. You were pleased because they up there got a little taste of what it's like for us down here. It didn't even the score, not by a long shot, but it gave them a little taste.

That's what you Northerners will never understand. The real insurrectionists never fired a single shot.

Q: Did you fight any other battles during the course of the war?

A: No. I hiked east two days, hitched a ride near Cross Lake and ended up back in my hometown in southern Alabama. Waited out the rest of the war there, and the plague that followed. By the time it was all done, most everyone I'd ever known was dead.

Q: Do you feel any lasting resentment, bitterness, or ill will toward the Union or the Northern states?

A: [Laughter].

II

July, 2081
Iuka, Mississippi

CHAPTER FIVE

The layout of Camp Patience resembled that of a circle drawn into quarters. The Mississippi slice occupied the northwest quadrant, Georgia the southwest, Alabama the northeast, and South Carolina the southeast. Refugees were assigned tents according to their native state. The Chestnuts, interlopers, had lived in the Mississippi quadrant since they first arrived, six years ago.

The camp's four sectors met at a focus composed of administrative offices: the camp intake, the school, the chapel, the medical clinic, and the cafeteria hall. Outward from the buildings, a centrifugal flare of tents blanketed the land.

To the west, Camp Patience bordered the blistered remains of the Tishomingo County Game Refuge. To the north, beyond the highest, most daunting fences, lay Tennessee. On a clear winter's day the occupants of the northernmost tents could make out the vague tree-camouflaged towers of the Blues in their forward operating bases, and at night hear the taunts and curses of the Union-aligned militias, stalking from the brush, hunting those who dared make a break for the North.

Some tried anyway, and were shot down. Others came and went, opting instead to take their chances in the city slums surrounding the Southern capital of Atlanta. The only exceptions were the refugees from South Carolina, who made something akin to a permanent life in Patience. South Carolinians had no hope of ever going home, because the South Carolina they knew was no more. Infected by Union agents with a stunting virus early on in the war, part of an effort to quell the fierce secessionist uprising in that state, it was now a walled hospice. The sick remained, imprisoned behind the quarantine wall, and the healthy could never go home again.

MARTINA'S NEIGHBOR Lara knocked on the door of the Chestnuts' tent and stepped inside. She found Martina where she usually was, seated at a salvaged plastic patio table. The table anchored the makeshift office in which Martina spent most of her days typing letters of appeal and myriad requests on behalf of illiterate refugees.

"How did the interview go?" Martina asked.

"Same," Lara replied. "You know those journalists from the Blue, they always ask the same questions. Insurrectionists this, secessionists that. Made a few bucks for the cantina, though. Can't complain about that."

"Come, sit a while," Martina said. "Get some water in you, it's burning up out there."

Lara opened the small refrigerator by Martina's desk and took from it two bottles of water. The water bottles arrived in boxfuls on the tenth of every month, a few days after the aid ships docked in Augusta. Their crumpled remains were the most ubiquitous form of litter in the camp.

"What is it this time?" Lara asked, taking a seat on a folding chair beside Martina and looking over her shoulder at the screen of an old, barely functional tablet.

"New girl in Alabama 36:12 wants to ask Atlanta to let her husband out of jail a year early," Martina replied. "Says he was recruited to the Copperheads at gunpoint, never fired a weapon his whole life."

"You trying to time it with Independence Day?"

"Yeah."

"Is it going to work?"

"Of course not. But she offered a whole pack of Yuxis for it, I ain't gonna say no."

"That reminds me," Lara said. "That girl Madison I told you about in the Georgia slice, turns out she changed her mind about getting you to write that appeal to Mr. Sharif."

"She find some other way to get her boy's cleft lip fixed?"

"Nah. She said she came around here looking for you the other day and saw that thing." Lara pointed to the cracked statue of the Virgin that rested on a couple of water bottle boxes near the front of the tent.

"What about it?" Martina asked.

"Guess she don't like Catholics."

"You kidding?"

"No ma'am."

Martina shook her head. "Some people," she said. "Fine by me. Let her get that snake-kisser from Birmingham to fix her son, if she's so devout."

Lara laughed. "They don't let him in here no more. Too hot for their taste. Got some soft-boiled Baptist from Atlanta instead. You know the kind—God's heavenly plan this, God's heavenly plan that." Lara checked the time on Martina's tablet. "That reminds me," she said. "You coming to the service?"

"No time," Martina said. "Gotta finish this one then get started on the Buckhorns' one."

"The hell the Buckhorns want now?"

"Guess the fighting's died down in east Georgia along the border. Atlanta declared their town safe again."

"They want a ride out there or something?"

"No, they're asking to stay here."

"That's a new one," said Lara.

"Can't say I blame them. They've been here longer than us. Probably nothing waiting for them back there but a big old hole in the ground."

The conversation was interrupted by a knock at the door. Lenny, a seventeen-year-old who was the camp's most well-connected fixer, entered, a wad of cash in his hand.

"Mornin' ladies," he said. "Now, don't you say you ain't glad to see me, for I know it not to be true."

"Glad to see what you're holding, anyway," Lara said. "How much did you get out of him?"

"You'll be pleased to know, Mrs. Boswell, that I got the standard rate," Lenny said. He counted three hundred dollars from his roll of bills and placed it on the table. "And this despite the frankly shameful way you treated our guest this morning."

"Oh, I'm supposed to sing and dance for them now too?"

"You ain't supposed to curse them, for a start."

"I didn't curse nobody."

"You called him a liar," Lenny said. "To a fancy Northern journalist, that's worse than cursing."

Martina put her hand out. "What about my girl's cut?" she said.

"Huh?"

"Don't huh me—turn your good side this way."

"All my sides is good sides," Lenny said. He handed Martina two hundred dollars.

"That it?" Martina said. "They filmed her for damn near an hour."

"That's it for now. But don't you worry, that Dana Chestnut gonna be a star. Foreign hacks will pay all kinds of money to film themselves a pretty little Southern refugee girl, and you got the prettiest little refugee girl anyone's ever seen."

"We're not making a habit of this," Martina said.

"Your call, but they will be back for more, I know it." Lenny knelt by the Chestnuts' fridge and emerged with a bottle of water. He sat at the table with the two women and wiped the sweat from his face.

"I think you're wrong about that Blue reporter," he said to Lara. "I think he might just use some of what you told him, even though God knows you were rambling and incoherent half the time."

"What do I care what he uses?" Lara said. "There somebody left up there doesn't know there's a war happening?"

Lenny chuckled. "You know he keeps asking me to take him to the Carolina slice. I told him they'll cut your throat the minute they see you, but he's convinced they're gonna—what'd he say? That's right, they're gonna recognize his neutrality."

"Oh, they'll recognize something," Lara said. "They'll recognize real quick."

Lenny finished the bottle in two quick gulps and set it on the table. He was short and skinny in a way that suggested stunted growth. Through years of practice he had committed to muscle memory a slight dip of the shoulder and shift of the body, such that the devastated half of his face, where the skin lay molten and the ear curled in on itself, was always partially shielded from view. He wore, almost exclusively, faded QQ T-shirts and hiker's pants in whose various pockets he kept notebooks full of names and addresses, as well as three of the only working phones in Camp Patience.

"A pleasure as always, ladies," he said, rising. "I'll be seeing you both again shortly, I'm sure. Stay well south of the fence, much as you can. My guy says the militias up north are getting riled up again."

When he was gone Martina put her tablet to sleep and sat back in her chair. In six years she'd developed a sense to prognosticate the weather;

another dust storm was coming. There was a familiar aridity, an accretion of invisible weight in the air. In the next day or two a gradient of bronze fog would once again take the sky, and for a week afterward the cantina would be fully sold out of air canisters and wet wipes.

"How long's that boy been fixing?" she asked Lara.

"Lenny? Since he was ten or eleven, at least. Started out running cigarettes for Blue grunts stationed near the border, figured nobody would shoot a kid that small, and got lucky I guess because nobody did. From there he started working with journalists. That's how he lost half his face. Guess one of those reporters wanted to see up north of Corinth where the rebels killed all those Blues with car bombs, so he takes him up there, and wouldn't you know it . . ."

"You saw all those bills?" Martina said. "Boy must be sitting on a small fortune by now."

"Doesn't spend none of it, either. He's got plans. Every time he does a job for a Northern reporter or one of the Blue soldiers he asks them to write him a reference letter so he can apply for a permit to get the hell out of the Red. They all say they will but hardly any do. He doesn't even use his real name with them. Got a whole other identity just for his dealings with Northerners. They think his name's Christian something."

"He still does work for the Blue soldiers?"

"Yeah. Guess they figured a while back if you're going to barge into a Southern town and you want the locals to cooperate, it's best to have a Southerner there with you."

"I'm surprised the rebels haven't strung him up for it."

Lara shrugged. "He's the kind can make friends with anyone, and he's got a lot of them," she said. "It'll catch up to him one day, but at least he's working toward something, not like the rest of us, sitting still day after day till they bury us here."

Lara stood. "You sure you don't wanna come to the service?" she asked. "They have a reception afterward where they serve that orange juice that tastes like oranges."

"You go on," Martina said. "I'll catch you at the game tonight."

Lara shook her head. "Nothing as sad as a lapsed Catholic," she said.

☆ ☆ ☆

AFTER HER FRIEND LEFT, Martina opened her tablet and set to finishing the letter of appeal she'd been commissioned to write. But the words wouldn't come. She set the tablet down and retreated to her bed in the back of the tent. She lay on her cot, the metal springs squeaking under her weight.

She'd written hundreds of these letters over the years—leniency requests; admissions of petty guilt; appeals by growing families for bigger and better-situated tents; letters to the editors of faraway papers; Northern travel permits; love letters; eulogies.

Other than the eulogies, most of what she wrote proved useless; perhaps one out of every twenty achieved what it was intended to achieve. These successful letters, the demonstrable fruits of her work, she printed out and stored in a small filing cabinet by her bed. It was those letters that marked her place in the entrepreneurial ecosystem of the camp—alongside the likes of the man in the Alabama sector who could move any sum of money anywhere in the country in four days or less, or the grandmother in Georgia whose fortuitous real estate allowed her to leach a wireless connection from the administrative offices. Work provided purpose, a sense of place, a sense of agency.

In the course of her letter writing, she'd learned a few things about the subtle peculiarities of the South's power brokers. The Mississippi Sovereigns, like most other rebel groups, preferred to be addressed as Brothers; letters to Mr. Sharif, the director of Camp Patience, were exclusively read and acted upon by his secretary, but could never be addressed to his secretary; the Free Southern State government in Atlanta had a perfect record of responding to every letter, but no sooner than two years after the fact.

She learned which methods of attack worked and which didn't. Any familial relation between appellant and recipient, no matter how tenuous, was to be ruthlessly exploited; pictures of dead relatives or horrific war wounds never did any good, although the refugees in possession of such images invariably demanded they be sent anyway; a direct offer of bribery was more likely than not to elicit an insulted response, but an offer to make a donation to a cause of the recipient's choosing got the same message across more tactfully.

It was, in the end, hopeless work, the letters almost always doomed to fail. But for the refugees who paid or begged Martina to write these pleadings on their behalf, hopelessness was no impediment to hope.

☆ ☆ ☆

LIKE THEIR OLD HOME by the banks of the Mississippi Sea, the Chestnuts' tent was sectioned into thirds. Martina's room occupied the back third, anchored by a steel hospital cot and an old chest of drawers.

In the middle third of the tent the twins lived in opposing beds. On Dana's side there were the salvaged trappings of teenage girlhood—a straightening iron; a makeup kit composed of various brands and shades of concealer and blush and lipstick and eye shadow. Near these things lay a stack of dog-eared, yellowing copies of *Belle Magazine,* a publication out of print for decades.

On Sarat's side of the tent there were no posters and few possessions. In a large plastic bowl she kept a potpourri of war seeds—bullet casings and wild-toothed slivers of shrapnel. They were given to her as presents by the sullen grunts charged with scouring the Northern boundary of the camp for land mines. She liked watching the soldiers work, their frames hunchbacked, their ancient metal detectors helplessly beeping.

In a small space ahead of the girls' room Martina kept a kitchen. The area between the kitchen and the tent's front door was Simon's room. It was a chaotic space, thick with the dank smell of unwashed clothing that sat in a heap at the foot of the boy's bed. A blanket lay tucked under the bottom of the bed's mattress, creating a makeshift curtain that hid whatever was stored beneath the bed. On the wall there hung an old poster of pristine Texas desert, unspoiled and unmarked. It was a form of protest. The desert poster became popular among the teenage boys at the camp after the administrators banned posters featuring a particular brand of long-discontinued, fossil-run muscle car. Before that, it was snakes of any kind; and before that, the rebel rattlesnake; and before that—in the beginning—posters bearing the names of any of the rebel groups. Soon the administrators would get around to banning Texas pastorals, and the boys would move on to something else.

Everywhere in the tent there were piles of accumulated things—hot plates, standing fans, two mini-fridges, half-empty bottles of rubbing alcohol; moisturizer; paperwork from the camp and from the Free Southern State; can openers; first-aid kits; and, more than all of these things, blankets.

Blankets saturated every aid shipment to Camp Patience, boxes upon boxes of burly fabric that scraped the skin like sandpaper. Even in the deadest of winter there was no need for blankets, so instead the refugees fashioned from them room dividers and tablecloths, foot mats and drawer-lining. Still, there were more blankets than anyone knew what to do with. Folded piles of blankets lay beneath the twins' beds and above the filing cabinet. They were useless as bartering currency, subject to an inflation even worse than that of the Southern dollar. And yet the anonymous benefactors across the ocean in China and the Bouazizi Empire kept sending more. For the life of her, Martina could not imagine what the foreigners thought the weather was like in the Red, but then she couldn't even imagine the benefactors as people. They existed in another universe, not as beings of flesh and blood but as pipes in some vast, indecipherable machine, its only visible output these hulking aid ships full of blankets.

☆ ☆ ☆

MARTINA RESTED on her cot. She closed her eyes but could not sleep. The midday heat was building. She sat up and went outside.

She walked south, away from her tent, into Georgia. She followed the paths between the tents until she reached the place where the woman with the cleft-lipped baby lived. It was one of the newer tents, near the southwestern edge of the camp. The woman was alone, changing her child on the bed.

He was a pristine baby boy, his skin smooth as alabaster. Even the malformation that split his upper lip looked flawless, as though it were everyone else that was built the wrong way.

"Mornin'," Martina said. "You got a minute?"

The woman said nothing. She was in her early twenties. She wore an FSS shirt and a plain gray skirt that ran to her ankles.

"Lara told me you're not interested in a letter for the camp director anymore," Martina said.

"That's right," the woman replied.

"You got some other plan?"

"We'll make do."

"Look, I don't know your story, and I don't care," Martina said. "But in this place we don't have the luxury of inventing enemies. Let me write that letter for you. I don't need any payment."

"No. Thank you. We'll make do," the woman said. She lay her baby on a small scrap of aid blanket. The child grasped at the air with chubby little limbs.

"For Christ's sake," Martina said. "We're not even Catholic. That statue belongs to my husband."

"So your husband's Catholic."

"My husband's dead."

The woman did not respond. Her baby gurgled and spat and stared transfixed at the ceiling.

"Fine," Martina said. "Do what suits you. Just remember that it's that baby boy who's paying for your made-up grudges."

"Thank you for your concern," the woman said.

Martina left the tent. Her anger at the young woman's stubbornness quickly prompted recollections of all the times she'd found herself on one side or another of these meaningless, bigoted demarcations; all the times she'd been made to feel alien to some stranger's expectation of what constituted the right and normal world—the color of her skin, the ethnicity of the man she'd chosen to marry, even her tomboy daughter. And no matter how much she tried to fight it, every now and then it still made her venomous. Stay mean if you want to, you stupid little girl, she thought. Cling to that tiny piece of power you think you have. But I hope every time you see your baby's ruined lips you think of me.

She walked back to her own neighborhood in Mississippi. On her way she caught sight of Sarat playing tag with a gaggle of boys a few years younger than she was. They dodged around the tents and under the weighted clotheslines, giggling and screaming. Martina called her daughter over.

"Stop rolling around in the dirt," she said. "You look filthy."

"We're just playing," the girl replied, catching her breath as the rest of the children sprinted onward.

"Where's your sister?"

"I don't know," Sarat said. "Out with the older kids in Missy's tent, probably."

"I thought I told you to keep an eye on her."

"They're not gonna eat her."

"How 'bout your brother? I haven't seen him all morning."

"I heard he and Mark and them all snuck out to Muscle Shoals. Don't tell him I told you, he'll get mad."

"Muscle Shoals? How'd they get out of the camp?"

"Same way smugglers get in," Sarat said, pointing east. "Through Sandy Creek on the Alabama side."

"How do you know that? You been going out with them?"

"Like they'd ever let me."

"So you just know, then?"

The girl shrugged. "Everybody knows."

Martina brushed some of the dirt off the side of Sarat's sleeveless summer dress. At twelve years of age she was already wearing hand-me-downs—gifts from the parents of children three years older than she was. And even these seemed to shrink daily around her growing frame. Her growth spurt was so rapid over the last three years that her mother feared it might be the result of some chemical imbalance, a sickness. She was the same height now as her mother, with a frazzled head of hair made stiff by sweat and dirt.

"Go find your sister, and then the two of you come home and get cleaned up," Martina said. "You've been out enough for one day. And stay away from the north side."

Sarat nodded. "OK, Mama."

☆ ☆ ☆

SARAT WATCHED HER MOTHER retreat into the tent. In the time it had taken mother and daughter to talk, the rest of the children had galloped out of sight, and it seemed pointless now to try to catch them. Sarat returned to the women's shower tent, on whose moist and mildewing front steps she'd left her sandals so as to run more freely.

Like the crevices of a body, the shower tents radiated a damp, human-scented heat. This was most evident in the early morning hours when the water was coolest and the showers most bearable, and a trail of groggy-eyed refugees could be seen shuffling like pilgrims in their plastic sandals to the stalls. As they washed, the runoff spilled from the drains into a wastewater trench fifteen feet wide and five feet deep. The trench ran in a circle around the camp and was nicknamed Emerald Creek. In its slow journey to the purification tanks, the brown sludge of human waste produced a stench so overwhelming that the refugees, en masse, refused to live in any tent within fifty feet of it.

Sarat put her sandals on and walked east into Alabama to find her sister. Deliberately against her mother's wishes, she veered north and walked along the fenced boundary. It was near this fence where she spent much of her free time, alone and watching the young men charged with de-mining the land between the northern end of the camp and the Tennessee line.

They were hopeless-looking men, sub-privates by rank, and because they were technically in the employ of the Free Southern State they were not allowed to wear the white vests stamped with the red crescent; those were reserved for the neutral aid workers. Instead they wore yellow cycling jackets and helmets covered with reflective decals, and these they hoped would signal to the Blues across the border a kind of unofficial noncombatant status.

Even with these uniforms, it was too dangerous to do the work at night, and so the men worked in the daytime. They became friends with the girl watching them, and offered her whatever interesting false positives their detectors uncovered. She was a curiosity to them—a big-limbed, wild-haired girl who'd taken an insatiable interest in their slow, wartime metallurgy.

In Alabama, Sarat came across a boy playing with a washtub half-full of brown water. By the northerly location of his tent and the rattlesnake on his T-shirt—for which he had not yet been reprimanded—she knew him to be a recent arrival. He had green eyes and light brown hair in a neat part down the middle. He appeared about twelve years old, if a bit runty for his age. But in fact he was two years older than Sarat.

"What are you doing?" she asked.

The boy looked up, startled. "I'm making water clean," he said. "My father said you can do it with just some plastic wrap and the sun."

Without asking, Sarat took a seat in the dirt beside the boy, her curiosity piqued. In the tin washtub the boy had poured a couple of bottles of water and a few handfuls of dirt. In the middle of the tub stood one of the empty water bottles, weighed down with a couple of pebbles. The boy had sealed the tub with a layer of clear wrap, also weighed down at the center with pebbles, such that the wrap dipped just above the mouth of the bottle.

"The heat's gonna lift the water, but not the dirt," the boy said. "And since the clean water can't get out, it just slides down and falls in the bottle."

Sarat inspected the tub. She saw droplets moving slowly down the wrap, the sun fashioning tiny rainbows in their bellies.

"It's called heat evaporation," the boy said.

"You just moved here?" Sarat asked.

"Yeah, two days ago," the boy replied. "We don't know anybody yet."

"My name's Sarat Chestnut."

"My name's Marcus Exum," the boy said. "You Alabaman?"

"No. We're in the Mississippi slice. Been here six years."

"Six years!" Marcus repeated. "My dad says anyone who stays more than a month is gonna die here."

"It's not so bad. Pretty boring most days. They got a schoolroom but they don't care if you go or not."

The children's attention turned to a nearby tent, from which Marcus's father emerged. Like many of the men in the camp, he was potbellied and possessed an unruly beard that hid the contours of his neck. And like all the men, he registered as vaguely anomalous in a place inhabited predominantly by women and children. He wore brown overalls and a white undershirt recently washed but to which the old stains still held. The man approached his son.

"This is Sarat Chestnut," Marcus said. "She been here six years."

Sarat waved hello. The man looked her over, neither warm nor cold.

"How old are you?" he asked.

"Twelve," Sarat replied.

"You don't look it."

"I'm big for my age. Grew five inches last year."

"You been here six years, you say?"

Sarat nodded. The man pointed to the northeast, where the remains of old Highway 25 ran straight into a phalanx of razor wire, guards' quarters, and bright red signs warning against trespass.

"You know where that road goes?" the man asked.

"Sure. It's the northern gate. Leads up to the Tennessee border. They get real mad if you go anywhere near it. My brother says the Blues got snipers in all the trees right on the other side, and they'll shoot anyone who crosses, don't care if it's kids or women or anybody."

The man watched the gate a little longer, squinting in the midday sun. He walked a few feet toward it and then changed his mind and turned south, to where a group of four recent arrivals were arranged around an upturned cardboard box, playing cards.

Marcus turned to his new friend. "They really got snipers on the other side?" he asked.

"Yeah," Sarat replied. "You wanna see?"

Marcus nodded. Sarat led him to a spot along the northern fence where three of the links had broken, leaving a gap just big enough to fit a head through.

"Look here," Sarat said. "Up at the tallest tree over there. You see it?"

Marcus inspected the horizon. Up-field the trees were thin but in one place the foliage thickened. In this small patch of forestland there rose a tree about ten feet higher than the rest.

"The minesweepers say that's not a real tree, and that's not real leaves or anything," Sarat said. "They call it like a bird's nest but for snipers. They're up there all day and all night, just waiting on someone to try to cross. Then they shoot them dead."

Marcus watched in silence for a moment.

"Should we be looking at them like this?" he asked. "Won't they shoot us?"

Sarat had never considered this possibility before. As she thought about it, a squirrel jumped somewhere in the trees and the branches shook. The two children nearly jumped out of their skins.

☆ ☆ ☆

SARAT FOUND HER SISTER and four of her friends near the camp's administrative buildings. They were perched on the closed lids of large garbage bins in the narrow alleyway between the cafeteria building and the director's offices. For much of the day, the alleyway was deserted—at this hour especially, as staff and refugees alike congregated within the camp's easternmost building, the chapel. No matter the position of the sun, the alleyway was always draped in shade, and on summer days was often ten degrees cooler than any other outdoor space in the camp.

Dana waved at her sister as she approached. "Hey, beautiful girl," she said. In the moments before Sarat's arrival the children had been looking at something on an old tablet, but they covered it now.

Sarat waved back. She recognized the others as tenth graders: the Mailer girls, who were the only other twins Sarat knew of in the camp; a boy named Avery and another named Bishop, both of whom she knew as friends of Simon and frequent escapees through the badly guarded marina near Sandy Creek.

In almost every other way, the older children were alien to her—possessed of a dramatic concern for things that seemed inane and devoid of adventure: the color and style of skirts, the arrival of facial hair, the mysterious topology of flesh.

"Mama says we have to come home now," Sarat said.

"Why us?" Dana replied. "Simon's been out all day and he doesn't get in trouble for it."

"I don't know. That's just what she said."

"They let boys do whatever they want," said one of the Mailer twins. A beauty spot on the left cheek distinguished one girl from the other but Sarat could not remember which was which. "Last year Bill and Mark Hernandez tore down half the loudspeakers in Alabama and threw them in the creek, and they didn't do a thing to them."

"Didn't they get sent home in January?" asked Avery.

"Yeah, but that was just because their parents had to go," said the moleless Mailer. "It wasn't because *they* were being punished."

"It's easy, really," Dana said. "All the boys, when they turn fifteen, they give them a gun and send them out the north gate. You have to survive out there one week, and if you come back you can stay."

"Why do we have to go?" Bishop said. "We didn't do anything."

"But if you wanted to do anything, you could," said Dana. "That's why."

"All right, all right, how about this?" Bishop said. "Can I send Sarat in my place?"

"You would, wouldn't you?" Dana replied.

"I'll go," said Sarat. "I know where the snipers are."

At this the boys and the Mailer twins laughed wildly.

"You hear that?" Bishop said. "Give her a chance. She'll end the war tomorrow!"

Dana made a gesture at Bishop that Sarat had been taught by her mother never to make. She stood up. "I'll see you losers tomorrow," she said.

"We'll be out by the snipers. Bring Sarat," Bishop replied, to a roar from the Mailers.

"Screw you, Bishop," said Dana.

☆ ☆ ☆

THE CHESTNUT TWINS RETREATED from the alley, headed in the direction of Mississippi. They walked in the shadow of the cafeteria building's tin awning, against the tide of departures from the chapel. Men and women in their Sunday best shuffled toward their tents, orange cups in hand, talking about all the things the Baptist minister had said—*Beloved, do not be surprised at the fiery trial when it comes upon you to test you, as though something strange were happening to you. But rejoice*—and here he said it twice more, with his hands as much as his voice—*Rejoice! Rejoice! Insofar as you share Christ's sufferings, that you may also rejoice and be glad when his glory is revealed.*

The men leaving the chapel wore prewar suits and ties—not the cheap, three-star ties manufactured in bulk and handed out by the Free Southern State at every opportunity, but fine ties of wool and sometimes silk, imprinted with smooth gradients or arabesque geometry or even just the logos of old American football teams. The women wore their least faded floral dresses and swoop-brimmed sun hats they decorated with pressed flowers or paper made to look like flowers. In these last vestiges of older, better lives the refugees sweated and were terribly uncomfortable, but they wore the clothes anyway, because there were no other occasions to wear them except Christmas or Southern Independence Day.

Sarat and Dana sat on the steps of the now deserted chapel building. They watched a couple of camp workers lead a shell-numbed woman and her baby girl to their new home in the furthest outskirts of the Mississippi slice.

A Tik-Tok, marked with a large red crescent, rumbled along the dirt remnants of Highway 350, which split the camp almost down the middle. A couple of FSS soldiers sat inside and another two stood on the back fender. The tiny, three-wheeled vehicle struggled for traction, its feeble motor squealing, its tires kicking up dust.

"I bet they're going to repair the gate," Sarat said. "Bet a militia rocket hit it again."

"You've got to stop talking like that," Dana replied.

"What? You wanna go see? I'll bet you five bucks."

"I don't mean them, I mean like today, with Bishop. Like you'll believe anything anyone tells you, like you don't know when the joke's on you."

"I don't do that."

"'I know where the snipers are . . .'"

"I do!" Sarat protested. "The minesweepers showed me."

"You have to grow up, Sarat. You're not a little girl anymore. Look, just try not to give anybody reason to make fun of you, is all. You'll make more friends that way."

The two girls sat in silence. Soon the Tik-Tok returned, missing three of its original passengers but carrying a new one, a vaccination officer from Atlanta. Accompanied by a bored-looking soldier, the volunteer moved from tent to tent, asking for the immunization records of any child under the age of five.

"I made a friend today," Sarat said. "His name's Marcus. He lives in Alabama."

"Oh yeah?"

"Mmm-hmm. You can ask him about the sniper, if you don't believe me. I showed him."

Dana shook her head and chuckled. She watched the health worker. She was a woman in her early twenties. She was a Northerner, a volunteer with the One Country Coalition, doing her year of service.

"You remember when they gave us that stuff?" Dana asked.

Sarat nodded. "Told them we were too old for it. Probably didn't do anything."

"Maybe it did. Maybe we'd be dead if we didn't take it."

"Marcus's dad says anyone who stays in the camp too long is gonna die here," Sarat said. "You think we're gonna die here?"

Dana thought for a while. Across the road, the health worker was shooing away a gaggle of children she knew as repeat customers, trying to get their hands on the caramel candies she handed out after every vaccination.

"No," Dana said. "Well, maybe a hundred years from now. But not, like, *tomorrow.*"

"All right," Sarat said. "A hundred years is all right."

In the face of the children's pleading, the health worker relented and gave all the candies away. Soon the children began to dissipate, their small jaws mining hard for sugar.

Dana leaned close to her sister, resting her head on Sarat's arm.

"I'm sorry for saying you should grow up," she said. "Don't ever grow up. Don't ever change, beautiful girl."

☆ ☆ ☆

THE HEALTH WORKER PASSED from tent to tent. She asked the children their ages. Some knew and others didn't. Those who didn't she asked to raise their right arms over their heads, such that the crease of the elbow rested somewhere near the top of the head, and the fingers dangled around the left ear. The children whose fingers touched their ears she estimated to be older than five years of age, and for them the vaccine would do no good. On this basis the vaccines were administered: a few drops of clear liquid to ward off the viral paralytic that had long ago been defeated but now, riding the saddle of war, returned.

☆ ☆ ☆

LATE AT NIGHT, when the weather cooled and the camp's ragged bustle gave way to the hard, graceless sleep of the dispossessed, Martina visited her friend Erica Yarber's tent for a game of cards. For the better part of five years, this had been a ritual, practiced three or four times a week by Martina, Erica, their friend Lara, and whichever women from the neighboring tents decided to join them on any given night.

It was a large tent, near the border between Alabama and South Carolina, once occupied by Erica, her husband, and her teenage son. But the son had moved west to join the fighting and the husband's heart gave out one morning and now she lived alone.

Martina arrived with a jar of pickles, red in their Kool-Aid brine. Their taste repulsed Martina, conjuring cherries marinated in sweat, but the other women enjoyed them. The women almost always brought with them something to eat or drink: boiled and dry peanuts, day-old cafeteria bread massaged with oil or bacon grease, sweet ears, kettle chips, a mason jar of corrosive, tent-made Joyful, in addition to whatever else the women managed to acquire that day through serendipity or altruism.

The game was Fight the Landlord. Ten bucks a point, first to a hundred. They used three decks, and in this way the game moved more quickly and opportunities for bombs and rockets were increased. They played by the light of rainbow candles made from melted crayons and shoelace wicks. On a nearby tablet, a Dixie Radio broadcast trickled from the speakers. It was a big-lunged, brass-backed man singing. *Young love has made me old, tired, restless, and blue.*

"Mag on Mag, nines on eights," Martina said, laying six cards on the shaky plywood table.

"Nope," Lara said.

"Nothing," Erica followed.

Martina swept the hand and set it facedown in a neat pile in front of her. Lara's Joyful was starting to do its work.

It had become, over the years, the South's wartime drink. Joyful, a Frankenstein hooch, made from whatever was on hand, no two jugs ever the same. Martina took another swig. She tasted the ingredients of this particular batch: a festering, months-old orange juice, and beneath that an aftertaste of corn and mouthwash. She felt the onset of drunkenness; every once in a while the candle flames stood still and it was the room that flickered.

Soon the game was called and Martina collected her winnings and the ladies retreated to Erica's small, makeshift living room. Here there were arranged a set of cushions made of stitched charity blankets and foam. With no couch to use as a base, the cushions were arranged flat on the ground in the style of a Bouazizi majlis. The arrangement was sectioned with low tables made of the discarded cardboard boxes in which the camp's water bottles came.

The women sat on the cushions and left the door of the tent ajar to let in a little breeze. Soon Erica was fast asleep where she sat.

It was quiet, Erica's snoring their only accompaniment. Between the Joyful and the good tobacco, a warming balm washed over Martina's body, and the pains of the day began to recede.

"You know I had a sister once," she said.

"You never told me that before," Lara replied.

"Never told no one. Never told my husband, even. She died when I was five. I don't remember nothing about her anymore, except she had thumbs that could bend both ways. She used to show that off all the time, soon as she figured out nobody else could do it."

Lara sat upright against the cushions. She blinked a few times to shake off the weight that had been building on her eyelids.

"How'd she die?" she asked.

"Got a cold one day playing in a creek that ran by our house. By nighttime she was shaking and coughing up blood. She was dead by morning. Didn't even take a whole day. I remember my parents wouldn't let me in the bedroom, didn't want me seeing her the way she was. But I was out in the hallway and I could hear it, the sound she made when she was fighting so hard to breathe. I wish they would have let me see her. I think just the sound of it alone is worse than if they'd let me see her."

"I'm sorry," Lara said. "That must have been hard."

"Ahh, it's all long gone now. Time buries time, my mother used to say. It broke my father, though. For months afterward he just went round talking about how there used to be drugs that could have fixed her right up, but everybody used them too much and they didn't work anymore. And what did work, we couldn't afford. He kept saying it over and over, like saying it would change things."

Martina stamped out her cigarette butt in her empty measuring cup. "I remember the day we buried her. We brought this preacher out to the farm to say a few words. Man must have been a hundred years old, half-blind and pretty well senile. He walks up to the grave—my parents dug a plot for her right there on the farm, made a cross out of fence posts—he walks up to the grave and we stand behind him, all dressed up in the finest clothes we own. And we think he's just going to read a passage or just say a couple nice things about heaven or the

Lord calling her home or whatever. But he doesn't do any of that—you know what he does? He starts singing. He had this song like, We're all children in the kingdom of Jesus. He sings that line a couple times—I think he just made it up in his head, none of us ever heard this song before, we're just standing there like idiots behind him, none of us saying a word—and then he starts with: the boys and the girls are children in the kingdom of Jesus, the cats and the dogs are children in the kingdom of Jesus, the mules and the antelopes . . . just keeps going and going, like he's taking attendance on the Ark. Finally I can't help it anymore, I start giggling. My mother smacks me on the back to shut me up, but I can't help it. I'm trying, damn near wetting myself trying, but I can't. And then suddenly it hits me that I'm laughing at my own sister's funeral, and I get this guilt right in my gut—hits me like a train. And I start crying harder than I ever cried. But that old man doesn't care, he just keeps on going—the frogs and the horses and the squirrels and . . ."

Martina chuckled and shook her head. "I'll never forget that goddamn senile old preacher. How's he gonna go and make a little girl hate herself at her own sister's funeral?"

"Jesus," Lara said. "Maybe ya'll really are Catholics."

Soon the first blue of dawn began to leak into the charred sky. After the Joyful buzz wore off, Martina excused herself and walked back to her tent. In these hours the camp was at its calmest, and the tents running afield in all directions were beautiful in a rugged, delicate way—strange desert fauna reticent and frozen, a harvest of life.

When she reached her tent she opened the door slowly so as not to wake the children. She stepped inside and saw her son knelt down, pushing something under his mattress. At the foot of his bed his boots were caked in fresh mud.

"May as well show me whatever it is you got under there," Martina said.

The boy jumped at the sound of his mother's voice. He started to say something, then thought better of it. He reached under the bed and dragged out a black hard-shell guitar case. The strap showed signs of wear but the case itself was immaculate for its age, and appeared to Martina to have been at one time used prolifically but also with great care.

"They give you that?" Martina asked. "Some kind of gift or something?"

"No," Simon replied. "Found it in an abandoned studio."

"Don't lie to me."

"I swear it."

"Sit."

Simon sat on his bed. His mother sat beside him. She saw he'd cut himself across the left side of the forehead. She inspected the cut with her thumb. Simon pulled back.

"You know what they want in return when they start giving the kids round here gifts, right?"

"Mama, I just stole it, is all. I swear. It's not like it was really stealing, anyway. It was just sitting there—nobody was ever gonna come back for it."

Martina sighed. "If that's what you tell me, that's what I'll believe," she said. "But just the same, you're getting old enough that I won't have much of a say in what you're doing or where you're going anymore, so let me say it now: If you want to fight, if that's where you're headed, go to Atlanta when you turn seventeen and sign up with the Free Southerners. Put on a uniform, fight by the rules. I won't like it, but you'll be a man then and the decision's yours to make. But not the rebels. I don't care what they give you, I don't care what they promise or how they make it sound, you and I both know what they recruit the camp people to do, and I won't have you do that, you understand?"

"Mama, c'mon. I'm not gonna join any rebels, I'm not gonna blow myself up, I won't do nothing like that."

"No matter what they tell you, some things are just wrong, war or no war."

"I know, Mama."

Martina hugged her son. Then she smacked him on the back of the head.

"And it is stealing. Don't do it again."

"All right. I'm sorry."

She kissed her son good night and tiptoed past the sleeping twins in the next room. She reclined on the mattress into which her scent and shape had seeped over the years. She closed her eyes. Sleep came easy.

Excerpted from:

NEITHER BREATHE NOR HOPE: THE UNTOLD STORY OF THE SOUTH CAROLINA WARTIME QUARANTINE

In Cairo, the capital of the Bouazizi Empire, the old gray buildings of the Students' Quarter loom over alleyways of stone and brick. They are tired, pre-revolution buildings, their roofs laden with pigeon coops and thatched janitors' shacks and cracked solar panels. It is frighteningly hot, even in January. For much of the year it is too hot to be outside; soon even the hardest-bitten residents will retreat northward to the Mediterranean seaside, or to the burgeoning indoor and underground cities that have largely replaced the ancient ones above the ground. It is too hot to live the old way. But traditions die hard and, at least in the coolest winter months, many still try.

The cacophony of the alleyway bazaars rises from below: the dangling din of the silversmiths; the embers exploding off soot-lacquered grills; the indignant howls of tourists haggling for a bargain. And beyond that, the sounds of the greater metropolis: the airplanes circling Mathlouthi Airport, the Bouazizi Empire's largest hub; a symphony of horns from the unmoving cars along the August 14 Bridge. Old and new Cairo endlessly colliding.

It was in this very neighborhood, three quarters of a century earlier, that the students rushed the alleys of Khan El Sisi and the soldiers met them with rifles drawn. Today, there is little to commemorate that massacre but a tired, sputtering fountain whose alabaster tiles leach the rust from the tourists' coins.

In his small apartment overlooking the Martyrs' Fountain, Mahmoud Abd-el-Ghafur sits and listens to these sounds coming through the arabesque window coverings. This is not his real name, and this not his real country. His name is Gerry Tusk, and his country is America. He is a traitor.

☆ ☆ ☆

On January 14, 2075, the day after Southern rebels killed 38 federal workers in Lexington, the President called a half-dozen government researchers to the Executive Building in Columbus. They were tasked with devising a way of pacifying the population of the country's first rebel state. Three months later, a group of War Office agents (who were themselves told the effects of the sickness would end harmlessly in a few months) arrived at a rebel rally at the South Carolina statehouse with canisters of invisible disease tucked under their jackets. Along the state's northern border, the Blues formed a phalanx larger than any seen during the war. Everyone in the besieged state expected an incursion, but it was in fact a quarantine. Within a month, the sickness had spread across the state, and the fiery core of the Southern rebellion had been cooled. The rest of the Free Southern State, after seeing the effects of the virus, quickly put up a quarantine wall of its own.

By the time Gerry Tusk arrived at the government labs in Lynchburg ten years later, the war had turned in the North's favor. And the rebel state whose induced coma turned the tide for the Blues was now a glaring embarrassment, the shame of a nation. The young virologist, still new to his work and enthusiastic, was tasked with finding a cure.

Unlike most Americans, he would have seen the effects of "the Slow" firsthand. On the last Friday of every month, an armored convoy traveled five hours south from Lynchburg to the Carolina quarantine wall. Once across, they found themselves among the comatose.

For his guinea pigs Tusk picked both children in whom the sickness had yet to manifest, and adults fully consumed by it. In this way he was able to test both cure and inoculation; an alchemist in search of living metal.

Most came willingly, ushered into the isolation vehicle by soldiers in thick protective suits. The younger Carolinians, who knew full well what they would soon become, begged to be chosen. The older ones, who were by the age of thirty barely able to do anything more than breathe, eat, and breed, sometimes cursed the Northerners, but were easily compelled. And the eldest were wheeled without protest into the bus, their limbs paralyzed, stiff as stone.

Every month, for the better part of a decade, Gerry Tusk would have taken this trip. He would have seen those children plead desperately for a cure he could not give them. Perhaps over time it turned something within him bitter.

How cathartic it must have been then, on that April day, when finally five of those near-vegetative subjects momentarily came alive, their faces breaking into ecstasy, their fingers gingerly uncurling. How the young scientist must have wept with delight that one of his potions finally worked. How he must have wanted, against his better judgment, to open the fortified door and lead his patients out to the laboratory's great central lawn, to show them off like prize crops in spring.

And how cruel the universe must have seemed by the end of the same week, as the bodies of the momentarily unfrozen subjects were cast lifeless into the incinerator. In time, the thing Gerry Tusk created would come to be known as the Quick—a virus even more contagious than the one that put Carolina to sleep, and universally lethal. But at the moment of its genesis he knew it only as he knew all his failed creations, by a simple serial number: 032-072.

There exists no written record of the scientist's own thoughts. But it is difficult to imagine those two days in April, when so bright a light so quickly turned to darkness, and not believe that it was at that moment that Gerry Tusk made the decision to trade his old life for something—anything—else.

It is all but known now that the Bouazizi Empire, eager to prolong the American civil war as much as possible, arranged the deal that granted the virologist his escape. On the morning of December 3, 2094, Gerry Tusk boarded the merchant vessel *El Fattah* at the Richmond harbor, bound eastward. His lethal creation paid his fare. The following year, the monster he bred would come alive on the steps of Reunification Square in Columbus, Ohio, and the first of more than one hundred million people would die.

CHAPTER SIX

By the banks of Chalk Hollow, Sarat hunted for pet food. She moved in graceful rampage over the broken branches and dried-up leaves, the dead things emitting a satisfying crunch beneath her bare feet. The branches were sharp and the leaves dusted with nettles but the girl felt none of it, her soles tough as leather.

She knelt and dug into the soil near where it met the water. On the surface the soil was warm from the sun but below it was cooler. She dug an elbow-length hole, looking for the little burrowing worms she recalled from her childhood. But there were none. Soon the bottom of the hole began to fill with river water, and she abandoned it.

Nearby, Marcus Exum picked at the fungi growing on the bark of stunted sweetgum trees. He slashed with a penknife at the roots of the wide, white-fleshed mushrooms and placed the bounty in his stitched blanket knapsack. One tree, collapsed completely, was barely visible beneath a second skin of mushrooms. Marcus picked at the parasitic growth until his bag was full, and a small segment of the tree's coal-black bark was bare.

"He'll eat that for sure," Sarat said, climbing over the dead tree. "Heck, I'd eat that."

"I don't know," Marcus replied, bending the edges of the mushroom back and forth. "Maybe it's poisonous. My dad says a lot of the stuff growing out here is. Says anything growing out here people can eat, they already ate."

"We're feeding it to a turtle," Sarat said. "A turtle ain't people."

"Yeah, but poison's poison. It don't know who's eating it."

"Well, she's gotta eat something around here. Keep looking."

Sarat wiped the soil from her hands on the sides of her COSCO Shipping T-shirt and scrambled back down the ravine in the direction of the creek.

She was confined to boys' clothes now, there being no girls and hardly any women in the camp as tall as she was. And although it limited her to the worn-through jeans and scuffed shirts that once belonged to Simon and his friends, she found it liberating to no longer be measured against the unbearable standard of her sister, who counted in her sprawling wardrobe not a single piece of clothing fit for adventures like these.

She picked the green leaves and tiny flowers of an Alabama supplejack perched low against the water, its branches limp and thirsty. On the ground she discovered a small tangle of sweetgum seeds and black peppervine fruit. All these she deposited in her knapsack.

A few feet away, a clearing led down to the water's edge. Sarat scrambled down until she was ankle-deep in the warm, muddy creek. A fine sheet of blue-green scum covered the surface of the water. She brushed it away and dipped a thermos into the river and filled it. The water below was tinted brown and, lifted to the light of the sun, glistened with fine particulate.

A hundred feet beyond, the sheltered estuary of Chalk Hollow fed into Sandy Creek, and a mile further to the east, Sandy Creek met the Tennessee River. Sarat could see the rebel skiffs in the far distance, docked near the ruined wharf of an abandoned marina. When the daylight began to fade, they would cross.

Many times the children had seen the rebels, and the rebels had seen the children. Often they crossed paths at Chalk Hollow, where the camp's feeble fencing was bent and torn to shreds. Over the years, the camp's residents had learned not to venture this far east, where the rebel boats docked, nor to the north, where clashes between the rebels and the Northern militias had grown more and more frequent.

But to Sarat this place was a small paradise—a land teeming with life, away from the human pollution and unmagical monotony of the camp itself. Soon the rebels became used to the site of the broad, fuzzy-haired girl and her runty friend. They ignored the children, saw in them neither threat nor enticement; the boy was too small, the girl too big.

Marcus clambered down the embankment to where Sarat stood. "We should go," he said.

"Relax. Have some fruit." Sarat picked two black peppervine pebbles and offered one to Marcus, who declined. She shrugged and popped both into her mouth. The skin was mushy and broke open with little resistance.

The children marched back inland. For a while they followed the broken, sand-covered remains of Highway 25. Not a mile to the north lay the severed bridge to the Blue country.

They walked west, toward the now abandoned tents that marked the northern end of the camp. From experience they knew which tents to avoid—the ones that, though unoccupied, contained the rebels' illicit cargo ferried nightly across Sandy Creek.

Officially, these tents near the fence were assigned to refugees long since dead or relocated. And newly arrived refugees, when given assignments here, were quickly warned by more senior residents; inevitably they found some way to relocate further south, closer to the camp's interior.

The children arrived at a tent near the border between the Mississippi and Alabama slices. It was indistinguishable from all others in the area but for a rectangular gash on the east-facing canvas, cut there by Sarat so as to let more sunlight in.

Using the Phillips head on his knife, Marcus had learned to turn the door's metal bolt from the outside, and in this way the children believed they could keep the tent's contents secret from prying eyes. He wrestled with the bolt's screw head for a moment, and the bolt unlocked. The children stepped inside.

In the center of the tent, four cots were stationed on their sides in the shape of a rectangle, forming a makeshift pen. The inside of the pen was lined with charity blankets.

A yellow-and-black-shelled turtle shuffled glumly in one corner of the pen. It was a small, rotund animal, about six inches in length. The yellow markings on its back were split with black lines in patterns that resembled the fractal aesthetics of butterfly wings. It moved on ancient, leathery feet, at the ends of which grew sharp pointed claws that tore softly into the blanket.

The animal watched the children approach with a muted consternation. Gently it retreated into its shell.

"Is he ever going to like us?" Marcus asked.

"She's a girl," Sarat said.

"How do you know she's a girl?"

"I found her, so she's a girl."

"Is she ever going to like us, then?"

"She's gonna like us when she sees all the food we got her," Sarat replied.

"Maybe we should just take her back to the creek," Marcus said, but Sarat brushed him off. She reached into her sack and began laying out the leaves and berries in small mounds on the far end of the pen from where the turtle had backed itself into a corner. Reluctantly, Marcus followed, setting the mushroom heads on the blanket.

"Not like that," Sarat said. "They're bigger than she is. Break them first."

The children lay the food in the pen and then backed away a few feet. Eventually the turtle reemerged from its shell. It observed the spread on the other side of the pen, but did not move.

"Maybe she's lonely," Marcus said.

"Can't do anything about that," Sarat replied. "When's the last time you saw another turtle anywhere around here? Or a lizard, or crickets even."

"Well she must have come from somewhere. She was born, so she must have had parents, maybe brothers and sisters too."

"Just because she had them doesn't mean they're still there."

The children waited a while longer but the turtle refused to move. Soon Sarat could no longer stand the sight of nothing happening.

She marched to the far side of the pen. As she approached, the turtle once more ducked into its shell. Sarat picked the animal up and carried it to the other end of the pen and set it next to the food. Then she stepped back.

The turtle reemerged. It observed the children again with its orange-backed eyes, and then turned and shuffled away.

"Dammit," Sarat said.

"Maybe we should try my idea," Marcus offered.

"I'm telling you, it won't work," Sarat replied. "That rat is almost as big as she is. She's just gonna get more scared."

"What have we got to lose by trying?"

Sarat acquiesced, and quickly Marcus left and sprinted to his own tent further south. In a few minutes he returned with a galvanized steel bucket. He held the bucket over the pen and tilted it. A small brown field mouse skittered down the side.

All four of the tent's occupants stood frozen, eying one another.

Then the mouse scurried to the pen's bountiful corner and began eating the berries.

"Well, least she won't be lonely anymore," Sarat said.

The children left the tent. They parted in southern Alabama; Marcus returned home. Sarat said she'd come by later in the evening so they could check again on the welfare of their pets.

"You know we're not supposed to go up near the fence at night," Marcus said.

"We're not supposed to go up near the fence in the day, either," Sarat replied. "You scared?"

"No."

"Then there's no problem."

Sarat said goodbye and left. She walked south through the western part of Alabama and then into Mississippi. Before she reached home, a couple of boys cut across her path, high with excitement.

"I'm telling you, he lost it in the shit," said one of the boys. "Came off his arm when he was swinging at a fastball, and landed right there in the shit."

Curious, Sarat followed the boys.

They led her to the banks of Emerald Creek. A crowd of perhaps a dozen boys and girls from the nearby tents were assembled near the foul-smelling sewage ditch.

In the center of the commotion was a boy named Ethan. The forlorn boy, who was a year Sarat's senior, was pointing to something in the ditch and arguing with a handful of other boys, all of whom seemed to be talking at once.

One of the girls, holding her nose against the stench, caught sight of Sarat approaching.

"Hey, maybe Sarat can get it," she said. "She's bigger than all y'all."

"Get what?" Sarat asked. The boys looked her over in a way she'd gotten used to: a cautious curiosity at the girl who was not like the other girls. She ignored them and pushed her way to the banks.

In the ditch the wastewater flowed brown and thick as gravy. It was the pungent soup of the camp's excrement and filth. Small crescents of the blue disinfectant that the cleaning staff flushed twice daily down the bowls swirled along the surface. Cigarette butts and empty cans and ration wrappers littered the banks and floated in the effluent.

An ancient heirloom wristwatch lay upon a rock in the middle of the creek. Like so many of the functionally deceased things the refugees carried with them—the washed-out photos and the obsolete or corrupted stores of memory and the keys to homes long since bombed or otherwise demolished—it bore a vital link to some distant, happier past.

"Used to be my grandfather's," Ethan said. "My mom's gonna kill me if I don't get it back."

"So go in there and get it," Sarat said.

"Don't be gross. I'm not gonna step in shit."

Another boy whispered something in Ethan's ear. He listened and nodded.

"Why don' you get it, Sarat?" he said. "I'll give you fifty bucks if you do."

Sarat shrugged. "All right."

Once more she pushed the boys aside and walked away from the creek, toward the nearest tents. A few of the children followed, among them Ethan, who held Sarat by the wrist and warned her against telling any grown-ups.

"I'm not telling anybody," Sarat said, shaking the boy's hand loose. "Stop being so scared of everything."

She walked between two tents, where an unused clothesline hung. She unhooked the metal holders on either tent and rolled the line around her fist. Then she returned to the creek. The children followed.

At the banks she uncoiled the line and tossed it into the ditch. On her first try she fired too far left and then overcompensated. But on the third throw the hook landed just past the rock on which the watch was stranded. Slowly she pulled on the line.

"Careful, careful!" Ethan cried from behind her. "You're gonna knock it in."

"Be quiet," Sarat said.

She tugged gently on the line until the metal hook rested on the rock just beside the watch. With surgeon's hands she edged the hook closer until it dislodged the watch from its place. The watch began to slide down the polished side of the rock toward the stream, but caught on the edge of the hook. A couple of the children yelped in triumph.

"You got it!" Ethan yelled. "Pull it in, pull it in."

"Hold on," Sarat said. "Give me that bat of yours."

One of the boys picked up a baseball bat nearby and handed it to Sarat. With the line still in her left hand, she lifted the bat with her right. She held it as far out in front of her as she could without losing her balance. Slowly she began lifting it up underneath the line to create a pivot point. Then she reeled in the catch. The hook lifted, the watch rising with it. As it came off the rock the watch swung and skimmed across the surface of the creek. Coiling the line around her wrist, Sarat pulled the watch in and set it on the ground.

She turned to Ethan. "Pay up," she said.

The boys stared at the watch on the ground as though it had landed from outer space. Finally Ethan pulled a wad of Redbacks from his pocket and paid Sarat what he owed her.

The children began to disperse. Some of the boys revived their baseball game, a little further away from the creek this time. One of the younger girls, whom Sarat did not know, offered to return the clothesline for her.

As she made to leave, Sarat was approached by another of the boys, a fourteen-year-old from Georgia named Michael. She knew him only tangentially. He was the older brother of a boy named Thomas, who as a toddler had suffered a shrapnel injury that had frozen his mind at the age of two. The older brother had been sleeping in the same bed the night the Birds came, but through blind chance had escaped uninjured.

"Hey, Sarat—wait, girl, where are you going so fast?" Michael said. He pointed at the creek. "I'll give you another fifty if you go in."

The departing children halted. Sarat eyed them, and then Michael. He was wiry and lanky, swimming inside his too-big Sinopec Solar T-shirt, a hand-me-down from the Augusta docks.

Sarat said nothing.

"C'mon now," Michael said. "You ain't scared, are you?"

He had pasted on his face a smirk with which Sarat was well acquainted. She'd seen the same look on so many of the other boys' faces over the years. A self-satisfied grin. It was the smirk of knowing he'd left her with an impossible choice—step into the river of filth or be labeled a coward.

Even then, at such a young age, she understood that smile for what it was: a mask atop fear, a balm for the crippling insecurity of childhoods deeply damaged. They were fragile boys who wore it, and their fragility demanded menace. Sarat knew the boys better than they knew themselves. And she knew there was no winning this dare. That was the point—for there to be no winning, only different magnitudes of losing.

"How do I know you're not lying?" she said.

Michael pulled a wrinkled Redback from his pocket. He held it up to Sarat. She inspected the gray pastoral of McCoy Auditorium—the place where Julia Templestowe spit in the Northerners' eyes all those years ago—drawn on its back.

"She's not really gonna do it, is she?" said one of the boys in the crowd. Another boy elbowed him and told him to shut up.

Sarat turned away from Michael and took a step down the embankment, easing down with her backside braced against the slope. She descended slowly, the dirt gradually becoming cooler against her feet as she neared the fetid pool. In all her years at Camp Patience, the smell of Emerald Creek had never bothered her, but as she came closer now there was a thickness to the stench she'd never known before; it overwhelmed the borders between the senses and soon she could almost taste the acrid sweetness on her tongue.

Her throat tightened and she felt the urge to gag, but fought it. Everywhere in the camp the bustle of daily life continued unhindered but here the children stood watching, silent and entranced.

Where the embankment met the creek, Sarat's foot disappeared into the brown sludge. She felt the liquid stick to the short hairs of her shin, syrupy and warm. A sharp sigh broke out among the children behind her as her feet went through the surface. She heard a young girl say, Gross.

She realized then that she hadn't agreed beforehand with Michael what stepping into the creek really meant. However deep she went, he'd argue she should have gone deeper.

Her feet found solid footing on a polished rock when she was knee-deep in the waste. It was shallower than she'd expected. Gently she eased her backside off the bank and stood upright. She turned to face the boy who'd dared her. Michael stood at the edge of the creek. He had the same smug smile plastered on his face but behind it she could see a tightly reined astonishment, a disbelief that she'd actually gone and done it.

Satisfied she'd met the terms of the wager, Sarat eased herself back against the embankment, this time facing forward, her hands braced against the dirt. As she pushed herself up, she heard a muted crack beneath the surface. The rock on which she stood came loose. Suddenly she was sinking.

In an instant the brown water swallowed her. Instinctively she closed her eyes and in the darkness felt the warmth of it in her hair and on her face. For a moment she believed she was drowning. A panic reflex unlike anything she'd ever felt before took hold of her muscles.

Before her eyes were open she was clawing at the bank, her nails scraping against the rocks and dirt. Like a cornered animal she thrashed wildly, the fear alive inside her.

She climbed back out of the creek, her arms and legs slick with brown muck. It was on her now, the stink. She could smell nothing else. She saw the children laughing at her, the boys most of all. Michael made a big show of it, keeling over, pretending he couldn't breathe from laughing so hard. It was his way of showing he'd won; the smart-ass girl who'd shown all of them up with her little fishing line was now covered in shit.

Sarat climbed up on hands and knees until she was back on the flat ground.

"I did it," she said. "Give me my money."

Michael backed away as she approached. He tossed the bill in her direction. It landed in the dirt at Sarat's feet.

"Jesus Christ," Michael said, still laughing. "You stink."

Sarat picked up the money. She walked past the children, who parted to let her through. A few of them hovered in her periphery as she walked back to her tent. Others, like forward scouts, ran ahead of her to tell their parents and siblings what had happened.

The filth stuck to her legs, drops of it trailing behind her in the dirt. She felt something in her hair, moving like tiny insects.

When she reached her tent she found that the news beat her there. Her mother stood outside, waiting.

"What did you do to yourself?" Martina said.

"Nothing," Sarat replied. It was an instinctual reply—the word came out of her mouth before she knew she'd said it. And as soon as she'd said it her mother stepped forward and slapped her across the face.

"You think we don't have enough problems?" she said. "You think it's not enough that we're stuck here in this hell, killers all around us? You think I don't have enough to deal with, you gotta go make an embarrassment of your family, make them all laugh at us too?"

Sarat shook her head. Tears welled in her eyes. Most of the children who'd followed her home had left, and now the remaining few were also leaving. Whatever novelty there was to be had in the spectacle of her had suddenly dried up.

"You're not coming in here covered in shit," Martina said. "You did this to yourself, you go get yourself cleaned up. Nobody fixing your messes from here on in but you."

"Fine," Sarat said. "I didn't ask you to fix anything."

She turned and walked away. She walked east. Dusk settled over the camp. Some of the men who'd slept through the hot middle of the day were now emerging from their tents to sit on their box-crates and drink and play cards. Sarat walked past them and although the breeze carried her smell ahead of her, the men did not notice or seem to care.

Near the northern edge of Alabama, she saw a group of about half a dozen men seated around an old folding table. Upon the table sat a tablet connected to a small speaker.

The men were watching a recording of the previous week's Yuffsy. It was a title fight at the Citadel in Augusta, one of the better ones in recent memory. All twelve fighters had managed to stay on their feet for the first seven and a half minutes before one was finally knocked out.

One of the men watching said there had been a boy from Patience who came close to making the undercard, but lost a fight two nights earlier in the qualifiers.

"It was one of the Carolina boys, a kid named Taylor," the man said. "Mean as hell, they say."

"Yeah, but I bet you the whole time he was busy being mean, the other guys were busy fighting," another replied. "Mean don't mean nothing."

Marcus Exum stood on the periphery of the men's viewing circle. He was perched on an upturned laundry basket, craning for a look at the screen. When he saw Sarat he jumped down and ran to her.

"Hey, hey," he said, tapping her on the elbow. "What are you doing?"

"Don't touch me," Sarat said. Marcus recoiled. She saw in his eyes a sudden burst of confusion and hurt.

"I don't mean it like that," she said. "I'm covered in shit. I stink."

"So what?" Marcus said. "Take a shower, then."

"Got no clothes to change into. My mom won't let me in the tent. Says I embarrassed her."

"I bet if you go say you're sorry she'll—"

"I'm not sorry," Sarat said, loud enough that a couple of the men watching the fight looked up. "I'm not sorry and none of them can make me sorry. They're liars and cowards, all of them. They pretend like this is normal, like it's normal to live this way. But it's not normal. Your dad's right. We're just waiting to die, waiting for the Blues to come up over that fence one day and kill every last one of us. I'm not sorry. I'm not the one who's wrong."

"I don't think you're wrong," Marcus said. "I've never thought you were wrong. Go to the shower trailer. I'll get you some clothes from our tent. My dad's not that much bigger than you anyway."

Sarat walked up the dirt path to the northernmost shower trailer in the Alabama slice. It was a rusted metal and vinyl shack on blocks. Inside, it smelled of mildew and the candy-cardamom scent of the cleansing lotion packets that arrived by the boxload every month from the Augusta docks. They were small clear packets like the kind condiments come in. They littered the ground, caught in the drains, and stuck to the undersides of feet. All but the most well-connected of Camp Patience's residents used the packets to wash their hair and skin, and yet none of the residents ever smelled like the slimy amber liquid, only the shower trailers did.

Sarat entered the trailer and stripped down. She piled her clothes on the ground under the showerhead in one of the three stalls and turned the hot water tap. In a minute, steam began to churn about the room. The water melted the crust of filth from the clothes, and a briny, sulfuric smell filled the trailer.

Sarat stepped into the adjacent stall. She turned the tap. The water was cold; her skin erupted in goose bumps and the fine hairs on her forearms rose.

She stood with her head bowed, watching the milky-brown water swirl around the drain. On the back of the stall door there was all manner of graffiti: symbols of the Southern militias, genitals drawn cartoonish and grotesque, addresses of tents in which lived the whores and thieves and traitors. Soon the water ran clear.

Sarat heard the trailer door open. She heard Marcus walk inside, his footsteps almost indecipherable under the rush of water and squealing pipes. She heard him set the clothes on the bench by the wash basin, and then she heard the squeak of the trailer door once again opening and closing.

But when the sound was gone she knew Marcus had not left. She knew he was still standing inside the room, and through the tiny sliver where the door hinges met the stall, she could feel his eyes on her.

With her head still lowered she saw what he saw. The topography of her body: the shoulders wide and thick; the breasts that on any other girl her age would have stood as mounds but on her frame were modest; the hips in line with the shoulders, in line with the thighs, the body big and uncurved. A brick of a girl. And to his eyes she knew the strangest prize was the place between the lines, the place that had in this last year turned against her in a way so sudden she thought at first she was dying. The place that in an instant made her a stranger to herself.

And she knew that if she were simply to look up and catch his stare, the boy would flee, would not even beg forgiveness later but instead would die right there of shame. For the first time in her life she owned a pair of eyes other than her own, and with her head bowed she kept them locked upon her. In the thick sweat of steam both boy and girl for a moment were entranced by the same skin.

The flow of water began to weaken and the pipes let out a rumbling whistle. Sarat shut the tap. As the water died she heard Marcus scurry from the trailer.

Outside the stall she found an Alibaba shirt and a pair of slouch jeans worn white at the knees. The shirt fit her well enough but the pants were loose around her hips. She picked her old shirt from the soaked pile on the floor and tore it apart. She took one half of the ruined fabric and braided it; wringing the water out as she did. Then she ran it through the belt loops and tied it tight.

When she stepped out of the shower trailer she found Marcus seated on the bottom step, his arms hugging his shins. She sat beside him.

In the early nighttime hours the camp was alive with chatter and wandering flashlights and the fungal sweat of cooking. The sounds of the Free Southern Radio came high and tinny through portable speakers.

She looked at Marcus but he looked at his feet. She sensed that between her and her friend one wall had come crumbling down but another, different one had taken its place. And although she couldn't define it, she knew what it was. She knew it to be a cousin of that low-lit language her sister spoke so well. It lived in that strange fevered place between curiosity and desire.

And it thrilled her—not the sex of it but the newness, the realization that she could not only manipulate these feelings within herself but also without; that she could turn the gears inside another so forcefully.

Finally he spoke: "My dad, when he falls asleep, nothing can wake him."

"I'm not staying in your tent," Sarat said.

"Then where are you gonna stay?"

"I'll go bunk in the pen with Cherylene and that rat of yours, if she hasn't eaten him already. Plenty of room there."

Marcus turned and held Sarat by the forearm. "Please don't stay up there. You know it's not safe. My dad says the Blue militias are going to tear through that fence any night now."

"And I believe him, but what are the odds it'll be tonight?"

"What if it is tonight?"

"Then we'll all be dead anyway. Where you want me to stay, then?"

"Go down to the sick building," Marcus said. "Tell them you got the flu or something—they'll let you stay the night there."

"The sick building hasn't been open since last Christmas," said Sarat.

"They still got a couple of bunks in there. Nobody's using them for anything."

They were jolted from their conversation by a crack of gunfire, a single shot ringing in the air somewhere to their north. It was a sound they'd heard a million times before, a sound unanchored and without destination.

"Please don't stay up there tonight," Marcus said.

"All right," Sarat replied.

The two friends sat together at the foot of the stairs and watched an old woman patch a square hole in her tent with some thread and a piece of blanket. Sarat squirmed.

"What's the matter?" Marcus asked.

"My hair's itchy," Sarat said.

"Didn't you wash it?"

"Yeah." She scraped her nails against her scalp until she worried it would bleed. Still, trails of invisible ants marched through the fuzzy corkscrews of her hair.

"Your dad have clippers?" she asked.

"Yeah."

"Go get them."

Marcus sprung up and ran back to his tent. Soon he returned with an old electric clipper and three attachments.

Sarat fit one of the attachments and turned on the clipper. It buzzed and vibrated in her hand. Cautiously she set it just above her forehead and for a moment she felt nothing. Then came a slight tug at the roots and soon she saw the rough strands float gently past her to the ground.

She moved the clipper slowly, in part out of caution but also to prolong the act; the shearing felt good against her skin. Soon the clipper glided along smoothly, and no more hair fell.

"Did I miss anywhere?" she asked. Marcus shook his head.

Sarat set the clipper on the stairs, its teeth still clogged. She rubbed her hand against the felt of her scalp. She stood.

"You're a good friend," she told Marcus, and then she left.

☆ ☆ ☆

SHE WALKED to the administrative buildings. She sat by the infirmary's back door and waited. Across the nearby walking path she saw the southernmost of the Alabama tents. Among them was one whose entire east-facing side had long ago been torn beyond repair. In its place the old woman living there had tied down a large flag of the Free Southern State. In time the flag had faded, the red bars made ghostly pink, the three black stars barely visible.

Sarat observed the flag. She'd seen it a million times, decorating the tents and strung high on poles and etched into a currency whose worth eroded by the day. But she'd never paid much attention to it. It had always seemed to her that the South was the governing ground of two different powers—the official Free Southern State government, headquartered in Atlanta, whose soldiers did almost no fighting, and the vast array of rebel groups, who did nothing but fight.

She knew the three stars on the flag represented the three states of the Mag, and she knew if South Carolina hadn't been turned into a forest of living dead, there would be a fourth.

Looking at the flag, Sarat noticed the black stars were slightly asymmetric. The right-pointing sides were longer than the others. She recalled hearing one of the older refugees say that in Atlanta, in the first year after declaring independence, the Free Southerners scrambled to create a flag and compose an anthem. In their panic they botched the stars, and never could agree on an anthem. And so in his address at the revealing ceremony, President Kershaw made up the famous line about how the pained wail of the South's anguished people was the state's only song, and never mentioned the misdrawn stars.

Sarat thought about how easy it would be to fix the mistake, to simply redraw the stars properly. But she knew that even broken history is history. The stars, cast wrong, must remain that way. It would be more wrong to change them.

She fell asleep thinking about it, seated against the wall, curled up like a cashew with her knees for pillows. When she woke it was well past midnight, and the camp was quiet.

She walked around the infirmary building to where a large waste disposal bin sat below a small window. She climbed up and stood at the window. The pane made a square barely big enough to accommodate her circumference, and she worried that even if she managed to slide the glass open, she would get stuck trying to climb inside.

The lights overhead glanced sharply off the window. Sarat saw her reflection in the glass.

With her hair shaved, her face looked fuller, rounded in a way that unveiled its symmetry. There was a smoothness in how the jaw became the skull, and the skull an almost polished half-mirror to the light.

Sarat observed her new face a long time. In the back of her mind swirled all manner of looming irritations—her mother's wrath, the ceaseless teasing of the children who'd seen or by now heard what she'd done. But in this moment, alone with her reflection, she felt new and impossibly light.

The pane was of a flimsy plastic and gave slightly when Sarat pushed on it. But in the groove on the other side there was a thick wood block, and it prevented the window from sliding open. She tried to dig her fingers in and lift the pane out entirely. She became so caught up in this task that she didn't notice the shadow climbing up the wall, a shadow in the shape of a man who now stood behind her.

"Whatever it is you're looking for," he said, "I doubt you'll find it here."

Sarat jumped and stumbled back, nearly falling off the waste bin. She turned to see a man of about sixty, dressed in a black prewar suit lined with white thin stripes. She'd never seen him before.

He was short, a half-foot shorter than Sarat, even aided by the thick heels of his polished dress shoes. He wore a stiff black homburg. Its brim kept the overhead lights from illuminating his face.

"I'm not stealing," Sarat said. "Are you gonna tell?"

"Don't worry, I won't tell on you," the man said. "What's your name?"

"Sarat."

"Hello, Sarat. My name is Albert Gaines." He had a slightly low, even voice with a sliver of Mississippi drawl, one wide vowel cozying up to the next. It reminded Sarat of the announcer on the *Peachtree Variety Hour* her mother liked to listen to on Friday nights: a soothing, familiar voice.

"How old are you, Sarat?" he asked.

"Twelve."

"And why are you dressed in someone else's clothes?"

The question caught her off-guard, and for a moment she wondered if the old man had been watching when she went in the creek. But she knew he hadn't. Every face that watched her was etched in her memory now; she'd remember every single one, every smile, every snicker, forever.

"I jumped into Emerald Creek."

"And why would you do that?"

"A dare."

Gaines smiled. Along the skin between the ends of his lips and the dark crescents beneath his eyes Sarat saw small craters, markers of time and damage.

"Come down from there," he said. "I have a business proposition for you."

Sarat climbed off the waste bin and approached the man. She imagined him a dignitary—one of the representatives the Free Southerners dispatched from Atlanta every now and then to gauge the mood of the refugees and spread word of recent concessions by and humiliations of the Blues. But those were different beasts; they dressed in cheap, formless shirts and wore pins in the shape of the Southern flag and stammered for hours without saying anything of value. In the eyes of the refugees, those men were little more than dull sparks launched off the gears of some distant machine.

Gaines retrieved a small yellow envelope from his breast pocket. "I have an acquaintance to whom I need this letter delivered," he said. "His name is Leonard and he lives in row nine, tent nine, in the South Carolina sector."

"All right," Sarat said.

"You're not afraid of going to South Carolina?"

"No."

"Don't you want to know how much I'm willing to pay?"

Sarat paused. The man chuckled. "Don't worry, this isn't a dare, it's a job. Jobs pay." He handed her the envelope. "Go on, then, let's see how you do."

Sarat took the envelope. On its back the name Leonard was written in impeccable cursive. She walked southeast, past the administrative buildings and in the direction of the camp's main gate.

Like the rest of the refugees from the other states, she'd never ventured into South Carolina. She had only heard stories of it: of mean, bitter people, the last uninfected remnants of their quarantined state.

Once, years earlier, the South Carolina slice was the largest in the camp. But over the years the sector had shrunk, ceding its northern and western borders to Alabama and Georgia—because from those states there was still a regular flow of refugees, but nobody else was leaving South Carolina. The whole state was walled off, sealed.

Sarat walked past unadorned tents, their tears left for the most part unmended. A few men sat on plastic chairs, reading and playing dominoes. They observed her as she passed.

She reached her destination to find a couple of boys playing cards on a rice sack table. They were perhaps fourteen or fifteen, the one with his back to her a buzz-cut redhead, the other a spindly blond naked but for a pair of Double Star shorts.

Beyond them, and beyond the tent in the distance, the soft white lights of the camp's main gate burned. And beyond those gates the great Southern world, its cratered cities and salt-eaten coasts and parched, blistered gut, lay waiting. It was a world that for Sarat now existed only in the fiery sermons of radio preachers and the lyrics of war songs and the bucolic pastorals of Free Southern State propaganda. It was an abstraction, an idea, nothing more.

The blond boy, when he saw Sarat approach, sprang from the mandarin-crate box on which he was seated.

"What do you want?" he said, approaching.

"I'm looking for Leonard," Sarat replied. "Got a letter for him."

"This ain't your place. Leave."

The boy was pale, as though he'd spent no time under the Southern sun. A pink streak ran from the left side of his neck down to near his belly button; Sarat could not tell whether it was a rash or some natural imperfection or the remains of burned skin. He was three or four inches shorter than she was, and at least thirty pounds lighter, his hip bones like the blades of cleavers.

"I'll leave after I give this to Leonard," Sarat said, holding out the letter.

"You deaf?" the boy replied. "I said get out, now."

He came to push her, his hands landing in the space between her shoulders and her breasts. It was then that something deep within her snapped. She felt a searing inflammation, a fire in the cavities behind her eyes.

With a guttural roar she leaped for the boy, palms turned to vises around his throat. He tumbled back onto the ground and she jumped on him, his arms pinned beneath the thick planks of her shins. Her first punch landed square; the boy's nose cracked. Sarat threw another, and another, until her limbs felt as though they were not her own. With each punch she exhaled and the exhales soon turned to screams. In the wide, blood-splattered eyes of the wiry Carolina boy she caught, for an instant, her own rabid reflection.

A moment later she was lifted, her limbs still moving but her body caught by a pair of handless arms. She was set down on the dirt by a man nearly seven feet tall and wide enough to momentarily eclipse her view of the retreating boy. She tried to scramble around the man's legs but he held her firm, his stumps hard against her shoulders.

"Enough," the man said. "Stay."

Sarat tried to break from the man's hold but could not. She turned to see his face. It was ruined, the lips gone and in their place thin slivers of brown-crusted skin, the cheeks wrinkled and charred. She saw the cavernous aperture where his right eye once was and she was hypnotized by it.

"What's this about?" the man said.

Sarat held out the envelope. "I have to give this to Leonard," she said.

The man took the envelope, pinned it between his wrists. "You've done it," he said. "All right?"

"All right."

She saw the boy standing behind the man, blood still running from his shifted nose. There was a wild fear in his eyes but it was not the girl he was looking at, it was the man.

"You tell Gaines something for me," Leonard told Sarat. "Tell him there's two families that got no one to provide for them no more." He held up the envelope. "And this alone don't make that right."

"Fine," Sarat said. She turned to leave.

"Hold on," Leonard said. He turned to the boy.

"Did I raise a coward?" he asked.

"No sir," the boy replied, his voice hushed and mechanical, his eyes lowered.

"Sure looks like it right now. Apologize."

The boy stepped forward. "I'm sorry," he said.

Sarat said nothing.

"It's all right," Leonard said. "You don't have to accept it—he just has to say it."

☆ ☆ ☆

WHEN SHE RETURNED to the administrative buildings Sarat found Albert Gaines seated on a bench by the central office. He was reading an old paper book whose cover bore the curled scribblings of a language Sarat recognized but did not understand. There was no illustration on the cover, only a geometric pattern and swooping, saber-curved lines. The writing resembled a more elaborate version of the same script Sarat had seen a thousand times before, on the sides of the food and water containers, the aid packages, and the Red Crescent vans. The language of foreigners.

"Leonard says to tell you this don't make up for the other two families who got nobody to provide for them," Sarat said.

Gaines looked up from his book and smiled. "Leonard has earned his fictitious chivalry, I suppose."

He pulled a bill from his wallet and held it out to Sarat. "As we agreed," he said.

Sarat stared at the money. It was a Northern twenty, a genuine greenback stamped with the portrait of some long-dead president. The bill's holograms were of an ancient, granite-columned mausoleum, its contours shimmering in the light.

"Go on, take it," Gaines said. "I know, I know, it's Blue money, right? Well, remember this: there's no sin in using what's theirs against them."

As she reached for the bill Gaines held her wrist. She saw he was looking at the reddened, blood-marked knuckles.

"Well, I assume it wasn't Leonard," he said. "His boy?"

"He pushed me," Sarat replied.

Gaines removed from his breast pocket a gray silk handkerchief and wiped the blood from Sarat's knuckles.

"Good girl," he said.

He released her wrist. Up close, Sarat could better see the pockmarks in his face. They put more years on him, and yet he did not look as aged nor as tired as the men who lived in the camp. There was a vibrancy about him, a burning bulb of confidence lighting his ashen blue eyes. He sat different, the spine stiff and tall. He had about him a kind of calmness that reminded her of her father.

"Thanks," she said, pocketing the money. "I'll see you around, I guess."

She turned to leave.

"Sarat," Gaines said. "Would you like to join me for a late dinner?"

"You got a tent here?" Sarat asked. "I thought you were one of those Free Southerners here from Atlanta."

"I do not and I am not," Gaines said. "But I do keep an office here, and I suspect you'll find the few provisions I keep there, meager as they are, to be a welcome respite from the sludge they feed you in this place. Come."

Sarat followed him to the back of the main administrative building. He unlocked a side door. Since the day she arrived at the camp, she'd only set foot in the supervisors' offices a handful of times. It was a dim, unremarkable building, the walls painted the sickly pinkish ivory of fingernails.

They descended a staircase she'd never seen before, and past a metal door to a small basement. Here the single hallway was narrow and the concrete unpainted. At the end of the hallway was a door. Gaines unlocked it and held it open.

Sarat stepped inside. The room smelled of mahogany and citrus. Behind her, Gaines flicked the light switch.

"Make yourself at home," he said. "It's always a pleasure to receive visitors."

It was a low-walled room, narrow but long, with a couple of small windows that were level with the ground outside. To her left Sarat saw a desk of thick chocolate mahogany, its legs like the bottom halves of hourglasses. On the desk was a neat stack of manila envelopes and an old teardrop-tipped fountain pen from a previous century. Next to those lay a letter opener with a golden blade.

On the wall adjacent to the desk there were a series of maps—one Sarat recognized as the Mag, another seemed to detail the Tennessee line, where so much of the worst fighting took place. The third and fourth maps were alien, covered in strange circular doodles and large painted swaths of red and blue and brown.

The two maps furthest down the wall Sarat had seen before, in a book long ago. They were maps of the whole world—one from a hundred years ago, one from today.

"Do you know where you are?" Gaines asked, standing behind her.

She pointed vaguely at the square of land on the left side of the map.

"That's Georgia," Gaines said. "But that's very close." He took her hand in his and moved it a few inches northwest.

"And do you know the places where the aid ships come from? The places that send us all those blankets and all the food that ends up in the cafeteria?"

Sarat stared at the map.

Gaines pointed first to a big mass of land on the right side of the map. "Some of it comes from China." Then his finger moved to the center, to a country whose sprawling borders covered the northern third of one continent and the rectangular peninsula to its east. "And some of it comes from the Bouazizi Empire."

"What's an empire?" Sarat asked.

"An empire is when many small countries become part of one big country, willingly or otherwise," Gaines said. "An empire is what we used to be."

Sarat looked over at the old map, the one from a hundred years earlier. The area Gaines had pointed to was, in this map, a mess of doodled borders, some describing countries so small, their printed names overlapped. On the new map, the entire mass simply bore one word: Bouazizi.

"Back when I was your age, the people in these countries had a revolution," Gaines said. "It failed. Then they had another one, and another, and on the fifth try, they finally won."

He pointed to a stretch of blue that marked the boundary between the Bouazizi Empire's northern edge and the European continent.

"If you ever stand anywhere on this shore, say in New Algiers, you'll see fleets of ragged little boats headed southward from the European shore," he said. "Boats full of migrants from the old Union countries, looking for better lives.

"That's what an empire is," he said, "an orchestrator of gravity, a sun around which all weaker things spin."

As Sarat continued to study the map, Gaines retrieved something from a small refrigerator nearby. A moment later she was interrupted from her thoughts by the smell of toast.

"Have you ever tasted honey?" Gaines asked.

"Yeah," Sarat replied. "They give it to us every few months with the rations. It's fine, I guess."

"That's not honey. That's mush, grown by scientists in a lab in Pearl River."

Gaines set the toast on a plate and the plate on the table. Sarat watched him unseal a small glass jar in which sat two hexagon-gridded sheets, sunk in a caramel-colored liquid. He spooned some of the honey on the toast.

"This comes from something living," he said. "What you get from the living you can never truly copy, you can never fake. Taste it."

Sarat sat at the table and took a bite. Instantly the sweetness set off fireworks on her tongue. She moved the honey against the roof of her mouth and found the quieter undercurrents beneath the sugar: a slight hint of coffee, an earthiness, something faintly metallic and damp. Somewhere in the caverns of her mind awoke memories of the place where she was born: the mud banks, the hot tin box, the mouth of the Mississippi. Like a stranger to herself, she was surprised to discover she'd started softly crying.

"We forget, sometimes," Gaines said, "that there are still beautiful things."

He asked her where she was from.

"I was born in St. James, Louisiana," Sarat said.

"I have always loved Louisiana," Gaines replied. He pointed at the old map on the wall. "Do you want to know what your home state once looked like?"

Sarat nodded. She had seen it before, seen the tentacles of marsh and swamp and the boot-shaped expanse of land they'd once formed. But she wanted him to show her. She followed him to the map. He pointed to the place where Louisiana's shattered hourglass figure brushed against the western edge of Mississippi.

"You see here, where the river meets the Gulf? That used to be land. Beautiful land. And here, near where the eastern shore is now, there used to be the loveliest city in all of America."

The girl observed the map. On the newer one on the wall beside it, the place where the man pointed was a uniform blue.

"Where were you born?" she asked him.

"I was born in a place called Rome," Gaines said.

"Where's that?"

"Well, the famous one was in a place called Italy, but the one I came from is in New York."

Sarat watched the man's eyes for signs of a lie, but there were none. She realized then that, save for the dwindling number of journalists who showed up at the camp every now and then and who always made great effort to appear geographically neutral, she'd never met a Northerner before.

"You're a Blue," she said.

"I didn't say that," he replied. "You asked me where I was born, and I told you. Had you asked me where I call home, I would have told you something different."

"What are you, then?" she asked.

Gaines sat at the table. "Well," he said, "when I was young, I was a soldier. This was back when there was no Red and no Blue, just the one military of the United States of America. Then when I was through being a soldier, I studied to become a doctor, and for a while I worked as a plastic surgeon. Do you know what plastic surgery is?"

"You made people look pretty."

Gaines laughed. "I suppose I did, in a way. I spent most of my time helping people who had been very badly burned. I specialized in repairing damaged skin."

"You still do that now?"

"I still practice medicine, you could say. I volunteer at the field hospitals along the Tennessee line; I worked for a while near your old home in Louisiana, out by the oil fields."

"You help rebels."

"I help Southerners."

"It doesn't matter to me," Sarat said. "My brother's just about set to join the Virginia Cavaliers. He thinks he's keeping it a big secret, but I know all about it."

"Then for his safety you shouldn't go around telling everyone, should you?"

"I didn't tell everyone. I told you."

Gaines smiled. "You know, before I practiced medicine, I wanted to become a mathematician. I was obsessed with very large numbers, and the way you can use them to tell secrets. But my father was a doctor, and he wanted me to study medicine. He used to say the only truly stable profession is blood work—the work of the surgeon, the soldier, the butcher. He said all industries rise and fall but as long as there's even a single man still alive, there will always be use for blood work. And I suppose he was right."

"So what are you doing in Patience, then?" asked Sarat. "I've seen the man they bring here once a week to hand out pills; you ain't the camp doctor."

"No, I don't come here to hand out pills. What I come here to do—what you could say these days is my chief occupation—is something I don't talk about with most people. But since I've taken a liking to you, Sarat, and since you were so kind to make that delivery on my behalf, and since you shared the secret of your brother's affiliation with me, I think it's only fair that I, in turn, share a secret with you. Isn't that right?"

"That's right," Sarat said instinctively.

"What I do is travel around the Southern State—sometimes to camps like this, or towns along the border where the Blues and their Birds have caused terrible carnage, and I look for special people."

"Special how?" asked Sarat.

"Well, courageous, I suppose," said Gaines. "But courage isn't enough. How do I say it? Let me ask you something. Do you ever see people in this camp who've been hurt by the Northerners, who've lost their limbs or their sight or a family member?"

"Hell, most people here are like that," said Sarat.

"That's right. And doesn't it make you angry to know that the ones who did that to your people got away with it?"

"I guess."

"And don't you wish you could do something about it?"

Sarat paused, silent.

"I suspect right now you're thinking, What can I do? I'm stuck here in this camp that may as well be a prison. What can I do against a whole army full of grown men with guns? Maybe there's nothing I can do, nothing at all."

"I didn't say that," Sarat replied.

Gaines laughed. "Of course you didn't, of course you didn't! And that's my first inkling, Sarat, that maybe you're one of the special ones. So let me tell you what it is I do. I seek out special people—people who, if given the chance and the necessary tools, would stand up and face the enemy on behalf of those who can't. I seek out people who would do this even if they knew for certain that it would cost them dearly, maybe even cost them their lives. And then I do everything in my power to give them the tools, to give them their chance."

Sarat waited for him to say more, but he sat quietly watching her. She struggled to think of a reply, some means of convincing him she understood exactly what he had said, even though she did not, even though she was mystified by almost all of it. The silence grew leaden around her; she blushed.

"Ah! Never mind all that," Gaines said suddenly. "We'll have plenty of time for that sort of talk later. For now, what say you we listen to some music?"

"All right," Sarat said.

Gaines stood and walked to a set of bookshelves on the other side of the room. The shelves were full of old paper books. Some were impossibly thick, others bound in leather and inscribed with delicate golden script. While his back was turned Sarat ate another spoonful of honey.

At the bottom of the middle shelf there was a small, flat contraption Sarat had never seen before, and two small speakers connected to it. Gaines ran his finger along a row of thin plastic cases lining one of the shelves. He pulled one case out and opened it. Inside was a round disk whose underside turned the light to rainbows. He pushed a button on the contraption and its top sprang open. He set the disk inside, closed the lid, and pushed a button. A faint whirring sound followed.

"Does your family still have many old things?" he asked Sarat. "Things from before the war?"

"Not really," Sarat said. "We used to have a few of my grandparents' things back home, photos and a wristwatch and a couple of letters, but we left most of them behind when we came here."

"That's a shame, isn't it? The first thing they try to take from you is your history."

A soft stringed lament silenced their conversation. The room filled with music.

At its heart was an instrument Sarat had only heard once or twice before. Low, earthen strings, dampened as though filtered through the bones of deathbed oaks.

"This was my grandmother's favorite song," Gaines said. "Listen."

A woman's voice emerged from behind the waning strings. It was a voice unlike anything Sarat had ever heard before, full and deep and ciphered in a language she did not understand.

"'Son qual stanco pellegrino,'" Gaines said. The words meant nothing to Sarat but their phonetic echoes clung to the walls of her mind.

She listened, enchanted. And afterward, when Gaines said he would like her and him to become friends, and that he would like to teach her about music and art and many other things from the vast and varied world beyond the gates of Patience, she nodded without thinking. Gaines smiled.

"I think you'll find a place for yourself in this world, Sarat," he said. "I think you'll make a place for yourself in this world."

Excerpted from:

A NORTHERN SOLDIER'S EDUCATION IN WAR AND PEACE: THE MEMOIRS OF GENERAL JOSEPH WEILAND JR.

I was only 29 years old when President Daniel Ki was assassinated. At the time I was a Compensation Claims Officer in Columbus, working in a small department within the War Office. The war of Southern secession had only just begun.

Not coincidentally, the earliest days of the war were also some of the most prolific lawmaking and nation-building years in American history, rivaling only the years during which the capital was relocated inland from storm-ravaged Washington, D.C.

It was during those early wartime years when the federal government succeeded in passing the Clean Fission Act, restarted the Eastern and Western Seaboard Decommissioning Initiatives, laid down the first thousand miles of the Sunbelt Transit System, and greatly expanded the overfill suburbs around Pittsburgh, Indianapolis, and Lexington. War is movement, my father likes to say.

At the time, the department I worked at was located about two miles east of the Executive Building, where my father worked in an office down the hall from President Martin Henley's briefing room. He used to call me up from time to time, usually to discuss some compensation claim I had recently approved. I remember one such meeting, early on in the war.

On my way to see him that day, I passed the Threat Map in the lobby of the Executive Building. On that morning, a portion of the southern fortification was pulsing the black-and-red color that indicated an attack had taken place. By my count it was the third such attack in three weeks. I learned later that it was another homicide bomb, aimed at the more vulnerable defenses of the capital's outer wire. No insurrectionist has ever managed to penetrate the Blue Square itself, but it is an unfortunate reality that there have been many cowardly attacks against the outer wire, attacks that have taken the lives of many brave guards. We lost four guards that day.

When I reached my father's office, I saw that he had been reading my latest compensation decision, regarding an Alabama claimant who alleged Incidental Property Damage from an Un-Oriented Drone.

I watched him skim the pages of my report, looking over the assessment of facts, the reasons for judgment, and the compensation amount. His face was, as always, unreadable, serene. He asked if there had been any collaterals. I said there were none, but that the man had lost all his belongings, and was forced to seek shelter in the camps near Atlanta, which were known to be poorly managed by the insurrectionist government.

"I thought we had a policy on Un-Oriented Drone damage," my father said.

"We do, but I made an exception in this case," I replied. "It's the second time his house has been hit."

"Struck twice by lightning? So either he's a liar or he's got terrible luck. Seems like either one shouldn't be enough to prompt a violation of policy."

I came to reply, but he'd foreseen my argument, and preempted me. "The amount doesn't matter," he said. "Every compensation claim is a statement. When you compensate a UOD strike claim, you take responsibility for a crime committed by your enemy. It was the insurrectionists who destroyed the server farms. They're the reason we have no more control over the drones. Do you see them handing out compensation claims for UOD strikes?"

I argued that the claimant's residence was in a strategically important area near the Tennessee line, and that by paying his claim we could help shift the perception among some Southerners that the federal government was unsympathetic to the plight of those living under corrupt insurrectionist rule. My father smiled.

"Tell me," he said. "Do you have an opinion about whose cause is right in this war?" he asked.

"Of course," I said.

"And how much would I have to pay you to get you to change your mind?"

Eventually I came to accept my father's reasoning. I knew,

despite how many soldiers he had lost in the war, he held no grudges against the people of the South. Let us not forget that it was his decision, made against the fierce objections of many federal politicians, to assign refugee Southern patriots to guard the Blue Zone's outer wire, a job they perform with supreme courage.

CHAPTER SEVEN

A faint evening rain fell over Camp Patience. Back in Sarat's childhood home the rain used to make a sharp sound as it hit the shipping container's roof. But here in the camp it was a whispered admonition, a soft *shh* against the tattered tents.

Sarat listened. She lay in her cot, her mother and sister asleep nearby. Through the window flap a soft line of silver moonlight illuminated her sleeping sister's face.

Their mother once said they were two birds hatched from the same egg, the same bones and blood inside them. And although Sarat had read one of Gaines's books on genetics and now knew that wasn't entirely true, she still liked to believe it. Whenever she got to thinking about why Dana's skin was light and hers dark, or why Dana's hair fell straight and bright and hers, before she shaved it, was fuzzy, she told herself that these things didn't matter. What mattered was bones and blood.

She watched Dana sleeping, her face cast in alabaster light. She did a thing she'd done since they were little children: she held her breath, manipulated it until it synchronized with her sister's, until their chests rose and fell in time. She lay still and breathed as her sister breathed and listened to the whispering rain.

At around four in the morning Simon stumbled through the door. He tried to move quietly but he was drunk and in the dark he stubbed his foot against his bedside locker. At the sound of his muffled cursing, a light went on in the back of the tent. Martina got out of her bed, as did Sarat and Dana.

"Go back to sleep, for Christ's sake," said Simon, struggling to get his boots off.

"Where were you?" asked Martina. "You haven't been home in four days."

"The hell it matters where I was? There a sign-in sheet I didn't know about?"

Sarat could smell the reek of Joyful on him, could see he was that aggravated kind of drunk where even your own skin feels itchy as wool. She'd seen a lot of men at Patience get that kind of drunk.

Martina walked to the front of the tent. She reached for her son and grabbed the pendant she saw hanging around his neck. It was a bullet casing pierced near its top with an iron nail—the symbol of the Virginia Cavaliers. In the South every rebel group had its own symbol: coiled snakes or Texas oil drills or words drawn in barbed wire. The Virginia Cavaliers had a bullet with a nail through it.

Everyone already knew. For months Simon had been out with the rebels along the Tennessee line, sneaking in and out of Patience through the inlets near the northeastern border. And for months both he and his mother had simply pretended it wasn't so. But on this night there was no use pretending.

"How can you go and do the one thing you promised me you wouldn't do?" Martina said, looking Simon over like he was someone else's son.

"Do I look like I blew myself up?" Simon replied. "I didn't do a damn thing."

"You've gone and joined them," she said. "Joined the same ones who blew up that permit office in Baton Rouge, the ones who killed your father."

At the mention of his father Simon's face crumpled. He snatched the necklace from his mother's hand. "You killed him," he screamed. "You killed him with all your nagging about going north, going north. He was happy where he was, happy in his home, but you pushed him to do it. It was you who killed him, nobody else."

She slapped him across the face and at the sight and sound of it Sarat and Dana were jolted but Simon did not move.

"What kind of child says something so cruel to his own mother?" Martina said.

"I'm not a child," Simon replied. "I'm a man." His voice was louder than his mother and sisters had ever heard before, as though the louder he said it the more true it became. "I'm a man, I'm a man, I'm a man."

He tore the front door open and stumbled back out of the tent and when he was gone his mother sat on his bed and wept. Instinctively Sarat and Dana sat by her side to comfort her and in that moment

Sarat had never hated anyone more than she hated her only brother. In the weeks and months to come both mother and son would dismiss what happened that night; both would say that it was just one of those fights every family has, that they didn't really mean what they said. But Sarat knew each had meant every word.

Soon that old hardness set in and Martina was herself again. That night she stayed up well into the morning talking with her daughters. She told them about that day when Benjamin Chestnut went up to Baton Rouge and never came back. She told them about the night she went to see the rebel commander about refuge, and the night the falling bombs chased them from their home.

SARAT WOKE AROUND NOON, drenched in sweat from the midday heat, to the sound of Marcus at the door.

"You been sleeping this whole time?" he asked, handing her a juice cup he'd smuggled from the old cafeteria building.

"Long night. What's up?"

"I was out by Chalk Hollow looking for turtle food for Cherylene and I saw a whole bunch of rebels out by that island across the lake," Marcus said. "They had a ton of stuff with them, boxes and boxes."

"They're out earlier than normal," Sarat said. "Can't be coming into the camp in the daylight. People will see."

"That's right. I heard one of them say they'll come back for their stuff after sundown."

It took Sarat a moment before she realized what her friend meant. "So, you wanna go see what they got in those boxes?"

Marcus smiled.

They walked to the eastern edge of the camp. They passed Marcus's tent, where his father sat on a plastic garden chair, a sweat-soaked rag over his balding head. With a pair of binoculars he was watching the Blue soldiers who lay hidden among the trees beyond the northern fence. Every few minutes he'd mark something down in an old notebook, like a birdwatcher deep in observation.

Marcus entered the tent and returned with a small Donald Duck backpack, into which he'd stuffed a couple of water bottles and apricot gel sandwiches. He walked briskly, a step ahead of Sarat. She was a full foot taller than he was, and the manner in which he walked—almost hunched, his eyes focused on the ground—only exacerbated the difference in height between them.

When he was with her he was a little more confident, but otherwise he seemed perpetually hobbled by shyness and anxiety. Some of the boys in the camp had started a rumor that, because of his size, he was forced to wear hand-me-downs from some of the girls in Patience. To Sarat, this kind of drive-by cruelty was a normal part of camp life (and even if it were true he wore younger kids' clothes, what did it matter? Who cared?), but Marcus seemed especially distraught by it—so much so that she'd seen him walking around a few times dressed in jeans and shirts that were entirely too large for his frame, a decision that prompted a whole new round of ridicule from the boys.

But when he was with her he was himself. She enjoyed the feeling it gave her to know it, to be his protector, his confidante.

But there was something else, a comfort he unwittingly afforded her. It was the comfort of his smallness. The meekness and harmlessness of him allowed her to explore without fear her fluid feelings on attraction and companionship and boys, the hormonal gauntlet of adolescence. Other than him, she had almost no friends her own age, but she wondered if the thing he gave her wasn't friendship's only useful purpose—a testing site for new and unfamiliar emotions, free of hazard, free of judgment.

When they reached Chalk Hollow they climbed over the fallen trees and down to the bank. Marcus pointed to the small uninhabited island north of Smith Branch, about a quarter-mile ahead of them in the water.

"You see it?" he asked.

Sarat squinted. Barely visible beyond the shore was the edge of a raised tarp, although the things it covered were hidden.

"They said they wouldn't be back till after sunset?" she asked.

"Yeah," Marcus said. "I don't know how we get over there, though."

Sarat shrugged. "We swim."

Marcus's courage seemed suddenly to abandon him. With trepidation he looked out at the water, thick and murky, its surface the color of the soil.

"Well, how did you think we'd get out there?" asked Sarat.

"I don't know," Marcus replied. "I thought we'd get a boat or something."

Sarat laughed. "What boat you ever see round here didn't have a man with a gun on it?" She stripped down to her underwear and stepped onto the remains of a small dock, whose planks teetered unevenly into the water. "C'mon," she said. "It's not so far."

"But my bag will get wet."

"Give it here, then." Sarat held the bag high over her head like a sacrificial offering. She stepped off the edge of the plank and into the water. Marcus took off his clothes until he too was only in his underwear, and then he followed.

The water was as warm as the children's bodies and so thick with soil and mud that it hardly felt like water at all. With Sarat leading and Marcus struggling to follow, they shuffled along like paddling dogs. Marcus's arms flailed wildly as he swam, but Sarat appeared to move with little effort, the backpack held high above her head, her legs doing all the work beneath the surface.

When they finally arrived at the island's shore they collapsed on a small stretch of beach. Marcus lay as though crucified, breathing heavily. Sarat lay beside him, her legs burning.

The island had no name. It was small and had never seen much use. Once it was covered end to end with thick foliage, but now only the detritus of trees remained: browning stalks of deadwood, waist-high weeds, and ancient leaves, brittle as crackers. Near the middle of the island some of the tree trunks were still thick and tall, but nearer the shoreline they were short and sickly.

The children walked inland, following footprints in the soil. The trail led them along a jut of land that curled around the island's western shore like a comma, partially hiding a small parcel of beach from the sightline of anyone standing on the other side of the water.

There they found the large blue tarp, held up with branches and planks of wood. The tarp covered about a half-dozen wooden crates. Most of the crates were nailed shut but one sat on the ground with its lid slightly askew.

The children approached carefully, listening for the sound of nearing boats. Sarat eased the crate's lid aside, and peered at its contents. Marcus stood behind her, his attention split between the crate and the path leading inland.

"What's in it?" he asked.

Sarat picked up one of the metal disks stacked inside the crate. It looked familiar, but she couldn't quite place where she'd seen it before. It was heavy and circular, like a thick dinner plate, colored the same shade of brown as the land on which they stood. Its edge was lined with equidistant markers and in its center there was something that looked like a fat black button.

"I don't know," Sarat said.

"Maybe there's something inside," Marcus replied. "Can you open it?"

Suddenly Sarat remembered watching the hopeless Red grunts with their metal detectors, clearing the earth near the camp's northern fence.

"It's a bomb," she said.

"What?"

"It's a bomb. They bury them under the ground and when someone steps on them they blow up."

She could feel Marcus freeze behind her. "Walk away," she said. "Go on down that path over there. I'll be there in a second."

"I'm not just gonna leave you with a bomb in your hand," Marcus said.

"Just go, for God's sake. What's the point in both of us getting killed?"

"Better that than you getting killed and me having to explain what happened. I ain't leaving."

With Marcus peering from around her shoulder and her heart pounding, she carefully set the land mine back in the crate. A few inches from the bottom of the crate, it slipped out of her hand and dropped. Sarat watched it, waiting for the inevitable explosion, and then in an instant she turned around, grabbed her friend by the hand and sprinted toward the island's interior.

They ran blind and mute through the thicket for five minutes without pause, until their exhaustion and the dawning realization that there had been no explosion brought them to rest.

"What . . ." said Marcus, gasping. But he couldn't form an end to the question, and finally he just said, "What the hell? What the hell?"

Sarat couldn't help but laugh, and quickly they were both in hysterics over their brush with death. Since their arrival they'd been careful not to make too much noise, but now they cackled.

They found themselves near the middle of the island, where the tree cover was thickest and the ground cool under the shade of the branches. About twenty feet up one of the tallest trees, Sarat saw a wooden observation platform, a lookout of sorts. Without a second thought she started to climb the thick hemp rope that dangled from the tower.

"What's up there?" Marcus asked.

"Don't know, but I bet you can see the whole camp," Sarat replied. "Bet you can even see the Blues."

She climbed to the platform and Marcus followed. Their view was obstructed a little by some of the nearby trees, but otherwise they were above most of the canopy. The world, Blue to the north, Red to the south, spread out before them.

They unzipped the backpack and ate their sandwiches and watched the vast horizon. In the distance to the north Sarat saw more acreage of browning forestland and a few dilapidated marinas and even the skeleton of a creek-side condominium near where the Tennessee River flowed.

From Albert Gaines's many maps she had learned that there were natural borders and political borders. To the north the land looked the same but she knew there existed some invisible fissure in the earth where her people's country ended and the enemy's began.

They sat silent for a while, letting the sugar from the apricot gel slowly revive them.

"You mad at me?" Marcus asked.

"Why would you think that?" Sarat replied.

"Haven't seen you lately. Came by your tent a few times, but you weren't there."

"Been busy, I guess."

"Doing what?"

"Learning. Got a new teacher, comes by a few times a week."

"I thought you said they don't teach you anything worth knowing in Patience."

"They don't," Sarat said. "But he ain't one of them useless teachers the Red Crescent folks bring in. He's teaching me all kinds of stuff they won't. Stuff they're too scared to teach."

"Like what?" Marcus asked.

Sarat pointed northward. "Like about them. About all the things they've done to us over the years. All the times they've put what's good for them ahead of what's good for us. You can go to school a million years down here and they won't have the guts to tell you a single thing about Northerners. But now I'm learning what they're really like."

Marcus observed the land to the north with indifference. "My dad told me the other day that my grandfather was a Northerner," he said.

"Like, he fought for them?" asked Sarat.

Marcus shook his head. "Nah, just worked up there, on the oil trains up in some place called Williston. Died in that big explosion in '69. My dad said the North didn't care about prohibition too much before that, said if the same thing had happened in Texas they wouldn't have done anything about it, even if it had killed a thousand. He said the thing about Northerners is, when it's good it's their good alone, but when it's bad it's everybody's bad to share."

"If your dad hates them so much, how come he's always talking about sneaking out of here and going up to join them?" Sarat asked.

"Just because he wants to go there don't mean he likes them," Marcus said. "Just means it's safe. If you had a chance to go where it's safe, wouldn't you?"

Sarat thought about the question. It seemed sensible to crave safety, to crave shelter from the bombs and the Birds and the daily depravity of war. But somewhere deep in her mind an idea had begun to fester—perhaps the longing for safety was itself just another kind of violence—a violence of cowardice, silence, submission. What was safety, anyway, but the sound of a bomb falling on someone else's home?

"I don't know," she said.

The sun began to set over the far side of Camp Patience. Sarat and Marcus descended from the lookout and walked back along the path to the edge of the island. Their underwear had dried on their bodies but it felt good to slip into the water once again. With nothing inside the bag, there was no point in holding it above the water; Sarat slipped it on her back. Her hands free, she swam with ease, gliding.

She'd learned recently that solid land was not the natural skin of the world, only a kind of parasitic condition that surfaced and receded in million-year cycles. The natural skin of the world was water, and all water on earth was connected. In this way she was able to make believe she was swimming not in some offshoot of the Tennessee River, but in that muddy place by the banks of the Mississippi. For a brief moment she was home.

☆ ☆ ☆

AFTER NIGHT FELL she ate dinner alone in her tent and then she went to see Gaines. They'd settled into a thrice-weekly ritual: every night he visited the camp she would come to see him in his office. Sometimes he'd give her errands to run, envelopes stuffed with cash to hand out in the South Carolina slice. Eventually the Carolinians got used to the sight of the tall, bald-headed girl crossing into their neighborhood. In time the boys in South Carolina gave her the nickname Payday. But although anytime she walked through the hermit sector she had on her person more money than most of Camp Patience's refugees would see in a lifetime, not once did she worry about theft or harassment. They all knew who she worked for.

After she ran the errands she would return to Gaines's office and listen to him teach. Every night was different: sometimes they discussed the natural world, a textbook spread open on the table before them full of pictures of all the plants and animals that didn't survive the planet's warming. Most often, they talked about the way things used to be.

He fed her the old mythology of her people—the South of Spanish moss and palmetto fronds; of magnolia trees dressed up in leaves of History and History's step-sister Apocrypha; of unmatched generosity and jubilant excess; of whole pigs smoked whole days and of peaches and pecans and key lime pie. She gorged on it all, delighted not only that such a world existed but that she held to it some ancestral claim. How much of it was real and how much pleasant fantasy didn't matter. She believed every word.

He said that her country once occupied the most fertile land in all of the world; mother of sugar and mother of cotton and mother of corn. He taught her about the first time the North had torn her country to shreds. He said people think of that war now the way they think about most wars: just a bunch of young men killing young men on the orders of old men. But he said it was women who were left to clean it all up in the end, women who rebuilt the scorched Southern country and nursed what was left of those young men. He said there were even some women who fought and killed, disguised themselves in the clothing of men if they had to. Women who defied.

Sometimes he gave her what he called lyrics—a script of sorts, relating to something they'd discussed that day. Then she'd go home and read it over, until she learned her part of the conversation. And the next time he returned to the camp, they'd talk through it, as naturally as though they'd had the same conversation a thousand times.

What is the first anesthetic?
Wealth.
And if I take your wealth?
Necessities.
And if I demolish your home, burn your fields?
Acknowledgment.
And if I make it taboo to sympathize with your plight?
Family.
And if I kill your family?
God.
And God . . .
. . . Hasn't said a word in two thousand years.
Good girl.

Sometimes the meaning of the lyrics escaped her. But she committed them to memory anyway. She was certain one day they would suddenly reveal their meaning; one day there might come reason to sing, and sing she would.

☆ ☆ ☆

SARAT STOOD by the side of the administrative building, waiting for Gaines to arrive.

He was the only man she had ever known who could enter and leave Patience whenever he pleased. No refugee was ever afforded such privilege, and even the camp's administrators and guards were forced to sign in and out every time they ventured into the Red. But Gaines floated past the gates at any hour of the day or night, carefree and without hassle, as though the gates marked not some severe wartime perimeter but the entrance to his own summer home.

Once she had been passing near Patience's front gate when Gaines arrived. She watched the young soldiers at the gate smile and shake his hand, inquiring about his health and the health of his family. He in turn asked them about their families, about their wives and parents and children, and whether they were comfortable in their apartments in Atlanta. Then the soldiers, in a sheepish way, made it clear that times were hard for them and their families, that the Free Southern State was late again in paying their wages, but that, anyway, what was the use in complaining?

She watched as Gaines discreetly passed each of the soldiers a small envelope. The soldiers, even as they protested that they couldn't possibly accept such kindness, quickly snapped the envelopes from his hand. In that moment Sarat saw the only sincere expressions of gratitude she had ever witnessed on the soldiers' faces. Watching the interaction, she needed no one to explain to her that, between the flag sewn on their uniforms and the money in Gaines's envelopes, there was no question where the young soldiers' loyalty lay. It seemed perfectly reasonable then that Gaines should come and go through Patience whenever he pleased.

A little after eleven o'clock, she saw him walking up the path from the southern gate. Every time they met he had come alone but on this night he was joined by another man, a man she had never seen before.

"Sarat, I want to introduce you to a close friend of mine," said Gaines. "I've known him for a long time, since we were both not much older than you are now."

The man standing next to Gaines extended his hand. Sarat shook it. He appeared about the same age as Gaines, but his skin, the same caramel shade as Sarat's father's, was smooth and almost entirely free of wrinkles.

"It's a pleasure to meet you, Sarat," the man said. "Albert has told me a lot of very nice things about you. My name is Joe."

There was an exotic quality to his accent, the phonemes leaden, birthed a little lower down in the throat. She recognized quickly that he was a foreigner.

Gaines led Sarat and Joe into the administrative building and down the stairs to his office. Like Gaines, Joe appeared out of place in his neatly tailored suit and green silk tie. And like Gaines he seemed to take pleasure in the rigidity of his posture, his shoulders level and proud, his spine a ruler.

Inside, Sarat and Joe sat at the table while Gaines made coffee. He turned on the stereo and played the old classical song he liked, the one he called the song of the weary pilgrim. For Sarat he slathered honey on warm toast. She felt self-conscious in front of her unfamiliar companion, and ate slower than usual. But he simply smiled and observed her as though he'd known her since birth.

"Albert tells me you are originally from Louisiana," Joe said. "Is that correct?"

"Yeah," Sarat said, "that's right."

"It's a very beautiful part of the world. I went there, some years ago. Very proud people there, very proud."

"And how about you?" Sarat said. "Where you from?"

Joe seemed taken aback by the question, but quickly he regained his calm demeanor. He smiled at Gaines, then he pointed at one of the maps on the wall. "I am from the Bouazizi Empire. Do you know very much about the Bouazizi Empire?"

Sarat shook her head. "Just what Albert said, that it used to be a bunch of different countries and now it's one."

"That's correct," said Joe. "It used to be that all those different countries were ruled by kings and generals who treated a few people very well and a lot of people very badly. So we had a revolution, and finally we forced out the kings and forced out the generals and formed a republic, a democracy."

Even more so than Gaines, Joe projected an air of serenity when he spoke. He was bald but for silver wings above the ears, clean-shaved but for a thick mustache that perfectly described his upper lip. Sarat tried to pinpoint what it was about him that imbued him with such calmness and finally she decided it must be because he was a visitor, an interloper, removed from the immediate consequences of the war raging all around him.

"So what you doing all the way out here," she asked, "if you're from over there?"

Joe nodded. "That's a very good question. I am here because my country supports those who fight for freedom, wherever they are in the world. And that's what your people are doing, isn't it, Sarat, fighting for freedom?"

"Yes sir."

Gaines rose from the table and walked to the bookshelves. He retrieved a book, one volume in a hardbound, green-covered collection. The writing on the spine and the cover was intricate and indecipherable to Sarat, the letters all conjoined, their peaks and loops like the road map of a hallucinated city. But Joe seemed to recognize the book.

"My God!" Joe said. "You kept them, all these years?"

"Of course," Gaines replied. "It's one hell of a gift." He turned to Sarat. "When we were young men, Joe gave me a present, a collection of old Arabic poetry called the Book of Songs. It's a very old, very rare gift, probably the only one of its kind in the Red or the Blue."

He opened the book on the table and flipped through it until he came to a photograph slipped between the pages. He handed it first to Joe, who whistled in disbelief at the sight of it. Then he showed it to Sarat.

"Be kind," he said, "and tell us you still see some resemblance."

Sarat looked at the old photograph. It was of two lanky young men, one shirtless, the other wearing a uniform of brown camouflage, standing in a desert encampment. A little nameplate was stitched to the uniform's shirt; it read: Joe. The two men looked to be in their late teens, about the same age as Sarat's brother. They were smiling and had their arms around each other's shoulders. The shirtless one was leaning on the butt of his rifle, the other one carried no weapon.

"How long ago was this?" she asked.

"Must have been '21 or '22," said Gaines. "Around the time they sent us over there for the third time, right before the Fifth Spring."

Joe leaned close to Sarat; he looked at the photograph again. "That's right," he said. "I remember, I remember when it was still your guns and our blood."

For a moment Sarat thought she saw Gaines wince. He took the photograph from her and placed it back between the pages of his book and put the book back on the shelf. Then he sat beside Sarat.

"A few weeks ago we spoke about what you think you might want to do one day, when you're older, when you leave this place," he said. "Remember?"

"Sure," Sarat replied.

"Well, that's why I wanted to introduce you to my friend Joe. Because when you settle on what you want to do for yourself, what you want to do for your people, Joe might be able to help you. I know you said you might want to go to Atlanta one day and work for the Free Southern State, but you might change your mind. And then you might find that you need things, things that are hard to obtain, things even I can't procure for you. But Joe might be able to help you. So I want you and him to be friends, and I want you to keep your friendship a secret, because there are lots of people who would want to hurt him if they found out he was helping Southerners. Do you understand?"

"All right," Sarat said, even as she wondered what kind of help Joe might provide. "I won't tell."

"I'm happy to have met you, Sarat," said Joe. "I hope we'll be able to assist each other one day."

She stayed with the two men until it was almost dawn, listening to them reminisce about the old war during which they first met. Much of the world they talked about was long gone, the old dynamics of power now inverted, but she enjoyed listening to it.

They talked about the years they spent in the part of the Bouazizi Empire once called the Arabian Peninsula, a place whose desert heart, once home to glittering oil-funded kingdoms, was now too hot for human habitation. Sarat knew from her geography and politics textbooks that these parched sandscapes were now lined with wave after wave of solar panels—blinding amber nets that caught the energy needed to feed and finance the empire. But the old men swore there had been cities—entire countries even—in these places. Millions once lived here, they said, before the temperature soared and the oil ran out.

In the early morning Joe said goodbye and left the camp. Gaines and Sarat were alone together in the office.

"There's nothing quite as tedious as old farts droning on about the days of their youth, is there?" said Gaines. "You were generous to indulge us."

"That's all right," said Sarat. "Every grown-up in this place talks all day about what it was like when they were young. At least your stories happened someplace far away."

Gaines chuckled. "Well I guess that's some relief." He stood and lifted the blinds and opened the window to let a little air into the room. It was still dark outside.

"I'm glad I was able to introduce you to Joe," he said. "I owe that man so much."

"He save your life or something?" Sarat asked. "Back when you were soldiers?"

"No," said Gaines. "I mean yes, I'm sure he must have, many times over. But that's not all."

He sat beside her at the table. From his wallet he produced a small wrinkled photograph, a high-schooler's graduation portrait. The girl in the picture had Gaines's smile, his deep-set eyes.

"Even back then, you could see it coming," said Gaines. "Before the first bombs fell, before the slaughter in East Texas, everyone knew this country was getting ready to tear itself to shreds. I was worried for my family, worried about whether I could keep my wife and daughter safe. It was Joe who helped me. He found a safe place for them to live in the Bouazizi. They hated me for sending them away, but they're safe there, and that's the only thing that matters. That's what Joe did for me. That's the gift he gave me."

Gaines folded the picture of his daughter and placed it back in his wallet.

"You know, I'd like to say you remind me of her, or that you two would have been good friends. But the truth is it's been so long since we've spoken. Maybe if we met now she wouldn't even recognize me. Maybe all she'd see is some old fool, some foreigner."

He seemed then not to be speaking to Sarat, or even to himself, but to nobody at all. He stared out the half-open window.

They heard the faint patter of footsteps overhead: the camp's administrators and volunteers, preparing for the morning shift.

"Why did you side with the South when the war came?" asked Sarat.

"You were born a Northerner, you fought for the Northern army when it was still one country. Why not side with the Blues?"

"Well, after they finally brought us back from Iraq and Syria for the last time, I wandered around for a while before settling down in Montgomery," said Gaines. "You see, we have a habit in this country of deciding the wisdom of our wars only after we're done fighting them, and I guess we decided the war I'd been sent to fight wasn't a very good idea after all. In the North, whenever anyone found out I'd been a part of that war, they'd want to debate it all over again, as though I was the one who ordered myself to go over there. But in the South, they don't do that, or at least nobody ever did that to me."

"So that's it?" asked Sarat. "They were good to you here, so you sided with the Red?"

"No," said Gaines. "I sided with the Red because when a Southerner tells you what they're fighting for—be it tradition, pride, or just mule-headed stubbornness—you can agree or disagree, but you can't call it a lie. When a Northerner tells you what they're fighting for, they'll use words like democracy and freedom and equality and the whole time both you and they know that the meaning of those words changes by the day, changes like the weather. I'd had enough of all that. You pick up a gun and fight for something, you best never change your mind. Right or wrong, you own your cause and you never, ever change your mind."

"So you think we're wrong?" Sarat asked. "You think what we're fighting for is wrong?"

"No," said Gaines. "Do you?"

"No."

"But if you did. If you knew for a fact we were wrong, would it be enough to turn you against your people?"

"No."

Gaines smiled. "Good girl," he said.

The sound of footsteps grew. Soon they could hear the workers upstairs delineating the day's tasks: who was to oversee distribution of rations, who was to escort the immunization worker around the camp, who had to deal with the South Carolinians.

Sarat stood to leave.

"Hold on," said Gaines. "I want you to take something with you."

He opened one of the desk drawers. When he turned around Sarat saw he was holding a small folding knife. He opened it; the blade was of slightly blemished steel and smooth except at its lower end, where it turned to serrated teeth. There was a monogram etched into the handle: "YBR."

"Do you know how to use a knife?" asked Gaines, pointing the blade toward her.

"Everyone knows how to use a knife," said Sarat.

"No, everyone knows how to stab." He flipped the knife and offered her the worn leather handle.

Sarat turned the knife in her hand. It was light and its lightness made it seem insignificant. She pushed her finger against the edge of the blade.

"It's rusted," she said.

"It's not rusted," Gaines replied. "It's dull. But that can be remedied."

He retrieved a sharpening stone from one of the drawers. The stone was black and rectangular. One of its sides was coarse, the other smooth.

He set the stone on the table in front of Sarat, and then he guided her hands until they held the knife against the coarse side.

"Resistance and stress," he said. "All it takes is resistance and stress."

He moved her hands with his. The knife scraped against the stone, even and rhythmic. The sound of it filled the room.

"How do you know when it's ready?" asked Sarat.

"It's ready," said Gaines, "when it does what you need it to do."

☆ ☆ ☆

FIRST LIGHT CAME. Sarat said goodbye to her teacher and made for home. Outside, a soft morning breeze lifted swirls of dust off the ground. Sarat looked across the vast sea of tents; they looked not all that different from the ones that littered the background of the old photograph of Gaines and Joe. Maybe all tents looked the same in wartime.

In the distance, she saw two refugees fighting. One man, drunk and stumbling, had knocked over the other one's jug of fermenting Joyful. The two men cursed and threw feeble punches at each other but Sarat did not stick around to watch. It seemed such a petty thing to fight over, so inconsequential.

Excerpted from:

REMARKS BY KASEB IBN AUMRAN, PRESIDENT OF THE BOUAZIZI UNION, DELIVERED AT OHIO STATE UNIVERSITY (JUNE 4, 2081)

I have tested your patience, speaking for so long on such a warm day. But I want to say this again: the government of the Bouazizi Union has no desire to impose its will on the affairs of any other nation. I believe we are all in agreement that the end of the troubles your country faces will come at the hands of the people who call this country home, nobody else. (Applause.)

But I also believe that all reasonable people of the world—regardless of race or ethnicity or religion—yearn for the same right to liberty, democracy, and self-determination. These are truly universal human ideals, and what we do today to advance them is the most important gift we leave for our children. Wars are temporary; these principles are not.

I remember the first time I came to America, many years ago. I was a young university student, a student at this very campus. At the time, my country was undergoing a bloody but necessary revolution, a revolution that claimed the lives of many martyrs but granted my people the freedom they had, for almost two centuries, been denied.

I remember all the things that fascinated me about America—its vast and beautifully diverse geography, blessed with some of the most awe-inspiring natural wonders on earth; its equally diverse people, living alongside one another in peace, regardless of the superficial differences among them. I saw in the people of this country a spirit I had rarely seen elsewhere, a dedication to liberty so overpowering, it made of many, one. (Applause.)

I say to you now, in closing, that I see that very same spirit here today. Whatever challenges America faces in this troubled moment, I am sure the people of this country can overcome. They have done so many times before (Applause), and they will again.

And I say to you that my people, the people of the Bouazizi Union who decades ago demanded from their rulers the very same liberation your revolutionaries once demanded of theirs, stand ready as allies to assist in any way we can. We are, all of us on this earth, drawn instinctively to peace, and I believe peace will prevail.

Thank you, and God bless America. (Applause.)

CHAPTER EIGHT

Two days before the massacre, there was a heavy storm. It lasted from dawn to dusk, the gray-muddled clouds oscillating between torrent and trickle. The hardest rain came early. By the time a convoy of Free Southerners' trucks arrived with sandbags, many of the camp's older tents had already washed away. The refugees sought shelter in the administrative buildings. Outside, in the stream of mud and wastewater, a doomed armada of clothes and cooking implements and irreplaceable keepsakes floated helplessly. The runoff fed into the ditches and beyond the ditches the creeks and beyond the creeks the now roaring Tennessee.

As the Free Southerners packed the sandbags along the banks of Emerald Creek, cursing and gagging at the smell of the overflowing filth, Sarat and her girls chased after the water-swept mementos.

Soaked to the bone, they scooped up anything of practical or sentimental value: picture frames, coils of fishing line, flags of the state and of the rebels; and keys, most important of all, keys.

The girls worked solemnly. At Albert Gaines's urging, Sarat had, a few weeks earlier, started a small club of sorts—her very own version of a scout troop. Already she'd wangled four young recruits—the Singleterry sisters from Alabama; Charlie from Georgia, who went by her dead younger brother's name; and Nadine from Mississippi. Two months before she arrived at Patience, Nadine lost her lower jaw in a Bird strike on Holly Springs. In its place now was a mash of mangled skin and a metal plate that held together what was left of her jawline. Nadine didn't speak. Of all the girls, she was Sarat's favorite.

When the girls' satchels were full, they took the contents to the administrative buildings. There, Sarat unlocked the side door and led them down the stairwell to the hallway leading to Gaines's office. In the hallway they set the salvaged items down on towels to dry, and then they returned to work.

By sundown the rainfall started to ease; a couple of hours later it was little more than a sprinkle. Sarat ran to the northernmost tents and watched the low gray clouds fall back to the Blue country. In the north the tents were new and largely unused, but none of the refugees had sought shelter there.

The next morning, Sarat instructed the girls to begin taking the salvaged debris out of the hallway. Her recruits laid their findings out on the ground by the side of the building. By the time the camp's staff became aware of what the girls had done, a mass of refugees had descended on the impromptu lost-and-found. They sifted for things they thought were gone forever and when they found them they cried and hugged the girls and called them angels. By noon there was not a single item left unclaimed.

☆ ☆ ☆

MARTINA CHESTNUT STOOD for a long time in front of her pristine tent. She observed the corners where the fabric hugged the scaffolding. There wasn't a single tear, not even a sign that a rainstorm had come through at all. The ground surrounding the tent was a thick stew of mud, and all her neighbors' homes were collapsed or nearing collapse, but Martina's home was untouched.

For a moment she was taken with thoughts of divine providence. She began to entertain the notion that some higher power had held its cupped hand over her home. Surely it was no mere chance; surely she had suffered enough to warrant this small act of mercy. Of course others had suffered; some arrived at the camp missing limbs or sight or kin and some were nothing but hollow shells in the shape of the living, but she had suffered too. She had suffered too.

Inside, she found Sarat and Dana on their cots, reading. Dana held a tablet; on the screen there was a *Tumble* magazine feature on Black Sea chic and the newly resurgent fashion scene of the far northern Bouazizi.

Sarat sat upright on her cot, an old Southern history book in her hands, on loan from Gaines.

"How did you two get back here so fast?" Martina asked. She breathed in deeply; the air inside the tent smelled bittersweet and acrid, a chemical scent.

"She was out all night saving everybody's trash," Dana said. "I was in here."

"Why didn't you come to the building?" Martina asked. "This whole tent could have been swept right out in the storm."

Dana chuckled. "You kidding? Simon and a couple of his friends came by a day ago and sprayed the whole thing down. They got chemicals that make the water bounce right off of anything—makes it like it never rained at all. It was a loud storm, though, I'll tell you that. Barely got any sleep."

Martina observed her other daughter, who had yet to take her eyes away from the pages of her book.

"You knew 'bout this?" she asked.

Sarat shrugged.

Martina fell silent. She walked past her daughters to her own room. In the last year the woman and her twin daughters had come to occupy the entirety of the tent, as Simon had taken to living outside the camp, only returning for a night or two every few months.

On her bed Martina found another care package from her son. It was a cardboard box that had once held a kitchen mixer. Its top flaps were sealed tight with packing tape.

Martina lifted the box. It felt heavy, perhaps twenty pounds. Without opening it she carried it past the blanket curtain to her daughters' room. She set it beside Sarat's bed.

"Take this and give it out to the people who lost their tents," she said.

"What's in it?" Sarat asked.

"I don't care. Just give it to someone who needs it."

"There's lots who need it. You want me to stay in Mississippi or . . ."

"Just do it, Sarat."

"All right."

Martina went back to her room and lay on her bed. The sheets were cool and the pillow felt good against the back of her neck. Soon the girls heard snoring from behind the curtain.

Dana, lying still on her cot, cast an eye at her sister.

"Go on then," she said.

"She's gonna change her mind when she wakes up," Sarat replied. "She'll want it back."

"And she'll get mad at you if it's still there. Open it up—let's take some of it and tell her we haven't given away the rest yet. Then everybody's happy."

Sarat retrieved from a sheath in her pocket the small folding knife Gaines had given her. When she first received it the blade was dull, but she had scraped it against the sharpening stone night after night. Now the blade was rough and uneven from being overworked, but Sarat mistook this for sharpness.

She slit the tape and opened the care package. She picked the first items she saw inside—a couple of stunted, Blue-grown oranges—and tossed one to her sister. Dana pierced the skin with her fingernail and held the fruit to her nose and inhaled deeply.

"They must have gone all the way up to Virginia for these," she said.

Sarat shook her head. "Simon says they've only been fighting around the southern end of the Smokys. Picking out those militias around there. Get any further north and the Blue soldiers proper will get you."

"Can't grow these in Tennessee," Dana said. "Too hot. Gotta be Virginia at least."

"They don't go get them where they're grown. They just pick them up at the ports in Augusta. You can get whatever you want there. Stuff you can't even get in Atlanta."

Dana smirked. "What do you know about all that? You can't even point Augusta out on a map."

"Yeah I can, and it's true. Nobody keeps track of what's on those charity ships. You can steal half the boat before anyone notices."

Sarat sifted through the rest of the package. She tossed a small can of cashews to her sister, and kept a packet of apricot gel for herself. She set aside a tube of superglue and a roll of twine and some knitting supplies to hand out to other refugees, and left the rest for her mother.

"Hey, give me some of those," Dana said, pointing to a small container of painkillers. "Mama doesn't need those."

"Nobody needs those," Sarat replied. "They're for broken bones. What have you got that needs these?"

"I got bored," Dana said, raising her feet to the air and flicking her toes at the ceiling. "I got ten broken bones' worth of bored."

Sarat observed her sister on the bed. She seemed younger somehow. For as long as she could remember, Sarat had felt that her twin had a head start on her, an innate understanding of what it means to be grown up. But in the last few months, she had come to feel the opposite. Now Dana suddenly seemed to her impossibly juvenile, and the things that held her interest girlish and trite.

Sarat set the painkillers in the package and then slid the box under her bed. She turned back to her book. Dana picked at her orange, savoring each segment and setting a strip of the fruit's skin atop her upper lip like a mustache. She hummed the first bars of a popular Redgrass song called "Julia's Right," which the summer prior had been the biggest hit in all the Mag and was universally banned anywhere north of the Tennessee line. The song was by a country star called Cherylene Cee, after whom Sarat had named her pet turtle.

Dana turned once more to her sister. "So when are we gonna tell Mama?" she said.

"Tell Mama what?"

"You know what. About you and me going away. About Atlanta."

Sarat sighed. When she had first told her sister her ambition to one day travel to the Southern capital and work with the government of the Free Southern State, Dana had chuckled at the thought. What use do you think they have down there for a refugee girl from Louisiana? she'd said; you gonna run for president too? But as the months passed and the camp continued to fill well beyond its capacity, its occupants subjected daily to new and varied indignities, the idea of running to the city began to appeal more and more to Dana. She started boasting to her friends about it, until Sarat regretted ever having told her anything about Atlanta.

"We're not just leaving our mother here and running away," Sarat said. "Who's gonna take care of her?"

"Simon's been taking care of her just fine," Dana said, pointing at the box under Sarat's bed.

"Simon doesn't spend more than one night a month in this tent—you know that."

"So, what, we're just gonna live the rest of our lives in this place? Wait for another storm to come and wipe the whole place away, or the Birds to come by and bomb it to hell? I thought you had all these plans about working for the government, letting the world know what the North's been doing to us, all that stuff. You keep talking about how you're gonna change things. You can't change a damn thing living in Patience."

"We're gonna go, Dana, I promise. But we gotta think about our people too."

Dana snorted. "Our people? In this camp, are you kidding me? You think if it weren't for everyone knowing Simon was with the rebels and you now being Albert Gaines's pet, they wouldn't have come through here and stolen every damn thing we got? Ain't nobody in this camp our people. Only thing we got in common is we all on the losing side of the same war."

"We're not losing the war," Sarat said. "And I'm not Gaines's pet."

"C'mon, girl. You spend every damn night with him, he's got you reading all those books and running all those errands. You know well as I do he's just an errand boy for all them rebel groups. Comes to places like this looking for anyone dumb enough to strap on a farmer's suit and blow themselves up outside some Northern checkpoint. Won't be long before he tries to put a farmer's suit on you too."

"He's a teacher," Sarat said. "Nothing more."

Sarat stood up. She lifted her messenger bag off a hook on the wall and slung it over her shoulder.

"I'm gonna go look for Simon out by the creek," she said. "It's getting 'round sundown—they should be coming in. Don't tell Mama nothing about Atlanta, and don't take any of those pills."

☆ ☆ ☆

THE AIR SMELLED of mildew. Everywhere there were signs of damage from the storm, but also signs of recovery. With nowhere else to turn to, the refugees began to rally around the rain-damaged tents like antibodies to an infection.

On her way to the northeastern end of Alabama, Sarat passed countless lines of clothes and sheets and flags and blankets, all drying in the wind; tablets and radios and phones planted like seeds in bags of rice. The sky was a matte purple. Another warm, dry evening was coming over the Mag. The puddles began to dry.

She walked through the northern tents, where there were some signs of damage but no signs of life. She passed the tent in which her pet turtle lived and reminded herself to check on the animal later.

When she approached the remains of Highway 25, she saw a man and a boy, both hunchbacked with heavy baggage, walking north toward the ruined bridge and the gate to the Blue country. She approached and saw that it was Marcus Exum and his father.

The two carried overstuffed packs on their backs and grocery bags in their hands, and the father wore around his neck a pair of birding binoculars. Sarat watched them for a minute as they approached the place where the road once crossed low over the creek.

Before the war, the road ran straight into Tennessee, but now the only things visible above the waterline were two slim concrete barriers that once marked the edges of the highway. They peered just above the surface like stone tightropes. In the distance, beyond a series of large red signs prohibiting passage, the razor-wired fences and tree-camouflaged snipers' towers marked the beginning of the Blue country.

Sarat approached Marcus and his father. When the man saw her he turned hurriedly to see if there were others watching, and when he saw none he motioned for the girl to leave.

"What are you doing?" Sarat asked.

"It doesn't matter to you what we're doing," he said. "Go on now, this doesn't concern you."

"It's all right, Dad," Marcus said, setting his grocery bags down. "Let me just say goodbye."

"No time," his father said. "They'll be back at the gates soon."

"Just one minute, promise."

Marcus eased his backpack from his shoulders. He'd grown a little in the last year, but still stood only as high as Sarat's chest. He put his hand on her arm. "We're leaving, Sarat," he said. "We're going to the North tonight. We're not coming back."

"Are you crazy?" Sarat said. "You go anywhere near that gate, they'll shoot you dead."

Marcus shook his head. "Dad's been watching. There hasn't been a single guard at the gate in the last two days. Not one Blue soldier anywhere along the fence. I don't know where they've gone, but they've gone."

Sarat looked out at the gate in the distance. The foliage-covered towers and the old chicanes looked the same as they always did.

"Something's going to happen," Marcus's father said. "They're getting ready to storm the fence—they're getting ready to finally come through here."

"You've been saying that for years," Sarat said.

"They've been getting ready for years."

Sarat turned to Marcus. "You were just gonna go like that? Without even saying goodbye?"

"I knew you were busy with what you've been doing," Marcus said. "We haven't really talked much in the last little while. I didn't wanna bother you."

"But you're my best friend," Sarat said.

Marcus turned from her gaze, his eyes to the ground.

"Pick your bags up," Marcus's father said. "We got no time to stand around."

She watched Marcus pick up his belongings. One of the grocery bags was weighed down with ration packs and a water thermos and a couple pairs of underwear; the other had a headlamp and a small camping stove.

"You'll take care of Cherylene, right?" Marcus said.

Sarat nodded.

"Don't tell nobody," Marcus's father said. "They'll come back and kill us all if everybody starts trying to get through."

She watched the man and his son as they traversed the concrete tightrope to the forbidden country. The path jutted only a few inches above the waterline and was a little more than a foot's width across. They walked carefully, their arms occasionally rising from their sides in an effort to keep balance. As she watched them pass the warning signs, Sarat waited for the snipers' rifles to ring out, for the man and his son to fall dead in the river. But no shots came.

Soon they crossed past the chicanes and disappeared into the brush. Sarat stood for a long time after they were gone, watching the unmoving land on the other side of the water.

She tried to imagine where her friend and his father would go. Perhaps beyond the brown and scrubby ridge there lay bustling Northern towns brilliant with electric light. Or vast fragrant rows of farmland full of oranges and mandarins and exotic Blue-grown fruit of which she'd never even heard. Perhaps the two pilgrims would find refuge working in one such farm, or maybe their accents and sun-cracked skin would give them away and they'd be shot dead at the gates of the very first town.

And as she imagined these possibilities, Sarat thought of something else: of desertion, of treason against one's own. But what the man and his son had done didn't feel to her like treason, only the grim work of the hopeless. As she'd learned from Albert Gaines about her people's history of mistreatment at the hands of the North, Sarat had grown to loathe the enemy nation beyond the Tennessee line. But in this moment, as she watched her closest friend disappear into that alien land, she wished only that he be safe there. That he live, that he simply live.

☆ ☆ ☆

AFTER MARCUS and his father disappeared behind the distant foliage, Sarat walked east in the direction of Chalk Hollow.

The rebels were at the edge of the creek. She heard them before she saw them, a cackle of singing and laughing and loud conversation. Usually they were quiet when they came in across the creek at dusk but this evening they made no effort to hide their presence.

They were Simon's clan, the Virginia Cavaliers. But in reality there was nothing much to distinguish them from the Mississippi Sovereigns or the New Zouaves or any of the other rebel groups. They were simply boys with guns, fanned out across the border, picking fights with Northerners.

She found them, about a dozen in all, at a clearing a few hundred feet past the broken highway. They had come over on three Sea-Toks and a larger fossil-powered skiff, all of which were docked now in the sandy beachfront, partially hidden among the sweetgum trees. Beside the boats the men were unloading box-crates sealed shut with nails.

"Hey, Sarat!" yelled a half-drunk Cavalier named Eli, a boy of about nineteen who'd come to the camp from Dalton four years earlier. "Hey, Simon, your sister's here."

"Yell a little louder," said Simon, lying on the sand with his back against the black-painted hull, the lapping creek water at his feet. "They didn't hear you in Tennessee."

Eli was perched over a small bonfire, grilling. A set of thick steaks sat atop the fire on a charred cookie tray, the flames licking at its underside. The juice of fat and blood set the fire dancing; the tinder crackled and burst.

"Where did you get that meat?" Sarat asked.

"One of their generals was kind enough to hand it over," said Eli, a wide smile across his face. He was missing one of his upper incisors; his hair was unwashed and matted across his forehead in an oily wave. Like the others he went days without cleaning himself but on this evening the reek of him was overwhelmed by the warm sweetness of the fire and the intoxicating scent of grilling meat.

"You know those pigs up there, they eat like this every night," said Eli. "Girl, tell me, when did you last eat steak like this?"

"Maybe once back in Louisiana," said Sarat. "Never had it here."

"Those pigs eat it every single night," said Eli.

He leaned down and cut a piece of the steak. It was dense with fat and severed easily under the blade of his bowie knife. He handed it to Sarat. She chewed it slowly, savoring the warmth and the way the marbled flesh both gave and resisted against her teeth. The taste of wood smoke was thick in the charred exterior, the meat beneath it pink and tender.

How could it ever be, thought Sarat, that a person could eat this well every day and not die from the very shame of it—when just a few miles away there lived so many subsisting on so little.

"You gotta be careful," said Sarat. "They smell that in the camp, they'll come running."

"Oh we got some for them too," said Eli, pointing at the crates along the bank. "We can't go around handing it out like it's Christmas or nothing, but we'll get it to them. God knows they deserve it."

Eli pierced the steaks with his knife and turned them over; the fire hissed and set its curled fingers upward. He leaned close to Sarat over the flame.

"Hey, are those Southern State boys they sent up here after the storm still around?" he asked.

"Nah," Sarat replied. "Soon as the rain stopped they were gone."

"That's good," Eli said. "Goddamned if they're gonna get any of this. Let them go back to Atlanta. They get fed well enough there."

"So did you steal this, or what?" Sarat asked.

The smile momentarily left Eli's lips. He was a scrawny boy—all the rebels seemed to either be scrawny or muscle-bound, never regular-set—and the orange glow of the fire put dark shadows in the hollows beneath his jaw.

"Didn't steal nothing," he said. "We fought them for it and we won. You've been watching too many of their shows, reading too much of their news. They have you thinking they can't ever be beat. Well they can. Take away their tanks and their Birds and all those toys they hide behind like cowards, make it so it's just us and them eye-to-eye, and they can be beat."

"Calm down," Sarat said. "I didn't mean nothing by it."

Eli's smile returned. "I know you didn't, girl. Hell, I heard you're learning from Gaines now." He laughed. "And he *loves* you. Says you got more balls than most men out here."

Eli sliced one of the steaks width-wise. "Here," he said. "Take half of mine."

Sarat thanked him. She walked to where her brother sat at the creek-side.

A couple of rebels sat nearby on a felled log, playing guitar and singing an old folk song whose popularity had recently been revived by some firebrand folk star in Atlanta, who set the old music to new lyrics. The boys, drunk on Joyful, slurred the words and cackled at their own musical ineptitude. The one playing guitar stumbled through four open chords with uncoordinated fingers, muting half the strings.

Mama take this flag from me
Ain't my country anymore . . .

Sarat sat on the sand beside her brother.

"Hey, lady," he said. He had a goofy grin on his face, a half-empty jug of Joyful beside him. The drink's reek hung over the beach: a honeyed perfume of fruits left to rot, old bread, creek water, and whatever else the boys could find to give the dark juice muscle—from antifreeze to turpentine to ground-up painkillers.

"You're celebrating something, I hear," Sarat said.

"You could say that," her brother replied.

"I don't mean to put a damper on it, but Mama's mad at you."

"What's she mad at me for? Didn't that stuff we sprayed on her tent work?"

"Yeah, but she thinks you should have sprayed it on everybody's tent. Thinks her neighbors are all looking at her funny because all their tents collapsed but hers looks good as new."

Simon chuckled and spat. "What's she think? We got time to spray everybody's tent down? Anyway, tell her we're coming around tomorrow to help all those folks fix the place up. Just couldn't be there when the Free Southern State soldiers were there, or else we'd have to put those government boys in their place. And then the Blue reporters would have a field day saying, Look how the South's fighting itself."

Simon poured a capful of hooch from his jug and offered it to Sarat. When she reached for it he swooped it into his own mouth and smiled.

"Very funny," said Sarat. "That stuff will make you blind, anyway."

"If it's any good, it will," said Simon.

He dug his heels into the sand and watched the boys singing on the log nearby. He'd grown in the last year; not taller—she still had three inches on him—but bulkier. In the rebel camps out by the banks of the Tennessee, he and some of the Cavaliers passed the time curling milk jugs full of sand; he had biceps on him now like rolling hills.

Sarat envied the malleability of boys' bodies, the way they could, while still boys, cast their physical shapes forward into adulthood like reconnaissance scouts. All her life she'd had little interest in the working of boys' minds, which she imagined only as a set of flimsy pinwheels turning in the direction of obvious things. But she longed to have such a malleable, predictable body—one that could grow big and strong and yet not raise a single stranger's eyebrow.

In the amber glow of firelight the boys sang drunkenly. Simon turned to his sister. "We got one of them yesterday, Sarat," he said. "We got a big one."

"Who?" Sarat asked.

"A guy named Pearson," said Simon. "A general, commander of half the troops along the Tennessee line."

"Jesus. How?"

"We were out in the forest, all the way out east, past Chattanooga. We'd been there for days, camped out by a path the Blues had been using to run supplies in and out of Big Frog. Eli set a trap, a big mine deep in the ground, a little mine just above it. The big mines don't go off under the weight of a man, but the little ones do, so you make it so that one sets off the other. Then we lay a tree trunk across the path and we just waited. Waited for three days till finally this convoy comes rolling through. Usually they run in fours but this time it was just two LAVs. We thought it was just grunts rotating through the forward base at Halfway Branch. But when they came out to take a look at the log, well, Eli's looking through the binoculars and he says, 'One of them got stars on his shoulders.' And we're watching as he walks out ahead of all of them, like he's making a big show of leading, and he steps right on it. The little mine sets off the big mine and takes all but two of them out right there. We came running down there soon as it went off, and in the back of these LAVs were nothing but crates of supplies. So many, we couldn't even carry them all."

Simon pointed to the sky. "I'm telling you, He was watching over us, Sarat. He was watching over us, I know it."

"Simon, you can't be out here celebrating," said Sarat. "You gotta hide. They'll come after you."

Simon laughed. "Who are they gonna come after? They don't know nothing. All they know how to do is build walls and send the Birds to do their dirty work for them."

"You gonna keep all this stuff in the camp?"

"Most of it is just food," said Simon. "We're gonna keep some of it up north in the empty tents, but most of it we'll just give out. People deserve to eat."

"They'll know," said Sarat. "Word will get out. You can't have a whole camp eating steak and nobody hears about it."

"It'll be all right," Simon said. He put his arm around his sister and pulled her close to him, her smooth-shaved head resting against his shoulder. "Christ, lady, when did you get so nervous? What happened to the girl who jumped into Shit Lake on a dare?"

"Just be careful."

"We got one of theirs, Sarat," said Simon. "Every day they get a hundred of ours, but this time we got one of theirs."

☆ ☆ ☆

SARAT RETURNED to the center of the camp. She entered the administrative building through the side door that led to Albert Gaines's office.

On this night she found him leaning over the table, placing delicate spoonfuls of something black and glistening on a plate. He was dressed as she'd always seen him dressed: his single-breasted suit unblemished by wrinkles. He wore a double-Windsored tie of matte gray decorated with a crest of three stars atop an armored knight's head and a red-striped shield. His hat lay on the table.

"Come in, come in!" he said, smiling. "I have something special for you."

Sarat inspected the small flat canister on the table. Its tin lid had been pried open and inside lay a clump of small black balls. The writing on the side of the canister was foreign: letters similar to English but oddly misshapen, as though mutated somehow. The logo on the label was of a fish and a king's crown.

"In Columbus the Northerners pay more than you would ever believe for pale imitations of this," Gaines said. "Tonight you get the real thing for free."

Sarat poked it with her pinky finger. The amount on her plate seemed impossibly small for a meal, and she wondered if it wasn't some kind of vitamin pill, like the ones that came in the aid shipments.

"What is it?" she asked.

"Try it first. I don't want you to be disgusted beforehand."

"I won't be."

"It's caviar," Gaines said. "Fish eggs."

"Hmm."

Sarat tasted the caviar. It whispered to her tongue an awful, briny secret. It spoke of something very far away, fruit of alien trees. Instantly she loved it.

"Where did you get this?" she asked.

"The Russian Union," Gaines said. "The other side of the world. A present from our friend Joe."

He walked to the office's small kitchenette. Sarat heard the tick-tick-tick of the toaster oven, and soon he returned with her favorite, honey on toast. He sat beside her and watched her eat. He seemed to have an endless capacity for watching.

"I have a new book for you," he said. He went to the bookshelves and returned with a hardback. Sarat inspected the book. It was brand new, as though it had been published that day. The book was called

A Northern Soldier's Education in War and Peace. It had a picture of a handsome man on the cover. Most of the books Gaines had given her to read until then had nothing on their covers but the names of the authors and the names of the books. But on this one, the image of the man dominated the cover, as though his face itself were the subject of the book. The portrait of the man was cropped at his chest; Sarat saw the medals and marks of a military uniform on him.

"The man who wrote this book is named Joseph Weiland Jr.," said Gaines. "He's the son of the Blues' most senior general."

"What do I have to read a Northerner's book for?" asked Sarat. "It's all lies, anyway."

Gaines pointed at the picture on the cover. "This man, quite recently, decided to run for office. And it's customary that when a man like him runs for office, he puts a whole lot of words on a whole lot of pages and stamps his picture on the cover and sends it out into the world. That way, by the time election day comes around, a very well-manicured version of himself has already been foisted onto the people who do the electing.

"But that's not why we read it. We read it because he's our enemy. And half that book that's supposed to be about him, it's really about us, because we're his enemy. We read it to read beneath it, and in doing so, find out what it is about us that scares him."

Sarat watched Gaines intently. She loved to hear him speak, loved the cadence of his voice and the vast unseen world of which his diatribes so often hinted. Even when she lost track of what he meant, even when she failed entirely to understand him, she smiled and listened and wished only for more.

Gaines rose from the table. "I have one more thing for you," he said.

He retrieved something from his briefcase. And then he was behind her, his hands and what they held brushing against her neck.

It was a hemp necklace, made of black and white and red threads purled tight. He clasped it around her neck and gave her a small hand mirror. She looked at her reflection; the necklace felt rough and worn against her skin.

"What's it mean?" she asked.

"It used to belong to my daughter," Gaines said. "I want you to have it."

"Thank you."

The girl looked in the mirror a while and for a moment she no longer saw the necklace, only the old man's hands on her shoulders: the knuckles weathered and cracked, the fingernails cut down to the nub. His palms seemed to radiate and the heat slowly filled the space between Sarat's shoulder blades and spilled down her back.

Before he let her leave, Gaines gave Sarat more envelopes to distribute among the refugees. He paid her in advance for the errands. She slipped the crisp Northerners' currency into her messenger bag and bid her teacher goodbye. At night she made her rounds. By dawn she was back in her tent. There, for the last time in her life, she slept soundly.

☆ ☆ ☆

WHEN SHE WOKE in the afternoon, Sarat saw her tent was empty, her mother and sister gone. She sat up and reached under her bed for the box of rations. She retrieved the tube of apricot gel from her bedside drawer and squeezed some of the saccharine paste into her mouth. A few minutes later the grogginess disappeared.

She changed into her jeans and an Orascom T-shirt and left the tent. Outside, the refugees were busy fixing their homes, assisted now by a few of the rebels. The smell of mildew hovered in the air but also the smell of steak and the sound of singing and pleasant, drunken conversation. All the acrimony of a day earlier seemed now to have melted away.

Men and women sat on chairs and tables made from sandbags, drinking Joyful and eating meat with their bare hands, the juice running down their chins. Sarat joined them for a few hours, and for a few hours she was well-fed and happy and a little drunk.

In the evening, after the alcohol had worn off, she walked north to check on her pet. When she arrived she saw the same empty tents of northern Alabama, but beyond them something was different.

The massive floodlights of the Blue checkpoint to the north were alight, their beams blanketing a million shadowed outlines in the ground ahead. Sarat hid behind one of the tents and peered out, watching.

She saw the men at the gate. Hundreds, perhaps a thousand, clad in black, their faces covered. They arrived in a sloppy formation of old trucks, carrying rifles and pistols and machetes. In the floodlight the men appeared as shifting inkblots, black limbs on black torsos. In their totality their movement was of a single squirming organism, writhing under and through the gashes in the fence. She saw them and at once she knew.

As the men approached, Sarat sneaked out from behind the tent and sprinted back into the heart of the camp. She ran in the shadow of the tents, faster than she'd ever run before, the air a maelstrom in her lungs. Where she saw men and women she screamed at them to run, to hide. She said the militias were coming, but no one seemed to listen.

As she approached her tent, Sarat heard the first crack of gunfire—not the distant rifle shots she'd become acquainted with over the years, but a close burst, a deafening metal rattle. And then she heard shouting; a high-pitched scream; more shots, this time closer.

Sarat burst through the door to find her sister sitting on the bed, tablet in hand. She was watching footage of a charity concert in Kennesaw to benefit the Mothers of the Southern Republic. The old country star Cherylene Cee sang her hit song. Dana sat on the bed, eating Virginia oranges and singing along.

"You remember how we used to go nuts for her, back when we were little?" Dana said. Then she saw her sister's face. "What's wrong?"

"The militias are here," said Sarat. "They broke through the northern gate."

"How many?" asked Dana.

"Hundreds. Get up, quickly. Where's Mama?"

"I don't know. Playing cards at Erica Yarber's tent, maybe. Maybe out with Lara. I don't know, I don't know."

Sarat grabbed her sister by the arm and together they ran from the tent. Outside, the sound of gunfire echoed, its source ever closer. Some of the refugees stepped out of their tents and asked about the commotion, but this time Sarat said nothing.

She led her sister to the administrative building's side door, and unlocked it with Albert Gaines's key. She locked the door behind them and they ran down the stairs to the office in the basement, turning the hallway lights off as they went.

When they were inside the office, Sarat and Dana pushed one of the large bookshelves against the office's front door, and then the table against the bookshelf. Sarat turned off the lights in the room. She led her sister to the closet, and then made to leave.

"No, no, you can't go out there," Dana said, holding on to her sister's arm.

"I gotta go find Mama," Sarat replied. "I'll nudge the shelf and the table enough to open the door a little, and then you push it closed behind me."

"Please, please," Dana begged. "You know you won't find her before they find you. They'll kill you out there. I can't lose my whole family, I can't lose everyone I love. Please don't go out there."

Sarat looked at her sister, astounded not by the black-glistened tears on her face or the panic in her voice, but at the dark calculation she'd already made. Sarat led her sister into the closet; they huddled together on the floor.

The gunfire grew closer, screams drowned in its echo. It came at times in a rapid back-and-forth. Sometimes there were only single shots, or a parade of single shots, short silences between them.

The sounds continued into the night. Then in the earliest morning hours came a brief pause. And in that silence Dana, exhausted and delirious with fear, slept.

Sarat remained by her sister's side. In the blackness the twins were only the hushed sigh of their breathing, the rise and fall of their chests. Outside, the sound of gunfire had faded but there were still other sounds.

Sarat listened: boots against dirt; a militiaman asking something unintelligible and his superior responding: you know exactly what to do; the sounds of pleading, of cursing; a line of feet shuffling in unison, drawn closer, closer, ordered to kneel; more pleading, a man saying: I'm not with them, I swear, I swear. His voice coming through the walls of the building in which Sarat hid, clear as though he were pressed against it. Then nothing. Then a line of single gunshots, one after the other. Then nothing.

The shots were closer than any that had come before, and for a moment Sarat believed the men had entered the building.

If it's going to happen, then let it happen, she thought, but I won't die crouching.

She eased quietly away from her sleeping sister. She pulled her folding knife from her pocket and stood up. She eased the office door open just enough to slide through, then she closed it behind her.

The corridor that led from the office to the stairs was dark and the walk seemed endless. As she approached the door, she tried to imagine what the killers looked like. She pictured them as the Northerners she'd seen on television, who always appeared tall and muscular, their complexions ghostly. In her mind they were of a different breed, a different species.

She climbed the stairs to the building's side door and she put her ear to the door and listened. There was no sound. She opened the door and peered outside.

For a moment she believed she'd mistimed the day. She had thought it was two or three in the morning, the slaughter closing in on its twenty-fourth hour. But the sky above was midday bright.

Then the light began to fade, quickly, giving way to a black sky. It stayed dark until, from somewhere far to the north, she heard the whistling arc of another flare, and soon the fraudulent daytime illuminated the camp once more.

Sarat walked slowly, keeping near the wall. There were sounds of men cursing in the distance to the southeast and southwest, in Georgia and South Carolina. There were sounds of chaos too: of tents being torn apart, of women muffled mid-scream. Sounds of gunfire, but not as rapid or sustained as it was a day earlier.

A great fire burned in the gut of the Alabama slice. The flames curled around plumes of black smoke. There were men in the distance, burning bodies. They brought kindling in the form of tent covers and clothes and mattresses. The fire skipped and cracked and traced higher and higher into the sky.

Sarat turned the corner to find a line of bound corpses near the wall. They were men, young and old. They'd been lined up against the wall on their knees, and where the bullets had gone through them there were splatters of dull red on the wall.

Sarat stood frozen. She looked at the bodies. Most lay flat on their fronts or on their sides facing away from her, but those she could see had grotesque, unrecognizable faces, cracked open at the forehead, contorted in silent agony.

The bodies made damp pools in the dusty ground. There was a heat to them. Sarat felt it against her skin, damp and real as steam from a boiling pot. She knew what it was. It was the heat of life extinguished. The heat of something leaving.

In the mass of crumpled bodies she saw a face she recognized. It was Eli, the Virginia Cavalier she'd seen when she went to talk to her brother. Quickly, the faces surrounding him began to register in her memory: they were rebels from her brother's clan.

Suddenly all her courage disappeared. She stood paralyzed with terror, incapable of unseeing the pile of corpses at her feet, among whom she was now certain her dead brother lay. The sounds of burning and of screaming and of killing continued relentless around her, the sky overhead beating dark and light like God's great heart itself.

The sound of men approaching from behind the far corner of the wall shook her from her paralysis. She knew from the soft thud of their boots and from their voices that they were militiamen. She heard one of them say: "They said there's no rules before sunrise. It's all ours till then."

She knew that when they turned the corner they'd see her. Without thinking, she fell to the ground. She wriggled into the mass of dead men, camouflaged herself within it. The heat that had touched her body now wrapped itself around her, sunk into her pores. She lay among the blood and sweat and shit and piss of the murdered. She thought nothing of the fluid that seeped into her clothes, or of the odor or of anything except her small desperate prayer: Please God, don't let them see me. Don't let them kill me.

She held her breath. The boot steps grew nearer.

She waited, unmoving as the dead that surrounded her. The men passed.

In the stillness that followed she heard another sound, close by in the tents across the road. It was the sound of guttural heaving, the crack of bone on bone. When that sound subsided there was another scream cut in half.

From a sliver of sight between the limbs of the dead, Sarat saw a man leave the tent across the road. He wore black jeans and a black shirt untucked. His balaclava hung limp from his pants pocket.

She saw his face. He looked no different than the men who lived in the camp. He looked no different than anyone Sarat had ever seen. He was of the same species, the same breed.

She lay frozen in place and watched the man walk in the direction of Georgia, where there was now another pyre aflame. When he was gone and she heard no more boot steps, Sarat rose and ran in the direction of the tent from which the man had just emerged.

Inside she saw a woman named Sabrina, a refugee from Mississippi, a survivor of the firebombing of Hopewell. She recognized her despite the bloody, swollen pulp of her face. The woman's jaw had been shifted violently to the right, the skin around her eyes made puffy and purple. She lay on the floor of her tent with her skirt hiked high and her stomach butterflied open. Her chest moved.

When the woman caught sight of Sarat she raised her hand and beckoned her to come close. Sarat took the woman's hand and sat beside her. The canvas beneath her was soaked. The woman moaned and said a word Sarat could not understand. She took it as a pleading for comfort and, not knowing what else to do, Sarat reached for a nearby charity blanket and covered the woman's gaping stomach. The woman muttered the same word a few more times and then fell silent.

Sarat remained inside the tent. She held the woman's hand but the hand was now simply weight. She listened as the men returned north toward the gate from which they'd first entered. They passed close to her tent. It seemed an endless procession, thousands strong. She imagined them not as men, not even as human, but as a dark, daylong season: a primal winter.

When the boot steps had passed and there was only the distant crackling of fires, Sarat peered out the tent's front door. She saw the wall where the pile of bodies lay.

Then came a straggler, a young militiaman with his rifle slung loose over his shoulder. As he passed the dead men he stopped and faced the wall and unzipped his pants and began to urinate.

Sarat watched. She pulled her knife from her pocket and unfolded it. She walked outside, toward the man, who had his back to her. She was no longer afraid. She moved as a wraith, a cold conflagration in the skin of a girl. She approached the man and when she was upon him she reached around his neck and slashed open his throat.

The man reached for her arm and caught it. She pushed him against the wall. They both fell, she on top of him, he on top of the corpses. A cascade of blood erupted from where she'd cut him open. She pinned him down and kept slashing, the neck slippery now with blood. Soon the man stopped fighting, but she kept moving the knife back and forth, back and forth, until she hit something deep within the body she could not sever. She screamed. She stabbed at the back of his head and when the knife hit the hard bone of the skull it held. Sarat's left hand slipped from the bloody handle and slid down the blade, cutting a deep gash across her palm. The pain was anesthetic. The heat of life left the man but this time Sarat did not feel it.

☆ ☆ ☆

THE FREE SOUTHERNERS ARRIVED at dawn: a convoy of soldiers dispatched from Atlanta. They rumbled through the gates and into the camp. Behind them came trucks and aid buses bearing the symbol of the Red Crescent, and behind those came a couple of journalists.

The soldiers disembarked from their trucks. They were boys and young men, many of them having never seen a day of fighting. They walked among the corpses and the pyres, dumbfounded, their weapons drawn at phantoms. Quietly, the foreign observers and the journalists began to count and document the dead.

The sun rose over Patience. The survivors, some mutilated, others dumb with shock, crawled from their hiding places and the places where they'd been discarded. The staff who'd hidden in the administrative building emerged holding the flag of the Red Crescent above them, screaming their affiliation.

Sarat walked around the building and when the Reds saw her they raised their weapons and told her not to move. One of the soldiers ordered her to get down on her knees. Sarat stood, soaked in blood.

When one of the camp's staff saw her she told the soldiers to lower their weapons.

"She's one of the refugees, she's one of the refugees," the woman said, rushing toward the girl.

"Sarat, honey, put that knife down," the woman said. "It's done. It's over."

Sarat turned her gaze from the boys and their guns to the woman.

She pushed the woman aside and walked into the administrative building. She descended the stairs and walked to the office where her sister hid. She knocked on the door three times, then twice, then once—a secret knock they'd shared for years. Slowly there came a shuffling sound from the other side of the door.

"It's me," Sarat said. "They're gone."

Dana opened the door slowly. She saw her sister.

"Oh God," she said. "What did they do to you?"

"Let's go," Sarat replied.

She led her sister out of the building. The Southern soldiers were in the courtyard, putting out the fires and searching the tents.

The soldiers covered the bodies and what was left of them with white cloth and then placed them on stretchers and carried those stretchers to the beds of the waiting trucks. Men with masks over their mouths and noses kept a tally on clipboards. The journalists took pictures of the dead and asked questions of the survivors, who looked straight through them with flint-lacquered eyes. The handful of unharmed survivors were ushered quickly onto waiting buses.

When she saw the carnage, Dana screamed. Sarat took her in her arms and buried her head against her chest.

"They killed them, didn't they?" Dana cried. "Mama and Simon. They killed them."

Sarat guided her sister in the direction of one of the buses, where a handful of survivors sat in silence.

"Go with them," Sarat said. "If Mama and Simon are alive, I'll find them. If they're dead, I'll find them."

One of the surviving camp workers came to where the twins stood. "You can't stay, Sarat," she said.

"I'm gonna bury my people," Sarat replied.

"The soldiers are taking care of them. They'll be treated with respect. But you have to leave here, Sarat. It's not safe—they might come back."

"I'm staying. If you don't like it, have them shoot me."

Sarat turned to her sister. "We'll be together again soon, I promise."

Dana retrieved a handkerchief from her pocket and tied it around the wound on Sarat's left palm. She hugged her sister.

"Beautiful girl," she said.

Dana boarded the bus. Sarat walked to Mississippi, toward the smoldering remains of a fire. She walked past the tents, many of them slashed open, their doors broken down. She choked on the smell of burning.

She reached her own tent. The door had been kicked open and the Chestnuts' belongings lay strewn on the beds and on the floor. But there was nobody inside.

Sarat crossed the dirt footpath to another tent down the way, the place where she believed her mother might have gone the night before to see her friends. Here too the door had been broken open.

Sarat paused at the threshold. She tried to steel herself for what she might find inside, tried to preemptively imagine her mother's body, the life gone from it. But she was incapable of making herself imagine it. Instead, her mind recoiled and offered only a feeble, child's defense: My mother cannot be dead because she is my mother. Everyone else can die but not my mother.

Sarat stepped inside the tent. There was blood on the floor and blood on the walls, but there were no bodies.

Outside, by the tent's broken door, she saw lines in the dirt. Wide swaths, like the beginnings of infant canals. Without following the trails, she knew where they would lead. In the distance, not far away, smoldered the blackened remains of a large and dying fire.

☆ ☆ ☆

THE SOLDIERS WORKED QUIETLY. She worked alongside them, numb to the world around her. She helped cover the dead in white cloth and carry them to the waiting trucks. The bodies were placed atop the beds and when the beds were full the trucks were dispatched south and new ones came to take their place. By nightfall the murdered had been cleared and the fires quenched and the survivors dispatched to some far-off hospital.

Most of the soldiers were ordered back to Atlanta but some were left to stand guard over Patience. The ones who were ordered to remain cursed their luck for having to spend the night in the camp. The dead were gone but the smell of them lingered. The echoes of them lingered.

Sarat walked north. In Alabama there were also soldiers stationed at the now gutted fence but one was asleep in his chair and the other was watching a movie on his tablet and neither noticed her presence. The soldiers seemed certain the men who'd done the killing would not return. In the distance behind them the floodlights of the Blues, so bright one night ago, were dark.

Sarat entered the tent in which she and Marcus had kept their pets. She saw that the mouse had fled, but Cherylene the turtle remained in her pen.

She picked the animal up, but it did not retreat. She walked with it back to the center of the camp and placed it on the seat of the last remaining bus. There were only a few people left in the camp now: men and women with gloves and face masks who continued to document the killings. They took pictures of bullet holes in the sides of the buildings, of dried stains in the dirt.

Sarat returned to Albert Gaines's office. She closed the door behind her. In the camp the smell was of fire smoke but in this room it was of other things: fine wood and old ink on paper and patent shoes and well-ironed suits.

Sarat closed the door behind her. She tore the maps from the walls. She flipped the table. She pushed the bookshelves over and pulled the fine prewar suits from their hangers and smashed the plates on the floor. She ripped apart the old antique books, shredded their pages and broke their spines. Then she sat on the floor and wept.

In a while the door opened and Albert Gaines entered the room. He stepped over the broken bookshelves and around the upturned table and sat on the floor opposite Sarat. He appeared as though from another world, his prewar suit immaculate, untouched by dirt or blood.

"I came as soon as I heard," he said. "Did your family survive?"

"My mother's dead, but I can't find her body," Sarat said. "My brother's dead, but I can't find his body."

"They call themselves the Twenty-first Indiana," Gaines said. "They're a militia, not enlisted, but there's no doubt the Blue commanders knew what they . . ."

"Stop talking about them," Sarat said. "I don't wanna hear about them anymore. I don't wanna read about them or memorize their capitals or learn how they did us wrong."

"Then what do you want to do?" Gaines asked.

"I want to kill them."

Sarat buried her head in her hands. She never saw the faint smile that, in that moment, crossed her teacher's lips.

Excerpted from:

WAR OFFICE—

FINAL COMPENSATION RULING ARCHIVE

Case Number: 091682

Applicant Name:
Chestnut, Martina
(Deceased/NOK Application)

CASE SUMMARY:

A) Claim Agreement

The Final Compensation Ruling issued by the Condolence Payment Department of the Joint Compensation Office (hereinafter referred to as "Payer") is issued under the Domestic Claims Act in the case of MARTINA CHESTNUT and 3 dependents (1 FA Male; 2 Pre-FA Female) (hereinafter referred to as "Payee"). The Ruling is accepted by both parties and constitutes final and irrevocable settlement in relation to the incident outlined in Section B. The Ruling and claim payment determination are made at the sole discretion of the Payer and are nonnegotiable.

B) Incident Details

Payee was impacted by an incident at a Red Crescent–administered Mississippi refugee facility ("Camp Patience"). As determined by the Investigation Office, the incident is classified as Class 2—Serious; Contained. Incident Attribution is Other/Undefined.

C) Nature of injuries

Chestnut, Martina (FA Female): Deceased
Chestnut, Simon (FA Male): Displacement; Class 1 Injury (Head)
Chestnut, Dana (Pre-FA Female): Displacement
Chestnut, Sara (Pre-FA Female): Displacement; Class 4 Injury (Left Hand)

D) Payment Schedule

Payee is hereby granted residence allotment (Charity House 027, Lincolnton, Georgia) for Displacement (3 or more). Payee is also granted $5000 for Death. Payee is also granted $2500 for Class 1 Injury. Payee is also granted $100 for Class 4 injury.

E) Release and Withdrawal

This Ruling implies no admission of fault by any arm or agency of the Federal Government (See Appendix A "Gesture of Regret Policy: Terms and Conditions"). The Payee hereby relinquishes any right of recourse in relation to this matter.

III

October, 2086

Lincolnton, Georgia

CHAPTER NINE

There was a mark where the devil left him. They came from miles to touch it, to kiss and caress the fissure in the forehead, to see the broken Miracle Boy. Sometimes they sat in silence, the only sounds coming from the kitchen, where the caretaker Karina Chowdhury hummed ancient gospels as she worked. Other times the men and women who came to see the boy prayed, and other times they too sang. And sometimes in the grip of paroxysm they cried and called him by their own children's names. The boy let himself be their vessel. He sat unspeaking, the shivering hands upon him, serene as a cloud.

The house was built by the river, near where sunken Joy Road once met Chamberlain Ferry. There were others like it, northwest as far as Elijah Clark and southeast almost to Augusta. They were simple ranch houses of cheap wood and vinyl siding—prefabricated homes: the material brought in on barges that floated down the Savannah. Only thirty had been built since the start of the war, and in the years that followed, one had burned to the ground at the touch of lightning and another was erased when a war Bird fell from the sky, defunct but still deadly. The rest of the Charity Houses were occupied by refugees from the furthest reaches of the Southern State—winners of a dark lottery; survivors.

In the spring, when the storms were weak, the Savannah ran brown with mud. Although Augusta marked the last deepwater port along the river, often the smaller carriers went as far inland as Hartwell. They moved upriver in the shadow of the quarantine wall that sealed off South Carolina. The ships moved slowly, their cargo of grain and solar panels and smuggled weapons guarded by Mag soldiers or rebels or freelance arms.

☆ ☆ ☆

KARINA ARRIVED in the morning, her Tik-Tok bouncing along the dirt road that led from Lincolnton to the edge of the spit where the Chestnuts lived. She arrived at the house to find its occupants still asleep.

She turned off the television and cleaned up the plates from the previous night's dinner, then she went to the kitchen. Everything was in its place, just as she'd left it the night before. A dusting of sorghum flour lay on the island counter. Every night she sprinkled a little on the counter and memorized the shape in which it rested. And every morning she checked the landscape of the flour against her recollection, and in this way was able to deduce the passing of ghosts. She looked at the flour; none had come.

A back door and three sagging steps led from the kitchen to the sloping riverside yard. It was not a yard, in truth, but an expanse of land—seemingly unlimited in all but the river's direction. It stretched outward from the home's small garden through the shrubbery and into the spits and slivers of nearby woodland through which the Savannah constantly cut new avenues of egress.

There were no neighbors for miles, no spillover from the fierce fighting up in Tennessee, and no visiting townsfolk from Lincolnton or anywhere else. But for the people who came to touch Simon's wound and pray, there were almost no visitors of any kind. The only eyes that watched this place belonged to the family that lived there, the guards manning the towers along the Carolina wall on the other side of the river, and the rebels who came by boat every week with food and supplies.

Once, during a rare moment of candor, Miss Dana told Karina that all their lives the Chestnuts had lived at the feet of rivers and walls. Always bounded, always trapped—trapped by movement, trapped by stillness.

In the yard, the morning light burrowed deep into the gray trunks of the maples. The trees were thin and sickly and shivered in the passing breeze. Every once in a while the branches would shed a blood-colored leaf, and Karina would chase after it for safekeeping. Secretly she set her collection to dry between the pages of an old Bible she hid under Simon's bed. When the leaves were crisp and brittle she crushed them into the boy's chamomile tea. She believed the red leaves healed, and she believed Simon was healing.

This was her job—a caretaker of the Chestnuts' home and a caretaker for Simon Chestnut, the Miracle Boy. She was, nominally, an employee of the Free Southern State, although she could never rely on Atlanta to pay her wages on time or pay what she'd been promised. But still she did the work. She was a nurse by training and in the early and middle years of war she nursed Southern survivors.

☆ ☆ ☆

ON THIS MORNING the river was blue and rippled white with the reflected undersides of clouds. The air was moist and smelled of earth and exhaust and the other smell, the one that came from beyond the wall. A dredging barge lumbered slowly upriver, a black tail in its wake. In the months following the storm seasons the barges moved up and down the river, altering the geography of the riverbed.

Karina slipped off her sandals and walked to the edge of the river. Here the soil was caramel and cool against the soles. She watched the sweep of the current, the vast lumbering arm. On the other side of the river a young man in a decrepit Sea-Tok was anchored near the base of the Carolina wall. He tagged the wall with red spray paint: "KAB."

In the Augusta docks the quarantine wall was a vibrant mural, but this far inland the dull gray concrete was largely untouched. Overhead, the guards at the towers looked at the young vandal, indifferent. Had he decided to run a hook up the thirty-foot barrier and climb over into the Slow country, they probably would have let him. It was only the people trying to leave South Carolina they cared about, and whenever the rifle fire rang out in the night it was always only on one side and only for one purpose. In Lincolnton they said the ragged riverside forests here were overrun with the ghosts of near-escaped Carolinians, but in truth this was some of the safest country in all of the Red.

Karina stepped back from the riverbank. She checked on the vegetable garden. A week after she had told Miss Sarat she planned to try growing vegetables, a rebel skiff arrived with bags of thick black soil. It was rich eastern soil, and in it Karina tried growing beets and radishes and rhubarb and lettuce and southern peas. But even when she watered them dutifully and the heat and deluge did not overwhelm them, their roots refused to take hold in the foreign-born soil.

But on this morning she saw a shootlet: a single fetal sprig had broken forth from the earth. The green of it was pale, ghostly, and she knew it would not survive. But perhaps somewhere beneath, where the roots grew, it would leave behind some kind of genetic inheritance, a map marking, and perhaps the next thing she planted in that place would grow a little more.

☆ ☆ ☆

SHE TURNED FROM the garden. She saw Cherylene shuffling slowly across the yard. For a while, when she'd first started working for the Chestnuts, Karina wondered why the weekly supplies so often included boxes of snails and crickets. Then one day she saw the turtle waddling in the garden.

Karina returned to the river. Near the banks there sat a portable desalination box. It was the size and weight of a refrigerator; the rebels had to use an old fossil tugboat to bring it upriver. It sat on a block of two-by-fours, its snout dipped into the brackish river.

Karina unfolded the butterfly panels and set them in the direction of the morning sun. Slowly they inhaled the light. The machine awoke, and soon the vacuum started to whirr. The machine began to cleanse the river water, soiled with salt far outland, where the ocean intruded on the sunken country.

On solar power the box produced two gallons of drinking water an hour, the contents dripping slowly into blue jugs. On old fossil fuel it ran twice as fast. Karina knew Miss Sarat ordered that the house run only on old prohibition fuel, but the panels did the job well enough, and whenever the young woman disappeared for weeks into the northern forest along the Tennessee line, Karina made do with the givings of the sun. Miss Dana was only equally adamant on the topic whenever her sister was home, but seemed not to care one way or another when Miss Sarat was gone. So whenever Miss Sarat returned, the house rumbled again to the sound and smell of the decrepit diesel generator. There was no use arguing about it. Miss Sarat had no interest in compromise.

A rebel skiff approached. Karina recognized the young man at the helm as Henry the Alabaman, a former Cavalier. In the last six months, the United Rebels in Atlanta had managed to bring most of the insurrectionist groups under a single banner, but some of the men still held fast to their old affiliations, and as a form of protest had taken on their states of birth as family names.

Henry steered into the muddy bank near where Karina stood and threw the anchor down.

"Morning, sweetheart," he said.

"Good morning, Henry," Karina replied. "You're late again."

"What, you having a bad day or something? It ain't even an hour."

Karina pulled her skirt up to her knees and stepped into the river. She sidestepped Henry and picked up a large grocery bag of supplies. The rebel followed with three more.

"Set them here," Karina said, pointing to the ground near her vegetable garden.

"I'll take them inside for ya, no trouble."

"Here's fine."

Henry put the bags down. He returned to the boat and retrieved two locked steel boxes. He set them carefully by the bags. Then he and Karina offloaded a diesel drum from the skiff and carried it to the storm shelter by the side of the house. Karina removed the padlock and the two of them descended the stairs.

Here the Chestnuts kept the croaking generator hidden. The room, dark and dank, smelled overwhelmingly of that sweet bile, that old fossil fuel smell. The scent always jump-started ancient memories in Karina's mind, memories from a childhood spent on the other side of the world: army jeeps refueling, well fires wild and unquenchable, wounds tended to by the light of headlamps. To her, the smell of any old-world fuel was invariably the smell of war.

They returned to the riverbank. Henry stood for a while, eying Karina. He smiled.

"So you gonna come back with me or what?" he said.

"Go on home, Henry," said Karina.

"Just come out to Augusta for a couple days, just one time," he pleaded. "Let me show you around the boardwalk. They know me in all those bars. You'll have a good time, I promise."

"How about we see how this war shakes out first," Karina said. "I don't want to end up going with someone from the losing side."

"Christ, the boys were right," Henry said. "You really are too old to have fun."

Karina smiled. "Thanks for the groceries, Henry. I'll make sure to tell Miss Sarat you dropped by."

The impish grin disappeared from his face. He slunk back to the skiff and waded into the river's middle and soon he was gone.

Karina carried the steel boxes to the edge of the yard, where a woodshop cabin stood, its doors hanging on rust-bitten hinges. The doors were held closed with a crowbar through the loops.

The cabin had been there a long time, longer than the house, longer than the trees, even—from a time well before the sea ate the coastal cities and the river ran roughshod over its old banks. The boards that formed the cabin's exterior were of pale, knotted wood and stained with streaks of reddish brown, as though the wood itself had rusted.

Karina loosed the crowbar; the doors sagged open. She carried the steel boxes inside and set them down on a workbench, as she'd been instructed to do. But for the workbench, the cabin was empty—the shelves barren, the windows covered up with old charity blankets. Soon Miss Sarat would return, unlock the boxes and take their contents to someplace far away, and the cabin would be empty once more. Until then, Karina was instructed to leave the boxes untouched and replace the crowbar with a combination lock. Otherwise, she was never to set foot in the cabin, nor let Simon wander near there whenever she took him for his daily walks.

She knew what the contents of the boxes were. And in a vague, unspoken way, she knew what Miss Sarat was. Many people did, although none would ever talk about it. In Lincolnton the Chestnuts walked around town hallowed as saints: survivors of the massacre and champions of the Southern cause. In Atlanta, politicians wrote them letters of solidarity. In Augusta, there wasn't a dockhand that didn't know their names or a bar owner who'd take their money.

Karina knew. But unlike everyone else, she didn't admire Miss Sarat or hold her in some reverent esteem. The girl was still a child—at seventeen, less than half Karina's age. She knew from experience that there existed no soldier as efficient, as coldly unburdened by fear, as a child broken early. And she knew from the news and from townie gossip what the girls had been through. And because she knew, she understood. But that didn't mean she had to admire it.

Karina carried the bags into the kitchen. They were full of esoteric supplies, things she couldn't get from town: Oolong tea; shrimpshell bandages; the painkiller they called Bonesetters; anticonvulsants for Simon; caviar from the Russian Union.

Karina made breakfast. Simon would only eat his eggs scrambled and runny, without salt or butter. At noon, when his eyelids began to droop, she made him a sandwich of chocolate spread and apricot gel. He inhaled it and for a couple of hours afterward was ebullient and electric.

In these hours, after the weeping pilgrims who came to see him had been ushered away, she took him for walks through the forest. Many days, when Miss Sarat was gone to her secret places and Miss Dana was off in the docks in Augusta, it was just the two of them alone, walking hand in hand.

He delighted in the curling wakes of the barges and the crackle of dead leaves underfoot and the way the sunlight felt on the place near the back of his head where the hair no longer grew.

Sometimes he saw purple and orange flowers in the ground—strange life that grew in spite of the heat and the frequent storms. Sometimes he pointed at the flowers, and Karina, who did not know their names, would invent names for them: Bigwics, Morning Hallows, Laviolas, Southern Laviolas.

After she finished making breakfast, Karina woke Simon. Like the rest of the house, his room was barren. There was only a nightstand, a closet, and the bed he slept in. Miss Sarat had a rule about decorations in the house: there were to be none. No paintings or photographs on the wall, no flower vases in the living room, not even a welcome mat on the porch. There had once been an iron weather vane on the roof, a rooster atop a spinning arrow—the day after the Chestnuts moved in, Miss Sarat climbed up and tore it down.

The only exception to the rule was an ugly ceramic statue of the Virgin of Guadalupe, which sat on Simon's nightstand. The statue was cracked in a million places and seemed to accumulate dust faster than any other surface in the house. But Miss Sarat ordered Karina never to touch it.

Simon woke to her smell before the rest of her entered the room—an oversweet lavender and vanilla perfume she knew he loved. He woke smiling, reaching for her. She wore the colors he liked. Warm, bright colors—reds and yellows, a sunflower print on her flowing skirt. She knelt by his bedside and instantly his hands took hers. He leaned up and kissed her on the cheek, a sloppy kiss, the spittle of sleep still wet on his lips. It was progress—a step she'd kept hidden from the twins. They knew he'd started to remember names and return greetings and they thought he'd started to dress himself, but they didn't know he'd gained a sense of affection.

"Good morning," she said.

"Good morning," Simon replied, echoing her cadence, her inflection.

She helped Simon out of his pajamas and into a fresh white T-shirt and a pair of track pants that stretched around his growing waist. She took his recent weight gain and the new wheel of fat around his gut as more signs of healing. In the first few weeks following his arrival at the house, he had taken in nothing but milk and mashed apple paste. And on one ugly morning, the family discovered that he'd developed a crippling fear triggered by the smell of cooked meat. Now he was eating—picky and tedious as a toddler, but he was eating.

She guided Simon to a chair at the kitchen table. Then she went back to his room and made the bed. The bed was dressed with fine, rebel-smuggled sheets of the best Bouazizi cotton.

☆ ☆ ☆

AT NOON the women came to see him. They arrived a few minutes early. Karina saw them from the living room window, idling at the small gate at the end of the road. She let them wait—she knew if she allowed them in just a few minutes early, soon they would start arriving to their appointments even earlier, and others would learn of it and start doing the same, until the schedule Karina worked so hard to maintain would be rendered irrelevant.

At noon exactly she walked the length of the dirt driveway and met the women. They were sweltering, packed into their Tik-Tok: the driver was a woman whose first name was Kristin but who demanded everyone call her the Widow Bentley. Her daughter, Leslie, sat beside her, and her mother, Eleanor, sat in the back.

Karina opened the gate. For a moment the Tik-Tok's tires spun impotently in the dirt. Then the car fumbled along toward the house. Karina followed. She took her time walking back. When she got there, the Widow Bentley and her daughter were helping the widow's mother exit the carlet. The eldest woman, Eleanor, was hollow with a cancer of the lungs, and, although her daughter and granddaughter took pains to constantly assail her with hope, she seemed resigned to the fact she was dying.

The Widow Bentley had taken to wearing black, long-sleeved blouses and black skirts since her husband died a year earlier in the botched rebel raid on East Ridge. She'd forced her mother and daughter to do the same; the clothes hung limp on the eldest woman's wasting frame, still and slack as a waterlogged flag.

Karina hated to see the widows in black. They struck her as relics of their own making, frozen in permanent deference to reckless or foolish or simply unfortunate men who were nonetheless dead and sealed away in the earth forever.

Husbands never wore black. Husbands were never confined to that kind of passive declaration, were never compelled to sulk across the world for the remainder of their lives, walking signposts of mourning. Husbands were permitted rage, permitted wrath, permitted to avenge their loss by marching out and inflicting on others the very same carnage once inflicted upon them. It seemed to Karina further proof that wartime was the only time the world became as simple and carnivorously liberating as it must exist at all times in men's minds. Some of the women she met never used their own names again—she knew them only as the Widow This or the Widow That—but she'd never met a Widower Anything.

She had lived more than half her life in the South and yet often she still felt like a foreigner. She was the daughter of doctors—analytic, razor-minded natives of the Bangladeshi Isles who overcame great poverty and strife and had no time or patience for sentimental things. From a young age her parents had seen the worst of war—the northward death marches in retreat from the rising seas; the Arunachal

Massacre; the four failed Springs—and had dedicated themselves to alleviating that suffering wherever they found it.

Karina's earliest memories were of field hospitals and blood-caked bedsheets, the great thundering barrel of war. She witnessed the last of the Russian Expansion, the wars of conquest at the furthest edges of the Bouazizi. She stitched her first suture at fourteen, tied her first tourniquet at fifteen. She knew war, knew it better even than these delusional, totem-grasping widows.

And what she understood—what none of the ones who came to touch Simon's forehead understood—was that the misery of war represented the world's only truly universal language. Its native speakers occupied different ends of the world, and the prayers they recited were not the same and the empty superstitions to which they clung so dearly were not the same—and yet they were. War broke them the same way, made them scared and angry and vengeful the same way. In times of peace and good fortune they were nothing alike, but stripped of these things they were kin. The universal slogan of war, she'd learned, was simple: If it had been you, you'd have done no different.

☆ ☆ ☆

SHE LED THE WOMEN into the living room. "Something to drink?" she asked.

"Water," Leslie said. The teenage girl slumped on the couch on the end furthest from where her mother and grandmother sat. She stared out the window at the moving river.

"We're just happy to see Simon, sweetheart," the Widow Bentley said. "You can bring him in now."

Karina left the women and went outside to the backyard. She found Simon sitting at the muddy landing where the rebel skiffs docked, tossing broken branches into the current.

"You know I told you not to sit this close," Karina said. He looked up at her and smiled. He had chubby, hairless cheeks and when he smiled the smile displaced them in a way that made him look awestruck.

"You got guests," she said, helping him to his feet and brushing the wet mud from the back of his pants. "Paying guests."

"Paying guests," Simon said.

She led him back into the house. When he entered the living room, the Widow Bentley nearly jumped from her seat to touch him.

"Hello, Simon," she said

"Hello, Ms. Bentley," Karina told Simon.

"Hello, Ms. Bentley," he mimicked.

The Widow Bentley put her hand on Simon's face. "How are you feeling today, honey?"

"He's doing real well," Karina said. She knew the Widow Bentley hated it when she interjected, so she did it as much as possible.

"Karina, sweetheart, could you make Mama and I some tea?" the Widow Bentley said. "She's had a bad throat all morning."

Karina left the women with Simon and went to the kitchen. She set the water to boil and took a couple of bags of Mississippi Breakfast from the pantry; she had no intention of wasting the good Chinese stuff on the visitors. In the living room, the Widow Bentley continued to stroke Simon's cheek.

"How did you sleep, honey?" she asked. "Did you sleep all right?"

"Like a baby!" Karina yelled from the kitchen.

When she returned to the living room, the women were already engaged in the ritual. The Widow Bentley, a Bible on her lap, took her mother's hand in her own and placed her other hand on Simon's forehead. Together the three of them resembled the centerpiece of some spasmodic faith healer's sermon, the evil cast out, out from the soul.

Karina set the teacups on the table but the women ignored them. The Widow Bentley recited the same prayer she recited every time she came to visit, the psalms she knew by heart:

For you will command your angels concerning me to
guard me in all my ways;
They will lift me up in their hands, so that I will not
strike my foot against a stone . . .

The Widow Bentley closed her eyes as she spoke and her hands shook and her voice quivered. Her mother looked on with resigned tolerance; her daughter stared out the window at the moving river.

When they were done, the Widow Bentley wiped her eyes and,

gripped by a deep, post-cathartic ennui, sought to remain as long as possible in Simon's company. But the time she'd paid for had run out.

Karina walked the three women to their car. Before she left, the Widow Bentley paid the visitation fee: five hundred Redbacks. Karina took the money and thanked her.

"There's one more thing," the Widow Bentley said. "A favor we wanted to ask."

The woman reached under the Tik-Tok's backseat cushion and retrieved a shoebox. She opened it for Karina. Inside were rolls upon rolls of Red currency—a hundred thousand dollars, maybe more.

"We took it all out of First Southern this morning," she said. "Bank manager put up one hell of a fight, but we said, It's our money, you can't hold it hostage."

"What do you want me to do with this?" Karina asked.

"Just keep it for us, is all," the Widow Bentley said. "Ever since what happened at Patience, things have gotten bad again. In Atlanta you got the Free Southern State and the United Rebels fighting over who's gonna run the country, but neither of them got much control over anything no more. The fighting's gotten real bad and everybody's just waiting on the Blues to push south past Tennessee. Then you know there's gonna be a run on the banks and President Kershaw's gonna lock us out to keep the whole Mag from going broke. All we want you to do is keep it for us—just keep it where the boy is. That's all. Don't think we won't pay you for it."

The woman put the shoebox in Karina's hands. From the corner of her eye, the helper could see the look of disdain on the widow's daughter's face.

"He's just a boy, Kristin," Karina said. "He's not a bank. He's doesn't pay interest or buy stocks or anything else. He's just a boy."

The Widow Bentley pulled out another five-hundred-dollar bill from her wallet. "We don't need no interest, we don't need no stocks. We just need it to be where he is, that's all. What watches over him is enough."

Karina watched the women leave along the dirt road. At times she despised people like the Widow Bentley for believing so fiercely in their prayer bead gymnastics and credulous supplications. But most of all she despised them because, in the years she'd spent tending to their ranks, she'd come to believe in similar things—in superstitions: invocations meant to ward off the wrath of the Birds and the sickness of the walled Carolinians; the flight paths of ghosts through the sorghum.

When the three women were gone she went back inside the house. Simon was curled up on the couch with his knees pressed to his chest, asleep.

For a while she wondered what to do with the money. If she had any interest in honoring the widow's wishes, she'd slip it under Simon's bed, next to the Bible and the drying leaves. Otherwise she could hide it in the storm shelter next to the fuel drums. But in all these places, Karina worried Miss Sarat would inevitably find the money. And then she would berate Karina, in that charcoal, humorless voice of hers, about taking liberties that were not hers to take. Or, worse, she would say nothing, and one day the money would simply be gone, given as alms to the cause of glorious Southern rebellion.

As she thought it over, she saw through the kitchen window a black shadow reflected on the river. Instinctively she knelt down under the kitchen counter, waiting for the Bird to pass. She knew they rained down death at random, and that if today was the day they chose this place, she'd already be dead—and yet she ducked under the counter anyway, a survival reflex.

Minutes passed. She stood and looked out the window. The black shadow was gone from the river. She stepped outside into the yard. She knelt by her lifeless garden and dug deep into the soil. She dug past the places where fruits lay fetal in their seeds, until finally she reached the dirt below. She set the widow's shoebox in the grave, and covered it.

IN THE TOWER the young soldier moved, slow and rhythmic, tethered to the beat of her heart. Sarat knew him better than he knew himself: a child of the North's poor country—the son of dirt farmers, perhaps, or escapees from the torched California parchland or denizens of the ruined Dakotas, the post-prohibition fossil belt. She knew he had become a soldier not in service of God or Country, but Escape—a chance to become something other than his father, to dodge a life spent soldering the backs of solar panels or wading ankle-deep through shit in the vertical farms. Anything, anything else. And if that meant picking up a rifle and throwing on the brown-speckled camouflage, so be it. She had never spoken to the soldier, had never even seen him before this very moment. And yet she knew him down to his soul.

Sarat peered through her rifle's eye. The soldier's head floated in the cross-hairs, a buoy adrift.

☆ ☆ ☆

THE FIRST WEEKS AFTER the massacre at Patience had been the darkest. The house they were given as blood money felt alien; every night the sisters slept together in a room fully lit, the windows sealed shut with boards. For the first few nights, Dana could not sleep. She lay frozen by Sarat's side, certain that the men who'd taken their mother and brother would return to take them too. And on the fifth day, when the Free Southerners came from the hospital and brought with them a living shell of the brother both Sarat and Dana thought was dead, Dana screamed, because in a way the massacre was now unending.

It was only after the Chestnuts' new life settled into some kind of routine that Sarat began to leave her siblings and venture into the outer world—first to Atlanta, where she petitioned the committee investigating the killings at Patience for some information about her mother's remains, even though she knew in her heart that all that remained was ash. One by one, a smug parade of Southern dignitaries offered her their thoughts and prayers and the contact information of their assistants. They commended her on her stoicism, on how well she was handling it all.

She soon learned that to survive atrocity is to be made an honorary consul to a republic of pain. There existed unspoken protocols governing how she was expected to suffer. Total breakdown, a failure to grieve graciously, was a violation of those rules. But so was the absence of suffering, so was outright forgiveness. What she and others like her were allowed was a kind of passive bereavement, the right to pose for newspaper photographs holding framed pictures of their dead relatives in their hands, the right to march in boisterous but toothless parades, the right to call for an end to bloodshed as though bloodshed were some pest or vagrant who could be evicted or run out of town. As long as she adhered to those rules, moved within those margins, she remained worthy of grand, public sympathy.

But none of it mattered to Sarat. When the weeping widows came to see her brother and touch the wound on his forehead, she let Karina, the hired help, deal with them. When Free Southern State politicians from Atlanta drove up to present the Chestnuts with plaques and framed declarations of solidarity and to have their pictures taken with the survivors of the Camp Patience massacre, she left through the kitchen door and wandered out into the forest and stayed there until they were gone. In the few of those photos that survive today, scattered in myriad Southern State archives and the collected files of long-dead politicians, only Dana appears alongside the glad-handers from Atlanta, her smile radiant and wholly counterfeit.

In the months that followed, after Dana's nightmares subsided and the storm of attention surrounding the Camp Patience massacre was over and the journalists and politicians moved on, Sarat turned her attention to the only thing that still mattered: revenge, the unsettled score.

For weeks at a time she went out to the forest in Talladega, where Albert Gaines kept a ramshackle cabin. There he taught her to shoot. At first he'd asked her if she preferred to make herself a weapon, to become what the Northerners called homicide bombers. It didn't scare her to consider it, but the thought of abandoning Dana, of leaving her alone to care for what remained of their brother, was too much for her conscience to bear. Yet she wanted to kill. So Gaines pulled his ancient hunting rifle from its rack and set her to sniping soda cans on fence posts.

At first nothing he taught her stuck—not only because the weapon itself barely functioned, its sight cross-eyed, its trigger unreliable, but also because the memory of what she'd seen was still too vivid. Onto the tin cans her mind painted the faces of those Northerners that night in Patience, and at the hallucinated sight of them she was overcome by anger and a rabid desire to ruin those who'd ruined her. Rage wrapped itself around her like a tourniquet, keeping her alive even as it condemned a part of her to atrophy.

The hardest thing to learn was stillness. Even after she finally started hitting the cans and graduated to sniping rats, she struggled most with Gaines's order that she learn to stay in place for hours at a time. Sometimes he had her sleep where she lay, the forest insects crawling over her. He said the most important part about this kind of hunting was fusing yourself to your surroundings, becoming the earth. But she wanted to move, she wanted desperately to move.

One day Joe came to the cabin. In all her time there, Sarat had never seen Gaines receive visitors, but Joe appeared as though he'd been to the cabin many times, as though it belonged as much to him as it did to Gaines.

"I have a gift for you," he told Sarat. "Something to help you in your work."

The rifle he gave her was a fine weapon, a QBU-20 smuggled in on the charity ships, packed into a sack of rice. What Gaines's old gun saw wrongly it pinned with surgeon's precision.

She learned to strip it, reassemble it, gauge its temperament. She painted little check marks in red fingernail polish on the black shoulder stock, immortalizing the times when the soul of the gun and the soul of its shooter aligned, even if all that died as a result was a helpless rat.

She named her weapon Templestowe, after the first true rebel of the Second Civil War, the girl who'd killed the crooked Union president in Jackson.

"These are the ways in which I can help," said Joe. "In the end, it's up to you what you do with such assistance. The guns are ours but the blood is yours."

Finally she understood what he meant.

☆ ☆ ☆

SARAT LAY MOTIONLESS at the flat peak of a hill, hidden in a skin of brush and reeds. Behind her the hill rolled gently down to the Georgia border, the land etched with a network of rebels' tunnels. A mile ahead of her stood the southern wall of Halfway Branch, the largest Northern operating base on the Tennessee line, and beyond it the dusk-burned sides of the Smoky Mountains.

It had taken her the better part of a week to draw this close, shuffling slowly through the flint tunnels—listening for the footfall of passing patrols—and then the brush. She moved by night amidst the hickories. When she finally arrived at the spot atop the hill, she waited another three days, living off dry rations, burying her waste in the dirt. For three days she set her sights upon the southern gate of Halfway Branch and waited.

She put the rifle down and cast her binoculars upon the horizon. The hastily asphalted road leading to the gate sent upward a heat mirage, and in its untilted rise there were no signs of wind. She scanned the forest between her and the base, looking for the same things the soldiers in the towers looked for: unnatural shadows, straight lines, the glimmer of a shiny black nickel in the brush.

Gaines had trained her to see these things. In his cabin he laid out a table of items—books, cutlery, a flywheel, a packet of cards fanned out. Every time the items were different and differently arranged. He covered the table with a bedsheet and brought Sarat into the room. He uncovered the table for ten seconds and covered it again. Then he asked her to describe everything under the sheet to the most granular detail: the order of the fanned cards, the number of holes on the flywheel.

The sun set behind the mountains. Halfway Branch lay seared in the dying light, a box fortress of shipping containers and long-drawn tents. The soldiers milled about in their guard towers.

Sarat lay still. There was a residual dampness in her pants from when she'd urinated without moving, and now that dampness cooled and hardened. She felt it in the hairs of her legs, down to where her bare ankles rubbed against the earth.

Four soldiers ascended the guard tower. She recognized two of them as muscle, bodyguards watching over the third man. He was older than the others, his hair silver and smoothly parted. He wore the same uniform as the men who surrounded him but he was not of them; there was a calmness in the way he carried himself, the way he nodded as the fourth man and the guard tower grunt pointed out markers on the horizon.

Sarat knew the soldiers were pointing to the places from where the martyrs came—men and women who walked out from among the black gum trees with the makings of hellfire strapped to their chests. Rarely did they get to within a hundred feet of the gates before they were shot down. And when they came with rocket launchers on their shoulders, the Blues had turrets that gauged the trajectory of those rockets in midair—before the projectiles landed, the ones who'd fired them were already dead. The rebels knew these things, knew the futility of their assaults, and yet every few days another walking weapon emerged from among the black gum trees.

Sarat took Templestowe's eye off the young soldier in the tower. She set it on the old man. He had about him an aura of distance, of remove. He was smaller than the men who surrounded him; compact, his fatigues unblemished. She saw the dusk light gleam off four stars on his shoulder. Her informant had been right. It was a general from Columbus.

The officer's head came under Templestowe's eye. Sarat breathed in deep. She eased her chest off the ground; she was still. In a moment Sarat and her black-mouthed girl were aligned. At a pull of the finger, Templestowe let loose a muffled sigh, and before the reeds by her lips had stopped their shaking, Sarat knew.

Excerpted from:

ONE SHOT AT HALFWAY BRANCH: THE LIFE AND DEATH OF GENERAL JOSEPH WEILAND

They laid the General's body to rest on a Sunday, and all of Columbus came out to see it. Thousands lined the sidewalks as the funeral procession crept slowly up Daniel Ki Drive, past the Executive Building, toward Trinity Episcopal Church. The flags atop the federal government offices—not only in the capital, but across the wartime North—slumped halfway down their staffs.

From the hearse emerged a fine casket of straight grain and dark cherry hue—no one in the crowd could recall the last time they'd seen such fine mahogany. The pallbearers took their places, a representative from each branch of the United States military, and the President of the United States. Inside the church, Senator Joseph Weiland Jr. delivered the eulogy, speaking before an audience composed of every Union governor and federal lawmaker in the country, as well as countless foreign dignitaries from almost every one of the North's wartime allies.

In the early afternoon the gray, impenetrable rain clouds, long a fixture of Ohio autumns, momentarily lifted. The October sun cast a warm amber light on the cemetery grounds. A phalanx of Marines, stiff as granite columns in their Blues, stood watch, and it is said that when the ceremonial guns shattered the air, not a single one of them flinched.

The assassination of General Joseph Weiland at Halfway Branch marked in many ways the central turning point of the Second Civil War. Shot dead by an unknown insurrectionist sniper, he was the highest-ranking military casualty of the conflict.

But if General Weiland's killing marked a temporary victory for the South's insurrectionist rebels, it also set in motion the eventual demise of the Southern state. Popular opinion throughout the North, which for years favored compromise and reunion over an extended fratricide, seemed to harden overnight. From Pittsburgh to Cascadia came calls for vengeance. And in Columbus, the Union government listened.

By January of the following year, Joseph Weiland Jr.—only a few years removed from a low-level position in the Compensation Claims office, and a sitting Senator for less than a year at the time of his father's death—would assume Directorship of the War Office. Under his leadership, the rate of Northern military incursions south of the Tennessee line soared. In the year following the killing at Halfway Branch, more than 250 rebel fighters were captured throughout the South. And while many were ultimately found to have played only a minor part in the conflict and were eventually released, the surge nonetheless helped pave the way for the eventual eradication of the rebel menace.

CHAPTER TEN

The general fell dead. The echo of the gunshot rang in Sarat's ears. In a few seconds a wailing siren began to sound from the Blue fortress. Sarat lifted herself from where she lay. She turned in the direction of the Red country. In the darkness, she ran.

Soon she found the entrance to one of the rebels' tunnels. She scrambled through the underground clearing as the sirens blared above. The tunnel was low and dank and wholly unlit; she crawled blind.

A half-mile south, the tunnel broke at the foot of a steep incline. She emerged from a thatch-camouflaged cover to find the sky streaked with the red of tracer rounds. Something moved near the trees to the west, a mongrel from the border towns in search of food, perhaps. She watched as the gunners in the watchtowers eviscerated the brush.

Unseen, she scrambled over the hillside. She crossed empty creek beds and the rotted cores of bee gum trees. In the weeks before she set out into the forest, Sarat had studied the land: learned its folds and the crevices, the places where the cover was thickest.

In a few hours she reached the hills outside Chatsworth, where she knew the Blues would soon send a raid party. Most of those who remained in places like Chatsworth—the border towns that bore the brunt of the Northerners' incursions—were holdouts. Everyone else had gone south, mostly to the high-rise slums that circled Atlanta. But it was the last stubborn few in the border towns who moved the street signs every week to confuse the soldiers, who spat on the floor at the very mention of Blues.

She found her old Tik-Tok where she'd left it, by the side of Highway 76. As she traveled southwest into the protective embrace of Georgia, Sarat raised her head to the sky and screamed, victorious.

She took the small backroads home, arriving in the early evening. Alight with adrenaline, she walked east from the edge of the woodshed into the forest. She walked carefully, counting her steps until she counted five hundred. At the last step she stood in a clearing in the woods, near the riverbank. She knelt down and dug into the dirt. She buried her rifle. She left no markings of any kind, and padded the dirt until it was flat and plain. Then she walked back home.

From the edge of the yard she saw the maid Karina in the kitchen, kneading dough and humming "Jacob's Ladder." There was something about the woman she found foreign—more than her faraway place of origin in the Bangladeshi Isles, which left no markers on her mannerisms or accent. She smiled too often, carried herself too comfortably in a home and around a family that was not hers. Sarat could see that Simon had started taking a liking to her; she saw how his eyes and smile widened when she was near. She knew the woman had done nothing wrong, and yet Sarat felt a rabid urge to remind her that she was just a maid: that she was not of the Chestnuts, and never would be.

Sarat stepped between the trees and down to the water. She walked into the river. The water felt good against her skin. The night before, when she ran from the edge of Halfway Branch, she'd tripped and stumbled through a thistle bush that left cuts all over her arms and shoulders. Now the places where her skin was broken came alive, burning like flicks of oil against a hot iron pan. But this too, in its own way, felt good.

When she had walked far enough into the river, and the ground swept down and away from her feet, Sarat undressed. She let the river take the soiled clothes. She floated weightless, naked but for Albert Gaines's charm around her neck. The river smelled of dirt and algae but it also smelled of her: the stink of a week unwashed; a vinegar effluent that grew in the spaces under her arms and between her legs. She loved her scent, carried it like her own newborn child. Now, with her eyes wide open, she sank deep into the water and gave it to the river.

She felt the eyes of the guard in the tower, watching. There was only one tower along the quarantine wall with an unobstructed view of the Chestnuts' property. Therein sat a young Southern State private, charged with keeping the infected Carolinians from getting out.

When the family had first moved to the Charity House, Sarat refused to sleep another night under the watch of guard towers. Finally Albert Gaines took her to meet the Free Southerner who manned the tower nearest her house. He turned out to be a hopeless little boy from the Georgia coast; a kid one year younger than Sarat who'd lied about his age to volunteer.

It didn't take long for Sarat to understand that the boy, and all the other boys dispatched to babysit Carolina's living dead, was both Red-blooded and harmless. And in the months that followed, as she lay flat in the forest eying him through her rifle scope, she learned something else too: the watchtower guards were blind. It was a blindness fed by boredom and fear, by having at once too much and too little to observe. Often, when Sarat lay watching, the sleepy-eyed boy in the tower looked right back at her, and didn't see a thing.

The river took her smell. It loosened the grime caught in the hairs along her arms and along her legs. When she was very young her father told her that some of her ancestors were once buried near the banks of the Mississippi River, back when it was still corseted with levees. But eventually the river broke loose and took all the nearby houses and the farmland and even the dead in their graves. The river moves, he said, and as it moves it takes.

When she emerged from the water she found a fresh set of clothes waiting on a rock by the bank. Dana sat by the side of the woodshed.

There lay a straight razor and a small bowl of eucalyptus cream set atop a stump. Sarat sat by the river and shaved her head clean. She sat for a while watching the river move, savoring the crisp coolness of the cream against her scalp, the air against her skin. Then she stood up and dressed.

She joined her sister by the woodshed. There was almost a foot of difference in height between them, Sarat pushing six-foot-five and still, a year short of adulthood, not sure if she had another spurt in her.

She sat by her sister's side. Dana's hair smelled of coconuts and jasmine; it curled the way waves curl, tinting the sunlight chocolate. Sarat could already see the boys in Augusta leering.

"You should go inside and say hello," Dana said. "Simon's in a good mood today."

"He saying much?" Sarat asked.

"Echoes what you tell him. But it's not nothing."

Sarat shook her head. "Give me a minute," she said. "I still got lightning inside me." She held up her right hand, which shivered like a picked string.

Dana wrapped her arm around her sister's shoulder. Sarat leaned over and curled up like a child with her head on her sister's lap.

"Beautiful girl," said Dana. "I'm so glad you're home."

The sisters saw Karina in the garden. They watched her hang clothes out on the line by the riverbank. She pretended not to see them sitting by the woodshed. She sang as she worked: the same old hymn she always sang, playing her own choir, echoing each line—We are *we are,* climbing *climbing.*

"She's taking good care of him," Dana said.

"I don't trust her," Sarat replied.

"What's she done?"

"Nothing she's done, just something about her. I don't know what she really thinks of us. What she really wants."

"What do you care what she thinks of us?" asked Dana. "She's just working here, nothing more."

"She's in our home, isn't she? Anyway, she keeps talking to Simon and anyone else who'll listen about how she doesn't care who wins, North or South, just as long as there's no more war. Like she'd be happy if the Blues marched on Atlanta tomorrow. You know her parents live up in the North? Moved there right before the war started."

"So? Wouldn't you, if you had no stake in it?"

"Nobody has no stake in it," said Sarat.

☆ ☆ ☆

NIGHT FELL. A humid film spread over the air. Sarat awoke from a fitful nap with her sister's hand still caressing her head. She heard the sound of a motorboat engine in the distance, a rebel skiff from further inland.

"Why'd you let me sleep?" said Sarat.

"Wasn't long," Dana replied. "You were barely out an hour."

As the skiff landed, the sisters went to the woodshed and retrieved the most recent shipment of locked boxes. They carried them to the waiting boat.

The boy at the helm of the boat, a New Zouave from southern Alabama, thanked them. He took the boxes without checking their contents, knowing the arms promised him would be there, knowing from experience that the Chestnuts were as reliable a conduit as any along the Savannah smugglers' trail.

They watched him leave upriver. When he was gone and the grogginess of interrupted sleep had left her, Sarat became aware of the hunger eating at her stomach. The last of the apricot mush she ate in the forest had gone through her. She yearned for okra swimming in oil; pigeon grilled over charcoal; the cinnamon burn of tub-brewed Joyful.

"Let's go to Augusta," she said.

☆ ☆ ☆

DURING THE WAR Atlanta was the heart of the South but Augusta supplied the blood. Ever since the storms and rising seas swallowed much of the eastern coast, it was this place that functioned as the Red country's most vital port. Toward the end of every month, a hundred and fifty miles to the southeast, the foreign shipping vessels arrived from the far side of the world. The ships' captains waited there for reef pilots to come and guide the hulking freighters around the remains of the submerged coastal cities and into the Augusta docks.

In anticipation of the ships' monthly bounty, an assortment of opportunists descended on the city: ship hands, smugglers, rebels, reef pilots, foreign captains and their crews. They were joined by sailors on leave from the impotent Southern navy, whose skeleton fleet had long ago surrendered the ocean to the Blues. For a few days every month, the port's riverside bars and brothels and boardinghouses hummed.

At dusk the dockmaster flipped a switch and a string of Christmas lights hung along the boardwalk came to life. The boardwalk sat atop the flattened head of the Reynolds Street levee, which rose twenty feet high. The river-facing side of the levee was sheer, except in the places where stairs led to the reef pilots' house and the wharf. On the city-facing side, the concrete slope was of a gentle gradient, and it was on this side where, in the early morning, many of the passed-out drunks could be found sleeping.

☆ ☆ ☆

BY THE TIME Sarat and Dana arrived in Augusta, the bars overflowed—not only with those waiting on the aid ships but also with tourists from all over the Mag, in town to watch the Yuffsy.

The sisters went first to the Hotel D'Grub near 12th Street. There was a gaggle of dockhands and Atlanta boys gathered on the lawn of the repurposed Baptist church, drunk and cheerful. In the center of the lawn there stood an ancient Chevy fossil truck, mounted on bricks. The truck was brown with rust, its hood sheared off, a charcoal grill in the place where the engine used to be.

Billows of smoke rose from the grill. The retired freight captain Isaac, who ran the Hotel D'Grub, stood between the truck's lightless eye sockets, a palmetto fan in his hand. He was a large man, shirtless, sweaty but serene under his skipper hat despite the barrage of orange embers the truck spat in his direction. The smoke climbed from the blackened trays and made of the redbrick church behind it a distant dream.

"How are you, old man?" said Sarat.

The captain turned. "Well now, if it isn't the only real goddamn men in Augusta. Make way, for Christ's sake!" he said, kicking at two Atlanta college boys slumped on garden recliners near the grill. "It's a zoo around this time of the month—you know how it gets when there's money to be had."

"Don't worry," said Dana. "We're gonna go inside and clean you out anyway. Haven't had a decent meal in a week."

The captain nodded. "Go on in. I'll send some steak your way."

Sarat laughed. "Ain't nothing like that flying steak you got here. You shoot them down yourself?"

"I'll shoot you down, you keep running your mouth. Flying steak's better than none."

The captain pointed to the grand bullethead windows of the church's street-side facade. The original windows had been smashed long ago in one of the riots following the massacre at Fort Jackson, the insides stripped and looted down to the pews and the floorboards.

"Your friend Bragg is in there, by the way," he said.

"The old one or the young one?" asked Sarat.

"Ha! The old one can't get up to take a piss nowadays. It's the kid. Got his whole entourage with him too."

"Christ," said Sarat. "Well that's no fun."

The captain wiped the beaded sweat from his forehead and wiped his hand on the side of his jeans. "He gives you any trouble, you let me know. I'll go in there and kick his ass—don't care how united his daddy's little rebels are."

They thanked the old captain and went inside. Beyond the redbrick exterior, there was little left of the original church—only the words AND THEY WENT DOWN BOTH INTO THE WATER, painted in an arch along the wall, and below it a pale hollowness where once there hung a shining cross.

The captain was a collector of long-dead things, species that had once existed but could not adapt to the planet's unbreaking fever. Taxidermied heads of caribou and muskoxen and sea lions and white-faced foxes stared down from the walls with marbles in their eyes.

The dinner hall was full. The air was heavy with the smell of fryer oil and sawdust on spilled beer. The tables were arranged haphazardly throughout what was once a grand nave. In the rear of the room a frenzied herd of line cooks moved in chaotic ritual around stoves and bubbling pots.

The twins searched the room for a place to sit. Instantly, Sarat saw the men turn to watch her sister. Dana shifted the room's orbit, took charge of the air. The boys turned toward her like filings to a magnet's pole. Sarat waited for one of them to do more than look; secretly she hoped for it.

They found a table in the back by the kitchen. But before they sat, one of Adam Bragg Jr.'s bodyguards came over and asked them to join his party.

"We're good where we are," said Sarat.

"We'll be over in a minute," said Dana. When the bodyguard was gone she turned to her sister. "Just a couple of minutes," she said. "Just to make nice."

"You know it won't be a couple of minutes," said Sarat. "Why we gotta go make nice? We don't work for him, we haven't pledged allegiance to no United Rebels or anybody else."

"I don't give a shit 'bout the United Rebels or anybody else. But people like him won't suddenly stop being important because we ignore them. Better to have him on our side in case we need him or his daddy's help one day."

"Goddammit," Sarat said, rising. "Can't even eat proper around them. Let's get it over with."

They found the young man, who on this night was celebrating his twenty-first birthday, seated at a large circular table in a corner of the room. It was the only table in the place covered with cloth, and around it hovered a flock of bodyguards, rebel grunts, well-wishers, and hangers-on.

Seated at the table were a couple of faces Sarat recognized: a well-known smuggler named Henson; Augusta's deputy mayor; the head of the reef pilots' union; and three other men who, by the stiff pull of their ill-fitting suits, were probably government men from Atlanta. The fractured politics of the wartime South dictated that high-ranking members of the United Rebels and the Free Southern State should not be seen socializing, given the diverging tenors of each on the subject of peace. But in Augusta such rules were often temporarily set aside.

" 'Evening, ladies," said Bragg. "A true pleasure to see you. Sit, sit."

The sisters sat near their host. He introduced them to the table, loud enough so that the orbiting entourage could also hear.

"These are Dana and Sarat Chestnut," he said, "survivors of the Camp Patience massacre and proud patriots of the Southern nation. I'm honored to call them friends."

"It's great to see you two girls," one of the suits from Atlanta said. Bragg introduced him as the director of the Free Southern State's media operations for northern Georgia.

"Aren't you two the sisters of that boy Simon, the Miracle Boy?"

"Yeah," said Sarat, "and whose sister is you?"

The man looked at his host, the smile fading from his lips.

"Enough small talk," said Bragg. "Let's eat."

From the kitchen came a parade of bowls and silver trays: chicken liver; cracklings; rice smothered in redeye gravy; corn chips and Mississippi caviar; beef that was not really beef but pigeon, charred black on the outside and pink within. The table descended into a glutton's silence, the only sound that of jaws and silverware. In the lull, Bragg leaned over to his guests.

"I heard you were out in Halfway," he said. "That true?"

Sarat said nothing.

"Well, at least you made it out alive. Not many my father sends out there can say the same."

When the guests were done, the plates were cleared and in their place came others: trays of sliced peaches and watermelons and cantaloupes; jugs of ice water and lemonade and artillery punch. Until finally those seated around the table could eat and drink no more.

Tipsy and slurring his words, one of the Atlanta men rose to make a toast. He started with something about the Southern spirit and the great and noble cause of freedom, but soon he talked himself into a pretzel, until finally Bragg interrupted him: "Let's just say: To the South, victorious."

"To the South, victorious!" echoed the man. The table raised their glasses.

The men from Atlanta soon left. A few of Bragg's people took their place at the table. Among them were two of the Salt Lake Boys, Trough and Cornhill.

There had been six when the rebels first found them: orphans in the battle of Spanish Fork, where the Blues, Mexican troops, and even a few misguided Texas outcasts fought to a standstill near what became the very northwestern edge of the Mexican Protectorate.

They were rumored to be the brood of Mormons. In the aftermath of the battle, the rebels found them hiding in a piggery on the outskirts of town, and named them after the places they found them. Eventually they were taken back south and drafted into the Bragg family's bustling orbit.

The staff cleaned the tables and then brought out cigars and brandy. The cigars were from the old Caribbean islands, expensive and among the last of their kind. The haze that filled the air was sweet and earthy.

"You know my father sends me out here because he doesn't trust me," said Bragg, leaning close to the twins, high on the easy camaraderie of the freshly drunk. "He says it's to make sure the supplies get past the Blues out on the coast and into the right hands—to keep an eye on things. But I think he just wants me out of Atlanta as much as possible. Afraid I'll kill him in his sleep, all that palace coup shit old men worry 'bout."

Bragg laughed. He was looking at Dana but watching her sister. He carried an effortless charm wielded almost exclusively by those born into comfort or those who rose from nothing to achieve it. He smiled by default, teeth sheathed, eyes like pistol barrels, as though a camera lens stalked constantly on his periphery. He was gifted with a very rare and advantageous talent for seeming to speak intimately, every word a precious secret between old friends.

Others came to the table, but were turned away: rebels and would-be rebels and the kin of both, all in need of favors; dockhands and laid-off reef pilots looking for smuggling work; refugees wanting a room in the Atlanta slums, refugees wanting out.

And then there were those men aligned with the groups who'd refused to come under the United Rebels' umbrella—they watched from tables at the other end of the room, observing the delicate fracture lines of the divided, wartime South.

To Sarat, it was all nonsense, the petty turf wars of insecure men. Rarely a day passed without news of some fresh dispute between the Free Southern State and the United Rebels and the myriad fringe fighters who controlled swaths of territory in the border battlegrounds—disputes over who should run the schools, collect the taxes; whose dead should place first on the murals. She had seen them do these things both publicly—in defiant, chest-thumping speeches—and privately, pragmatically, in the backrooms of Atlanta and Augusta. She saw them do these things and she was disgusted by it. They were to her nothing more than prideful, opportunistic captains, arguing over the boundaries of long-obsolete star maps as all the while the opposing armada's cannonballs tore their hull to shreds.

For Sarat Chestnut, the calculus was simple: the enemy had violated her people, and for that she would violate the enemy. There could be no other way, she knew it. Blood can never be unspilled.

"Anyway, the old man will be glad to hear you made it out alive from Halfway . . ." said Bragg.

"Keep your voice down," said Sarat. "You want everyone in the place to know?"

"Don't worry so much," replied Bragg. "You're still new, still a ghost. Only people in this room who understand what you've been up to are at this table. And believe me, they'll have their tongues cut out before they say a word of it to someone who's not supposed to hear."

He turned to the two Salt Lake Boys sitting at his side. "Ain't that right?"

The boys said nothing. They sat as though encased in wax, no smile or frown on their lips. The elder of the two wore his hair parted down the middle—a child's haircut that made him look younger than his sibling, who had his hair buzzed close to the scalp.

"You know their two older brothers are already dead?" said Bragg, speaking as though the boys were not at the table. "One got taken during a FOB raid near Fayetteville—Lord knows what hellhole the Blues are keeping him in now, if they haven't already killed him. The other strapped on a farmer's suit and sneaked himself past the wire. Made it all the way up to Kentucky then got himself shot dead outside a checkpoint before he could even get the damn thing to blow.

"My old man signed off on both too. Neither kid had so much as fired a pistol in his whole life, but he okayed it anyway."

Bragg turned to Sarat. "But with you, he wouldn't hear it. Couldn't imagine a girl out there fighting. If it wasn't for Gaines's pull with him, no way he would have changed his mind. Anyway, he'll want to see you, so you can plead your case to him. Maybe he'll give you a second chance."

"I don't plead with no one," said Sarat. "Your old man is nothing to me. He ain't my boss, ain't my father. I don't need his permission. You got something you need to say to him, go on and say it yourself."

"I'd rather just wait for him to die, if I'm being honest," said Bragg. He waited on the sisters for a reaction and got none. "You know he was fifty-six when he had me? Fifty-six! There's a goddamn half-century between us—how am I supposed to bridge that? He's caught up in the old way of doing things, still thinks he's in the desert, still fighting that old, faraway war. All that tradition he's saddled with, it's too late to shake it off. Better just to wait him out and hope they haven't raised the Blue banner over Atlanta before he finally has the decency to die."

The conversation was interrupted by a chorus of hooting and applause on the other side of the room. A piece of gossip moved around the dining hall, and all those who heard it responded with happy cursing and calls for another round.

"What are they so pleased about?" Bragg asked one of his bodyguards. The guard inquired with a waitress and returned to whisper something to his boss. The shine came off Bragg's smile. He turned to Sarat.

"Was it you who did it?" he asked.

For the first time that evening, Sarat afforded herself a smile.

"Jesus Christ," said Bragg, and then he finally did lower his voice. "You poker-faced bitch. You've gone and changed the whole damn war."

Sarat winked.

Bragg turned to his bodyguard. "Free up another couple of seats at the Citadel," he said. "We got some real celebrating to do."

☆ ☆ ☆

A LONG LINE FORMED outside the doors of the Citadel. It was mostly young men, waiting on the fight. A roving squad of doormen monitored the crowd; whenever anyone got too loud, or an altercation broke out, the bouncers quickly removed all parties involved.

A couple of street vendors traversed the lineup. One sold Dixie cups of Joyful, brewed in the row houses down the street. Another hawked peanuts and roasted corn.

The young men waited for the doors to open, and when they finally did, they shoved at one another on the way upstairs to the nosebleeds.

The Yuffsy was fought at midnight on the turn of every month. There were other, smaller fights that took place at the Citadel at other times, but only on this night did all twelve contenders gather for the big-money bout. Some fans came from as far as Mississippi to see it, the great Southern spectacle of battering men.

The Citadel used to be the grand rotunda of an old museum. It was a fine and high-roofed lobby. Inside the ring, the floor was padded but the padding was thin, and a man thrown onto it with sufficient force could feel resonating in his bones the marble tiles below.

The rotunda's central circle was bound into an octagon by fencing that ran all the way up to the second-story balcony. Most of the spectators sat in the balcony. But on the first floor, ringside, there were two dozen seats reserved for Augusta's gilded class: Southern government leaders; celebrities from Atlanta; foreign captains in town for the weekend; and whoever else wielded sufficient cash or clout.

Bragg and the Chestnuts sat in those chairs; dead center and near the wide double-doors from behind which the fighters would soon emerge. Popcorn and wild invective rained down from the balcony seats.

The lights dimmed. A strafe of thundering rock descended from the speakers overhead.

The doors swung open to savage applause. The fighters walked barefoot, dressed only in shorts. Some wore bands around their heads and compression sleeves on their arms or legs. The sleeves were decorated in bright colors: reds and yellows and greens; adorned with lightning bolts and tigers' fangs and the stars of the Southern flag. The men bore tattoos of crosses and Bible verses and razor wire and the names of kin. They walked into the cage eyes dead ahead, as though no crowd existed. Soon the lights rose and the music died and the cage door was closed. The twelve men stood, sizing each other up, planning paths of attack.

Conventional wisdom said there was no way to win a Yuffsy in the opening minute, but plenty of ways to lose. Many fighters, when the bell rang, opted not to pounce on the weakest-looking of the bunch but the slowest—someone with whom they could safely spar without appearing cowardly, as the other men thinned their own ranks. But rarely did such tactics work as intended, and often two men who targeted the same sluggish Goliath would find themselves instead compelled to fight each other. The chaotic nature of the sport ensured that a dollar bet on any fighter was a dollar bet almost at random, and any man who managed to win even three or four fights before retiring was considered to have had a stellar career.

The ringside announcer read the fighters' names. A couple were new to the circuit, and had likely been included by the fightmaster simply because they looked big and granite-jawed enough to stay on their feet for at least a few minutes before going down.

The defending champion was a nineteen-year-old from Hattiesburg named Joshua who fought under the moniker Wraith. There was a rumor he had once spent time with the Sovereigns, fighting in East Texas when he was only thirteen. It was a lie invented by his manager, in part to blunt another rumor—started by a rival's camp—that the fighter was in fact the son of Northerners, and had signed a deal with a promoter in Pittsburgh in anticipation of war's end.

A victory on this night would mark three consecutive Yuffsys for Wraith, an unprecedented run in a contest where the previous winner always walked into his next cage match centered in eleven men's cross-hairs.

Only one contender interested Sarat: a veteran named Taylor. She'd heard of him a long time ago, in Camp Patience. He had lived there once, before the massacre. She knew little about him or his people—whether they had left with him and, if not, whether any of them had survived. She only knew that he'd lived once in the South Carolina slice and that now, almost a decade of fighting under his belt in a competition where the average fighter's career lasted four months, his body was irreversibly broken. Sarat ignored the other fighters and watched only him.

The bell rang. A cheer rose from the balcony. The men stalked one another and soon were sparring. In a Yuffsy a man left the ring only one of three ways: by tapping out, sustaining an injury brutal enough to warrant a retreat to the cage's only door, or by being knocked unconscious—in which latter case a couple of Octagon clowns were dispatched to drag the fighter out of the ring.

In order to maintain the Yuffsy's appeal as the South's true outlaw sport, the organizers were loath to put any rules on the books and, strictly speaking, the twelve men who entered the cage every month were bound by no written code.

But in reality, an elaborate system of unsaid conventions regulated the melee: an honor code concerning sucker punches and the length of time a man may avoid his opponents. A fighter clearly headed for the exit should be left alone, for example. But there was no actual punishment for violating these rules.

The night's bout raged on but no man fell. At the twelve-minute mark, all twelve fighters were still standing. The crowd applauded the dozen-dozen, a rarity. But by fifteen minutes, half the fighters had left the cage: four on their own power, bloodied and limping; two dragged out by the clowns, unconscious. The exits came as they always did, in a cascade. As soon as the shame of being the first fighter down was gone, the men's threshold for pain suddenly plummeted, and those who knew they had little chance of winning were almost happy to find themselves in a headlock or an arm-bar from which they could tap out.

Bragg leaned over to Sarat. "Your old neighbor has a busted foot," he said.

Taylor from Patience shifted hard onto his right leg, his left foot swollen and purple at the ankle. Only he, the champion Wraith, and one of the last-minute entrants, a behemoth named Grayson, remained.

As it did toward the end of every Yuffsy, the cage, whose padding was now streaked with drying blood, looked too large for its occupants. Instinctively, the men stepped back from each other and took a moment to catch their breath. A large gash had opened over Grayson's right eye; he wiped the blood with the compression sleeve on his arm. Soon the crowd grew tired of inaction, and began heckling the men, demanding action.

It was Taylor who moved first, limping toward Grayson. But before he got to him, Grayson raised his hand in surrender and made for the door. A chorus of boos erupted from the balcony, the crowd enraged that a man they believed still capable of fighting had chosen not to. They tossed peanuts and popcorn at the fighter as he left, calling him a coward and an embarrassment to the cage. Grayson made no response. Quickly he was shepherded beyond the great double-doors to the fighters' quarters, a repurposed exhibition room in the bowels of the old museum that once housed the bones of dinosaurs.

Two men remained, and although one of them had gone into the ring the favorite, the other now commanded the audience's affection. A few cheered because they knew the hopeless challenger came from the site of the famous Blue massacre, others because they knew he had failed to win a Yuffsy in twenty-three tries, a record. But most cheered because of an innate desire to back the underdog. That he stood no chance against his youth-armored opponent only endeared him further to the roaring crowd. Instinctively, they expected of him the same chivalrous defiance they believed they themselves, placed in the same position, would show.

The champ approached. He was wiry, his veins embossed in skin. The challenger struggled to hide his impairment. But it was more than the useless left ankle—which forced him now to skip and skitter where he stood—that hobbled him. It was an exhaustion in the very being of him, the weight of all his previous fights compounded.

The champ saw his advantage and played it. A swift kick to the swollen ankle brought the challenger down. Quickly, the champ jumped onto him and with a barrage of three quick punches, broke the challenger's nose along the bridge, where it had been broken many times before.

In such instances, when a Yuffsy was down to just two men, one of whom was obviously on the verge of defeat, a broken nose was the customary way to end the fight with mutual dignity. All the challenger had to do was tap out or lie still on the ground; the crowd would not begrudge him for doing either. The champion, kneeling atop the challenger, paused and waited.

But the challenger refused. Instead, the bloodied, broken fighter swung a fist upward at his opponent. So surprised was the champ by this that he failed to block it, and the punch landed square on his jaw, although it had so little weight behind it that it did no damage. The champ responded with another barrage; the challenger's head knocked side to side as though readying to come loose from his spine.

Once again the champ waited, and once again the challenger refused to submit. He swung from where he lay, this time unable to close his fist, such that he succeeded only in slapping the champ on the shoulder.

The crowd, now uncertain, grew quiet, nervous with the thought that the champ would inevitably lose patience.

But instead, the champ stood up. He left the challenger where he lay, a crimson halo on the padding near his head. He walked to the edge of the cage, near where the trainers were seated. He raised his hands in exasperation.

"What are you waiting for?" said the champ's trainer.

"I gave him a chance to go out easy," the fighter replied. "What do you want me to do, kill him?"

"If he don't want to get killed, he'll tap out," the trainer said. "Do your goddamn job."

As they spoke, the challenger stumbled onto his one working foot. He limped toward the edge of the cage and threw himself against the body of the champ. There was nothing left of him now but weight, and with it he knocked his opponent back against the side of the cage and onto the ground.

The champ screamed in pain as he fell. An unsmoothed protrusion in the mesh of the cage had cut a deep gash all the way along the length of his chest. Blood poured from the wound and spilled out the boundaries of the ring.

In a moment, the champ was standing again. Enraged, he knelt over his motionless opponent and beat him until the trainers and the crowd and all who watched knew he was dead.

☆ ☆ ☆

THE LIGHTS ROSE, the crowd dispersed. Usually the young men who came to watch the fight left afterward with adrenaline coursing through their veins, and were apt at the slightest provocation to start brawling with one another in the back alleys south of the boardwalk. But on this night the crowd was muted, and diffused quietly to the Imperial and the other Reynolds Street bars.

Adam Bragg Jr., fully drunk now, invited the sisters back to the Woodrow, where he and his entourage had booked every room for the weekend. But it was clear his interest lay in only one of the twins, and both declined.

Sarat and Dana stood awhile on the boardwalk, watching the docks. In the wake of the big winter storms, the wash often broke over the seawall. Tonight the water moved like black molasses. Even the massive freight ships, the first of which should have started to arrive at port by now, were nowhere to be seen.

"A guy at the fight said one of the gift ships ran aground all the way out at the Mouth," said Dana.

"They're here every month," Sarat replied. "How do they still manage to screw it up?"

"The land shifts under the water. Places that were deep one season turn shallow the next, and unless you're out there every day you can't know it."

Sarat watched the men down in the reef pilots' house. The lights were on. They were drinking and playing cards and passing time, hoping for the call to head out to the Mouth, the gaping waterway where the ocean met the river near the drowned remains of old Savannah. Others had already joined the tugboats dispatched to rescue the freighter, because it was a day's work and, even though the reef pilots earned a better living than almost any legal job in Augusta offered, they could still use the money.

"You going to meet that pretty boy of yours tonight?" asked Sarat.

"You know I am," said Dana. "Don't go making it a big deal when it ain't. We're just seeing each other is all. It's just fun. I'll be there when you get up in the morning."

"He's not even a real pilot."

"He's in training. Everybody's gotta learn to do a thing before they do it. Gotta get taught."

"He's not good enough for you."

Dana laughed. "You tell me one man you think is." She took her sister's hand and kissed it. "I'll see you soon, beautiful girl."

Sarat knew where her sister would be spending the night: the Fargo shipping building on 7th Street. It was a block-wide, bureaucratic-looking thing, and amassed within it were the reef pilot trainee dorms, the shipping authority and customs offices, the foreign crews' hostel, and the north Georgia branch of the Free Southern State.

Sarat despised the place. It spoke to her of all the unnecessary adornments with which her country's institutions justified their own existence. In truth, the customs officers were crooked, the hostel a thinly disguised brothel, and the temporary storage units in the basement used almost exclusively by smugglers.

It was, all of it, a lie—and the worst kind of lie: a charade of normality at a time of war. The thought of her sister inside that building—lying on one of those soiled bunks with one of those vacant, libidinous boys—made her sick.

Alone, she went to the Belle Rebelle to drink and then to sleep. It was a small bar, built inside one of the old row houses between 10th and 11th Streets. Upstairs, the owner, Layla Denomme, kept three rooms. Some nights she rented them out, but most of the time she let old friends and regulars stay there for free.

Layla's sixteen-year-old daughter, Layla Jr., had been pouring drinks there for the last two years, standing atop a Yuxi crate to see over the bar top. She knew the regulars by name and Sarat by more.

Of the Belle Rebelle's die-hard regulars, there were predominantly two groups—the first were stump-limbed war pensioners. They sat at the back tables, growing rust and getting eyes-shut drunk on Atlanta's dime. The others were river rats: reef pilots, tugboat and towboat captains, and the men who ran skiffs laden with contraband in the dead of night. These patrons sat at a corner of the bar, congregated near a large screen mounted on the back wall.

The screen showed the position and status of the freighters as they approached and navigated the river. Whenever one of the charity ships needed a reef pilot or a batch of dockhands to help with unloading, a notice popped up on the screen.

The simple screen was, for the bar owner, a coup—the result of a years-long relationship with the proprietor of one of the very few working commercial satellites that still covered this slice of the world.

On this night the screen showed that the freighters, which should by now have been working their way upriver to Augusta, were instead logjammed behind the ship that had run aground. The workers nursed watered-down Joyful and cursed their lousy luck.

"If he's got any sense, he'll stay on that goddamned boat and hope they take his ass all the way back to China," said one of the reef pilots. "He comes back here, they'll string him up on the boardwalk."

Sarat sat at the other end of the bar, where Layla the elder leaned on the bar top, eating frickles.

"Baby girl!" she said, hugging Sarat. "Gaines said you'd be coming around soon. It's so good to see you."

"How you been, Mama Layla?" said Sarat.

The bar owner shrugged. "The same. Bad night tonight. There's talk it might be another couple days before they get that ship moving. People are starting to worry about credit, about paying last month's bills."

"Is there a storm out there or something?"

"Nah. They had one called Walter, was a Cat Six coming in off the Gulf four days ago, but died real quick over the Florida Sea. Just some rain and wind now, gave the gift ship captains a little trouble out past the borderline, but nothing too bad."

"Then what's keeping them?" asked Sarat. "It can't just be that one stuck ship. Are the Blues tightening up inspections again?"

Layla shook her head. "Just the one stuck ship, can you believe it? They sent this new pilot out, kid named Brunswick—hasn't been certified no more than a week, and they send him out to guide the first gift ship in. Well don't you know, he's running off last season's map, and he guides them too far south. First damn ship of the month, and he runs them aground into Hutchinson Reef."

"So they're just sitting there?"

"Been there since dusk. FSS shipping authority folks being real hard-asses about letting other ones go round it. I think they finally saw a chance to flex their muscles. So now everybody's just waiting on them to pull her out and tow her in."

"Christ," said Sarat. "Can't run a ship up a river. How we supposed to win a war?"

She picked at the bowl of frickles. Layla, who swore up and down that nobody could tell the difference, made them with cricket flour. But Sarat swore she could. There was a stale aftertaste to it, a dishwater echo on the tongue.

Layla called on her daughter to bring over a carafe of Joyful. The girl poured Sarat a cup.

"How are those boys doing?" asked the mother, pointing to the reef rats at the corner of the bar.

"They're asking if they can start a tab on next month's ships, if these ones end up turning around."

"What did you tell them?"

"You know what I told them."

"Good girl."

Layla Jr. walked back to the other end of the bar. Sarat watched her. She had her hair in a thick, braided ponytail. Behind it, on the back of her neck, lay a small tattoo of the state of Georgia that her mother had yet to discover.

"How's your family?" asked Layla Sr.

"They're all right," said Sarat. "Gaines's friend Dr. Heller came by again last month, talking about how they're working on a program with the Red Crescent where they send injured Southerners up to the good hospitals in Pittsburgh. I told him I'd rather Simon die."

"What's the harm in it? It's not like you're turning on your people. What if they got something up there in those hospitals can fix him?"

"Unless they got a time machine in those hospitals, they ain't fixing him."

Layla sighed. She poured herself a glass of Joyful. "How about the letters? Gaines said you've been sending them back."

"We don't need donations," said Sarat. "Every week they come in from all over the Red. People I've never met before—some of them I know don't even have a pot to piss in, and they still send us envelopes stuffed with cash, like we're a church or something. Well we ain't a church—we don't need their charity."

Layla laughed. "Oh honey I know that. Knew it the minute Gaines first introduced us. But what you need to know is, it isn't about you. It's about them. You really think those folks are too dumb to know they're poor? Of course they know. And they send you that money anyway, because it means that much to them to be connected to you."

"What do they know about us?" Sarat replied. "What they read in the papers? What those FSS politicians said in those rallies? For all they know, they're mailing their cash to a hole in the ground."

"The only thing they need to know is you're clean," said Layla. "You and your sister and your brother. Especially your brother. You're clean because of what was done to you at Patience. All the politicians and the rebels and even the preachers, they might say the right things, but they haven't been made clean like you. That's why they send you money, that's why they write you those letters saying you're in their prayers. Because you're clean."

"That's not true," said Sarat.

"Oh it's true. It might not be reasonable, it might not be fair. But it's true."

"If they want to be clean so bad, why are they sitting in their homes writing letters? Why aren't they out fighting, or even saying they're proud of the South, proud of their own side? Every time I read the J-Con or any other one of those Southern newspapers, they've got some article about a new poll showing more and more people in favor of those cowards at the FSS and their phony peace plan—a plan that don't ask for nothing but free movement over our own land. If they're so worried about being clean, whatever that means, they'd hang those cowards in Atlanta with their pocket linings stuffed in their mouths."

A cheer erupted from the other corner of the bar. At first Sarat thought the river workers had been listening to what she said, but it was the movement of the ships they were cheering. The red dot that had been stalled atop Hutchinson Reef finally turned green, and to the east the waiting freighters began to move upriver. The month's parade of gift ships was under way.

"Won't be needing that credit after all, sweetheart," said one of the dockhands as he raced from the bar.

"Wasn't gonna be getting it anyway," said Layla Jr.

The dockhand blew her a kiss as he left, and she returned it with a finger.

Soon the bar was quiet save for the murmuring of the war pensioners. The men—a half-dozen on this night—were between ten and twenty years older than Sarat, but looked older. She knew them only vaguely: the one missing his legs was Nathan Something. The one next to him was named Jeb, and was paralyzed on his left side. Others who drank in the Belle Rebelle's dark corners on this and other nights were broken in other ways, some cracks visible, some not.

Layla Sr. pointed to the men. "You want people who'll never stop supporting the war? Talk to them over there. The war will never be over for them. The people who're sending you those letters, I bet you most of them aren't yet damaged that way. Maybe they've been touched by it, lost a friend or heard about some massacre, but it's not the same. The truth is, they're on the other side of the river from where you are, they haven't been through what you've been through. And they don't want to. They're not young like you; most of them are old enough to remember when it wasn't like this, when there was peace. And if you'd known that, you'd want it back too."

"It ain't coming back," said Sarat. "If they wanna dream, that's their choice."

Layla cupped her hands on Sarat's. There was a warmth to her palms that seemed to emanate from her eyes. "Maybe," she said. "Maybe. But let me ask you this, and be honest: if they did have a time machine up in that Northern hospital, and you had a chance to go back—back to a time when none of what happened to you happened, a different world altogether where there had never been any war—wouldn't you take it?"

"Doesn't matter," said Sarat. "They can't ever make that happen."

"But if they could . . ."

"They can't."

The bar owner smiled. It was a sad smile, and behind it Sarat suspected something akin to pity. "It's getting late," she said. "They're gonna be out on the docks unloading all night, and then tomorrow the shirt factory dealers are gonna join them, and it'll be a carnival for three days straight."

She passed a set of room keys to Sarat. "Get some sleep while you can," she said. "Room's all set up how you like it."

Sarat thanked her. They hugged and Layla retired to her own home, which stood about ten blocks south of the boardwalk, insulated from the riverside cacophony.

Layla Jr. rang the bell: Last call. Sarat finished off the Joyful in her cup and she stumbled off her chair. She climbed the stairs near where the pensioners were getting ready to leave for the dime-bag motels and the VFWs, repurposed now as VDWs. As she climbed the stairs, she leered at Layla Jr., who caught her eyes but said nothing.

The bedroom upstairs was small. The bed was made of a steel bunk salvaged from a ruined Southern destroyer. The bunk bed's frames had been severed from each other and reset side by side to make a crude double bed. A lamp lit the room, its light sinking into the brown-painted walls. A ceiling fan spun, its bamboo arms warped and wobbling. A small window overlooked the boardwalk and the docks and the river.

Sarat smelled the sheets. They'd been recently washed and they smelled of jasmine. It was the first thing she did whenever she stayed at the Belle Rebelle; the scent of other people on the sheets disgusted her. If she ever detected it—even the slightest remains of another body's signature—she stripped the sheets from the bed and slept on the naked mattress, or on the floor, where the dust tempered all other scents.

On the nightstand there was an old music-player, the kind that carried songs in its own memory instead of fetching them from the clouds. It had once belonged to Layla's mother, and had reached that useless middle age between novelty and antique—it was simply old.

Sarat searched it for a song she'd heard before, a slow number she liked. The player had a little display on its face but that had long ago stopped working. Instead she listened, and skipped past song after song until she found the one she wanted. From the speakers came the sound of bourbon-clouded piano keys. A shredded nightgown of a song. *You moved like honey, in my dream last night.*

Sarat undressed. She set her shirt over the lamp shade, and the soft light turned from amber to blood. The shirt depicted the flag of South Carolina, drawn against a red background instead of blue.

Sarat listened. Layla Jr.'s footsteps were light against the stairs outside. She opened the door. With her apron off she appeared even smaller, a milk-skinned apparition under Sarat's looming shadow. She closed the door behind her.

"Come here," said Sarat.

"Say it nicer," Layla replied.

"No."

Sarat smiled. She wanted Layla to stand her ground, and Layla knew Sarat wanted it. Because it made what came next sweeter, made the roughness sweeter. And it was the roughness Sarat craved. She wanted not love itself but the taking and giving of it; the parched hardness of her tongue scraping along Layla's skin, a harvest of goose bumps in its wake. She wanted her to feel love the way a bone feels a break, to make her scream in a language she never even knew she knew, a language deposited from her lips like secrets into the vault of a muffling pillow. She wanted it to hurt, and for Layla to want it to hurt.

The sound of them seeped through the brittle bedroom window and was drowned by the bustle of the docks. Outside, the river rats worked the cranes and the trucks, readying to relieve the gift ships of their contents. Soon the freight ships would arrive and their cargo of rations and tent materials and charity blankets would be moved throughout the Red. Then in the days that followed the ships would be loaded with their reward in the great barter: crate upon crate of clothing from the Southern shirt factories; cheap electronics from the sweatshops along the Alabama coast; fruits and vegetables from Atlanta's vertical farms. Then the ships would depart, and Augusta would grow quiet once more, the giving and taking complete.

Layla's heartbeat echoed in the springs. Sarat rolled away. The fan turned slow, easy circles overhead.

She felt Layla's finger on her back, tracing a wound. The cut was thin and long, running from the top of her left shoulder to the middle of her back.

"How did you get this?" asked Layla.

"Don't know," said Sarat.

"Yeah you do. You just don't want to tell me."

"That's right."

Layla sat up in bed. She leaned over and picked her shirt off the floor and put it on. It was stretched out a little around the collar from when

Sarat had pulled it off her. Outside on the boardwalk, there shone a great blinking lantern. A sliver of its light came in through the bedroom window. It cast Layla momentarily in a wash of white, and in this moment the places where her skin was red and flush were made porcelain and clean, the newness of her restored.

"This is my last year in this place," she said. "Come January, I'm gone."

"And where exactly you gonna go to?" asked Sarat, her back still turned.

"South to Valdosta, where my mother grew up. All her people are still there."

Sarat chuckled. "Everybody trying to get the hell out the south coast, and you're going back?"

"Better there than here," said the girl. "I'm not gonna wait on drunk river rats and clean up puke for the rest of my life. Wake up one day find out now I'm the Old Layla. At least down there I don't have to worry every day about whether this'll be the night the Blues finally come down from Tennessee, burn the whole place to the ground."

"Only reason Blues won't come all the way down to Valdosta is because there's nothing down there worth burning," said Sarat. "What are you gonna do, work in one of the farm slums? The shirt mills?"

"Maybe I will."

Sarat shook her head. "Christ," she said. "You still so young."

"Like you ain't?"

Sarat faced her. "Turn around," she said.

Layla complied. Sarat brushed aside her ponytail and kissed the place where Georgia's outline lay inked upon her neck. "Run off wherever you like," she said. "You mine tonight, though."

"I ain't nobody's," Layla replied. But she lay a while longer under the slow-turning fan.

Then she was gone, and Sarat slept. She dreamed of Patience, and of the knife coming loose from her hand too soon. In the dream the Blues bound her and took her north, to a place in the forest. They dug for her a prison well deep into the ground, a dark earthen hollow from which she could not climb. It was always the same. Every night she closed her eyes and was confined to the empty well, powerless and blind and alone.

She woke with the residue of the nightmare in her pores. For a moment she scratched at the mattress, but a warm hand patted her head, and a voice said: It's all right, beautiful girl, it's all right.

She let her sister's breathing calm her, and smelled the skin of her thigh. She let the lullaby wash over her—*it's all right, beautiful girl, it's all right, beautiful girl.* But she held her own eyes closed because she knew that the voice and smell and touch of her sister were not real. They were only imagined things, concocted by her mind to cleanse the aftertaste of the nightmare. When she finally opened her eyes, her sister would not be there.

☆ ☆ ☆

OUTSIDE, the docks rattled with the movement of commerce. All morning, the crews unloaded the boxes. By noon, when Sarat could no longer keep her eyes closed, the opposite process was under way.

Sarat walked to the window. The room was dank, despite the fan's slow circling. Still naked, she lifted the window open and leaned out to catch a little of the Savannah breeze. The boardwalk looked old and weathered in the clear light of day. A couple of drunks lay asleep in their vomit. A freight ship blocked the view of the river but Sarat could still see, on the other bank, the great martyrs' mural.

It was painted onto a stretch of the Carolina quarantine wall, about ten blocks long. Here the wall was covered with a collage of the South's unjustly killed. Not an inch of concrete was visible behind a mass of drawings and photographs. Almost daily, the survivors of Northern assaults were ferried on skiffs across the river and given a chance to paste or draw their loved ones' images on the wall.

Only the dead were allowed to grace the wall. In time, the ritual became so popular that the kids who ran the skiffs started mounting ladders to their boats to reach the topmost edges. The Red soldiers looked on from their guard towers, and no matter how close the mourners came to falling over into the Slow country of South Carolina, they did not intervene. Eventually, the center of the quarantine wall in Augusta was saturated entirely, and the mural began to spread up and downriver.

Only very special circumstances, such as the massacre at Camp Patience, allowed for the pasting of new martyrs on the old part of the mural in Augusta. But the very center of the mural, it was understood by all, was never to be touched. In that sacred place was painted a large portrait of Julia Templestowe.

A tipsy, whistling dockhand stumbled down the boardwalk, shirtless. He was a rookie, fresh off celebrating his first shift on the docks. He wore a child's toy Viking's hat, its plastic horns bright green. As he passed the Belle Rebelle he looked up and saw Sarat standing naked at the window. He stopped and stared, uncertain. Finally Sarat snapped forward as though to lunge at him. He flinched and fell back, nearly tumbling off the boardwalk and onto the wharf below. Sarat winked at the jolted dockhand. She closed the window.

She dressed and went downstairs. The bar was empty. She fixed herself a drink and ate the stale leftover frickles, and then she left.

The waterfront was as busy now as it was the night before, but it was a different kind of traffic. This was the busyness of work. By nightfall, when the month's business was done and the gift ships were moving back to the Atlantic, Augusta would once again be consumed in revelry, the temporarily flush dockworkers burning through their cash. Then it would grow quieter and quieter, until by the third week of the month half the bars wouldn't bother opening their doors at all.

She hitched a ride east to the coast on one of the trucks that ran back and forth along the Savannah highway, shuttling dockhands, foreign crew members, and packages to and from Augusta.

She arrived at Garden Sound in the late afternoon. The mouth of the river where it met the ocean was a desolate place, but beautiful in its own way. Great looming wharfs lined the edge of the land. It was here where many of the freight companies kept offices, and where the last remaining salvage divers set sail to search for bounty in the undersea heart of sunken Savannah.

In the distance, six miles outland, a line of glowing buoys marked the boundary beyond which the Blues controlled the water. Their coastal vessels circled, and whenever a gift ship arrived, they escorted it to a large floating customs platform, where the soldiers searched it.

At the very edge of the Red, near the light ships that provided guidance to the mouth of the river, another, smaller platform stood. A tiny building of welded shipping containers sat atop the platform.

It was a coffee shop, run by a man named Prince Wendell who was nearing his hundredth birthday and had lived on the Georgia coast his entire life. He was known as the very last holdout of the great Inland Exodus, the one man left who remained on his land even when it ceased being land.

For the better part of eighty years he had run this business. Mostly blind now but unwilling to retire to the dry world, he opened the coffee shop for business only on the first three days of every month. During those days, his customers were reef pilots, foreign crews, and Northern soldiers with the circling customs fleet.

Any other Southerner would have been strung up for serving Blues, but Prince Wendell was old and stubborn enough to be grandfathered into the peace of his youth, and the tiny confines of his floating coffee shop stood as the only place in the wartime country where the North and South maintained an unspoken truce.

In one of the warehouses near the shore, Albert Gaines kept a Sea-Tok docked in Wharf Twenty-one. Sarat took the tiny vessel out into the ocean.

It was a slow trip to Prince Wendell's coffee shop. She had chosen this place and this time to meet her informant because it coincided with a lull in the traffic at the mouth of the river. By nightfall the first of the gift ships would begin the crossing back to the other side of the world, and the coastline would once again become congested as the Blues searched the freighters for stowaways. But in these few hours the sea was clear.

Sarat docked at the foot of the platform and climbed the ladder to the deck. A neon "Open" sign buzzed on the door. Inside, the coffee shop was decorated with pictures of the old city of Savannah and of Prince Wendell's childhood home.

Sarat had seen many walls decorated with pictures like these—pictures treated by their bearers with ritualistic reverence, as though the memory of a thing, showered with enough devotion, could resurrect the thing itself.

Prince Wendell sat at the counter. For a while he stared at the door, trying to make out his customer. When Sarat was close enough for him to see, he smiled.

"Julia!" he said. "Good to see you again!"

Sarat hugged the old man, one of many acquaintances in and

around Augusta to whom she had given a fake name. "How you feeling, boss?"

"Can't complain," said Prince Wendell. "Good month, this one. Storm just missed us. Last month though, Christ, that was a bad one."

He continued describing the previous month's storm as he walked to the kitchen to fetch his customer a cup of coffee. Sarat sat at the table nearest the counter and waited. Soon she heard another skiff docking at the base of the platform. A Blue soldier climbed the ladder.

No matter how many times they met, the sight of her informant's uniform up close slipped a primal switch deep within Sarat's gut.

The soldier walked inside. He greeted Prince Wendell and soon the old man was back in the kitchen, preparing the soldier's usual order.

The soldier sat at Sarat's table. Every month, they met this way, briefly, no more than a couple of minutes. And every month she marveled at the sight of him—the way he had grown into a man seemingly overnight, even as his frame remained stunted. He had survived, he had lived; it was the only thing that mattered.

"You got him," said Marcus Exum. "Every damn one of them is talking about it. Highest-ranking Blue casualty since they killed the president in Jackson."

"Couldn't have done it without you," said Sarat.

Marcus looked over Sarat's shoulder at the door.

"You got someone joining you on this coffee run?" asked Sarat.

"No. But you never know who else might come by."

Marcus slid a cigarette across the table. "Only intel I could get this month. It's a convoy, four LAVs. They'll be passing near the Tennessee line at Russell Cave. Supposed to have some deputy secretary from the War Office onboard, getting a tour of the front."

Sarat looked at the cigarette—she could see the outline of words and a simple map drawn on the inside of the wrapping paper. "Thank you," she said.

"Can I ask you a favor?" said Marcus.

"Sure."

"Lay low a while. There's talk they're going to retaliate for what happened at Halfway. They're going to put the old man's son in charge of the War Office, everyone's sure of it. And he's going to tear the whole front apart. I don't know how or when, but I promise you he will."

Sarat touched her friend's shoulder. She felt the bars on his uniform, markers of his place in the hierarchy of what was once the most powerful force in the world, the military of her enemy.

"You're a good friend," she said. Once more he glanced at the door.

They heard Prince Wendell coming back from the kitchen. Marcus paid him and walked out without saying another word. Sarat waited a half-hour after he left, nursing her coffee and listening to Prince Wendell reminisce about the time George came through in '57 and took the entire eastern edge of the city with it.

Then she left for the docks. To the east she saw the Blue customs ships waiting, and she knew her friend would be there for another two days before returning to the base at Halfway Branch. She thought about that last time she saw him at Patience, about watching him walk that thin concrete tightrope to the alien country. And she begrudged him not a single one of the choices he'd made since.

Excerpted from:

ARCHIVES OF THE SPECIAL SENATE COMMITTEE ON INSURRECTIONIST AND SECESSIONIST ACTIVITY— TESTIMONY OF WAR OFFICE DIRECTOR JOSEPH WEILAND JR.

Perhaps the best way to explain it, Madam Chairwoman, is with a simple analogy.

In this country, we have elections. Our elections have strict rules, of which I'm sure every member of this committee is familiar. But, under special circumstances, we also have special elections. When President Daniel Ki was murdered, for example, we had a special election that was in fact not an election at all. It was an emergency measure taken in response to extreme and unique events. In other words, we set aside the normal guidelines because the circumstances themselves were far from normal.

And I think it's fair to say, Madam Chairwoman, that no reasonable person genuinely believed that by temporarily setting aside normal protocol and installing a President until the following election, we had somehow forever dismantled the foundations of American democracy.

Now, to return to your question. You asked about the methods we use to extract information from insurrectionist detainees, and I am happy to answer.

Since I assumed directorship of the War Office, insurrectionist terror attacks across the so-called Tennessee line—attacks similar to the one that cost my father his life—have plummeted. Certainly the primary credit for this goes to the brave men and women of our Armed Forces. But I believe that the dramatic reduction of secessionist violence is also a direct result of our strategic initiative to capture and interrogate known and suspected insurrectionist leaders in those regions where attacks have been most rampant.

Let's be clear, Madam Chairwoman: the people we target are no angels. We have focused our efforts intently on rebel recruiters—the cowardly men and women who have for years brainwashed young Southerners into violent, suicidal acts to further the cause of treason.

Now these recruiters, in most cases, never had the courage to take up arms themselves. So we were faced with a choice, Madam Chairwoman: either spend years trying to prosecute them for crimes that, while very much real, are nonetheless extremely difficult to prove—especially to the standards of a peacetime court in a wartime setting—or extract from them as much information as we could. I speak of information, Madam Chairwoman, that has subsequently saved American lives.

We do not act as monsters, Madam Chairwoman, even though we are often pitted against them. As is the case in any war, we use the tools available to us under the constraints of time and urgency to which we are subject. And in cases where information from insurrectionist recruiters has subsequently proven false or unreliable, we have responded accordingly. The mission of the War Office, above all else, is to protect our nation.

And I believe we have done so, Madam Chairwoman. I believe in the coming months the insurrectionist terrorists will abandon their doomed efforts at disunion, and this war will come to an end. And I certainly believe that, just as we have returned to the normal rules of Presidential elections, we will also return to the normalcy of peacetime. I'm sure all the members of this committee echo my desire that we reach that normalcy as quickly as possible.

I believe we are closer now to peace, Madam Chairwoman, than ever before.

CHAPTER ELEVEN

Sarat walked through the ruins of Lake Sinclair. She stayed close to the remains of Milledgeville Road. It was wrecked in places with craters ten feet deep, and in others with fallen trees and power lines and charred fencing.

As she neared the lake, Sarat veered from the main road to the smaller paths that led past an old bank branch and a dry jut in the lake bed. Here the fallen trees were densest, interspersed with the boathouses and the crumbling docks. Occasionally, rodents rustled through the undergrowth, but otherwise it was quiet. Sarat walked slowly to the site of the meeting.

The firebombing of Lake Sinclair happened early in the war, before it was known that the Blues had lost control of their airborne assassins. At dawn there came a buzzing sound, like a fly trapped in an upturned glass. All over the South, people had gotten used to the sight of the Birds, but no one had ever seen a flock before. They circled, a dozen or more with their wings outstretched, their shadows like fading bruises on the water.

Nobody in the South knew why the Birds had chosen to obliterate this place. Some said one of the Union pilots must have entered the coordinates wrong. Or perhaps the generals and politicians who decided which places to burn and which lives to end had been given faulty intelligence.

Nobody could settle on an explanation. But it was better to believe something, anything, than to accept that it had happened without reason—that the wandering Birds had simply congregated over this particular place on this particular hour and rained hellfire in accordance with no greater order than that of blind chance.

In the years since the firebombing, the lake had gone dry. But a strong storm had come through the week prior to Sarat's visit, and on this day the bed was still swollen with rainwater. A film of green algae covered the surface. Thick as carpet, the algae held the water so still that the entire lake bed appeared as emerald-tinted land, sturdy enough to walk on.

Everywhere around the edge of the lake, the waterside houses lay in ruins, the small roads warped, the trees ashen and still. When she reached the lake bed, Sarat walked down a short driveway that led to a small and badly damaged church: a home converted into a place of worship. An ebony cross held firm to the front door.

The house had been cleaved down the middle in the bombing. The ground under the lake-facing half of the home neared collapse. The back rooms—two bedrooms and a study—teetered precariously over the lake bed. The front half stood level on the land.

Sarat climbed through a gap in the side of the house where there had once been a windowsill. The house was dark but for the midday light that dropped through the broken ceiling like a curtain. Inside, the house smelled of old paper. Fine particulate floated in the sunlit shaft.

In the middle of every month she came here to meet Joe. But this was their first meeting since she'd shot the general at Halfway Branch five months earlier. In the time between, the Blue incursions into Southern territory had increased in frequency and severity. So much so that Joe had temporarily suspended their arrangement.

She saw him inside the house, sitting where he always sat, on a wooden kitchen chair just beyond the curtain of sunlight. She recognized him by his outline: thin-framed, his posture neat, his hands clasped and resting on the table.

"Good morning, Sarat," he said. "It's good to see you again."

"Mornin'," Sarat replied.

"Come in, sit. It's a beautiful day, no?"

She still liked the sound of his voice, his strange accent. He had a habit of pronouncing Ps as Bs, soft Hs as hard ones. Sometimes when he talked about his home he spoke words in his own language that relied on alien letters, letters made of sighs and careful curls of the tongue.

Sarat sat at the kitchen table. She felt the warmth of flooding sunlight on the back of her neck. Behind Joe, the floor began to slope sharply downward, and through the rear windows she could see the dull green surface of the near-empty lake.

"Finally, I have a chance to congratulate you in person," said Joe.

"It was nothing," Sarat replied.

"It was certainly not nothing. The single most significant Southern victory since the beginning of the war. And you did it, Sarat. It is your victory."

"It's no victory, it's one man dead. They got plenty more still living."

Joe shook his head. "Albert was right about you," he said.

"Have you seen him?" asked Sarat. "I've been trying to reach him for months, but he up and vanished."

"I haven't heard from him either," said Joe.

"You think they picked him up? He's been known to them a long time."

"I don't think so. Maybe if this were thirty, forty years ago, but he's an old man now, like me, and they don't care too much about old men. He was like this as a soldier too—he would disappear for days across the border into Ar-Rutbah without telling anyone. That was back when it was not a very good idea to travel carelessly in Iraq. He even brought me with him a few times to translate and drive. At first I thought he was doing something very dangerous, meeting with the enemy, committing treason. But he just wanted to see the land, to meet the people. I believe they eventually tried him for it—he spent a year in military prison. Did he ever tell you that?"

"He told me you saved his life a couple times," said Sarat.

"I did no such thing. I was just an assistant, what you would call a fixer. The Americans liked having locals around who could speak English and Arabic, who knew the people and the area. It is always better if you can have people from the same country do the work."

The sound of a twig breaking outside derailed their small talk. Sarat turned to look out the sliver of space where the front wall was cracked open. She watched and waited for footsteps, but none came. She turned back to Joe, who sat undisturbed, his green dress shirt washed white by the sunlight.

"If it had been the Blues, we wouldn't have had time to worry about it," he said. "Anyway, let's get to business. What do you need?"

"Lag'm," said Sarat, using Joe's word for the weapon. "Like the kind you brought last year."

Joe nodded. "All right. Big or small?"

"Both. Same as last time. There's a convoy coming down near Tennga next week. Got a colonel riding with them. I know the roads they're taking, I'll lay the mines down there."

"Same as last time, understood. Anything else? More rounds for Templestowe? Cash?"

"Just the mines," said Sarat.

"Consider it done."

"There's something else."

"Of course."

"I heard there were secret peace talks happening, that the Free Southerners had some of their people up in Columbus a few months ago. There any truth to that?"

"I believe that is correct," said Joe.

"That still happening?"

"From what my people tell me, the director of the War Office has suspended the talks."

Sarat smiled.

"I told you," said Joe. "It is your victory."

☆ ☆ ☆

WHEN SARAT RETURNED HOME from Lake Sinclair there was a stranger's car parked in the driveway, an old fossil-powered sedan. Standing beside it was Attic, the eldest of the Salt Lake Boys.

"Christ," said Sarat. "I thought they killed you at Fayetteville."

"Mr. Bragg wants to speak to you," Attic said. He was as tall as Sarat but thinner, emaciated to the point of appearing sickly. He had dead, distant eyes like his brothers.

"Which one," said Sarat, "the boy or his father?"

"Mr. Bragg Senior," said Attic. "He wants to see you and your sister."

"He doesn't need to see my sister. Let's go get it over with."

"He said he wants to see you and your sister . . ."

"You deaf or just stupid?" said Sarat, approaching the boy. There was a mechanical quality to him, a sense of removal. "You and I can go, or you can go back to Atlanta alone. Your call."

They drove west toward the Southern capital. The car had an old radio; Sarat turned the dial. Between bursts of static came dispatches from amateur broadcasters scattered nearby: disembodied Bible reciters; howling cultists preaching apocalypse from the confines of their cabins; madmen squalling into the void. She settled finally on an old man reading a list of names. In the background there played a patriotic Southern hymn Sarat remembered from her childhood. The old man spoke in monotone, barely pausing for breath, and it was impossible to discern whether he was reading the names of martyrs or traitors or simply inventing the names as he went along.

"So what happened to you up in Fayetteville, anyway?" asked Sarat.

"I was captured," said Attic.

"The Blues got you? And they let you go? Goddamn, you must have spilled your guts and then some. Old man Bragg must love you if he's keeping the rebels from stringing you up with your pockets in your mouth."

"I didn't say a word, and I wasn't captured by Blues," said Attic. "I was captured by terrorists."

It took Sarat a moment to realize he meant the other Southern rebels, the ones who had refused to come under Bragg's umbrella group. She let out a high cackle.

"You let your own people get you? Holy God! That's more embarrassing than the Blues just shooting you dead."

"They're not *my people*," said Attic. "They're terrorists. Mr. Bragg is my people. I'm free because of him."

"Terrorists, goddamn," said Sarat. "That word will work on anybody, won't it?"

But Attic wasn't listening. "I didn't say a word," he repeated. "I didn't say a word."

At the lip of the horizon, veiled with grime, the capital of the South appeared.

☆ ☆ ☆

A WALL OF TOWERING SLUMS pierced the sky, afloat in haze. The buildings marked the outer edges of Atlanta, a city impossible with size and growing, forever inching outward, metastatic with life.

Once, long ago, its landscape had been inverted. Skyscrapers dominated the downtown core, and beyond them stood the hospitals and the arenas and the sprawling university campuses. Further out, the skyscrapers gave way to the suburbs, lined with strip malls and parks and golf courses and a ring of highways.

Now the tallest buildings belonged to the slums that walled the outer reaches of the city, towers brown and dull as rotting teeth. Within them lived the refuse of the Southern State—refugees from the border towns and from places ravaged at random by the Birds; the poor of the southernmost coast who fled the storms and the scorching heat; soldiers and rebels and people who were born here and whose parents and grandparents were born here, people who knew no other home.

Near the ever-growing slums stood the electronics sweatshops and the shirt factories and the vertical farms. These were huge structures, wider than they were tall. The sweatshops and the factories were made of red brick and the farms were encased in thick glass. The glass was impenetrable to the eye, lacquered from the inside with condensation. Only the reek of manure escaped the walls and clung to the outskirts of the city like a coat of paint. Every dawn and dusk a bleak procession marched from the slums to the sprawling workhouses, and from the workhouses to the slums.

Closer to the heart of the city, the bureaucracy of the Free Southern State—a set of gray, identical buildings—acted as a moat around the innermost core. In the center was the Southern State Capitol; the residences of President Kershaw and of the senior secretaries; as well as the gaudy, gated mansions of the South's neo-grandees, who owned the sweatshops and the factories and the farms.

Attic drove slowly through the slums. The air smelled of smog and the exhaust of a thousand humming generators. A small group of children ran aside the old fossil car, knowing through instinct that the driver of such a thing must reside above the masses in the hierarchy of the Red. They tapped on the windows and asked for change. An old man limped from one car to the next, selling tissue boxes for five dollars apiece. Lone Star flags hung limp from the balconies overhead as the car inched through the alleys of Little Houston.

It took two hours to get from Sarat's home in Lincolnton to Atlanta, and another two to get from the outskirts of the city to the core. At the edge of the United Rebels' compound, the car stopped at a wire-fenced gate manned by a couple of boys in old jungle fatigues. The guards eyed Attic's passenger with vague disdain. They opened the gate and waved the car through.

It was a simple compound, made up of three squat buildings huddled under a highway overpass. The buildings bore no signage, and at the steps of each sat a few men and boys in plastic chairs, rifles by their sides.

Two of these men ushered Sarat and Attic to the second floor of the middle building. There they sat in a large room that resembled a living area. They waited for half an hour before Bragg Sr. arrived. He was wheeled in by his son and joined by three assistants. Even as Atlanta sweltered, the old man wore a buttoned shirt and a sweater vest, and yet didn't break a sweat, as though his pores had hardened and dried with time.

His son wheeled him close to Attic and Sarat, and then took a seat in a corner of the room.

Bragg Sr. waved his hand in Attic's direction, and quickly the boy stood up and left. Then he looked Sarat over from head to toe, a vague, strained look on his face, as though he were reading a book written in a language other than his own.

Finally, he turned to his son. "You're right," he said. "Maybe she isn't really." His son said nothing.

He turned back to his guest. "So you're the girl who caused all that mess," he said. "What's your name again?"

"Sarat Chestnut."

"Sarat Chestnut," Bragg Sr. repeated. "You from the Montgomery Chestnuts? Good people, those. Had a boy named Paul, fought and died in Beaumont early on in the war."

"No," said Sarat.

"Her people are from Louisiana," said Bragg Jr., "down by the Mississippi Sea near Old Orleans."

"Christ Almighty, she ain't even from the Red!" said the old man. "The child of swamp people, out on the front firing a gun. Is that what we've come to?"

He inched closer to Sarat. "You know, when Albert first told me about you, I thought he was playing games. That's what he's always been like, trying to rile everyone up with new things, recruiting more girls than boys. Every few weeks, another pet project."

Sarat winced. She had always known there were others; every time news came of some homicide bomber sneaking into the Blue country and turning one of their city squares to rubble, she always wondered if it wasn't Gaines who'd eased the farmer's suit onto the martyr's frame. But in another compartment of her mind she secretly harbored the notion that perhaps she was the only one—that, having found her, he had no reason to recruit anyone else to the cause. She knew it wasn't true—of course it wasn't true—but that was no hindrance to believing it.

"Ah, but still, I got a soft spot for that Gaines," the elder Bragg continued. "He's worked hard for the cause. Used to fight for the Northerners once, back when that Bouazizi was just a bunch of tribes tearing each other apart. But that was before all this, and I don't hold it against him . . ."

Sarat felt Bragg's ashtray breath on her face. It amazed her, the length at which old men could talk. She wondered if it wasn't the sound of his own voice, rather than the words themselves, that pleased him. He had small dull eyes and the only time they lit up was when he was speaking.

Suddenly he stopped. He turned to one of his assistants. "Get us some water, Noah," he said. "And get the boys to move the fans in from the office. It's hotter than hell in here."

The assistant left the room and soon a couple of young men entered with electric fans in hand. They set them up on opposite ends of the room, such that their crosswinds met where Sarat and the old man sat.

"And where's that sister of yours, anyway?" asked Bragg Sr. "I told them I wanted to see both of you."

"She's not a part of this," said Sarat.

"Darling, we're all a part of this."

The assistant returned with two glasses on a tray. The old man drank as though it were his first time seeing water.

"It's that goddamn Gaines," he said, wiping his mouth. "He does this to all his little kids, makes them think it's all about them—that the whole damn war turns on how they feel, what they lost, how they're hurting. But it doesn't. There's a whole great world out there, little girl . . ."

"Don't call me little girl," said Sarat.

"A whole great world, more than can fit in the eye of your Templestowe."

He smiled when Sarat's brows furrowed at the mention of her rifle's name. "That's right, we know secrets here too. But we're your friends, and a lot of them out there ain't."

He pointed toward a half-open window, through which a sliver of downtown Atlanta sizzled in the heat and grime. "Just down the street, there's FSS men who'd hand you over to the Blues tomorrow if they thought it'd buy them a little more favor with Columbus, or give them better odds of pushing forward that white flag they call a peace plan. There's cowards, there's rats, and now you're food for all of them."

"And you gonna save me, is that right?" Sarat said. "You and those little boys of yours? That kid Attic who got took by some of his own? The other one, couldn't even get his farmer's suit to blow before the Blues killed him? Look at this place—you're living in a goddamn cave under the highway, talking talk while those FSS cowards sell out the whole of the Red. Hell, you should be asking me for help, not the other way round."

Bragg Sr. laughed, his black gums showing. He turned to his aides. "She's dumb the way we used to be dumb," he said. "It don't ever change, don't ever change."

Facing Sarat again, he said, "Darling, don't you understand? You're here because I like you. There's not one of my men as man as you, none that managed to do what you did—a general! The biggest goddamn get since President Daniel Ki!—that's why you're here. I would like to keep you around, keep you from falling into their hands. Because, believe me, now that they got the son of the man you killed running the Southern offensive, he'll burn down whole cities trying to find out who did it. And if he finds out it was you, he'll string you up."

"So let him," Sarat said. "I'm not afraid to die."

"That's because you're young and you think dying's quick," Bragg Sr. said. "But they got ways to make dying take just as long as living."

"So what do you want me to do, then? Crawl in a hole and wait?"

"Yeah, that's pretty well it. Go on back to that nice little charity house you have by the river and stay there. Don't go anywhere near Halfway, don't go whoring around with that barkeeper's daughter in Augusta." He paused and smiled. "Yeah, we know about that too—and make sure your sister stays there with you, your brother, the whole damn family. Wait till the fire dies out from Junior's blood up there in Columbus, and then I promise we'll help you put a bullet in his head too, if that's what you want."

"You done?" Sarat said.

"Yeah, darling," the old man replied. "I'm done."

Sarat stood. "Thanks for the advice," she said, and left.

☆ ☆ ☆

THE RESIDUE of the conversation lingered with her as Attic drove her home. She felt emboldened by having stood up to the man whose whims turned the currents of the Southern rebellion. She shifted in the passenger seat of the old sedan, leaned her head out the window. Even the saline Atlanta smog felt like a mountain breeze.

"Let's stop in the Floordeelee for a drink," she said. "I know they don't pay you shit; I'll buy."

"I have to take you home," Attic said.

"What, they hire you by the hour or something? It's just a drink—won't take much time."

Attic shook his head. "They don't like me over there," he mumbled. "Not my place."

For a moment she thought he was talking about Bragg and his men, then she realized he meant something else altogether.

"Christ, are you serious?" she said. "So you got no fear about picking up a gun and going to the Tennessee line, but you're too scared to go into your own people's neighborhood because they got different skin?"

Her words seemed to shame him into acquiescence; soon they drove into the New Fourth Ward. It was a cramped mass of towers on the east side of the city, adjacent to the grounds of a sprawling electronics factory from which a steady high-pitched din emanated at all hours.

The housing complexes, high and gray, were barely an arm's length apart—such that, between them, the buildings formed a narrow labyrinth of alleys. The cramped streets were lined with shirt vendors and stalls full of produce smuggled from the vertical farms, as well as money-movers and Tik-Tok mechanics and Just-A-RedBuck Stores.

They parked on the outskirts of the neighborhood and walked in, traversing the narrow inlets of asphalt between the buildings. Power lines ran down from the solar panels that covered all the roofs and from one building to another, creating a latticework overhead. Some of the old men and women sitting in the street watched Sarat and Attic as they passed, but it was the tall, bald girl that caught their interest, not the thin Utah boy who walked with his head lowered behind her.

The Floordeelee was a brick shack. It stood at the end of a narrow peninsula penned in on three sides by residential towers. Outside, there was an open space littered with old card tables and folding chairs. At all hours of the day and night the tables were full or nearly full.

Sarat and Attic bought a couple of drinks and sat at one of the tables. She drank a Kingway and he nursed a Coke.

"So you're indebted to the old man for life now, huh?" said Sarat. "Since he pulled some strings and got you out of that mess you were in?"

"I was indebted to him before then," said Attic. "He saved me and my brothers in Utah. Without him we'd all be dead."

"So what ever happened to ya'll in Utah anyway? You just hide out in that farm the whole time? I heard they found one of your brothers in a pile of pig shit or something."

Attic said nothing. She tried to get him to talk about his life before the Red, but he wouldn't. In time she did manage to shame him into having a couple of beers. Soon his shoulders seemed to loosen. As dusk rolled over the city, both he and Sarat were pleasantly drunk.

"See, the problem with men like Bragg is they think it's their right to run the place," said Sarat, slurring the words but adamant in her conviction. "They never known what it's like not to run the place, think they can just tell you what to do and you gotta listen like you got no say, like you got no thoughts, like you ain't even *alive.*"

Attic seemed to look past her, at a group of small children running barefoot through the alley, playing tag.

"See, it's like what Albert Gaines told me once—you ever met Gaines?"

"No," said Attic.

"You should. He's got this whole war figured out—he ain't like them other old idiots. He told me once, he said, Listen, because I'm about to tell you the gist of every opinion that's ever been had."

Sarat leaned forward, as though imparting a great secret. "All these old men want it to be like it was when they were young. But it'll never be like that again, and they'll never be young again, no matter what they do. And it's not just ours that do it. It's theirs too. Imagine if the North had just let us be. Imagine if they didn't fight us tooth and nail, kill all those innocent people, just to keep us from having a country of our own and doing things our own way—would it really have been so bad? No, of course it wouldn't. But it wasn't that way when all those old people that run everything were young, so they can't let it be. But you and I"—she pointed at the children playing on the street behind her—"and them too: we're young, and we ain't bound by what they bound by. We're gonna pull the power from their hands, because when it comes down to it, they don't really care 'bout the Red. Only thing they ever cared 'bout was themselves. But us, we're *of* this place. We . . ."

"I'm not of this place," said Attic.

"But you care about it. About the Southern cause."

"I don't."

Sarat sat back in her chair, surprised by the nothingness in his voice. "Then why were you fighting for it, then?" she asked. "Why'd you pick up a gun and risk being torn to shreds by the Blues if you don't care for the cause?"

"I wanted to be something," said Attic. He looked past Sarat to where the smiling children played. "I just wanted to be something."

☆ ☆ ☆

IT WAS NIGHTTIME when they finally got back to her home. He was new to drunkenness and after a half-hour of swerving badly along the highways, she made him pull over and she took the wheel.

The old fossil car was not nearly as nimble as the sun-powered Tik-Toks, but it carried within it a beast of a motor. Every now and then Sarat pushed her foot against the pedal just to hear the ancient thing roar.

When she got home she found Karina and Simon in the backyard. Simon sat on a kitchen chair facing the river, wearing a silver bowl for a hat. Carefully, Karina sheared the hairs protruding from beneath the bowl. She'd hung paper lanterns between the trees. Their candlelight spilled through cutouts in the shape of snowflakes. Simon was laughing, squirming in his seat as Karina brushed the fresh skin on the back of his neck with the cold handles of her scissors.

"Where's my sister?" said Sarat, startling them both. The smile disappeared from Karina's face and in its place came something more neutral.

"I don't know," she said. "Left with her friend the reef pilot this afternoon. Gone to Augusta, I guess."

Sarat waved the maid inside. "Go fix him some dinner."

"All right," said Karina. "Soon as I finish cutting his hair."

"No. Do it now."

Karina set her scissors down. Sarat could see a trickle of venom in the way the maid looked at her, and she met it with the same. As Karina left, Simon looked back at her. "Don't worry, baby boy," she said. "I'll be back in a minute."

When there was nothing else left to look at, Simon turned to his sister. He seemed ridiculous to her, sitting in the yard with a silver bowl on his head like a little boy playing spaceman.

"She's trying to make you like a child," said Sarat, tossing the bowl aside. "She's treating you like a little baby. But you like it, don't you?"

Simon said nothing. She turned his head to face the river and started cutting his hair. She tried to undo the bowl cut, but Karina had already done too much damage, and she had no choice but to finish it.

"She's not family, you know," she whispered into her brother's ear. "She might treat you nice, but she's not family. She's a stranger, and you know full well what strangers can do."

As she leaned in to talk to her brother she breathed in the new smell of him, the smell he'd taken on since Patience. It was to her a sour, nauseating scent—the smell of curdling milk. She tried to remember what he smelled like before, back in the camp.

She recalled sometimes he'd come home drunk from one of his rebel excursions and she'd catch the Joyful on him, but that was a temporary thing, a costume for his breath. Had there ever been another? Did he ever smell the way she smelled, the way Dana smelled? She couldn't remember, and in her struggle to recall what her brother had been like before he was stripped of himself, she discovered she was angry at him. She was angry at him for not dying in Patience. Had he simply done what all the other men on the execution line had done, she would have forever known him as a martyr, not a marionette—a dumbstruck plaything for doting housekeepers and idiot widows. What was left now was a hollow stencil of the brother she once knew, his very existence polluting her memories of him, burying and displacing the fine, brave boy that was. He should have died.

Caught up in these thoughts, she failed to notice that Simon was crying. He made no sound, looked straight ahead, but she could see the tears in the lanterns' weak snowflake light.

"What is it," she said, "your own sister not good enough for you? You trust a stranger more? You happier with some woman you know nothing about?" As she spoke she could hear her voice rising, and she knew it would carry inside the house, but she did not care. "She ain't even from the Red. Her mother and father, they live up there in the North, with the Blues. The same Blues that did this to you, that killed our father and our mother, the Blues that kill and humiliate our people every single day. And you like her better? You like her better than your own blood?"

It was only when her brother, weeping openly now, recoiled with his hands against his face that she realized she had instinctively brought her own hand up to strike him.

Sarat threw the scissors in the dirt. She went inside, past where Karina stood in the kitchen. She went to her sister's room and shut the door behind her. She lay in her sister's empty bed, beneath the soft sheets that glared a pinkish silver under the light. The sheets smelled of beautiful things—of citrus and jasmine cream. But they also smelled of Dana, of her hair and of her skin and of her breath. The smell Sarat knew from childhood, the smell of Chestnuts.

☆ ☆ ☆

JUST BEFORE DAWN, she woke to the sound of a knock on the door. For a second she thought it was Dana, but instead she saw Karina.

"What are you still doing here?" said Sarat. "You're spending the night here now?" She chuckled bitterly. "You sleeping with him too?"

"Sarat, there's a man outside," said Karina. "It's about your sister."

Before the slick of sleep had gone from her eyes, Sarat was running out the door. She found another of Bragg's boys in the driveway. He had his head lowered as though he'd done something wrong.

"Speak," said Sarat. "What happened to her?"

"The Birds," mumbled the boy.

☆ ☆ ☆

THEY DROVE most of the way to Augusta. Just before they reached the hospital, she saw the wreckage by the side of the road.

A group of locals from the nearby town had gathered around the twisted remains of the vehicles, gawking at the carnage. The remains were of three cars and a bus. The bus was charred although the shape of its body held, but the Tik-Toks had been cracked open like fortune cookies, and no longer resembled cars at all. A crater severed the road.

They drove to the nearest hospital. It was more of a clinic, no bigger than a diner, and had once been an animal hospital before the war. Relatives of the dead and injured crowded the entrance and the lobby. Alongside them were members of the United Rebels, who had been dispatched from Atlanta to document the carnage. Sarat shoved past them all, yelling her sister's name, until Adam Bragg Jr. took her by the arm and led her to a room near the back of the clinic.

They passed a silent spectacle of the dead and dying. The bus had been carrying migrant Southern workers returning from the Blue border of South Carolina. They'd been hired as part of an agreement engineered quietly between Atlanta and Columbus to send workers to help fix cracks in the Northern quarantine wall. It was dangerous work for little pay, and no Union laborer would do it.

The men and women lay covered in stained white sheets, their relatives gathered around them. The nurses and doctors, greatly outnumbered, moved from patient to patient with grim resignation.

She found the room where her sister lay. Before she entered, she heard Bragg Jr. as he tried to tell her something—"It was just dumb luck," he said. "They haven't had control over those things in years." But his voice sounded very far away.

She closed the door behind her, and the sounds of the pained and wailing were muted.

The girl on the bed ended at the knees. The sheet on which she lay and the one that partially covered her were colored a red that, in places, had darkened to black. The clothing had been sheared off her, and the skin below was blistered and burned.

Sarat stood over her sister. She ran her hand along the skin of Dana's thigh. She felt the indentation in the skin where someone must have tried to stem the hemorrhaging wound. She saw the coal marking on her sister's forehead—"3:49," the time the tourniquet was tied.

She saw the chest rise and fall for the last time. She saw the eyes flicker, the lips move.

"It's going to be all right," said Sarat, but it was not Sarat making the words. They left her mouth but they belonged to an impostor. "It's going to be all right. Just stay with me, it's going to be all right." The room smelled of rubbing alcohol.

Sarat dropped to her knees and rested her head on her sister's chest. Dana's fingers curled around hers.

"Beautiful girl," Dana said. "I miss you already."

☆ ☆ ☆

FOR THE NEXT WEEK Sarat did not set foot inside her house, except to lock Dana's bedroom door and prohibit Karina from ever coming anywhere near it.

She slept outside, sometimes in the woodshed but other times on the damp soil by the river, near the plot where Karina's crops struggled to grow. At night she dreamed of drowning.

A month after she set her sister's ashes free in the Savannah, the Blues finally came for Sarat. One night she heard music among the trees; a whisper of hands against bark, of feet against earth, very faintly in the distance. The night was quiet but enveloped in the quiet was a murmur. Years later, she would recall a pinprick of red light moving across the woodshed wall. Then the door creaked open. A canister tumbled into the woodshed, and the room erupted in sound and light.

Excerpted from:

THE CIVIL WAR ARCHIVE PROJECT—
SUGARLOAF DETAINEE LETTERS (CLEARED/UNCLASSIFIED)

Dear [redacted],

I received your letter in February. [redacted] from the [redacted] humanitarian team delivered it to me. As usual, [redacted] read it first, so I don't know if I got the whole thing. But I am grateful to [redacted], who has tried [redacted] best to help me, and of course to you for writing.

I'm still in Camp Saturday. There are [redacted] of us here, I think, but it's hard to tell. We are still in isolation, and the [redacted] us every [redacted].

Since [redacted] took over, things have gotten worse. He [redacted], I think, but I've never seen his face. I think it was him who ordered them to take our books, our sleeping shades, our toothpaste packets, and everything else that reminded us we're still human beings. I know he had to give his permission for them to [redacted] us after we started our protest.

It happens at all hours. Day, night, there's no difference here. First they'll come in and tell you to quit being difficult, to just eat.

When you refuse, they take you to another room. There [redacted]. [redacted]. [redacted] [redacted]. [redacted]. [redacted].

[redacted]. [redacted]. [redacted]. [redacted]. [redacted]. [redacted]. [redacted].

[redacted]. [redacted]. [redacted]. [redacted]

[redacted]. [redacted]. [redacted].

[redacted]. [redacted]. [redacted]. [redacted]. [redacted]. [redacted]. [redacted]. [redacted].

I heard [redacted] believes one of us killed his father. But I've been here for years, long before any of that. I never even saw [redacted], never heard of him before one of the [redacted] told us what happened.

Everything else is the same. The days go by. [redacted], except for [redacted], when we get to see the sun.

I know they've stopped telling people how many of us are still being [redacted]. [redacted]. They've been trying everything they can think of to make us quit. There's a nurse here, and [redacted] does everything in [redacted] power to make [redacted] as possible. I don't know why. I told [redacted] it's a violation of [redacted] oath, but [redacted] doesn't care. I begged the guard, but he cares even less.

I heard there's talk of peace back home. I hope for your benefit that it's true, but I don't think it matters much for us. We've been here too long. Whatever we were before this is all gone. People here speak to themselves. They see ghosts. I dream about you and [redacted], and about [redacted], and about home. I hope to hear from you soon.

Yours with love,

[redacted]

CHAPTER TWELVE

They were brought to Sugarloaf in roaring airborne beasts, chained to the floors and chained to each other. Eye-masks and earmuffs severed them from their surroundings. Through their pores the captives took in what little information there was to be had about the thing that carried them—a vast metal cavity, scorching hot as it sat for hours on the tarmac of some clandestine airfield and, soon after the plane ascended, bitterly cold. When the mouths opened to beg for water or relief from the chains, the skin felt other things—the hardness of a rifle butt, the steel-backed tip of a boot. The mouths closed. The bodies flew, dumb as idols, over the Florida Sea.

Only the very crest of the hill remained above water, the last vestige of the peninsular state. Upon it was built an artificial island of stone and concrete, rounded and circled with high razor-wire fencing. A jut of unused land, about fifty feet in length, extended beyond the fence to the shore. Here, but for a strip cleared to build a dock, the grass ran wild and the ground was thick with weeds.

The grass camouflaged the island. When the storm clouds cleared and the residents of the southern Georgia coast were able to look far into the Florida Sea, they sometimes mistook Sugarloaf for a trick of the eye—a tropical sea-dwelling mirage.

The women were kept in cages while the camps were reordered and their male captives segregated. The cages were small and the taller detainees could not stand without crouching.

Guards in black masks patrolled the cages. The masks hid their faces but their youth was evident in the skin around their eyes. The guards called the women in the cages by the last two digits of their detainee numbers, and called each other by their initials. As such, whenever the senior officers ordered the guards to move the women to other cages or to the Non-Compliance Area, the instructions sounded like moves in a game of chess.

But sometimes the guards accidentally used their real names. This was how the women, who had little to do but sit and listen, learned the identities of the soldiers who walked hourly among them. The tall one with the blue eyes was Lillyman; the kind one with the accent, who used to smuggle water bottles through the fencing and was soon removed from duty, was named Izzy. The one with the thick neck—the cruel one—was Bud Baker.

In time the women learned other things too: the names of the guards' hometowns, of their children and their pets. They learned a feeble geography of the camps, and of the officers' suburb, which lay on the other end of the island. And although none of these things were useful to them in their squat, vacant pens, the women committed all the information to memory, held the things they learned close like yet-unsharpened shanks.

Sometimes the women complained about the blinding heat or about the size of their cages or the smell of their unwashed jumpsuits. When any woman did this too frequently or too loudly, a small team of armed guards would rush the cage and drag the captive to the Non-Compliance Area. A day later a woman so taken would return to her cage, and would not complain anymore. Soon, all the prisoners stopped complaining.

☆ ☆ ☆

SARAT CHESTNUT'S CAGE faced what she believed to be the sea. She heard the waves breaking against the shore, just beyond the guard towers and a forest of leaning reeds. In storm season, when the sky overhead thickened and lit up, the waves rose high and crashed into the stone beaches. Other times the waves were calm, and made a sound like a dog slowly lapping from a bowl. Chained and unable to stand upright in her tiny cage, she strained to glimpse the water, but the sea lay beyond reach.

In the first weeks of her captivity she did not speak, neither to the guards who watched her nor to the women nearby. The guards took her silence as a passive defiance, and often threatened to take her to the Non-Compliance Area. The women, put off by her refusal to talk, began to suspect her as some kind of foreigner—perhaps a spy, or a Blue banished to this place for treason.

Instead she listened to the sea. She nursed a broken rib suffered during the night the soldiers came to take her in Lincolnton. In time the pain in her chest dulled and breathing became less difficult, but the weeks she spent crouching and sitting in the cage began to inflame her knees and her back. To remedy this she knelt into a child's pose, which she held until Bud or one of the other guards came and ordered her to get up.

She waited on death. She had no doubt that soon the troop of masked guards would come to take her—not to the Non-Compliance Area, but to some courtroom in the heart of the Blue.

She imagined being led in, shackled, before rows and rafters full of indignant, jeering Northerners. She imagined standing before the firing squad, a line of young soldiers no different from the ones who once hovered in Templestowe's eye. She imagined facing their softly trembling hands and smiling. Because no matter what they did with her afterward—in which unmarked grave they buried her or wherever they scattered her incinerated remains—she would find her way to the river. She would find her way to her sister. She waited in her cage and thoughts of death sustained her.

At the end of the third month, the women were moved into the camps. The ones who had put up no resistance were issued white uniforms and taken to Camp Thursday, where they were allowed the privileges of communal living. Others were dressed in blue, and taken to solitary cells in Camp Friday or Camp Saturday.

Some of the women spoke of another place, Camp Sunday. The stories they told of that place struck Sarat as the stuff of depraved medieval fantasy, and at first she didn't believe the camp existed.

After three days in Camp Thursday, they took her to her first Visitation. She was led to a small complex of prefabricated offices, unmarked save for cameras hanging from the ceiling. The walls were plain and reinforced to keep the sound from traveling.

She was ordered to sit on a small metal chair next to a metal table. Her arms were chained to the arms of the chair and her ankles to shackles in the floor. Soon the guards were gone and the room was quiet.

She sat alone for three hours. A fire began to grow along her spine. She tried to shift her position but the chair was bolted in place, and no movement of her neck could keep her muscles from seizing.

The door opened. A short woman about ten years Sarat's senior came in. She was dressed like the women who worked for the government in Atlanta. She folded her suit jacket and placed it gently on the table. She sat down.

"We know exactly what you did, Sara Chestnut," she said.

It was only then that Sarat realized her captors had no idea what she did—not only because the woman had called her by her old first name, the one she'd abandoned so many years ago, but also because if the Blues had known about her crimes, there would be no need for an interrogation, no need to extract any confession. They knew nothing; perhaps they'd apprehended her on some vague suspicion, after seeing her visit the United Rebels' compound. Perhaps she was simply a part of some random sweep, a fishing expedition.

"If you talk now—if you tell us everything and give us the names of the people you worked with—I might still be able to help you," said the woman. She leaned slightly forward. "There's still time, Sara. There's still a chance for you to leave this place, to go back to Simon and to Dana. To do the right thing. All you have to do is be honest with me. Can you be honest with me, Sara?"

"I didn't do nothing," said Sarat.

The woman closed her eyes for a moment and shook her head. "Sara," she said, "I know you think I'm your enemy, but I'm here to help you. My bosses in Columbus, they want to lock you up forever, they want to keep you from ever seeing your home again. They look at you and this is all they see . . ."

From her briefcase the woman produced a set of glossy photographs. She fanned them on the table. The photographs were of wreckage, the charred husk of a car torn apart. For a moment Sarat thought the pictures were of her sister's death. But that couldn't be—the scenery was different, and the woman didn't even seem to know Dana was dead. She saw gutted sandbags strewn about, the remains of a checkpoint. In one of the pictures, the fortified center of the Northern capital hovered in the distance.

The confusion on Sarat's face must have been evident, because the woman quickly put the photos away.

"Of course I know you didn't do this, Sara, but this is what my bosses see," she said. "But I told them, Just give me a chance; I can talk to her. I read your file, Sara. I know you've been through some terrible tragedy.

And I know you wouldn't want innocent people—in the South or the North—to go through the same thing."

The woman looked over her shoulder, as though to check that no one was within earshot. "You know my grandparents come from Alabama," she said. "I guess you can say I've got the South in my blood. I know these values mean something to you, Sara—protecting the weak, telling the truth, doing what's right. What's *right.* I want to go back to my bosses in Columbus, Sara, and I want to be able to tell them what I know to be true: that you're not a bad person, that you don't have the blood of innocent people on your hands. And if I tell them that, they'll listen to me, and they'll send you home, and you can be with Dana and with Simon again in Lincolnton. I can help you, Sara, but I need you to help me."

"I didn't do nothing," said Sarat.

Some of the softness dissipated from the woman's face. Her voice, once soothing, hardened.

"You know some of the people you're protecting, we already caught them," she said. "They're right here, in this place, and they've already told us about you. They've already turned on you to save themselves. Do you really want to see them go free while you spend the rest of your life in a cell?"

"I didn't do nothing," said Sarat.

"Albert Gaines told us about you," the woman said. The mention of the name caused an involuntary twitch in Sarat, but she said nothing.

"That's right," the woman continued. "Albert Gaines gave you up. He told us you're an insurrectionist. Do you want us to believe him, Sara? Do you want us to treat you the way we treat insurrectionists?"

"I didn't do nothing," said Sarat.

The woman shook her head once more and rose from her seat. "This can be easy, Sara, or this can be hard. The choice is yours."

"I didn't do nothing," said Sarat.

The woman left the room. Soon a masked guard appeared. Even before he removed his mask, Sarat recognized him by his frame and by the thickness of his neck. Some of the guards were always careful never to show their faces to the detainees, but this one did not seem to care. He drew close and looked at her with hollow, contemptuous eyes.

Before she could turn her head, he slapped her across the face. Her head snapped but the rest of the body, chained in place, did not move.

"You dumb Red dyke," said Bud. "We're going to make you sing."

The soldier called a pack of four others into the room. They wore blue gloves and had covered faces and were made larger by the shells of their armor.

"Take her to the Light Room," said Bud.

She was transferred to a room in the basement of another building. The room was made of concrete and was empty save for two anchors bolted to the ground. A set of large white floodlights covered the entirety of the wall opposite the anchors.

The guards chained Sarat's ankles to her wrists, and both to the anchors in the floor, such that she was forced into a deep and immobilizing squat. The guards left the room, and for a moment nothing happened. Then the floodlights came alive with a loud electric pop, and the room was drowned in eviscerating whiteness.

Sarat closed her eyes. The white light now turned a hot red against her eyelids. She lowered her head and for a while the onslaught was bearable. But soon the room began to grow warmer. Sweat dripped from her skin, her knees burned with the weight of her body.

On the third day, the door opened. A masked guard stepped forward and dropped a bowl of food and another of water on the ground where Sarat was shackled. The bowls were made of a soft rubber and half their contents spilled on the floor where they landed. The guard left and the door swung closed.

One bowl contained a thin brown gruel speckled with white flakes. Unable to move her arms, Sarat struggled to get at the food. She grasped at it with her fingers and leaned as far forward as she was able. Feebly, she tossed it toward her mouth. The gruel tasted sulfuric, rotten. But she wolfed it down, deranged with hunger. Soon her jumpsuit and the ground surrounding her were splattered with remnants of the meal. Under the heat of the floodlights, the gruel began to decompose. Every other day, the guard returned and dropped two bowls on the ground.

By the tenth day, the throbbing in her head and her knees consumed her. The room filled with her shrieking, and the small red darkness she lived in while her eyes were closed now seemed to exist even when her eyes were open. On the twentieth day, the guards removed her.

In the Visitation room, the woman in the neatly pressed suit asked Sarat if she'd had a change of heart.

"I didn't do nothing," said Sarat, slumped in her shackling chair.

The woman stood and left the room. Soon Bud returned. In the fog of her damaged vision he seemed to move in place, blurry as a half-remembered dream. He grabbed her by the fuzz of hair that had grown back on her skull during her time in captivity.

"How do you think this is going to end?" asked the guard, his breath hot on the side of her face. "Do you think this ends with you winning? With us giving up? You're going to sing, I promise you."

He let her go and called the guards back in. "Take her to the Sound Room," he said.

☆ ☆ ☆

IN THE MONTHS BETWEEN VISITATIONS, Sarat lived in a cell in Camp Saturday. The cell was square, and standing in its middle with her arms outstretched, Sarat could brush all four walls with her fingers. The walls were of concrete and were painted the color of margarine. A metal cot and a metal toilet bowl occupied opposite ends of the cell, otherwise it was bare. An overhead light shone at all hours of the day and night, erasing the difference between them. Deprived of the cycle of the day (and, in time, the seasons), the mind made do with the only indicator of passing time available to it: the footsteps of the guards outside.

The guards walked up and down the corridors of Camp Saturday at all hours. Every three minutes, the slit in Sarat's cell door would open, and a pair of eyes would inspect the room, and then the slit would close again. In time the sound of metal slits opening and closing all along the corridor became a kind of metronome, against which Sarat measured the dawn and death of the day. Eventually she came to know the peering eyes by heart, and gave their owners names of her own invention.

Sometimes she heard screams from the nearby cells. Sometimes the women waited on a guard to open the slit in the door and then tried to throw cupped handfuls of shit and piss in their eyes. A few minutes later a small troop of masked guards would rush the agitator's cell, and the woman would be carried kicking and screaming to the Non-

Compliance Area. In a week or two she would return, and no more noises would come from her cell.

The woman in the cell next to Sarat's was named Elena. She was from Mississippi, and had lost her mind. Softly she spoke to Sarat through the concrete, in a voice that passed so clearly through the wall that for months Sarat believed it to be a fabrication of her own torture-fevered brain.

Elena said she had been born in this place, caged here from birth because the Blues knew her to be a terrorist from the day she entered the world. She said Sugarloaf had once rested on a vast outcropping of land and was free of cages and free of fences. She sang songs about alligators and swamps and talking rodents.

Amidst the shuffling of the guards' feet and the rambling screams of the women, Sarat listened to her neighbor's voice the same way she listened to her own breathing—passively, without thought. But at other times it was the only thing she could hear, a reminder she was still alive.

Sometimes Sarat talked back to the voice sliding softly through the walls, and in these times she lied. When Elena asked her where she came from, she said South Carolina, and invented an elaborate lie about her escape from the illness unleashed upon that state. She enjoyed lying to her faceless neighbor, and enjoyed that the neighbor seemed to believe it. During the worst of her Visitations, when after weeks of mistreatment she returned to her cell hallucinating with pain, it provided some small comfort to retreat into a wholly fabricated existence.

Still, she resisted. The Visitations came in waves—sometimes the woman in the neatly pressed suit didn't come to see her for months at a time, until Sarat allowed herself to believe that perhaps the interrogations had finally come to an end. Sometimes, the woman seemed a permanent resident of the island, and would call on Sarat almost daily. Weeks alone in the rooms of Sound and Light dulled her senses, until the world beyond arm's reach became a muddled nimbus she could no longer decipher. The positions in which they shackled her slowly wore the cartilage from her knees and warped her back into a curving column of pain. Still, she resisted.

☆ ☆ ☆

IN HER THIRD YEAR on the island, Sarat participated in a hunger strike. Elena said women from every camp were taking part, refusing to eat or drink anything but water. She said some women had already been doing it for weeks. She said one had even died from it—a suicide of sorts, something the guards called "Going asymmetric."

She said the women had a list of demands, chief among them freedom. Failing that, they wanted their loved ones flown in to visit; lawyers from the Red to represent them; and the right to something whose name sounded foreign to Sarat's ears (she assumed it to be a drug or a religious text). The women in the solitary cells demanded time in the communal yard, a chance to see the sun.

Sarat made no demands. She could no more imagine negotiating better treatment from her captors than negotiating the stinger away from a scorpion. Her silence was the one weapon they could not pry from her; to hand it to them in the form of hopeless appeals seemed to her an act of high cowardice, a tacit admission that the brutal kinetics of Sugarloaf obeyed some kind of law. For the same reason she refused to meet the ones they called humanitarian envoys, who swooped in on Sugarloaf every few months with looks of stern disapproval plastered on their faces, for the same reason she spat in the face of the woman with the neatly pressed suit, for the same reason she tore the pages of the one book they allowed her and glued them with smeared shit to the slit of her cell door—for the same reason, Sarat made no demands.

Instead she simply refused to eat. In starvation she took the levers of torture out of her torturers' hands and placed them in her own. In starvation she found agency, control.

A week into her strike and concussed with hunger, she was taken by the guards to the medical facility.

She was led into a room with high white ceilings. Black sheets covered the windows and muted the sunlight. The room smelled familiar to Sarat—it was the smell of rubbing alcohol. She remembered the last time she saw her sister.

A single cot, raised to the incline of a dentist's chair, stood in the center of the room. Laid out on a steel table nearby were a set of hypodermic needles, a coiled rubber tube, a box of disposable gloves, and two bags of clear fluid.

The guards lifted her onto the bed. She felt straps tighten around her wrists and around her ankles and around her chest. Viselike restraints locked her gaze to the white empty ceiling.

At the edge of her periphery she saw one of the soldiers standing at the table. He wore a white coat and a stethoscope around his neck but she knew he was a soldier. He uncoiled the rubber tube and affixed it to one of the fluid bags, which he then attached to a metal stand. She watched out the corner of her eye as he began applying a glistening, mucuslike substance to the end of the rubber tube, before Bud the guard stopped him.

"No need for that," Bud said. "She's a big, strong girl."

Amidst the convulsions that followed, they fed her. The white ceiling to which her eyes were locked began to fill with brilliant stars. The cot shook; she felt the hands of the guards holding her in place. The acidic aftertaste of the feeding fluid crawled up her throat and leaked out her slack mouth. It tasted of her insides.

Midway through the feeding, a gust of wind sheared the black sheet from one of the windows. A beam of sunlight entered the room. Sarat closed her eyes and felt the warmth that grazed the very ends of her toes. Faintly, very far away, she heard the sound of children playing.

☆ ☆ ☆

FOR THREE DAYS in January a storm rattled the island. The rain made a sound like the patter of huge insects crawling on the prison walls. The women huddled and screamed in their solitary cells.

The storm spared Sarat her daily feeding. Hunger returned this time as mercy. On the fourth day, her cell door opened, and Bud came inside. He arrived with the usual entourage of guards but he made them wait outside. He closed the cell door behind him.

She knew it was him before he appeared, the meter of his steps down the hallway a fingerprint. It amazed her sometimes, how much she knew about a man she was supposed to know nothing about—the way his cheeks reddened when he cursed her, as though the sound of his own voice infuriated him; the way his upper lip drew closer to his nostrils in a feigned expression of disgust whenever he told a lie. She knew him the way animals know the weather, and from some indefinable thing living in the very presence of him, she'd learned to divine the severity of impending storms.

But today she could not read him. There was a calmness about his hollow eyes; the veins of his neck untensed. She detected in his stocky face the expression of a child on the eve of Christmas, impatient and electric with anticipation.

He sat at the foot of the bed. Instinctively, Sarat recoiled. She smelled the mess tent breakfast on him, the smell of fryer oil. He looked at the place by the bed where Sarat's last trickle of vomit had dried into a sand-colored crust. He chuckled.

"Tell me, do you believe in any of that Hindu shit?" he said. "They got a book about it in the library here; got so bored one night I started reading it. You believe any of that stuff about coming back as a toad or an ant or something if you were real bad in your last life? I mean, I saw what you did with that Bible we gave you; I know you're no Christian, so maybe you believe in that stuff."

Sarat said nothing. Bud cracked his knuckles. She waited for the cheeks to redden, the vein to emerge, and she readied her mind to take her to a faraway place.

"I've been thinking about that for a while now," Bud said. "Because I got to thinking I must have done some real terrible shit in my last life—burned down an orphanage or something. That's got to be why I ended up here, stuck playing babysitter to a cageful of goddamned animals."

The slit in the doorway opened. A guard looked inside. Bud waved him away. In that moment Sarat imagined lunging at his sweat-glistened neck, digging into the skin with her teeth. But what her mind imagined, her body no longer had the strength to do, and when again he turned to her and put his hand on her knee, she spat in his direction but what came out was spittle.

"But see, then I got to thinking I couldn't have done anything too bad, right?" said Bud. "I couldn't have done anything too bad, because then I would have come back as you."

He patted her softly on the knee and then he stood.

"Remember when you first got here?" he asked. "Remember how you used to press your face against the cage like a dog, trying to get a look at the water? Well, guess what, Sara Chestnut? We're going to take you to the water."

☆ ☆ ☆

SHE WAS MOVED by the guards to a different place, a small building she had never seen before. The building was white and unmarked; it stood at the edge of a fenced and barricaded complex that resembled Camp Saturday but was much smaller. The complex lay near the edge of the island; as the guards led her inside, Sarat could hear the distant crashing of waves.

They took her to a windowless room, lit harshly by the halo of an old, prewar incandescent. The bulb hung on a string from a low white ceiling.

Just as in the place where they fed her, a cot stood in the center of the room. The same people were present: soldiers in guard uniforms and soldiers in white coats. But this time the ones in the guard uniforms stood near the cot, and the soldiers in the white uniforms stood in the periphery of the room; when Sarat looked at them they looked away.

Once again she was strapped in place, and although she caught no sight of the usual implements on the bedside table, she closed her eyes and waited to be fed. But instead she felt a sheet of soft cloth laid upon her face, and then she heard the voice of the woman in the neatly pressed suit.

"If you want this to stop, Sara," the voice whispered, "you'll cooperate."

The voice went away. The room turned silent. And then Sarat was drowning.

The water moved, endless. She entered and exited death, her body no longer hers. Spasms of light and heat encased her; the mind seized with fear and panic. She drowned yet death would not come. It was in this way her captors finally broke her.

To end the drownings she admitted to all the crimes with which they charged her—complicity in all manner of insurrectionist violence, things she'd never heard of before. She admitted her role in the killing of three Blue informants in the New Fourth Ward and in a car bombing on the outskirts of Columbus. When asked about insurgents she knew, she said all she knew; when asked about those she didn't, she made up plausible lies. The woman in the neatly pressed suit presented to her reams of written confessions and she signed every page. There was no lie too big that her fear of drowning couldn't make it true.

☆ ☆ ☆

THE MONTHS THAT FOLLOWED brought relief. Slowly she was allowed the small precious things previously denied her—packets of soap and shampoo; books other than the Bible; black shades to block the overhead lights; spider-venom painkillers to dull the screaming of her knees and her back. For an hour a day she was led into the recreation yard, where she lay on the warm concrete at the foot of the fence and took in the sunlight, content as a house cat. They brought her food and she ate it all, voracious. The food was fatty and bland; soon she began to gain weight, because there was little to do but sit in her cell and eat. But she ate every bite, and they never had to force-feed her again.

Every other Friday, when the guards came to cut her nails and trim her hair, she sat still and let them. And on the Thursdays before they came, when her nails were longest, she dug them deep into the skin of her inner thighs until she felt the warm trickle of blood. The guards who looked in on her every few minutes must have thought she was masturbating; they let her be.

The following summer, the guards rotated, and Bud Baker left for good—but it didn't matter one way or the other to Sarat when Elena whispered the news through the cell block walls, because the girl whose soul the thick-necked guard had slowly strangled was also gone. The day assimilated the dark, the dark assimilated the day. Years passed.

☆ ☆ ☆

ONE DAY, long after her last Visitation, two guards came to Sarat's cell and took her back to the old building in which she had confessed. As she was led down the hallway, she recognized the place, but it felt dilapidated, unused. There was now a fine layer of dust on the chairs and on the table. An old, handwritten sign on one of the walls read, "Clean Up After Yourself."

Once again they sat her down, but this time the guards did not shackle the prisoner to the bolts in the ground. The soldiers left and soon a woman Sarat had never seen before entered the room. The woman was young and dressed in a formal blouse and skirt.

Sarat was gripped with a cold, crippling fear at the sight of her new visitor. She stared mute and motionless at the woman, and quietly she resolved to herself that if they tried to take her once more to that small white room, she would claw her own throat out before she let them strap her again to the drowning chair.

The woman sat down and set a plain folder on the table.

"Sara T. Chestnut?"

Sarat said nothing.

"Are you Sara Chestnut?" the woman asked again. "That's your name, yes?"

Sarat nodded. The woman removed from the folder three small stacks of stapled sheets.

"Sara, my name is Gabrielle," said the woman. "I'm a repatriation specialist with the Peace Office in Columbus. I want you to listen carefully—are you listening?—to what I'm going to tell you, because this is important. All right?"

Sarat nodded. The woman had a singsong voice, a cadence fit for explaining things to children.

"I'm going to ask you to read and sign these three forms," Gabrielle said. As soon as she said it, Sarat began signing the papers.

"Hold on, hold on, let me tell you what they are," said the woman. "Now pay attention: the first one is a declaration from the Peace Office. It states that the government of the United States, in capturing and temporarily detaining you as a suspected insurrectionist, was acting in good faith on information from a source the government now believes was not credible. It further states that, upon review, your status has been changed to No Longer Combatant. The second form is an agreement of indemnity, covering all branches and arms of the United States government in perpetuity. The third form is a solemn declaration that you will not engage in any action, nor counsel any action, against any branch or arm of the United States government, nor any of its members or representatives."

Sarat looked from the woman to the forms and back. "What do you want me to do?" she asked.

The woman leaned across the table. She took Sarat's hands in her own. The sensation of a stranger's bare skin on hers felt alien to Sarat. The sensation of proximity without violence felt alien.

"Sara, the war is over," said Gabrielle. "You're going home."

She heard the words, but they failed to register in her mind. Three times the woman repeated herself, until finally Sarat pushed her hands off and retreated from her chair to the corner of the room. There she knelt into a fetal ball and would not look at the woman or listen to anything else she had to say. Soon Gabrielle, exasperated, left the room, and the guards came in and dragged Sarat back to her cell.

A few days later they returned and took her again. But this time it was not to one of the Visitation buildings, but to the airstrip. There she was made to board a small plane alongside a group of fourteen women. The women looked haggard and disoriented in the glare of the early morning sun, and said nothing to one another as they boarded the plane.

Soon they were flying. From her small porthole window, Sarat peered out at the vast expanse of glittering blue surrounding the place that had been her prison. Her eyes badly damaged, she had trouble making out the geography over which the small plane flew. But she knew exactly what it was: the lapping Florida Sea, its bed thick with carpets of sea grass and schools of blind lionfish. It was real even though she could not see it clearly, and would remain real even if every last pair of eyes in the world went blind.

The plane crossed the sea and descended upon the mainland. Sarat was coming home.

Excerpted from:

FOUND CAUSE: DIARY OF A FORMER SOUTHERN RECRUITER

Some of the other ones would try all kinds of silliness. I knew one who would take them out to the middle of nowhere in the dead of the night and have them lie in open graves. He'd tell them, "This is where you're going to end up, trapped forever in a black hole in the ground, unless you fight for the cause of your people. The Lord takes good care of those who fight for the cause of their people." And that sort of thing was just fine if you were trying to get some burnout from the southern coast to put on a farmer's suit, but a lot of the smarter ones saw right through it.

What I found worked best was a lie slipped in with the truth. What I'd do is tell them about all sorts of terrible things the Blues had done—show them pictures of the victims from the firebombing of Burleson, the massacre at Patience, things like that. But along with those things, I'd tell them about the slaughter at Pleasant Ridge. Now the funny thing is, not once, in all my years working for the rebel South, did any recruit bother to find out if there had ever been a slaughter at Pleasant Ridge. They just assumed it to be true. The Blues had done so much to our people, why couldn't they have done that too? After a while, even I couldn't remember if there had been a slaughter at Pleasant Ridge.

That's what made it so easy to lie later on too, when the Blue surge came and they rounded us all up for interrogation. They wanted names and crimes and we gave them both in droves. One guy I knew just listed off everyone who worked on his old block. A week later the incursion force went and rounded up a bunch of accountants and butchers and grocery store clerks.

Eventually, it got to be that the Blues had so much unreliable information on their hands, they had to let all those people go. But it was like a snake eating its own tail—by the time they got around to emptying those detention camps, they'd already turned most of the people there into exactly what they'd needed them to be in the first place. I always said the camps at Sugarloaf were the best recruiters the South ever had.

IV

January, 2095
Lincolnton, Georgia

CHAPTER THIRTEEN

I remember the day I first met her, the day she invaded my life.

There was an iron gate that bordered our property, its entrance at the crossroads where the road met the winding driveway that led to the house. My mother had the gate built after she found out she was pregnant. She also paid the contractors to add another foot of concrete to the seawall. She even had them put in a smaller picket fence around the house itself, a moat that split us from the greenhouses and the rest of the property. My father said it was overkill; babies aren't made of glass. But my mother, who had once given up hope of ever having a child of her own, insisted. My father said some nights she used to stay up till sunrise, imagining all the ways that fate and the devil conspired to take her only child.

The two arms of the gate were decorated with twisting, curling bars that, when the gate closed and the two arms met, formed a metal outline of a pineapple. Near the entrance stood an old-fashioned mailbox, an antique from the days of government mail. A decorative wooden plaque atop the mailbox read: "Karina and Simon Chestnut."

Once, when my father was in his clouded place, he forgot to hit the clicker as the car approached the gate, and accidentally drove right into it. There wasn't much damage—he never drove very fast—and none of us were hurt, but my mother asked him not to take the car out again after that. Most days he was fine, and in regular conversation you'd never be able to guess the damage that had been done to him. But my mother said you just couldn't tell when the clouds would come over him and he'd retract from the world. Even a pristine mind can fog over, let alone one hurt that way. You just couldn't tell.

There was a buzzer in the grand room downstairs that went off whenever the gate opened. My mother, sick of the sharp sound it made, had recently ordered it altered to emit a prettier ring, two soft chimes followed by a faint rustling, like the sound of leaves in a breeze. On the night the stranger arrived, I heard the chimes; I climbed out of bed and ran downstairs.

My father was standing on the front steps. At the foot of our home, the driveway ended in a circle around my mother's rose garden. The roses were a pale pink. It was said by many a visitor that no such flower grew anywhere else in the South; the magic that encircled the Chestnuts' place sustained them.

I stood near my father and watched the car approach. It was the middle of winter. I was six years old. I still remember.

"You should be in bed," my father said. "You'll give your mother trouble tomorrow if you don't get your sleep."

But I pleaded, and he was too distracted by the looming car and our new guest to argue. I hid behind his leg and peered out, fascinated by the arrival of this stranger about whom my parents had argued for weeks.

The car pulled up to the house. The asphalt was newly laid and the wheels crunched against it. When my mother came out of the car she looked exhausted.

I'd seen her this way before—the previous winter, when Zenith came through and devastated the greenhouses. The house, made of fine red brick, withstood the storm, but throughout the property there were shards of glass, solar panels twisted and cracked. For five days straight she worked with the laborers to repair the damage. I remember seeing that drained look on her face. It was in those moments when I think she secretly wished my father was well enough to help her, that his mind was healed enough not just to carry on pleasant conversation, but to hold important things in memory, to keep from wandering to his clouded place. Sometimes, when I refused to go to bed or played in the parts of the yard that were off-limits, my mother would yell at me. It felt then like she was yelling twice at the same time, once for whatever I'd done and again because she was mad that it was always her who had to do the yelling.

The passenger door opened and from the car unfurled a huge, hunched body. The enormity of it blocked out the light from the driveway lamp and for a moment all I saw of her was a limbed wall of blackness.

"Welcome home, Sarat," my mother said.

The stranger moved slowly out of the light. My father descended the porch steps. He looked confused, his eyes squinting as though he were trying to focus on a very faraway thing.

"For God's sake, Simon," said my mother. "Don't you remember your own sister? Come here and give her a hug."

My father stepped forward and hugged her; she tightened up at the feel of his arms around her, and did not reciprocate. When he pulled away from her my father had tears in his eyes but the stranger looked at him in a way I'd never seen before. There was a kind of vicious longing in her eyes, a recollection of something once tender, now poisoned. She looked at him as though he were a plaster mask of her own face, cast before the onset of some great deformity.

I ran in for a closer look at our visitor. I hid behind my mother's skirt.

"Benjamin, this is Sarat," she said, pulling me out from behind her. "This is your aunt."

I stared at the towering woman, dumbstruck. I had seen a picture of her once. In the picture she must have been a teenager, lean and bald-headed, a menacing smile on her face. But what stood in our driveway bore almost no resemblance to that image. This woman was fat, her gut pressed against her dirty gray shirt. But it was more than that. All of her seemed oversized—her limbs trunklike, her nose flattened and wide.

She looked old; I'd been told she was my father's younger sister—she was not even thirty years old—but she looked older than him; older than my mother, even. As a child I imagined there were only three ages anyone could be—young like me, old like my parents, or very old like my grandparents in the North or the women in black dresses who came to see my father. But this woman was none of these things.

My mother ushered me toward our guest. I waited for her to lift me—to hug me and pinch my cheeks the way all our visitors did. Rarely did anyone come by the house without a present for me. The very old women in the black dresses—who called me the miracle of the miracle—would often take me aside and give me crisp hundred-dollar bills. But this visitor did nothing. Not knowing how to respond, I hugged her leg.

She stood motionless. I felt my mother lift me up.

"It's past his bedtime," she said. "I'm gonna take him upstairs. Come in, Sarat, come in."

Our guest looked at the house as though it were made of thorns.

"Whose is this?" she asked.

"It's ours, Sarat," said my mother. "It's yours. We tore the old one down a few years ago when things got better, after . . ." She paused. "Come on in."

But she was looking elsewhere, to the eastern edge of the property, where the seawall curled south past three greenhouses and the broken old shed.

"Why's that wall there?" she asked.

"The levee? We put that in around '91," my mother said. "Used to be the river would flood and wreck the greenhouses three, four times a year."

"The river don't run that way," our guest said. "That's land for another ten miles. I used to walk out there."

"Sarat, the river moves," said my mother. "It ate all that land a long time ago."

I thought I caught a twinge flash across her face, but quickly it was gone.

She seemed to dismiss our home entirely. Everyone always said there was no finer piece of property in all of northern Georgia than the Chestnuts' place. But she barely noticed it at all.

"We got a room for you all ready," said my father. "It's a nice room." He looked to my mother, who nodded.

"That's right, a nice room," my mother said. "I think you'll like it, Sarat. It has a view of the river, just like your old room did."

Our guest seemed to retract slightly at the mention of the river, as though some primal mechanism of defense deep within her had been triggered. I had no idea then of what water had done to her.

She pointed at the old shed. "I'll stay in there," she said.

"Sarat," my mother pleaded, "there's nothing in there but old glass panels and leftover wood. Come inside."

"I'll be fine in there."

I saw my mother look at my father, who seemed not to find our visitor's request at all unreasonable. I wondered if he even heard what she said, or if he had drifted to his clouded place.

"All right, Sarat," my mother said, "wherever you're most comfortable. We'll bring the spare bed out from the basement, and some sheets."

"No," she said. "It's fine as it is." And then she was walking past the rosebush to the shed I'd only ever seen the gardener use to store his mower.

I watched her move. She shuffled on stiff knees, the soles of the feet barely lifting. She reminded me of my pet turtle, every step a pained, deliberate undertaking. I wanted to stay up all night and see whether she would really sleep in that leaning, weathered shed, but my mother ordered me back to bed.

My bedroom faced the rose garden and the driveway. The eastern side of the house obstructed my view of the shed. My bedroom window, which my mother always kept locked, made faint the humming of the solar panels and the sound of the river.

But I lay awake in the dark, listening. Not long after our guest disappeared into the shed, there came from the place a loud cracking noise, like the structure itself was coming undone.

Eventually I heard my parents whisper-arguing about it. I couldn't make out any of the words, but I could always tell when they argued—it was something in the sharpness of the sounds, but only the ones from my mother's mouth. I'd never known my father to be anything but tranquil, his keel perfectly even no matter the situation. The way other grown-ups treated him—alternating between overt gestures of sympathy and barely suppressed impatience—made it seem as though he was not supposed to be this way, that there was a fault, a failing deep within the workings of him. But in my eyes he was simply kind.

I heard my mother go down the stairs. I heard the front door open and close.

☆ ☆ ☆

MANY YEARS LATER, when her letter led me to the place of her buried memories and I read the pages she left behind, I learned all about the moments that filled in the blanks between those things I'd witnessed with my own eyes. And by the time I was done reading, I'd learned every last secret my aunt had to give. Some people are born sentenced to terrible inheritance, diseases that lay dormant in the blood from birth. My sentence was to know, to understand.

☆ ☆ ☆

MY MOTHER WENT to the shed. Inside she found our visitor tearing the floorboards from the ground.

"What are you doing, Sarat?"

"I want to sleep on the soil," she said. "Go back inside, Karina."

"All right, that's fine," my mother said. "You want some help? I think we have a crowbar or something in one of the greenhouses."

"I'm fine—go back inside."

My mother ran her finger along the underside of the upturned planks resting against the wall. The wood was filthy and bleached a faint green from years pressed against the soil.

"You remember back when you first hired me to take care of the old house?" my mother said. "You sat me down and you went through this long list you'd written of all the things I couldn't do: 'Don't go near the shed, don't go near the cellar, don't open the boxes those boys on the boats deliver, don't wake Miss Dana when she's sleep . . .' "

My mother paused. "Anyway, I remember when you were finally done, I didn't know if there was anything left for me to do. Only thing you never said not to do was take care of that brother of yours. Guess I've been doing that ever since."

Our guest looked up from where she knelt on the floor. "How much of him is left?"

"You don't have to say it that way, Sarat."

"How much of him is left?"

"He has plenty of good days," my mother said. "He has plenty of really good days, when you wouldn't even know it. Sometimes he gets lost in himself a little, sometimes he has trouble remembering new things, a few times he'll forget old things. But he's not . . . he's good."

Our guest stared at my mother, unflinching. Then she returned to ripping the boards from the floor.

☆ ☆ ☆

WHEN I WOKE the next morning she was still in her shed. I sat on the steps of the kitchen door and waited for her to come out, half-convinced the image of her in my head from the night before was the doing of some strange dream. Inside, my mother and father sat at the counter.

"It's coming up on noon," my mother said.

"Just let her sleep, Karina," my father replied. "It's her first night out of that place in seven years."

"It's not sleep I'm worried about. How do you know she hasn't"—my mother caught sight of me on the steps—"how do you know she hasn't done something?"

My father stood and kissed my mother on the forehead. I knew she hated when he did that during their arguments, as though it were some kind of counterpoint to whatever she had to say.

"It's going to take a long time," he said.

"Fine," my mother replied. "But I'm not cooking a second breakfast. She wakes up now, she wakes up at midnight, she gets this."

A plate sat on the kitchen counter, piled with fried eggs fresh from the coop my mother kept near the rows of our numbered greenhouses, as well as asparagus from House Six and strips of real Virginia bacon.

"Fair enough," my father said. "I'm not asking you to wait on her. Just treat her as if she was your family."

"That's not fair." I could see my mother getting angry. She had a habit of digging her thumbnails into the skin of her middle fingers when her patience stretched. "I married you, didn't I? She *is* my family."

My father recoiled a little, surprised that my mother had taken offense. He was least clouded at the start of the day, least likely to forget or repeat himself, but most often he suffered from an inability to predict how the things he said sounded to ears other than his own.

"I'll take it to her," I said, stepping into the kitchen.

My parents looked at me, and then each other.

"Sure, why not?" said my father. "She's your aunt—go ahead."

Triumphant, I took the plate. The kitchen counter was a buttercream marble veined with black, and I had just that year grown tall enough to reach it. On my way out I took an oatmeal cookie from the jar on the table and set it on the plate. It seemed incomprehensible to me that so little food could possibly satisfy a body so big.

At the shed I found the doors slightly ajar. I wedged my hips between them and budged them open. Inside, the old prewar bulb was still on—I could feel the heat of it—even though sunlight seeped in through a thousand cracks in the wood. The air smelled of dust and mothballs and the wetness of recently disturbed earth. It also smelled of her.

She was still sleeping, her frame curled into something like a question mark upon a space in the floor where there was no floor—as though the very foundations of the shed had backed away from her quietly in the night. She was snoring and the thumb of her right hand twitched.

As slow and quiet as possible, I set the plate on the workbench. An old black toolbox had been taken down from the shelves—a dust outline still visible in the place where it had sat unused for years. Its contents were strewn about: a screwdriver, a set of pliers, and a folding knife. The knife had a black aluminum handle engraved with initials I couldn't decipher. There were a few strands of hair on the blade.

I was transfixed by the knife. At home, my mother would not let me near anything with a blade, not even the butter knives whose edges were dull as soap. But something about the confines of the old musty shed made me believe that this was a wild, sovereign place, where my mother's rule had no power. I was so mesmerized by the rust-streaked blade on the workbench, I didn't notice when the snoring stopped.

I heard something like a sharp inhale. I dropped the knife and turned to find her on her feet—moving faster than I ever thought possible for someone of such size. Lunging.

But it was not toward me. Like a frenzied prey she darted away to the furthest corner from where I stood. She backed into the walls with such force that the shed itself shook, and I thought the whole rotting thing would come down on us.

Fear of her pulled me toward the door, but something kept me where I stood. I saw the rise and fall of her chest. She looked at me as though I had stingers for limbs.

"Breakfast!" I blurted out. "I brought you breakfast. Look, look!"

I pointed at the plate on the workbench, but she never took her eyes off me.

Slowly, she approached. When she was close to me she knelt down. She leaned in until her face was close to mine and I could feel the milky breath of the newly woken on my cheek.

"I forgot your name," she said.

“Benjamin,” I replied. “My name’s Benjamin Chestnut.”

She took my chin in her hand and inspected my face. “You look like your father did, when he was young,” she said. “You got none of your mother in you.”

I saw that she had shaved her head, and that there were fresh cuts on her scalp.

“Why do you want to sleep here?” I asked. “It smells funny. We have lots of nice rooms in the house. My parents say you can stay there as long as you want.”

She let me go. Her eyes were red and her face stained on one side with soil. She wore the same clothes she had on when she arrived. It occurred to me then that not a single piece of clothing in our home would fit her.

“Listen very carefully to what I’m about to tell you,” she said. I nodded.

“Don’t ever come in here again.”

☆ ☆ ☆

SHE DIDN’T LEAVE the shed until dinnertime. In those days, whenever the weather wasn’t too hot, my mother liked to have dinner in the backyard by the levee. We had a beautiful table on the deck, made of real Cascadia redwood. And although the levee blocked our view of the river, we were able to enjoy its breeze.

My mother saw her in the yard. “Come have some dinner, Sarat,” she said. “It’s a gorgeous night—don’t get too many of those anymore.”

She looked at the old plot where my mother once planted her first seeds, back when she was still the help, still an interloper.

“Look familiar, don’t it?” my mother said. “It’s from before, from the old house. You remember how you used to get me that good foreign soil? That’s all we use now, in all the greenhouses. That very same soil.”

☆ ☆ ☆

IN THE WEEKS that followed, we settled into routine. Our guest spent most of her days and nights in the shed. Sometimes she came outside and walked among the greenhouses, but only late in the evening, when my parents were asleep. I lay awake some nights looking for her out my window.

Whenever I brought her meals to the shed and set them on the ground outside, I peeked in through the doors. I always saw her hunched over a table made of a plywood sheet on stacked paint-can legs. The shed was littered with cheap paper diaries you could only still get from the last dead-tree store in Lincolnton. She was writing in the old way.

My mother said if she didn't want to be part of this family, it was best to just ignore her. But I couldn't. Whenever the old widows came by with toys for me, I made sure to play with them out in the backyard from a spot where I could see through the ajar shed doors. But nothing enticed her to notice me.

She seemed to exist in her own wild space, unshackled from the rules and decorum of life as my parents had made me know it. It amazed me to think that she slept on soil and ate where she stood and had been on a trip to some secret place for seven whole years. My sheltered world shook with the realization that it was possible to live this way. I'd been raised in the shadow of walls; she was of the river.

We had fewer guests in the months after she arrived. The politicians who visited from Lincolnton and Atlanta stopped coming. But the old widows still came by every week like clockwork. Some of them wanted to see her, but she would never come to the house.

Sometimes, playing in the paths between the greenhouses, I'd hear the laborers gossiping about her in their strange far-south drawl. They called her a Bluenose and a Pocketmouth and I had no idea what those things meant. But the words sounded exotic, faraway, primed with the stuff of adventure.

☆ ☆ ☆

LATE THAT WINTER a new visitor came. Through my bedroom window I saw his small motorcade—three busted sedans, the old kind that ran on illegal fuel—at the far gate of the driveway. When I came downstairs I heard my mother say we shouldn't let a man like that anywhere near our home, that we should tell him to turn right around and go back wherever he came from, but my father said that would make us bad hosts.

The cars came up the driveway to the house. The sound of their old gurgling engines drew our guest out of her shed. From the cars emerged a somber-faced entourage of young men and women, all of whom orbited their boss, Adam Bragg Jr.

With the war coming to an end and reunion finally in sight, this was all that was left of the United Rebels.

"Simon Chestnut, you living saint," Bragg said. "The only man in the whole of the goddamn Red who deserves his good fortune."

"Hello," my father said, uncertain.

"What, don't you remember me? Remember you came down to see my father that time, got you a nice piece of change from the Martyrs' Fund?"

"What do you want, Adam?" my mother said.

But the man ignored her when he saw the big broad shape approaching from the woodshed.

"My God, Sarat," he said. "It does the soul good to see you free."

"I got nothing to say to you," she told him. "Go on, leave."

"I don't begrudge you that," Bragg replied. "Hell, I don't begrudge you anything, with what you've been through. All I ask is a few minutes of your time. Is there somewhere we can go and speak?"

"Say what you have to say."

Bragg looked at my parents. "Can we speak in private?"

"Go on inside," my aunt told my parents. "They'll be gone in a minute."

My father took me into the house, where my mother stood by the window of the grand room, watching.

Bragg took in the property. It was noon and the sunlight turned the greenhouses radiant. A few laborers toiled on the far edge of our farm; otherwise it was quiet.

"You know you're eating the same lettuce and potatoes the governor's eating?" Bragg said. "Your brother's done real well, Sarat. You should be proud."

"What do you want."

"Did they tell you how the great Chestnut Estate came to be, by the way?" Bragg asked. "You'll get a kick out of this. Turns out all those people who thought your brother was watched over by God, well they wanted God to watch over their money too. So they took it out of the banks and started keeping it here. And then the night the Blues came for you, everybody assumed they'd turn the house inside out and take all the money. But when they didn't, when they just took you and left, that's when people really started buying the notion that God watched over the Chestnuts' place. Pretty soon your sister-in-law over there was running a bank damn near as big as First Southern. And that's not even counting all those people who just sent money, donated it, didn't want a single thing in return."

He laughed. "You know, you should march right into that big old house and ask them for your cut," he said. "God knows you've earned it."

"I asked you what you want."

"I wanted, first and foremost, to see you," Bragg said. "When they told me you were getting out, I didn't believe it. I guess the war really must be ending, if they're clearing out Sugarloaf."

He pointed to the young men and women standing near the cars. "See that right there? What you're looking at is all that remains of the great Southern rebellion," he said. "All those ones who used to fight on the Tennessee line and in East Texas since the war first started have traded their swords for stump speeches—spending their time in Atlanta now, running election campaigns and talking about 'peace with dignity.' "

"You bitter they don't hold a table for you in Augusta no more?"

"Ha! Augusta the way you knew it don't even exist. Ships come up through the Northern ports now, and the Blues decide what we get to keep. Just one more concession the proud patriots of the Free Southern State agreed to in exchange for peace—the Great Reunification, they call it. Sold their country out for a seat at the kids' table in Columbus."

"The girl you came here to recruit is gone," Sarat said. "Go, and don't come back here again."

"Honey, you and I both know you're too broken to recruit," said Bragg. "I saw you hobble over here from that shed, and we all heard what they did to people in Sugarloaf. Three of the girls they set free with you are already dead, and no Northerner had to come down and kill them, they did the job themselves. Hell, even if I wanted to recruit you, half the rebels still left are dead sure you ratted out the cause in exchange for freedom."

He waved over one of the boys standing by the car. "No, Sarat, I didn't come to recruit you. I came to give you a gift."

The boy brought over a photograph. He was strange-looking, his skin too white and his hair buzzed close to the scalp. The rest of Bragg's entourage made an effort not to stare at Sarat, but this one looked at her dead on, shards of malice in his eyes.

"You don't remember him, do you?" said Bragg. She tried to recall why the boy looked familiar, but could not.

"This here is Trough," said Bragg, "the last living member of the Salt Lake Boys. Every single one of his brothers is dead or worse than dead. He keeps trying to join them, but I think they're watching over him from the next life, keeping him here with me against his will. Ain't that right?"

Trough said nothing.

Bragg showed the photograph to Sarat. She saw it and froze. She took it from him and held it close until even her feeble eyes had no doubt who the man was that stared back at her. Even blindfolded and bloodied, his face was more familiar to her than her own. It was the face of the thick-necked guard from Sugarloaf. Bud Baker, the man who'd drowned her.

"How did you find him?" she said.

"Damn idiot tried to take his wife and kids on a road trip to Zion and wandered into Mexican Protectorate territory," said Bragg. "When the Mexicans found out who he was, they shopped him around. I figured you two must have overlapped in that place, and that maybe you'd be interested in saying hello."

Her eyes never left the photograph. "Where is he?"

"We got him in a safe place down south," said Bragg. "You can tell us what to do with him, or you can come down and do it yourself."

☆ ☆ ☆

OVER MY PARENTS' OBJECTIONS, she left with Bragg. They drove five hours southwest to a cabin hidden among the stripped and bleached trees near Lake Seminole. The cabin stood at the edge of an algae-covered watering hole. A thin dirt trail led to its door. In the distance to the south, the Georgia coast gave way to the savage Florida Sea.

She found four people tied and blindfolded inside the cabin—Bud the guard, a woman who must have been his wife, and their two teenage children. All four were shackled to their chairs, their eyes covered with strips of black cloth. All their faces bore the blood and bruises of recent abuse, but none more so than the man she had come to see.

Bragg and his entourage waited outside; she entered alone. The blindfolded woman, at the sound of the door opening, broke into whimpered pleading, but Sarat ignored her.

She knelt near Bud. Up close, she could see the outer rings of deep black bruises around his blindfolded eyes. He was drenched in sweat, his heartbeat shook him.

She put her hands on his knees. He jerked back as though touched with a live wire.

"Just let my family go," he said. It was a different voice than the one she remembered—slightly thinner, free of resolve. "Just let them go, they did nothing wrong."

Gently she lifted the blindfold from his eyes. For a moment he looked at her as though trying not to recognize her face, as if by burying the memory of her he could bury the reality of her too. He closed his one working eye and when he opened it again and saw that she was still there, he straightened in his chair and tried to steel himself against what he knew was coming.

From her pocket Sarat retrieved her rusted folding knife. She cupped Bud's chin in her hand and stroked his cheek.

"Sweetheart, sweetheart," she said. "I'm going to make you sing."

☆ ☆ ☆

SOON THE SURROUNDING WORLD evaporated and with it the screaming that filled the room. Only her wrath remained, her unquenchable want. She wanted the blood inside him. He looked different now than when she'd last seen him: the early shadows of a beard growing on his face, his hair longer. But the blood inside him was the same.

She took it all. Rising, she looked at the hollowed remains of the guard and she felt the inverse of fulfillment—the empty undoing of a castaway who, rabid with thirst, resorts to drinking from the ocean.

When what revenge there was to be had was had, she turned and made to slit the throats of her other captives. She went first to the children. They looked about sixteen or seventeen: redheads, both with curly hair and the same jaws as their father. The shorter of the two had soiled himself and was shaking and sobbing. The other sat still, looking forward at his captor though he could not see.

When she closed in to kill them, she saw for the first time the mirrored contours of their faces.

"You're twins," she said.

The shorter boy said nothing. The taller one nodded.

They must have wondered why she did not kill them—why, with the knife so close to their throats, she stood and knocked the table over and screamed and left them there.

Outside, Bragg and his group waited. When they saw the color of her hands and the color of her clothes, some of them looked away and others smiled.

"We'll burn it down with them in it," said Bragg. "Nobody will ever know."

"No," she said. "The boys and their mother are still alive. Let them go."

"Let them go where?"

"I don't care. Smuggle them past the western line out into Blue country. Send them home."

"Sarat, they might have seen things. They might have recognized voices, they could tell . . ."

"Send them home," she said.

☆ ☆ ☆

ON THE LONG DRIVE BACK she saw Atlanta in the distance. It had grown during her years in Sugarloaf.

"I heard Albert Gaines killed himself a few years back," she said. "Where's he buried?"

"Oh, he ain't dead, or at least he's still breathing," said Bragg. "After the Blues let him go he went off to that shack of his in the forest, doesn't speak to nobody or go nowhere, just rotting away with none but his guilt for company. Let the maggots bury him when the time comes, goddamn Pocketmouth rat."

"So it's true that he's the one who told them?"

"He's one of the ones. Soon as they started rounding people up, suddenly all these proud Southern patriots started squealing. He didn't just give you up, he must have told them a hundred names. Truth is, I'd have killed him myself if my father hadn't made me promise not to. But that promise is binding on me—it sure as hell ain't binding on you."

They traveled slowly on the highways that circled the Southern capital, theirs the only old fossil car on the road. She saw now that all the other vehicles around them were distant descendants of the old Tik-Toks, powered entirely by the sun. She remembered the old wartime footage of hollering Southerners on the back of huge fossil trucks, revving their engines in defiance. All that was gone now, and looking at the roads you'd think there never lived a single Southerner who'd ever wanted anything to do with the old fuel that started the war. Drivers in nearby cars looked at the sluggish fossil sedan in which she rode, some with curiosity at the sight of the ancient thing, others with disgust. But none tried to stop them, none said a word.

She remembered something Albert Gaines once told her all those years ago in Patience. He said when a Southerner tells you what they're fighting for, you can agree or disagree, but you can't ever call it a lie. Right or wrong, he said, a man from our country always says exactly what he means, and stands by what he says.

Even that, it turned out, was a lie.

☆ ☆ ☆

SHE CAME HOME just before dawn, sneaking in over the eastern seawall. I cracked my bedroom window open and very quietly I leaned out to watch her. By the side of the shed she stripped naked and washed her clothes and herself with water from the garden hose.

Hers is the first naked body I remember. I looked on, mesmerized by the strange scars and disfigurements I assumed were the property of all adult skin.

Excerpted from:

REASONABLY SATISFACTORY AND ENCOURAGING TO ALL: AN ORAL HISTORY OF THE REUNIFICATION TALKS

DAVID CASTRO (Peace Office Senior Negotiator, 2089–2095): I remember the day their delegation came up from Atlanta. We spent six months preparing for it, so that by the time negotiations started, we had thousands of pages of notes on every conceivable topic. Border controls, restitution, prisoner swapping, you name it. Before we came to the table, we knew exactly how far the President was willing to go, how much he was willing to concede. We thought we'd covered all our bases.

Then the first day of negotiations came around. I remember we were meeting in a large boardroom in the basement of the Peace Office. There were five of us on the Union side, a small delegation because we had no real authority. Everything had to be approved later on in the Executive Building. But when the South's negotiating team showed up, there must have been two dozen of them. Each one had a different title, Director of Revolutionary This, Secretary of Patriotic That. One guy gave me his card; it said he was a Constitutional Defense Officer.

We thought they'd want to start with travel restrictions, or amnesty for all those rebels we had sitting in the detention camps. Or maybe they were desperate and would want to talk money. They'd held out for so long with their stubborn reliance on fossil fuels while the rest of the world moved on, their cities were falling apart, and we thought we could get them to make all kinds of concessions in exchange for infrastructure money.

We had a little agenda ready for them with a few proposed starting points to kick off the negotiations. But I still remember, the very first day, their chef de mission sits at the table, pushes the agenda aside without reading it, and says to us, "First thing's first: I don't want to hear a single one of you ever use the word Surrender."

It turned out they didn't give a damn about travel restrictions or prisoner swaps or any of those things. For three days straight all they wanted to do was haggle over the wording of the Reunification Day speeches and the preamble of the peace agreement. Every day they'd come up with something new they wanted included in the public record—one time it'd be some nonsense about courage in the face of aggression, the next time it'd be about the necessity of self-defense and the protection of long-cherished ways of living. Hell, I remember we spent a couple of hours one day planning out how the Reunification Day photo op would go. They wanted their President to be the one to extend his hand first, and ours then to take it. The next day, they changed their mind; now they wanted our President to reach out first.

Of course, the other negotiators on the Union team loved all this, because they were getting their way on all the strategic stuff. And the people in the Executive Building were happy to go along with it because they were looking further down the line, to a time when they'd have to campaign for all those Southerners' votes. I was the only one who put up a fight. I told the President's people if we go along with this, if we nod and smile while they parade some fantasy about this being a noble disagreement between equals, and not a bloody fight over their stubborn commitment to a ruinous fuel, the war will never really be over.

But in the end, Columbus went along with it. And even today, all these years later, we live with the consequences. They didn't understand, they just didn't understand. You fight the war with guns, you fight the peace with stories.

CHAPTER FOURTEEN

In the spring of '95 I broke my arm. It was a small break and the bone healed quickly, but it's the first I remember of pain.

It happened in May, at the tail end of what had been a bad few months. The stress of our new living arrangement—my aunt barricaded behind the doors of our woodshed—was starting to gnaw even at my father's tranquility. Many nights I lay flat against the cooling vent in my bedroom and listened to him and my mother argue downstairs.

"She hasn't said a word to us in four months," I heard my mother say. "Not even good morning, like we don't even deserve that."

"It takes time," my father replied. "She needs time."

"Stop saying that. What she needs is a doctor, a therapist, somebody they train to deal with people who've been through what she's been through. She needs help we can't give her."

"The man from the Red Crescent said she needs to learn how to be free," my father said.

"Does she look like she's learning?"

When they'd exhausted themselves arguing, they decided to drive down to Lincolnton for dinner. My mother didn't want to leave me in the house alone but she thought I was asleep and decided to chance it for a couple of hours. When I heard her coming up the stairs to check on me, I jumped up and ran back into bed and closed my eyes.

I waited until the taillights faded beyond the iron gate. I got out of bed and turned on the lights.

I left my room. I walked down the hall and down the stairs, past a row of hopelessly faded photographs on the wall. The photographs were of my grandparents, and the woman my parents told me was my other aunt.

One of the photographs depicted my grandfather, the man after whom I'd been named. It was washed out; only the faint outline of a man was visible, his face a cloud. He cradled something in each arm, but these things too were indecipherable. For a long time I thought it was a picture taken after his death, a picture of his ghost. I started to believe that there existed another class of age, older even than the oldest of the living—a class whose citizens lost the ability to speak even to themselves, and were confined to perfect, impenetrable stillness.

I walked downstairs, intent on solving a mystery that had tugged on my mind for months. A mystery hidden within one of our greenhouses.

I went outside. In the garden the air was warm and wet on the skin. The lights that hung on the side of the house lit up as they sensed my movement, and then went dark after I walked away.

I walked south to where our greenhouses stood in rows. The greenhouses were made of a translucent glass. Inside each pane were fine copper veins, part of the circuitry that pulled energy from the sun. At the time, translucent panels were still new and largely unavailable south of the Tennessee line; it took my mother many months of wrangling and many called favors before she managed to move them across the border. In the day they hummed and glittered, at night they were silent. And at all times, even while they worked, it was possible to look through them and see the things growing inside the greenhouses.

Near the southeast edge of the property, House Thirty-six stood unused. Instead of glass, it had plywood boards for skin. After Hurricane Zenith came through and damaged many of the greenhouses, my mother once again tried to have new panels brought in from the North. But she was only able to secure enough for eleven of the twelve damaged greenhouses. House Thirty-six was boarded up.

At night, I sometimes saw our visitor come here. Whenever she did, she carried one or two of her old paper diaries with her. But when she emerged from the greenhouse, the books were gone.

I arrived at House Thirty-six to find its door boarded shut and held with a small padlock. But along the roof there was a square of missing plywood, through which I thought I could peer inside.

The roof was too high for me to reach. I saw a ladder leaning against the side of House Thirty-five, where my mother grew fuzz-skinned okra and eggplants big as limbs. With a full-body heave, I managed to tip the ladder off the side of the greenhouse. For a moment it stood weightless in the air, and then fell back onto the side of House Thirty-six with a loud crack. I looked back toward the house and the woodshed to see if she heard, but there were no signs of movement.

I climbed the ladder. With every step it leaned slightly this way and that. But I had seen the laborers use it many times, and they were much bigger than me; I kept climbing.

When I reached the top rung I felt exhilarated. Beyond the boarded roof, the whole of our land lay visible. Not only our land, but the land surrounding it: the place where the river curved, where trees with braided hair grew straight out of the water. I looked to the south and saw the lights of distant towns.

But inside the greenhouse, I saw almost nothing. Under the silver cast of the moon, there was only the faint outlines of footsteps in the barren soil. I craned to see beyond the square of dirt lit by the moon, but there were no signs of whatever it was she came here to do.

As I readied to give up, a burst of red light caught my eye. It came from far to the north, from a place beyond the river. I turned to search for it but in an instant it was gone.

I stood perfectly still on the ladder, observing the boundary of our property. Past the levee, the river emitted a soft hushing sound as it moved. But there was something else, a break in the darkness on the far bank. It was almost impossible to see, but there was a demarcating line along the horizon—below it, the blackness was uniform and unnatural; above it was the imperfect darkness of sky, streaked with clouds and spotted with stars.

I stared at the line in the horizon, trying to make sense of it. Suddenly, the same red flash of light shone directly at me, sharp and blinding.

As I fell, I thought I saw the outline of a guard tower.

Then came the sky. I watched it as the ladder tilted. In the darkness I reached out with my left hand to break my fall.

A spear of fire unlike anything I'd ever felt before ran up my arm. I lay in the dirt and screamed. I looked away from my arm and toward the gate at the end of the driveway. I yelled for my mother, even though I knew she wouldn't hear. I was alone.

Then I heard footsteps coming from the direction of the woodshed. For a moment I didn't believe it was her, but when I saw that towering frame looming above me, I knew.

I was still crying in pain. I asked her to help me, but I had no idea what I wanted her to do. I only wanted the fire in my arm to end. She knelt down beside me.

"You broke your arm," she said.

The words terrified me. I had no idea then that broken things can be repaired. Whenever something broke on the farm—a vase or a lightbulb or a greenhouse panel—my parents did not repair it; they tossed it away and bought a new one.

"Look at it," she said.

I refused.

"Look at it."

I turned to look at the place from where the fire came. When I saw the unnatural way in which my right arm was bent, I passed out.

☆ ☆ ☆

WHEN I CAME TO, I was in my own bed. She was sitting beside me.

"Take this," she said, handing me a couple of white pills. "It'll make the pain stop."

I swallowed the pills and within a few minutes I felt a strange, body-wide bliss, a warmth radiating outward from my stomach to the end of every limb.

"Still hurts?" she asked.

I shook my head. The world around me was hazy and unfocused, but the fire in my arm was gone.

"What were you doing out there?"

"I was trying to look inside the greenhouse," I said.

"Why?"

"I saw you going there sometimes, and I wanted to find out what you were doing."

I knew she'd be angry at me, but I thought she'd be angrier if I lied. And I was certain she'd be able to tell if I lied.

But she didn't look angry, and she didn't say anything in response. Instead I thought I saw a passing flicker of admiration in the way she observed me. And then it was gone.

"You fell off that ladder?" she asked.

"Yeah."

She chuckled. "You really are your father's son."

I turned to my ruined arm. I saw it had been straightened against the spine of a wooden plank. The plank and the limb were tied together with strips of torn cloth.

It seemed such a crude prosthetic. I began to wonder if I'd ever be able to use my arm again. In all the times my parents had taken me to swim and play basketball with the other kids in Lincolnton, I had never seen a boy with a wooden limb.

"Have you ever broken a bone before?" she asked me. I bristled at the silliness of the question—obviously I hadn't; there were no other wooden planks tied around me.

"No," I said. I tried to lift my arm, but it was as though the lines from the brain to the limb had been severed.

"I can't move it," I said.

"In time," she replied. "The board's there so the bone sets right. It doesn't matter how a bone breaks, it matters how it sets."

"I'm sorry I looked at your things, ma'am," I said.

She shook her head. "Don't call me that," she said. "My name's Sarat."

"I'm sorry, Sarat."

"Why'd you do it?" she asked me.

"I just wanted to know."

"Don't ever apologize for that," she said. "That's all there is to life, is wanting to know."

We heard the sound of the doorbell chimes; the front gate opened. I knew my mother and father had returned, and although I dreaded their reaction once they learned what I'd done, I was unconcerned. The strange bliss that enveloped me remained.

My mother came upstairs and when she saw me her eyes turned wide as wells.

"What did you do?" she said, over and over. For a moment she ignored her sister-in-law's presence entirely, and I thought she was asking me. Then some accusatory deduction must have revealed itself to her mind, and she turned around.

"What did you do to him?" she said.

"He fell and broke his arm," Sarat replied. "I splinted it and gave him some Bonesetters. He'll be all right."

"You didn't call an ambulance? You didn't call a doctor? You didn't call us?"

My mother was moving toward her now. "What the hell is wrong with you?" she said. "A boy breaks his arm and you do nothing?"

Sarat grew silent. From the way my mother was standing before her I wondered if my mother would try to strike her. But instead she slammed the window shut and locked it.

"For God's sake, don't you understand? The war is over," my mother screamed. "This isn't Patience, this isn't the front, this isn't the prison they locked you in. You want to keep living in that world, go crawl back into that filthy little shed of yours and live it there. Don't you dare try to pull us into it, you hear me? Don't you dare."

I watched Sarat walk away. On the way out she passed my father, who'd been drawn upstairs by the sound of my mother's voice. She walked past him as though he didn't exist. It seemed impossible then to imagine the two of them as siblings, as having come from any kind of overlapping past.

When he saw my arm, my father came to my bedside.

"Oh no," he said.

"That's all you've got to say?" my mother asked him. "She breaks your son's arm and that's all you've got to say?"

"She didn't break it," I protested.

"She's damaged, Simon," my mother said. "She's a danger to us, a danger to your son. I don't know what it's going to take for you to see that."

This time, they didn't bother to argue in hushed tones. I watched them fight right there in my room. My father was upset and struggled to find the words he wanted to say, and this time my mother did not have patience. But I was not upset. At the time I had no idea it was just a chemical mirage, the Bonesetters coursing through my blood. Even later, when the warmth turned sour in my stomach and I threw up all over the floor, I still felt good.

In the clinic in Lincolnton, the doctor said the break looked worse than it was. He laughed when my parents brought me in, my arm still braced with the wooden plank. He asked if they'd found me in some old bunker on the Tennessee line, fighting the Blues.

He put a proper cast on and said in a month it'd be good as new. I was coming off the Bonesetters then, and embers were starting to glow again inside my arm, but I still remember the overwhelming sense of relief I felt when I heard those words: Good as new.

By the time we drove back to the house, it was almost dawn. My mother, who'd spent the whole car ride to the clinic digging her thumbnails into the skin of her middle fingers, had cooled enough to begin interrogating me about how I came to break my arm. But I held under the pressure. For some reason, the prospect of my parents entering House Thirty-six and discovering whatever it was that lived there was the outcome I most dreaded. When they finally laid me back in my bed, I fell asleep with a smile on my face.

ONE OF THE THINGS I remember most clearly about my mother is her capacity for stillness. Sometimes, when she was out planting strange new flowers in her backyard plot, or painting childlike pastorals on our riverside levee, she would suddenly become perfectly motionless. Once or twice I caught her doing it—frozen, as though trying to escape the attention of some passing beast. Once, after she went back into the house, I knelt by the levee and tried to mimic her, staring hard into the concrete. But wayward thoughts began to pile up in my mind, and in a minute or two I was ready to burst. I was young and I had no use for stillness.

The morning after I broke my arm, my mother went to see Sarat. The door to the shed was ajar and the light always on. Peering in, my mother could see her hunched on a stool over the worktable, sewing in the old way with a thread and needle.

"If you want me gone I'll go," Sarat said, her eyes still on her work, her back to the door.

My mother went inside. Even in the coolness of dawn, the shed was hot with the light of the incandescent bulb.

"This is where they kept us, the night they came for you," my mother said. "After they took you away and searched the shed, they locked Simon and me in here with rifles at our heads while they turned the house upside down. I never saw Simon like that before, the way he screamed when he saw those guns."

My mother sat on a stool near the bench on the other side of the shed. She inspected an old squirt can that once held oil and now served as a pen holder. "I always hated this goddamn shed."

My mother turned her eye to the thing being sewn—a shirt of gray cloth, big and baggy as a potato sack. The stitch lines were wide and ragged, the needle disappearing within the massive hand that held it.

"It's bad light for that kind of work," my mother said. "God knows how you can even sleep with that thing on."

"I forgot how to sleep in the dark," Sarat said.

My mother grimaced. The shed smelled of meat, a butcher shop stink. An ancient fishing box sat atop the workbench shelves, its tackles rusted and never used.

"I was wrong to yell at you the way I did," my mother said. "The doctor said it was good, as far as splints go, and Benjamin would have been hollering all night if you hadn't given him those painkillers."

"He's soft."

"Christ, Sarat, he's six years old."

"I didn't mean it as a bad thing."

"He told us he fell chasing a wolf away from the greenhouses," my mother said. "God knows there hasn't been a wolf around these parts in years. I think it might be the first time he's ever lied to us."

Sarat looked up from her sewing. "He's a good kid," she said. "He didn't do nothing."

"Oh I'm not mad at him," my mother replied. "He's lying because he likes you, and he wants to share whatever happened only with you. That's how little boys are supposed to feel about their aunts. He likes you, Sarat. In spite of everything you do to keep your distance from us, he still likes you."

"I thought they'd made a mistake when they told me about him," Sarat said.

"When who told you about him?"

"For a while, when they were still trying to get me to talk, every now and then they'd tell me they'd arrested Simon or Dana or Mama. That's how little they really knew—they had no idea which of us were dead and which of us were alive. Then one day they came in and said, If you don't talk we're gonna have to take Benjamin away. I thought, it's one thing if they don't know Mama and my sister are gone, but they don't even know Benjamin's been dead twenty years."

My mother smiled. The first blue of sunrise crawled through the cracks and illuminated the dust in the air.

"Your brother's a good man," my mother said. "He'll compromise on just about anything. But when we found out it was a boy, there was no way he'd have any other name. It's the only time he's ever put his foot down for as long as I've known him. Can you believe that?"

"Was he still like a child when you married him?" Sarat said.

My mother sighed. "So that's it, then? That's the grudge you decided to keep? All right, let's pretend he was. Let's say I took advantage of that simple little boy with the bullet in his skull, the boy I was paid to take care of. Let's say I raped him too, got my child out of him when he was too badly damaged in the head to even know what was happening. Let's say all of that was true—take it out on me, then. Be cold to me, hit me even, if that's all you know how to do. But Simon ain't to blame for it, and that little boy sure as hell ain't to blame for it."

Sarat folded the cloth and set it aside on the bench. From beneath the bench she retrieved a glass jug full of Joyful, made from the remains of mangoes and peaches and oranges pilfered from the greenhouses. She unscrewed the cap; a rotting sweetness laced the air.

"You know some of those old war widows still come by, every now and then," my mother said. "There's only a few of them still alive, but they still come by to touch Simon's forehead and do their little hocus-pocus. They still call him the Miracle Boy of Patience, like he never did any other thing his whole life. They still think the miracle is that he survived. But bad people survive too; lucky people survive. The miracle isn't that he survived, the miracle is that he's healing."

She rose from her stool and emptied out a couple of Southern Freedom Bond mugs that held a few nails dislodged from the floorboards. She walked to Sarat and held one out.

"Go on," she said, "it's my fruit you're stealing."

They drank until the sun was high and the walls bled orange. My mother spotted an old wind-up radio on one of the shelves and cranked it until it spat a hum of static. She searched the bands and found a piece of soft indecipherable jazz. A song crackled through the ancient machine.

"They ever let you listen to music in there?" my mother asked.

"Not like this."

"I want you to know we tried, Sarat," my mother said. "We filed petitions, we hired a lawyer. We gave money to the governor and the governor before him until they'd sit down with us. We talked to senators about your case. But none of them would do anything. They were terrified of having their name said in the same sentence as that place. But I swear to God we tried."

"You shouldn't have."

My mother inspected a soft line that ran down Sarat's left cheek, a scar her silence once earned her in Sugarloaf. It ended at the jawline, near a place on her neck where another line began.

"Christ, I can't imagine what you went through," my mother said.

"I never asked you to."

"But you want me to. I mean, you could have left already. You could have up and gone back to wherever you think the fighting still is, killed yourself a soldier or two. Killed yourself, anyway. But you're still here. I've seen it before, when I was a little girl watching my parents treat the wounded in all those hellholes we lived in. You suffered too much not to let anyone know it. You act like we're invisible, but you want us to know what they did to you. I think you need us to know."

Sarat threw the jug of Joyful across the room. It met the wall and turned to shards.

"What do you want me to say? You want me to say they broke me? Fine: They broke me. They broke me. They broke me. Does it make you happy to hear it? You're right, I can't bury it. What am I supposed to do, now that it's done—just snuff it out like a candle? Last night when you thought I'd hurt your boy you were ready to rip my throat out as revenge. But I gotta turn my back on what was done to me, on what's been done to me every day since I was your boy's age? Well let me make it clear for you: whatever part of me can do that is dead."

"And yet the rest of you lives," my mother said. "And yet you sew shirts from cloth and make booze from fruit and write whatever it is you write in those old books of yours. And yet you run out in the night to splint my little boy's arm. You're healing, Sarat. What's bitter in you might fight it, but you're healing."

My mother rose from her seat. "You're right if you think I don't find you worth loving," she said. "God help me, I know you're family and I know I married into your blood and know I should believe that you're worth loving, but I don't. So many terrible things made you this way, but I don't have to live with what made you, I have to live with what you are. And I know you don't find me worth loving either.

"But I'll love you anyway. And your brother will love you anyway. And your nephew will love you anyway. That's what family does. Take what time you need, Sarat. Heal how you want to heal."

☆ ☆ ☆

THE FOLLOWING WEEKEND, we went to the Saturday market in Lincolnton. I didn't expect her to come with us, but when I went outside I saw her in the car, the passenger seat pushed all the way back.

I remember thinking it was something important, a milestone—families take trips together.

When we arrived the market was in full swing. A throng of shoppers from all over northern Georgia descended on the town every weekend to buy fresh produce—so much so that eventually they started closing off a quarter-mile of Peachtree Street near the old Baptist church and turned the whole thing into a fair of sorts. I liked walking around the market with my parents, watching the sellers run out to greet them. We were rich everywhere in the South but only here were we a special kind of royalty, one of maybe five or six families in the whole state who still did the old small-batch farming, the kind you could hardly do anymore on account of the heat and the storms. I liked to watch the vendors leave their stalls, leave their customers mid-order, and race over to ask what Miss Karina was working on these days, what strange crops she'd managed to revive.

On this day, though, almost none of them came out to see us. I knew right away it was because of Sarat. Some of the sellers had been acquainted with the Chestnuts long enough to know exactly who she was, but most were scared away by the size of her, the way she shuffled, slow as stone.

After a while one of the fruit sellers did come over to say hello. He was one of my parents' bigger customers, exclusive purchaser of all Chestnut Farms cabbage, which he marketed as having all manner of restorative effects. At the sight of him approaching, my mother turned to my father and whispered, "His name's Sam."

The man came and shook my parents' hands. "Well, if it isn't my favorite people in all of Georgia," he said.

"Hello, Sam," my father said, smiling.

"How are you, Mister Simon? You're looking good."

"I'm all right, I'm all right."

Sam turned to my mother. "So I hear you've got something new."

"When have I ever let you down, Sam?" my mother said. "I've always got something new."

"So let me know! What is it? Tyler from Reunion Farms says you've figured out some way to make oranges that aren't so thirsty. That it?"

The conversation began to bore me. I looked around for one of the kids' stalls, where clowns built balloon animals and did card tricks while their makeup ran in the blistering heat.

It was only then I noticed Sarat had wandered away from us. She was standing by one of the lab-grown meat stalls, staring intently at something down the street.

I didn't realize it then, but she couldn't have known. She couldn't have possibly known that this was one of the conditions, one of the things the Free Southerners had agreed to as a precursor for peace. She didn't know that in return the Red got monthly access to a couple of Northern hospitals and the promise of slightly more favorable descriptions of the Southern cause in the Reunification Day speeches.

She wouldn't have known any of this. Instead, she simply saw a Blue soldier, in full uniform and gear, patrolling the market; patrolling Southern land.

I watched her reach for a butcher's knife on the stall table. And then she was moving toward the soldier. I'd only ever seen her move that fast once before, the morning she lunged away from me in the shed. The Blue soldier was conversing with a couple of clothes makers at a stall on the far side of the market; he didn't see her coming.

Somewhere in the depths of me I knew what was going to happen. I started to run, my damaged arm clunky by my side. When I reached her she was a few feet from the soldier's back. She raised the butcher's knife high.

I stepped in the space between her and the soldier. I screamed for her to stop.

The sound of my voice startled the soldier. He turned around. I had my back to him but I knew he'd raised his weapon, because Sarat froze where she stood. The knife dropped from her hand.

I began to imagine what would come next. She would be arrested, thrown back in that prison again. This time they'd put her there for good. I only hoped that the soldier behind me wouldn't shoot her dead right where she stood.

There came a silence. The rage on her face was gone, in its place a kind of disbelief. Behind me, I heard the soldier say her name.

"Sarat?"

And then I heard her say his.

"Marcus."

☆ ☆ ☆

ONE OF THE VENDORS had run over to the other end of the street and called the Blue soldier stationed there. He came running, rifle raised.

"On the ground!" he yelled at Sarat. But she did not move, did not look away from the man she had moments ago readied to kill.

"It's all right," Marcus said to his partner. "She's an old friend."

The other soldier lowered his rifle. He seemed unpersuaded, but Marcus waved him away.

Marcus looked around at all the people who were now staring.

"There a silent auction going on or something?"

A couple of people chuckled, more in relief than anything. As they went back to their stalls, Marcus nodded in the direction of a church nearby. He turned and walked toward it.

Sarat looked at me. "Go back to your parents," she said.

"Are you going to hurt him?" I asked.

"No," she said. "I'm not going to hurt him."

He was standing between the pews when she entered the church, his rifle and helmet removed. She saw then the fullness of his face. It was the same face, the same skin, the same boy. He'd grown a few inches taller in the years since she'd last seen him, but his smallness was the same. And in the way a soldier's gear is designed to puff out the chest and broaden the shoulders, he looked even more mis-sized, too dense for his height.

He was like a child in the way he looked at her. "I don't," he started. "Sarat, I don't . . ."

But she did not see him. She saw Chalk Hollow. She saw Cherylene's pen and the ugly little shower trailer thick with mist and the place high in the trees where you could see forever. She went to him and she held him.

"You're alive," he whispered. He kept saying it, and she didn't know which of them he was trying to convince. "You're alive, you're alive."

They sat together at the pews. The church was plain and musty and resembled the quaint courthouses of old Southern stories. There were seats in the balcony above them but no one sitting in them. They were alone.

"So they took you off the customs ships," Sarat said.

"Yeah, they do all that stuff up North now. Everything goes through the Blue first before it ends up down here. Cuts down on smuggling."

"And what about you? You here cutting down on smuggling too?"

Marcus laughed.

"You know, for a while I thought they stationed me down here because they secretly knew I was a Southerner this whole time. But now I think they really put me down here because I'm small. They think it makes all the people down here less hostile if the Union soldiers patrolling the place aren't the big brawny types you see in the recruitment commercials."

"Ain't true, though," Sarat said. "Hell, I saw you for ten seconds and I wanted to stab you."

He was smiling and when he smiled she felt as though she could walk to the doors of the church and open them and find a different world waiting.

He lifted his fingers to the place on her neck where one of her thin pink scars began. He traced it down to her shoulder.

"I did this," he said.

"No you didn't."

"You can't wear this uniform and not know what they did in Sugarloaf, Sarat. I've gotten by for a long time looking away, turning my head. And the truth is I never cared much about what either side did to the other because it's a war and maybe that's all war is, is shredding the rules. But I can't do that when it's you. I did this."

She took his hand, pulled it away from where it rested on her shoulders. She tried to remember how she'd gotten that particular scar, but in this moment the memory was unreachable.

"You never wronged me," she said. "You're the only one still living who never once wronged me."

☆ ☆ ☆

IN THE WEEKS that followed, my arm began to strengthen. Soon I was able to move it, although the cast was stiff and grimy. Where the cast ended I could smell the unwashed skin below. It had a rank smell that, for reasons I couldn't understand, I found strangely addictive.

After two weeks my mother let me play outside, but there were to be no trips to basketball or swimming practice in Lincolnton until the cast came off and the doctor declared the bone fully healed.

One morning I was playing in the backyard. My parents were on the other side of the property, busy haggling with a contractor who'd come to replace our front gate's busted motor.

There seemed always to be breakages and malfunctions in the small machines that moved our little riverside world—storms came through and wrecked the solar panels; the heat warped the circuitry of our lawn mowers and our generators. It never occurred to me until much later how exhausting it must have been for my parents, constantly warring with the land that housed them.

Sarat was in the kitchen, shucking corn for dinner. Slowly she had begun to make more frequent appearances in the house—sometimes she would sit awhile with us in the living room watching television. A few times she even stayed for dinner. Whenever she did, my parents said very little, trying to pretend like it was no big deal. But every time I could see my father struggling to restrain a giddy little smile. For a while she must have been alien to him, even if he remembered her name and her relation, but I think now he was starting to connect the woman he saw with the girl he knew before. And in doing so I think he was able, in some small way, to connect as well with the boy he used to be.

I watched her through the kitchen window. She worked in a monotone way, her eyes focused nowhere, lost in her own space. But then she looked up, and she saw me, and she came outside. Often she wandered around the property, walking among the greenhouses. But this was the first time I'd seen her come near the levee in the daytime. It was as though she was repelled in some invisible way by the river—not by the sight of it, which was hidden by the seawall, but by the sound of it, the sound of water moving.

"How's the arm?" she asked.

"It's fine," I replied. "In two weeks it'll be good as new."

"It'll be better than that. Bones that set right grow back stronger."

It was an amazing thing to hear, and whether it was true or not, instantly I believed it.

I stood up. "Do you wanna see something cool?" I asked.

"Sure."

"Come on, then," I said. Without thinking I took her hand and led her to a place near the levee protected by the shade of a hanging willow tree. It was there, in a small pen, that I kept my pet.

"This is my turtle," I said, pointing at the mounded, unmoving animal.

She seemed to forget me for a moment. I watched as she knelt down until her face was almost in the pen, inspecting the yellow, symmetrical markings on the shell.

"He's real slow," I said, embarrassed at my pet's reluctance to even show its head. "Some days he doesn't even move at all."

"She's a girl," Sarat said.

I asked her how she knew, but she didn't answer.

Finally she broke from her trance and stood up. I wiped the dirt from the knees of her pants.

"Is it true you were in prison?" I asked.

"Yeah."

"Why?"

"They never told me."

"How long were you there?"

"Seven years."

The number was incomprehensible to me; a lifetime.

"What are you gonna do when they get that cast off you?" she asked.

"Play basketball," I said. For weeks I'd thought about little else. "My team's in first place, and if we win the rest of our games, we get to go to the championship in Atlanta. They have a water park there, got the biggest swimming pool in the whole country."

"You like swimming?" she asked.

I nodded. "I go twice a week to the pool in Lincolnton. I'd be there today if I didn't have the cast."

"What you doing in a pool in Lincolnton when you got the river right here?"

I laughed. "You can't swim in the river, silly."

She looked at me as though I'd come from some other planet, and then that vague confusion turned to pity. She walked past me to the levee, shuffling slowly in that way of hers, the frame hunched and the knees threatening to give.

Where the seawall passed our backyard, my mother had painted a crude mural, the kind they have in kindergartens. It was of stick-figure children playing in the field among the apple trees, a smiling sun watching over them. She had given the children names and sometimes she'd talk to me about them as though they were real. I never understood why.

Sarat stood by the side of the levee. She was tall enough to see past the wall and through the willows. She watched the river. It wasn't until many years later that I understood the courage she was struggling to summon, the demon she had to bury before she could set foot once more into the moving water.

She turned to me. "C'mon, then," she said. "Let's go swimming."

Instinctively, I turned to see if my parents were around. Going over the levee was the one thing I was forbidden to do above all else. Beyond the wall lay death by drowning and death by disease and all the monsters that populated my mother's stern warnings. My feet froze to the soil.

"I can't swim with my cast on," I said, but it was not the cast that scared me.

"Yeah you can," she said. "C'mon, I won't let nothing bad happen to you."

Slowly she climbed down the other side of the levee, and soon she was walking among the willows to the riverbank. Suddenly the sight of her fading behind the braided leaves filled me with panic. I imagined she might step into the river and never return, taken by that green snake to the end of the world. My feet unfroze, a newfound courage took me, and I chased after her.

From atop the levee I saw her walk into the water. She walked barefoot and fully clothed. I climbed down the wall and ran with my head to the ground, following her footsteps in the soft riverbank soil.

And then I looked up, and the monster was upon me. For the first time in my life, I was at the river. Its sound and size astounded me, the banks wild and wide, the speed of the current readable in the branches and leaves that raced along its surface. I had never seen water move this way.

She stood waist-high in the river, the water curling around her. I remember the way she looked in that moment, that violent euphoria barely sheathed behind the lips. The water curled around her wounded body and as it moved it did not heal her wounds, it cauterized.

She was motionless. I waved at her to come closer to the riverbank, but she seemed not to see me at all. She was breathing hard though she had not run. She looked in that moment like a child, wide-eyed, uncertain. Then it dawned on me: she was afraid.

And then she was gone, fully submerged as though weighted with anvils. When she surfaced, her baggy shirt held fast to her skin and pins of light glimmered on her shaven head.

"Come here," she said.

I shook my head. "I'm scared."

"Good," she said. "Now you have something you can kill. Come here."

I faced down the river. Everything I had known of the world suddenly felt very far away. I saw that beyond the river there was a high wall, lined with razor wire and manned by guards. And although I wouldn't be able to articulate what I felt until much later, I knew then that the bulk of the world was just like this: wild, unvaccinated, malicious. I stepped into the river.

It was only a few footsteps before the soft polished floor fell from beneath my feet, and I was taken by the current. I screamed, but her hands were quickly on me. She held me afloat and carried me in further. The sound of water was like a million invisible mouths all whispering at once. The water was alive; I knew it because the water was moving.

I looked at her then, and I saw a thing I'd never seen before. My aunt was laughing.

Excerpted from:

**THE CIVIL WAR ARCHIVE PROJECT—
REUNIFICATION DAY CEREMONY
INVITATION LETTER
(CLEARED/UNCLASSIFIED)**

Governor Timothy Combs
391 West Paces Ferry Road
Atlanta, GA 30305

Dear Governor Combs,

At the direction of President Joseph Weiland Jr., it is my pleasure to formally extend to you an invitation to the National Reunification Summit in Columbus, Ohio, on Friday, July 3, 2095.

As the President has previously stated, the Summit will turn the page on a dark chapter in our great nation's history. Civic leaders, including yourself, from across the Union will gather in Columbus to declare what has been, since the dawn of this country, self-evident—that we are a nation forever indivisible.

For security and logistical reasons, travel to Columbus from several states, including Georgia, will be restricted in the months preceding and immediately following the Summit. As such, please respond at your earliest convenience with details of your travel party (maximum 4), so as to allow the Peace Office time to perform the necessary security checks and issue the required travel permits.

This is a momentous day for our Union, Governor. A day to celebrate the courage of all Americans who fought so gallantly for what they believed in, but also a day to put years of heartache behind us and begin the difficult but vital work of healing. A day to rejoice and to rebuild. I look forward to meeting with you and all the other delegates from the great state of

Georgia at the formal Reunification Ceremony and the grand parade to follow.

Sincerely,
Malcolm Kaysen
Deputy Secretary to the Director of Southern Affairs
Peace Office, Department of Defense
One Columbus Commons
Columbus, OH 43215

CHAPTER FIFTEEN

In late May, Scott came through and devastated Lincolnton. It was a small storm, but powerful, and although it just missed our home, it disrupted our daily routine. With the community center and the elementary school badly damaged, I found myself confined to the farm. I was thrilled with my good fortune—I had more time with Sarat.

One day I found Sarat in the woodshed, hammering boards. The night before, my parents had gone to a party hosted by the fledgling Southern arm of the New Reunificationists, who in those days were among the first to speak of peace as though peace meant victory. My parents decided to spend the night in Atlanta; my aunt and I had the farm to ourselves.

I found her kneeling by the place where once she had removed the floor to expose the earth. She had beside her a fresh stack of fake-cedar planks.

"What are you doing?" I asked.

"Putting the boards back in," she said. "You take any more wood from this shed, the whole thing will come down."

"Can I help?"

"Sure." She waved me over. I sat between her knees and she put the hammer in my hand. She held the nail in place.

"One soft one to set it, one hard one to drive it," she said.

I tried, but I couldn't bring the hammer down hard enough, for fear I'd miss and hit her finger. Finally, I cracked the nail with enough force to move it, but at an angle; it splintered the wood.

"Better, better," my aunt said. "At least that did something."

She had me practice on the damaged plank until I perfected the motion. In half an hour, I'd hammered the board into the floor with so many nails, no force in the world could move it. I beamed at my handiwork.

We covered half the hollow in the floor before the midday heat exhausted me. She suggested we go cool down in the river. With ease she picked me up and set me on her shoulders. We walked out to the eastern edge of the property and over the seawall and out to where the stunted trees met the water.

We stopped in a place where a soft beach of soil separated the willows. We sat for a moment while my aunt recovered from the long walk. I dug my hands deep into the earth. I learned, on one of our earliest trips to the river, that she liked to swim naked. The first time she'd taken off her clothes, she did so in the water, fearful I'd be frightened by the sight of her scars. But it didn't bother me—I'd seen them before, when I spied on her that night after she first arrived in our home. So I stripped down too, and from that day onward it seemed unimaginable that anyone should step into the water clothed.

We swam under the shade of the willows and the quarantine wall. On one of our trips to the river I had asked her why the wall was there. She said the people on the other side had been infected with a sickness, and the wall was built to keep them from making others sick. I asked her what kind of sickness. She said the kind where you don't ever get better, the kind you can't help but pass on to your children, and they to theirs.

To the east a guard looked on from the tower. I waved at him but he didn't wave back. At first the guards scared me, but my aunt told me they were not human beings, just a pair of eyes unable to harm or help anyone or anything. I thought of them now in the same way I thought of the stick-figure children my mother had painted on the levee, and I was no longer scared.

We dried ourselves in the sun, naked by the riverbank. Even now, her body astounded me: the strange rivulets of scarred skin that lined her upper arms and shoulders, dead-looking and paler than the rest of her; the way her breasts and stomach sagged; the smoothness of her shaved head. In her presence I could think of nothing strong enough to harm us. Not the river, nor the wall, nor whatever lay beyond the wall.

"Is Dana your sister?" I asked. The question had been weighing on my mind for weeks, ever since I heard her say Dana's name when she was talking to my father one night. I knew the woman in one of the pictures on our staircase wall was my other aunt, but my parents had never told me much about her.

The question seemed to take her by surprise.

"That's right," she said. "My sister and your father's sister."

"Does she live in Atlanta?"

"No. She's dead."

"How did she die?" I asked.

"You know the Birds that fly around here sometimes?"

"Sure."

"Well, they're empty now; they just fly around doing nothing until their solar panels break down or their wings crack and they crash in a field somewhere. But before you were born, they used to be weapons. They use to drop bombs from their stomachs."

It seemed such a ridiculous thing—birds that drop bombs from their stomachs. But like the squiggly things in the soil or the fish with whiskers or the old coastal cities now buried underneath the sea, I believed it. I believed it because she said it.

"You know, she lives right here now, my sister." Sarat pointed at the water. "After she died, instead of burying her in the ground, I buried her in the river."

"Why?" I asked.

"I wanted her to never stop moving."

"If I die, will you bury me in the river?"

My aunt chuckled. "It'll be a good long while before you die," she said. "I'll be gone before then."

"How about if you die?" I said. "Do you want me to bury you in the river?"

She was dumbstruck, as though she'd never considered it before. She smiled.

"Yeah," she said. "I'd be grateful if you did."

I leaned against her arm, and put my own arm around her. She was mine and I loved her.

☆ ☆ ☆

WHEN WE RETURNED from the river there was a man at the gate. He was a stranger to me, dressed in a fine prewar suit and a green tie. He stood just outside the gate, his car parked in the driveway, peering in. We walked up the road to meet him.

It wasn't until we were very close to the gate that my aunt's damaged eyes finally made out the stranger. She stood a long time staring at him, her face empty.

"Go on inside, Benjamin," she said. "I'll be in in a minute."

I asked her who the man was, but she ordered me inside again in a tone that let me know it was best not to ask any more questions.

She opened the gate. She inspected the man who stood before her, the man she hadn't seen in many years. He had aged, but he had aged well. The silver wings of hair and the thick black mustache, now also graying, were little changed from when she'd last seen him among the ruins of Lake Sinclair all those years ago.

"Hello, Joe," she said. "I thought you'd be long gone by now."

"Hello, Sarat," said Joe. Instantly she recognized his faraway accent. "I'm sorry I didn't visit sooner. I didn't know they had set you free."

She ushered him to the woodshed. I watched them from my bedroom window, hoping to catch a snippet of their conversation, but they walked silently and shut the door behind them.

I only learned what he said to her later, when I read it. By then it was too late.

☆ ☆ ☆

THEY SAT ON STOOLS by the workbench. She saw that he had not changed, his cool air of charm the same as it had been in their old clandestine meetings.

"He's a cute boy," said Joe, pointing in the direction of the house. "Is he . . . ?"

"He's my nephew."

"I see— How are you, Sarat?" he asked.

"Alive," my aunt replied.

"I want to say, first of all, that I didn't know what Albert Gaines had done. A long time ago he'd sent his daughter and her mother to live in the Bouazizi Empire, so they would be safe during the war, and I'm told his interrogators told him they'd learned of their whereabouts, and used it as leverage against him. He was not a coward when I knew him, Sarat, and I . . ."

"Don't," she said. "It doesn't matter."

Joe nodded. She saw that he was doing now what everyone she'd known from before her time in prison had done—he was staring, trying to reconcile the shape and size and damage of her now with the recollected image of the lanky teenager he'd once known.

Finally he said, "I know what they must have done to you in that place, Sarat, and I am truly sorry."

"You didn't come here just to tell me that."

"That's correct," Joe said. "I understand that you were able to meet one of your old prison guards. I understand that you were able to exact some measure of revenge."

Sarat laughed. "Revenge," she echoed. "Revenge, revenge. I hurt one man. Do you think it was just one man who hurt me?"

"If you would like, I can ask my contacts to look for others," Joe said. "Many of the guards who were stationed at Sugarloaf when you were there are back on the mainland now. Perhaps . . ."

"Why stop there?" she said. "Why don't you line them all up for me—can you do that, Joe?—you line up every man who made me what I am: the ones who killed my father, the ones who killed my sister, the ones who killed my mother, the ones who made it so my brother will never be whole again, the ones who drove us from our home, the ones who slaughtered all those people in Patience. You line up the whole lot of them for me, Joe. Then I'll have my revenge."

"And supposing I could?" Joe asked.

A grimace of light shone through the cracks in the boards.

"Say what you mean," my aunt replied.

"For several years, I cultivated a relationship with a young man in the North," said Joe. "A man named Tusk, a scientist who has dedicated his life to finding a cure for the disease the Blue government once used to silence the people of South Carolina. But even though he spent many years trying, he failed, and in the process he created something far worse—another disease of sorts, capable of wiping out entire cities, entire nations. He is in many ways a broken man, Sarat. And last year I arranged a deal with him—in exchange for the thing he created, I have offered him refuge in my home country, away from the war and everything he has had to endure.

"The Reunification Ceremony is coming up in a few months. The war will be over, and no matter what your new Southern politicians say, it will have been won by the North. But if someone were to go to

Columbus and release this disease, it would change the tide of the war, change the victor, change everything. I want to know if you wish to be the one to do it, Sarat."

A silence shrouded the room. Light turned to heat on the still uncovered soil. He waited on her answer.

"You don't need me to do it," she said.

"That's right. I could have one of my contacts in the North do it. It would be much easier to do it that way, I suspect. The Blues have thousands of new guards on patrol at the border crossings, and the ones I used to have some influence with are gone. But I wanted to offer it to you first, because I know how much you have fought and how much you have suffered. You want something the size of your vengeance, Sarat? This, I believe, is the size of your vengeance."

They heard a fleeting sound outside. A laborer wheeling fresh soil to the greenhouses. Then it was quiet again.

"Tell me your real name," my aunt said.

"My real name is Yousef Bin Rashid. I am seventy-one years old. I work for the government of the Bouazizi Empire."

"Yousef," Sarat repeated, letting her tongue whip every syllable. "*You-sef.*"

"It doesn't really matter to you, does it," she asked, "who wins this war?"

"No. It does not."

"Then why? Why be a part of it?"

"I come from a new place, Sarat," Yousef said. "My people have created an empire. It is young now, but we intend it to be the most powerful empire in the world. For that to happen, other empires must fail. I think by now you understand that, if it were the other way around—if the South was on the verge of winning—perhaps I would be having this conversation in Pittsburgh or Columbus. I don't want to lie to you, Sarat: this is a matter of self-interest, nothing more."

Sarat smiled at the thought. "You couldn't just let us kill ourselves in peace, could you?"

"Come now," said Yousef. "Everyone fights an American war."

They were both quiet, and in the silence Sarat was reminded of something Albert Gaines had told her. He asked her once if she knew how the word Red came to be shorthand for the South. She said it was politics, something to do with who voted for the old Republican Party back when it was all still one country.

But Gaines said it was older than all that, older than the country itself. He said it was about the dirt: in the South there's a mineral in the ground that turns the dirt red. He said when you've leached all the good from the earth, all the nutrients that a seedling needs to grow, the last thing left is the stuff that turns the dirt red.

She wondered now if maybe that was the only honest thing he'd ever told her.

"It'll kill everyone it touches, this sickness you have?" she asked Yousef.

"You have my word," Yousef replied.

"I'm never going back to that prison. No matter what happens, I'm never going back."

"You have my word."

She stood from her stool and walked to the doors and flung them open. Blistering daylight flooded the shed. She looked out at the new house that stood where the old one used to be, and at the wilting trees and the river imprisoned by walls. The world about her shook with heat.

"Do you ever get sick of this place, Yousef?" she asked. "Ever wish you could just be done with it, just go home, back to your family, back to the world you know?"

"Of course," Yousef replied. "I hope to go home one day soon."

"Me too," she said.

☆ ☆ ☆

FROM THEN ON she was distant. Once more she barricaded herself in that shed, just like she did when she first arrived. This time the door was closed and locked; I couldn't see inside.

I was so desperate to reach her that I spent hours kneeling outside the shed's back wall with my ear against the boards, listening. All I ever heard was the scratch of old pen on paper.

I lay awake at night wondering what I had done to drive her away. Was she disappointed in me—had I failed to defeat the river current one too many times? Had I nagged her with too many questions? Did I bore her? In desperation, I scribbled the word "Sorry" on a blank sheet of paper and slid it under her door. She made no reply.

☆ ☆ ☆

ON A SATURDAY in the middle of June, while my parents were at a farmers' trade show in Montgomery, she left the house for a day. We kept a used Tik-Tok on the property for emergencies; she took it.

She drove to the market in Lincolnton. It was a smaller crowd than usual, the town still cleaning up the last of the damage from Hurricane Scott. She walked past the half-empty stalls to the end of the road, where Marcus stood watch.

Without speaking they went to the church nearby. This time she went in first and he followed.

"Goddamn I'm glad you showed up today," said Marcus. "You know what I just heard from one of the Free Southerner boys? You remember that old man Prince Wendell, used to run a coffee shop out in the middle of the ocean? They're gonna name a street in Atlanta after him. Guess someone on one of those Reunification prep committees heard about him, and they decided to do it. Thought it would look good to honor a man who worked with both sides. I thought you'd get a kick out of—"

"Sit down," my aunt said. "I need to talk to you."

Marcus sat beside her on the pew. "Sure," he said.

My aunt handed her friend a small folded piece of paper. On it was written the name and contact information of a man.

"There's someone I know. I want you to go talk to him. He can arrange for you to leave this place, to leave all of this, and go start a new life on the other side of the world."

Marcus stared at the paper, confused.

"Sarat, it's all coming to an end," he said. "In a few months there's going to be no more war. It'll all be one country again. And then, I swear to you, you won't believe how quickly everyone forgets all about this."

My aunt shook her head. "Please, Marcus. Just go see him."

Marcus took the paper from her hand. "The war's over, Sarat," he said, and this time it didn't sound as though he was trying to reassure her.

"I know, Marcus," she said. She kissed him. She stood. "I know."

☆ ☆ ☆

SHE LEFT LINCOLNTON and drove west to the outer suburbs of Atlanta, in the shadows of the factories and the vertical farms. She went to Stone Mountain, on the easternmost outskirts of the city. Near the dilapidated, flat bungalows of the old village there stood an unmarked, redbrick storefront. It was to this meager slice of real estate that the United Rebels had been relegated.

When she arrived she found only Adam Bragg Jr. and Trough in the office. It was a small space—once a restaurant or a bakery—and longer than it was wide. Chairs stood upturned on their tables, except for where Bragg sat, nursing a cup of coffee.

He stood when he saw her. "Well hello there," he said. "Who'd have thought the great Sarat Chestnut would come visit us in our new home."

He beckoned her to the chair opposite him at the table. Even stripped of its old cash register and front counter, the place felt claustrophobic, the walls lined with cheap dark wood and decorated with ancient posters that urged: "Have a Coke."

Trough stood in the back of the room, near where the chairs and tables gave way to stacks of unopened moving boxes. The first time she had seen him after her release from Sugarloaf—on the day they took her to meet her old captor—she hadn't recognized him. But he looked familiar now, thin like his older brother; eyes numb and accusing.

"Can you believe it's come to this?" said Bragg. "Cast out into the wilderness, disowned by our own people. You know what they put in that building we used to be in—the one downtown, under the highway—after they forced us out? The new office of the Reunification Celebration Committee."

He laughed and shook his head. "They got a whole building of people deciding where to hang the balloons and send the marching bands to celebrate the day we surrender. Jesus, I wish my dad was alive to see it. It would have killed that old bastard twice."

"I need your help," my aunt said.

Bragg motioned for Trough to make more coffee. With his eyes still on my aunt, the young man complied.

"Name it," Bragg said. "We ain't got much, but what we got is yours."

"If I told you I could turn it all around—kill every last one of them who run the Blue, wipe out the North, make it so they don't see the sun for a hundred years—would you believe me?"

"Yeah, I'd believe you," said Bragg. "I wouldn't believe anybody else who said it, but I'd believe you."

Trough placed a cup of coffee on the table and returned to his post, watching.

"I need you to get me across the border," my aunt said. "I need to be in Columbus for the Reunification Ceremony."

"Christ, Sarat, it can't be done," said Bragg. "They got more men guarding the Tennessee line ahead of that goddamn ceremony than they did during the height of the war. Every crossing's a fortress, and they ain't letting a single Southerner through, probably not until the end of the year."

"What about the tunnels?" my aunt asked. "The ones we used to crawl through to get near Halfway Branch?"

"Sarat, they demolished those years ago. That world don't exist no more. Hell, other than Trough here, I got three, maybe four good men left. They wore our people down; everyone's tired and hungry and they all lost the will for war. Go see it for yourself on your way back home—drive into Atlanta proper, look at all those billboards the Free Southern State put up—'Peace With Dignity,' 'Respecting Our Past, Securing Our Future.' All that horseshit, and people eat it up. You know they don't even call themselves the Free Southern State anymore? They just use the acronym, never spell it out, like the letters don't mean nothing. They're waving their cowardice around like a goddamn flag—"

"I know a way," said Trough. "I know how you can get to Columbus."

Bragg fell silent.

"How?" my aunt asked.

Trough came to the table. "There's a medical shuttle that goes up north. St. Joseph's has a deal with a hospital up in Lexington. They get to ship a few people up there on the first of every month. They cap it at a dozen patients, and they keep it quiet. But I know the guy who runs it; he and my brother spent some time up at the Tennessee line together. He owed my brother a favor from back then, and there's no one but me left to collect. I'll tell him I got a friend who'll die if she don't get treatment up north. He'll bump someone and put you on. Then soon as you cross the border, you can make your way to Columbus."

Bragg stared at his lieutenant, dumbfounded. He turned to my aunt. "But if you're really gonna kill as many as you say, that means you're gonna take something with you—a weapon, a bomb, something. And just because it's a medical shuttle don't mean the Blues won't search it."

"They won't find what I'm bringing," my aunt said. "They can search me all they want, they won't find it."

"I have one condition," said Trough.

"What's that?" my aunt asked.

"I go with you."

"The thing I'm going to use, you can't aim it. It's a sickness, a kind that will spread to every last one of them in Columbus. Nobody going on this trip is coming back."

"I go with you," said Trough.

"No."

"Let him, Sarat," said Bragg. "He's been rotting here praying to be with his family for going on ten years. Give him what he wants—you owe it to his brother, just like that man from St. Joe's."

"I don't owe anybody a single thing," my aunt said.

Bragg sighed and rubbed his temples. "Let me ask you something, Sarat. During all that time you spent in Sugarloaf getting interrogated, did they ever once ask you whether you had anything to do with the killing of that Blue general, Weiland?"

"No."

"But that's the one thing you actually did. All that other stuff they must have asked you about, you probably didn't have a single useful thing to tell them. But the one guy you killed, they never once asked you about him. Why do you think that is?"

"I don't know," my aunt said.

"I'll tell you why. They didn't ask you about it because two days after they picked you up, that boy Attic walked right up to the Blue border guards at Harrogate and turned himself in. He told them it was him who killed the general. He made them believe it—told them all the details he knew from listening to us talk about it, except with him as the shooter. Now they got him locked away in Sugarloaf too—in a place called Camp Sunday where they keep the ones they won't even do the mercy of killing. That's why they never asked you about the one thing you did, Sarat. That's why you're free."

"That was his choice," my aunt said. "I never asked him to do it."

"Nobody asked him to do it, but that don't change the fact he did. And it don't change the fact that you're alive and sitting here now because of it."

Bragg pointed at Trough. "I know you've been through hell, Sarat. I know you had things done to you and I know you were a different girl before. But these boys never even had a before. They were dead before they got a shot at living. Give him what he wants. Let him be with his brothers."

Trough stood at the table, eyes blue and still, his face unchanged.

"Make it happen," my aunt told him, "and you can come with me."

Trough nodded. The last of the Salt Lake Boys left the old brick store.

Bragg stood. He walked to the back of the room, where the unopened moving boxes lay stacked. He began to rummage through them.

"You know, I always used to wonder what lines he used on you," Bragg said.

"Who used on me?"

"Gaines, when he was trying to recruit you. He had all these different plans of attack, you know, when he was trying to bring someone into the fold. Like if a kid was religious, he'd start talking to them about how it was God's will for the South to emerge victorious. Or if they were insecure, he'd talk to them about the ever-accepting rebel family. But he always told my father you were too sharp for all that. Too curious too—what was the word he used?—truculent. I had to go look that one up. He said if the course of life don't recruit her to the cause, no man will."

Bragg returned to the table, a small bronze star in hand. "Well, Sarat Chestnut, I thank God the course of life recruited you."

He set the star on the table and passed it to her. It was a pin, rusted and slightly warped.

"My father had these made a long time ago," said Bragg. "He had them cast in the style of the old Southern State flag. Did you know they drew the stars on that flag all wrong? Had the right-facing edges longer than the others; never bothered to fix it. My father had all these grand visions of a proper Southern rebel army. And so he had these little medals of valor made up so he could hand them out for 'Meritorious military service in the war against the Northern enemy.' "

Bragg chuckled. "Poor bastard didn't even get to hand out one."

My aunt held the rebel star in her hand. The pin in the back held fast to its catch with rust, and would not open.

"Is it really going to work, this thing you have?" asked Bragg. "When you set it loose in Columbus, it'll be enough to kill all of them—the Blues, the Southern traitors, the whole lot of 'em?"

"Everyone," my aunt said.

Bragg reached over and took my aunt's hand in his. "You're going to be remembered, Sarat," he said. "You'll be a hero to the Southern cause for as long as the South exists. When this is over they'll build cities in your name."

My aunt pulled her hand away. She tossed the flawed star to the ground. She stood.

"Fuck the South," she said. "Fuck the South and everything it stands for."

☆ ☆ ☆

SHE LEFT STONE MOUNTAIN. She drove west, through the capital and through the state, into Alabama. She went to the forest. For the last time, she went to see Albert Gaines.

The Talladega forest was thinner than she remembered it, the trees seemingly further apart. But the path to the cabin was the same, singed in her memory from all those times she'd stalked through this place, picking off cans, hunting rats.

She intended to gut the old man the way she'd gutted the guard who'd drowned her.

She opened the door and found him sitting inside, asleep in his chair.

Bragg had told her he'd suffered a stroke in the detention camp, right after he and the other recruiters had been rounded up. She saw the damage on the right side of his face. He was sitting in an old rusted wheelchair, wearing soiled pajamas whose stitching was coming apart. His hair was white and thin.

He looked old, ancient. His breathing was a fine whistle, the air leaking out of his mouth. She understood then why none of the remaining rebels had come out here to put a bullet in his head and stuff his mouth with the lining of his pockets. It would have been a kindness.

He woke at the sound of her footsteps. When he saw her he recoiled and his breathing grew quicker; his mouth opened but nothing came out. She saw his eyes, darting like gas lamp flames. For a moment he looked her over, unsure, but she knew he recognized her. Just like she knew she would always recognize him. Even if it had just been a pile of bones she found when she walked into that shack, she'd know it was him.

She looked around the room. Dirty dishes lined the table and filled the sink. There were clothes on the floor—not the fine suits she remembered, but undershirts and cheap pants from the sweatshops down south. In one corner of the room there was a bookshelf but it was empty.

On a table near the bed she saw the old stereo Gaines used to keep in his office in Patience. Of all the things in the cabin, only the stereo showed no accumulation of dust. She set it to play. The old classical number filled the room; the song of the weary pilgrim.

She knelt beside him. She drew in close. He was alien to her now, this feral, sickly old man. But what was inside him was still the same.

He looked at her. Between the soft heaves of his breathing he said, My daughter.

He said it again and again: My daughter, my daughter. Every time it sounded like an unfinished sentence, like there was more coming, but it was just those two words.

And then his breathing halted, and for a moment she thought that he had left her, that this was his final act of abuse: to die before her.

Then he exhaled and with the exhale came all of what he'd been trying to say.

"They said they would hurt my daughter."

She took the knife from her pocket, the knife he'd given her all those years ago. She opened his gnarled fingers to reveal the yellow skin of his palm. She gave it back to him.

IN LATE JUNE the storms subsided and new crops were born. For months my mother had tried in secret to grow strawberries in the greenhouses, and suddenly the plants began to deliver. The leaves sagged with berries thick as fists, dark and bursting with juice. My mother invited all her friends to come try the farm's newest produce, and all agreed the strawberries were the best they'd ever had.

One night, my parents got into an argument. Afterward my father went outside for a walk. Sometimes when he wanted to be alone, he sat on the levee, looking out at the river and the quarantine wall.

In a while his sister emerged from her shed and joined him.

They sat under the light of a copper moon. A westward wind made the willow leaves dance like charmed snakes. The river moved.

"She wants to go north, after they sign the treaty," my father said. "To Pittsburgh or upstate New York. She wants to sell the farm and the house and move there."

Sarat tried to gauge the state of her brother's lucidity, whether he was liable to leave her and wander to his clouded place.

"And what do you want?" she asked.

"I don't want to go."

The sound of humming motors came across the water. Somewhere, shielded by the night, a dredging ship slowly changed the shape of the river.

"I remember when we were kids back in Louisiana and Dad first said he was going to go up to the permit office in Baton Rouge and try to get a pass to the North," my aunt said. "I still remember how much you hated him for it. You kept telling Dana and me how anyone that wants to go up to the Blue country is a traitor. One time I even saw you packing a little bag and burying it in the dirt near that raft you had, like if Dad really tried to make us go north, you'd just take your things and sail off into the Mississippi Sea, go live on one of those man-made islands in the Gulf."

She chuckled. She turned to look at her brother and saw that he was smiling, his eyes cast down at his feet.

"You don't remember any of it, do you?" she said.

My father shook his head. "It just gets away from me sometimes. I can . . ." He rubbed his temple. "Truth is I'd be happier if I didn't remember any of it, if there wasn't anything left of it at all."

My aunt watched the guards in their towers on the other side of the river. She wondered if it was the same boys from her youth who still guarded the quarantine wall. The only signs of them now were small pulsing lights that blinked red against the darkness.

"It's strange, isn't it," she said, "what sticks with you and what doesn't, the things you decide to keep. The night after the massacre at Patience, I remember I'd sent Dana away, and the soldiers had taken you to the morgue, thinking you were dead, but I didn't want to leave. Some of the bodies were still there, you could still smell that burning in the air, from when they'd tossed the dead in the fire—but I wanted to stay. I wanted to find Mama, anything that was left of her, even if it was just ash. Finally the soldiers told me I had ten minutes to get my things before they were going to tie me up and throw me on the last bus out. So I went back, and you know what I took? I took Dad's old statue, the Virgin of Guadalupe; I took that turtle Marcus and I kept as a pet; I took a couple of old photos from Mama's bunk. I didn't take any clothes, didn't take any of the money Mama had saved up all her life. Not a single useful thing. Just junk."

"It wasn't junk," my father said. "It was our past."

"That's exactly what it was," she said. "There's this passage in one of the books Albert Gaines once gave me. It said in the South there is no future, only three kinds of past—the distant past of heritage, the near past of experience, and the past-in-waiting. What they've got up there in the Blue—what your wife wants, what our parents wanted—is a future."

"If we go up north," my father asked, "will you come with us?"

"Don't ask me that," my aunt replied.

An impotent Bird flew overhead, invisible in the evening sky. She remembered the first time she'd heard one of them after she'd been released from Sugarloaf—how she instinctively dove to the ground, covered her ears, breathed out lest the pressure wave of a nearby blast shatter her lungs. And then later, rising from the floor, wondering how it could be that in all her waking hours since the day they drowned her she felt not an ounce of will to live, and yet in that moment of perceived danger she had so quickly sought to protect herself, to stave off death. Why did the thought of violence against her only terrify her when it came at the hands of anyone but herself? She did not know.

"I want you to do something for me," she said to her brother.

"All right," my father said.

"I want you to forgive me."

"Forgive you for what?"

"For doing something terrible," my aunt said. "For taking so much away from you."

"You never took anything away from me, Sarat. You took care of me, after Patience. Karina told me how you came back for me, how everyone thought I was dead but you and Dana wouldn't give up . . ."

"That's a lie. I wanted you to be dead. The first time I saw you after they brought you home, saw how badly they'd hurt you, I wished you'd never survived. That's what I am, Simon. Makes no difference now how I got to be that way, it's what I am. I don't want you to love me, I don't want you to tell me I did nothing wrong. I want you to know I did wrong, and I want you to forgive me. Please, I'm begging you, just say you'll forgive me."

"I forgive you," my father said. "I forgive you."

She sank then into her brother's arms. And for the first time since she was a little girl at Patience, stained with the blood of the first man she ever killed, she wept.

She never saw her brother again.

☆ ☆ ☆

THE FOLLOWING MORNING I woke just before dawn, startled by the sound of our car moving up the driveway. In the twilight I saw my aunt park near the unused greenhouse in which she hid her secret things. I inched the bedroom window open and watched.

She opened the trunk, then she disappeared inside the greenhouse, shovel in hand. For a while I saw nothing, but soon she emerged, her hands black with soil. I watched her take dozens of dirt-stained diaries from the greenhouse and pack them in the trunk of the car. Then she drove away from the house. The front gate opened but the doorbell made no sound.

She was gone the whole day. She returned in the early hours of the following morning. In the darkness I heard her cavernous footfalls on the stairs. My bedroom door creaked open. There was no light but I knew it was her.

She came close to where I lay and knelt by my bedside. She turned on the lamp. It had been a long time since I'd seen her face so close. I felt the heat of her on me. I stared, wide-eyed.

"Hey," she said, "you want to go on an adventure?"

At the sound of that word, all the fog of sleep instantly left me. I nodded.

"Follow me," she said, "and be very quiet."

I watched her open my dresser drawers and pack a few changes of clothes into a small backpack. "Here," she said, handing it to me, "you'll need this."

Still in my pajamas, I trailed her to the car outside. Slowly she drove up the driveway, and I saw the wires hanging from the panel she'd broken, the one that made the doorbell ring. We slipped silently past the gate.

I asked her where we were going, but she said it was a surprise. We seemed to drive forever, away from the sun. The sky was blue behind us but black ahead.

Eventually I fell back asleep. When I woke it was early afternoon and we were in unfamiliar country. The highway along which the car raced was hugged by endless browning fields. I saw broken-down signs for motels and restaurants of which only wreckage remained.

We were coming up on water. I could see it in the distance—a vast brown river, thick as honey. Again I asked her where we were going, but she would not say.

Before we reached the water, she pulled onto a small dirt road that scythed a path through the myrtle trees. The trees had lost their color but the ground was littered with the remains of pink baptisia. We parked near one of the trees, around which a white strip of cloth had been tied.

She got out of the car. I followed. For a while she just stood there, saying nothing. I begged her to tell me what we were doing, but she simply told me to wait. I was still electric with the sense of adventure.

A dark sedan rolled up the road to meet us.

Two men emerged from the car. One was tall and burly, the other short, both bearded. The short one came to where we stood and looked me over.

"That him?" he asked.

"Yeah," my aunt said. "You know what to do?"

"Won't be a problem," the short man said. "Be about a month getting out to the coast, then however long the smugglers take, but we'll take good care of him, don't you worry."

I watched her give two envelopes to the man. He opened one and counted the cash inside. The other had my name on it, and was sealed.

"Don't give that one to him until he's a man," she said.

I asked her what was going on.

She knelt down to face me. "You have to go with these men for a while," she said. "They're going to take you to a safe place. Don't worry, everything's going to be all right."

"I don't want to go with them," I said. "I want to stay with you."

"I'm sorry, Benjamin," she replied. "It has to be this way."

The short man picked me up. I screamed and kicked at him, my heels driving into his shins. I begged her not to let me go.

As the short man carried me to the waiting car, I saw the tall one shake Sarat's hand.

"I just want to say it's an honor to finally meet you, Miss Chestnut," he said. "I heard what you did at Halfway Branch way back when. You're a true patriot of the South."

"Make sure he gets a good life up there," she said.

"Yes ma'am," the man replied. He returned to the car. We started moving. I slammed my hands against the rear window as the hulking frame of my aunt grew smaller and finally disappeared.

The men drove toward the Mississippi River. I cried and called out for my mother. As soon as we were away from the meeting place, the shorter of the men turned around and slapped me across the face.

"I don't give a shit whose nephew you are," he said. "You keep squealing like that and I'll break your goddamn jaw."

I slunk back, stunned. I tasted the dull iron of blood in my mouth. It was the first time anyone had ever hit me.

The men waited till nightfall to cross the river. They crossed in an old rebel skiff, under moonless night.

"Welcome to Purple country, kid," the short man said. "Nothing but cowards and traitors, far as the eye can see."

For weeks, we drove westward. The men refused to travel during daylight hours, or to take major roads. The landscape turned alien—vast trays of sand, pierced by mesas colored caramel and orange. The desert was endless and littered with the wreckage of tanks and planes and makeshift camps from the earliest days of the war. They fed me nothing but old ration packs: meat in the form of powder and sickly sweet apricot gel that was designed never to go bad.

Sometimes we stopped in small, run-down villages manned by soldiers whose uniforms I'd never seen before. The people spoke a different language and I couldn't read the street signs. Sometimes the soldiers pointed their rifles at my two kidnappers and asked them what their business was in the Protectorado. It was during these times I thought of screaming for help, but the shorter man told me if I opened my mouth he'd kill me.

One day the desert ended and a parched, desolate forest replaced it. The forest too seemed to stretch forever, but there was not a single living thing within it. Everywhere around me I was surrounded by the aftereffects of a fire.

By the time we reached the Pacific, I could no longer tell the days and weeks apart. The men camped in the concrete remains of a desalination plant half-submerged in the water. The sound of waves crashing against the side of the building became maddening as the weeks went by. I gathered from the two men's conversations that the smuggler's ship that was to take us from this place had capsized, and it would be another month before the next one came. We waited.

Every night, the men listened to a small radio for news. For weeks there was nothing, and then a burst of reports of a mystery illness radiating from Columbus, and then nothing again.

A vessel arrived in late October. It was an old fiberglass crabber, badly beaten and ill-suited for the ocean. From the moment the men dragged me onboard, I was green with seasickness.

The trip north was slow and rough. The captain kept close to the shoreline, and often the men cursed him and said he was going to run us ashore.

☆ ☆ ☆

THEN ONE DAY I looked out the cabin window to see a strange city alight with floating glitter. As we neared the port, I saw places in the water where previous ships had run into the submerged barrier reefs.

"You made it, kid," the shorter man said. "New Anchorage—the neutral state. Welcome home."

Excerpted from:

HEARING BEFORE THE COMMITTEE FOR TRUTH AND REUNIFICATION, ONE HUNDRED AND SIXTY-THIRD CONGRESS (DECEMBER 1, 2123)

Members Present:

SENATOR ELI THOMPSON (New Reunificationist—Arkansas) Chair
SENATOR BARBARA AIKENS (Democrat—Cascadia/Oregon) Vice Chair
SENATOR PETER JINDAL (New Reunificationist—Missouri)
SENATOR CLAY NORMAN (Democrat—Illinois)
SENATOR BERNARD WILLIS (Democrat—Indiana)

Witnesses:

COLONEL BARRET SINGER (Ret.)

SEN. THOMPSON: Good morning, everyone. If we can get the screen up and running, I think we can pick up where we left off yesterday. Senator Aikens?

SEN. AIKENS: Thank you, Mr. Chair. Colonel, before we go back to the surveillance footage, I just wanted to ask you about something you mentioned yesterday. About the two soldiers who were manning the Rossville checkpoint—Private Martin Baker and, what was the other one's name again?

COL. SINGER: Bud Baker Jr.

SEN. AIKENS: That's right, thank you. You mentioned yesterday that they were—let me see . . . in your words, "wired for kinetics," rather than border guard duty, is that correct?

COL. SINGER: Yes ma'am.

SEN. AIKENS: And what exactly did you mean by that, Colonel?

COL. SINGER: Well, certain young men, as soon as they arrive at the recruiter's office, you can tell . . . What I mean is, if it had still been a hot war, I wouldn't have assigned those boys to guard duty.

SEN. WILLIS: I think it's pretty clear what the Colonel is saying, Senator. Those two boys were mean sons of bitches.

COL. SINGER: That would be an accurate description.

SEN. WILLIS: Can't say I blame them, with what they'd been through.

SEN. AIKENS: Thank you, Colonel. Let's go back to the video. Now, my understanding is that this is the only surviving footage of the crossing on that day?

COL. SINGER: That's all we've got left, is the overhead. No ground-level, no audio.

SEN. AIKENS: So at the end of the day we're left with what, exactly? Conjecture? A guess?

COL. SINGER: Well, ma'am, what we do know is that, shortly before the first cases appeared in Columbus, the same sickness was noted in the hospital to which this particular bus was headed. So there is some reason to believe that the person responsible for the virus could have come across the border on that bus.

SEN. AIKENS: But we have no manifest, no hospital records. Colonel, we don't even know the name of anyone on this video except your two soldiers.

COL. SINGER: That's right, ma'am. Obviously the decade of the Reunification Plague decimated many parts of this country, and countless records were lost. We're left only with what survived.

SEN. AIKENS: Very well. Let's play it. So the medical transport bus arrives at the checkpoint that day at around noon, is that correct?

COL. SINGER: Yes ma'am.

SEN. AIKENS: And there were no other vehicles or convoys of any kind cleared for passage to the North that day.

COL. SINGER: That's right. It was two days to the Reunification Ceremony. The entire Southern border was on lockdown.

SEN. AIKENS: So the two soldiers at the Rossville checkpoint would have known ahead of time that this bus was to be allowed through?

COL. SINGER: They would have known it was an authorized vehicle, but we would never tell our soldiers to simply let a vehicle through. They would have known they would be expected to inspect the vehicle and check the paperwork of every passenger. Same as they would with anyone trying to come north from the Red.

SEN. AIKENS: So if we can go ahead and skip to the point where the passengers disembark . . . yes, thank you. Now at this point, one of the two young men—Private Martin Baker, I believe—is still inside the guard building. So what we have here is his brother, Bud Baker Jr., essentially ordering the passengers to line up for individual inspection. Is that correct, Colonel?

COL. SINGER: Yes ma'am. Again, standard procedure.

SEN. AIKENS: Now I see that, with the first two patients in line, Private Bud Jr. is perhaps a bit curt, but those interactions take just a minute or two. When he sees the third patient, however, I think it's fairly evident that his demeanor changes, wouldn't you say?

COL. SINGER: I suppose.

SEN. AIKENS: Any idea why?

COL. SINGER: Could be the size of the individual. You can see she appears to be a fairly intimidating woman, from a physical standpoint. Could be because she appears to be much younger than the first two people in line. Could be she reminded him of someone, or he thought he'd seen her before. Could be he just got a bad vibe from her—an instinctual thing.

SEN. AIKENS: So the young man who wheels her forward, he hands the travel permits to the Private for inspection. And now—if we can just pause it here—Colonel, can you tell me what the Private is saying here?

COL. SINGER: He's asking her what her illness is.

SEN. AIKENS: He didn't do that with the first two patients.

COL. SINGER: No ma'am.

SEN. AIKENS: And her reply?

COL. SINGER: The way she's facing, the overhead doesn't catch her face.

SEN. AIKENS: But is it a fair assessment, Colonel, to say that the Private doesn't believe her?

COL. SINGER: I couldn't tell you. Obviously he doesn't just let her pass.

SEN. AIKENS: That's right. He orders her to stand up.

COL. SINGER: That's what the lip readers tell me.

SEN. AIKENS: And when the young man pushing her wheelchair interjects, the Private doesn't hesitate to raise his rifle at him and order him to his knees.

COL. SINGER: Senator, you're talking about two boys who were bound and blindfolded and made to sit there while a Red insurrectionist—one who was never captured—tortured and killed their father. You're talking about two boys who lied about their age on the recruitment form so they could get out to the front, two boys who'd only been stationed at that crossing a few weeks. Obviously this isn't the way we train our border guards to perform inspections. Maybe he was having a bad day. Unfortunately we'll never know, given that, by the end of the week, everyone you see on that screen was dead.

SEN. AIKENS: That's not what confuses me, Colonel. If we could move ahead . . . so he turns back to this woman in the wheelchair, and it's safe to say he orders her to stand up once more. And when she doesn't, he kicks her chair over, sending her to the ground near where that young man is kneeling. Now he's got the rifle pointed at the two of them, and I would expect at this point that, at the very least, he's going to detain these two, if not the other ten patients as well. You stop the video right here and ask me what's going to happen next, and I would bet my bottom dollar that nobody's going to cross the border that day.

COL. SINGER: I suppose.

SEN. AIKENS: But then the other soldier, Private Martin Baker, comes out from the guard building. And he immediately lowers his brother's rifle, tries to defuse the situation, correct?

COL. SINGER: It appears so.

SEN. AIKENS: And then he looks at the medical permit—the same one his brother just inspected—and he looks at the young woman on the ground and the young man on his knees beside her. But he doesn't detain them, he doesn't interrogate them. He . . . well, I would go so far as to say he takes pity on them. He tells his brother to let them through. To let the whole convoy through.

COL. SINGER: Yes ma'am.

SEN. AIKENS: In fact, if my briefing notes are correct, I believe nobody else in line even had their paperwork checked after that. The guards simply ordered them back on the bus and let the bus through. If indeed the person responsible for the Reunification Plague was anywhere further back in line, he or she wouldn't have even gotten a once-over, is that correct?

COL. SINGER: Yes ma'am.

SEN. AIKENS: And that's what confounds me, Colonel. Here you have these two young soldiers. Both of them having suffered the horrific experience of witnessing their father killed by insurrectionists. Both of them, as you put it, "wired for kinetics." And yet one seems ready to shoot two of the patients and the other helps them back to their feet and waves everyone through. Don't you find that at least a little perplexing?

COL. SINGER: I'm not sure, ma'am.

SEN. AIKENS: I mean, I read the military records that survive, Colonel, and both these boys, in just a few weeks on the job, had been reprimanded numerous times for mistreating Southerners at that crossing, and this was at a time when hardly anybody was crossing at all. Obviously they joined the military because they were hell-bent on revenge against the people they held responsible for the killing of their father. And yet on this day, of all days, Private Martin Baker decides to show compassion. If indeed your hunch is correct, and in watching this video we are in fact watching whoever unleashed that terrible illness on our country, can you imagine how many millions of lives would have been saved if he hadn't?

COL. SINGER: Neither of these boys knew that millions of lives were at stake, Senator. At the time, the Tennessee line had been quiet for the better part of a year. The Reunification Ceremony was just a couple of days away. All those two boys would have seen on that day was a busful of sick people headed north for treatment.

SEN. AIKENS: A busful of Southerners.

COL. SINGER: Maybe so, Senator. But I don't think it would be unreasonable to expect that, in some circumstances, even someone hell-bent on revenge might find a temporary capacity for kindness.

SEN. AIKENS: No, Colonel. I suppose it wouldn't.

CHAPTER SIXTEEN

Five times in the first four years, I tried to escape. I tried to bribe the same smuggler who'd brought me here to take me back, to leave me anywhere along the western coast. When that failed I tried to go by land, and when the border guards brought me back to the orphanage for the third time, they said child or not, the next time they'd shoot me.

I knew my parents were dead. But that didn't stop me from inventing soothing fantasies—maybe they'd survived, maybe the plague never came to our home, maybe she'd done for them what she'd done for me. I tried to believe it, though I knew it wasn't true.

☆ ☆ ☆

BY THE TIME I was sixteen, I was working as a dockhand in New Anchorage. There was plenty of money to be had working alongside especially reckless captains on salvage trips to the barrier reefs.

Sometimes on my days off I stood at the same docks alongside the mob, cursing the newest refugees. By then the plague was starting to subside on the mainland, and most of the smugglers refused to ferry any more survivors northward, for fear of contracting the illness themselves. But a couple still ran quarantine houses near the California coast; anyone who lived a week in isolation without showing symptoms was deemed safe enough to travel.

Nativism being a pyramid scheme, I found myself contemptuous of the refugees' presence in a city already overburdened. At the foot of the docks, we yelled at them to go home, even though we knew home to be a pestilence field. We carried signs calling them terrorists and criminals and we vandalized the homes that would take them in. It made me feel good to do it, it made me feel rooted; their unbelonging was proof of my belonging.

On my eighteenth birthday, I came back to the dockhands' dorm to find an envelope passed underneath my door. The paper inside was old and yellowing. It was a letter.

Dear Benjamin,

There are things I want you to know, things that are your right to know.

When I first came to your home, I was empty. I believed there was nothing good in the world. Then I met you, and I learned I was wrong. The time we spent in the river together made me remember what it was like to feel joy.

I told you once that a well-set bone grows stronger. The opposite is also true.

I wish we could have met each other when we were both still children. I think we would have been best friends. I wish you could have seen my old home, our big brown sea, and the pirate ship your father built from clapboard. I wish you could have met your grandparents, who were good and honest people and would have loved you very much. You come from a long line of good hearts.

More than anything, I hope you have a good life in your new home, and that despite how I wronged you, you find happiness. I loved you.

Sarat
30727-83161

I tossed the letter into an old shoebox. I didn't look at it again for almost forty years.

☆ ☆ ☆

TIME PASSED. I went to school and earned a degree in history. It seemed preordained that I should spend my professional life studying the civil war. By the time the plague ended, the country was in a ruinous state, and so many of the source materials on which a historian might rely to piece together the past were lost forever. But that did not dissuade me, and I pursued with rabid stubbornness every document, every long-forgotten archive, the testimony of every survivor. My colleagues, who knew nothing about my past, never found my tenacity particularly unusual; it seemed a natural part of scholarly life to go chasing after questions for which no truly satisfying answers exist.

One day I was traveling back from a speaking engagement in Georgia. The passengers boarded the airplane and we sat waiting in our seats on the tarmac as the panels on the wings soaked up a little more energy from the sun. I was watching the monitor on the seat in front of me. It showed a map of the continent, the plane's flight path, and the numbered coordinates that marked our location on the earth.

Suddenly I realized the meaning of the numbers at the end of Sarat's letter.

As soon as I arrived back home, I rummaged through the storage boxes in the garage until I found it. The next day I flew back south. I went to the place they marked.

It was the destitute southernmost country, near the shore of the Florida Sea. Even with the car's air conditioner on high, the heat was overpowering. I drove past dust farms and shack-towns, places riddled with postwar poverty and the occasional three-star flag hanging limp from trailer-side posts—reminders that in so much of the Red, the war stopped but the war never ended.

I arrived at a small farmhouse with no farm, only a large dirt parcel out front and a barren lake bed out back. There was a man on the front porch, cleaning sand from the gutters. He was younger than me, I was sure of it, but years of unmerciful sun had aged his skin considerably.

"What can I do for you?" he asked as I walked up the driveway.

"I'm not sure, to be honest," I said. "I had . . . I had these directions. But I don't know—if you don't mind me asking, have you lived here a long time? I mean, before the plague?"

His mild cheerfulness suddenly turned to suspicion, and I regretted bringing up the Reunification Plague in a part of the country where brash young men still wear shirts bearing stylized, blacked-out profiles of Julia Templestowe's head.

"What's your name?" he asked.

"Benjamin Chestnut."

"Well goddamn," he said. "All these years I thought Mama was out of her mind. Come in, come in."

He led me into the house. In the living room, an old woman was seated on a decrepit couch, listening to old love songs. She was frail and thin, a wheelchair parked by her side.

"Mama, you got a visitor," the man said. "It's the one you talked about all those years. This is Benjamin Chestnut."

For a moment she eyed me as though I were an apparition. She covered her face with her hands.

"I was sure I'd die before you came," she said.

The old woman sent her son to fetch us drinks and called me to sit next to her on the couch. She touched my face as though she knew me. But I didn't recognize her at all.

"It's there," she said. "I can see it. It's faint, but you got some of her in you."

"I'm not going to lie to you," I said. "I don't know who you are, and I don't know why I'm here."

She laughed. "I think that's the way she wanted it."

The old woman shook my hand. "My name is Layla Denomme Jr.," she said. "I knew your aunt Sarat, a very long time ago. She used to come by the bar my mother ran in the old Augusta port, back before you were born."

Her son returned with a pitcher of lemonade. "I'm sorry for what I said all those years, Mama," he said. "You were right, I guess."

She shooed him away. "C'mon," she said to me. "Might as well show you what you're here for."

Her son tried to help her up but she told him to go back outside and clean the gutters. She picked a walking stick off of her wheelchair and motioned me to follow her out the kitchen door.

We came to a storm shelter built into the ground. The wood on the door had once been painted red, but had flaked away now to almost nothing. A padlock held the doors in place. The old woman wore a necklace on which hung the key. She gave it to me.

"Go on, then," she said. "They're your property, now. She willed them to you."

I opened the door. Sunlight flooded the storm shelter. I saw my aunt's old paper diaries stacked neatly on the ground below.

"There are two dozen of them in all," the old woman said. "I gave her my word that I wouldn't lose them, and I wouldn't read them. And on both counts I kept my word."

I stared at the books. A memory of them slathered in dirt within my mother's greenhouse suddenly came up like nausea. I was afraid I'd be sick where I stood.

"All these years, you held on to them," I said.

"That's right," the old woman replied.

"Why? Why would you help her like that, and for so long?"

"Why?" she echoed, bemused. "Because it was the right thing to do." She chuckled. "Sarat told me you were a sweet boy, Benjamin, but you must understand that in this part of the world, right and wrong ain't about who wins, or who kills who. In this part of the world, right and wrong ain't even about right and wrong. It's about what you do for your own."

She pointed to the west, out past the end of the property, where a few shacks and broken stables pockmarked an otherwise lifeless land. Dust swirled like cursive script under the sun.

"You know, three of the Georgia delegates to the Reunification Ceremony were from these parts," she said. "A few days after they came home, half the town was sick. That's why you don't see much of anything round here these days: plague came through and killed more people here than just about anywhere else in the South outside Atlanta."

She tapped the storm shelter door with her walking stick. "We lived in that little hole, Billy's father and I, for eighteen months," she said. "Lived off canned food, relieved ourselves in a little makeshift bucket we carried out once a week in the dead of night. Almost two whole years like that, until there were too many dead here for the sickness to keep moving."

"Jesus," I said. "That must have been hell."

"That's right," the old woman replied. "And we were the only ones from around here who survived, because we were the only ones who drove to every store from here to three towns over, buying every last can of beans and bottle of water we could find; preparing for it."

It took me a moment to realize what she meant.

"Even a cruel favor is still a favor," the old woman said, "and I repay what I owe. But now you have to take this burden from me. A woman can't die in peace, carrying a secret that big."

☆ ☆ ☆

THAT WINTER, I rented a small cabin by the lake in Nelchina. It was there I read the diaries, and it was there I wrote this.

During that winter I learned about the place where the Chestnuts first lived. I learned how my grandmother and my father and my aunts had fled their home. I learned what the women in black had meant when they said my father had been tested in Patience.

And I learned what had been done to her and what she'd done. In Patience, in Halfway Branch, in that floating prison in the Florida Sea. I learned about the day they'd drowned her, and the day that strange foreign man came to our farm and offered her the means to drown them back.

By the time I'd finished reading, there were no more means of escape, no more means of delusion. Laid bare on the page was the truth of it: she was not some accessory or accomplice. It was her that did it.

That was her last act of cowardice, all those decades later: forcing me to understand her, forcing me to choose what to do with the secret.

So I chose.

On the day I had finally taken from them all there was to take, I piled the diaries in a pyre and set them ablaze. If I had wanted to, I could have sold them for a criminal sum to one of the many wealthy history buffs who collect civil war memorabilia. I could have donated them anonymously to a museum, or to the Civil War Archive Project or to the Committee for Truth and Reunification. But I couldn't keep myself from burning them. It was the only way I had left to hurt her.

☆ ☆ ☆

SHE'S ALMOST GONE from me now. I've lived to be older than she was, older than my parents. But sometimes I still think about what she must have seen in the days after she gave me away, when she finally set foot in the Blue country.

On her way to Columbus she would have driven along the great Sunbelt highway, the road glimmering like a sheet of diamonds—past metropolises packed with the children and grandchildren of the original inland pilgrims. She would have seen the huge looming billboards commemorating Reunification, some of them vandalized with graffiti—the letters "KAR" painted big and blue—by angry Northerners who still believed the South was getting away with it all too easy.

I imagine her among the crowd at the Reunification Day Ceremony, silently wheeling herself to the site of the grand parade, the poison radiating from her hulking frame. The crowd would have parted to let her through—they would have seen her torture scars and her shaven head and her hunchbacked spine and they would have felt pity.

I remember once, when we were swimming in the Savannah, she tried to hold her breath underwater. I sat by the bank and timed her, counting the seconds as best I could. From the size of her, I imagined she would spend an eternity submerged. But her lungs were weak and quickly she surfaced.

As she sucked in the air, I saw a look on her face I'd never seen before. It was relief, as though she'd spent not a few seconds, but an entire lifetime suffocating, and was now finally free.

I wonder, sometimes, if that's the way she must have felt the moment she put the poison inside her and readied to wheel herself into Reunification Square—an overwhelming relief, the opposite of drowning.

THERE'S ONLY ONE PAGE from Sarat Chestnut's diaries I didn't burn. It's the first page of the first book. I carry it in my wallet, and every now and then I read the opening lines.

When I was young, I lived with my parents and my brother and my sister in a small house by the Mississippi Sea.

I was happy then.

ACKNOWLEDGMENTS

I owe Anna Mehler Paperny, Anne McDermid, and Sonny Mehta a debt I can never repay. They are the reason this book exists.

For their support during the two years it took to complete this novel, and more so for their friendship, I am grateful to Donald Richardson, Wesley Fok, Carolyn Smart, Daniel Dagris, Martin Lendahls, Missy Ladygo, and Isaac Pendergrass.

At Knopf, Edward Kastenmeier, Tim O'Connell, and Andrew Ridker guided this project through the editing process with patience and care. I'm a better writer for having worked with them. I am also indebted to Suzanne Smith, Leslie Levine, and Nicholas Latimer for their kindness, skill, and enthusiasm.

And to my mother, Nivin, the bravest, kindest human being I know. Whatever courage I possess is hers, whatever goodness I possess is hers.

And to Theresa, always, and for so, so much.

A NOTE ABOUT THE AUTHOR

Omar El Akkad was born in Cairo, Egypt, and grew up in Doha, Qatar, before moving to Canada. He worked as a journalist at *The Globe and Mail,* and his coverage of a 2006 terror plot earned him a National Newspaper Award for Investigative Reporting (Canada). His other journalistic work includes dispatches from the NATO-led war in Afghanistan, the military trials at Guantánamo Bay, the Arab Spring revolution in Egypt, and the Black Lives Matter movement in Ferguson, Missouri. He now lives with his wife in the woods just south of Portland, Oregon.

A NOTE ON THE TYPE

This book was set in Minion, a typeface produced by the Adobe Corporation specifically for the Macintosh personal computer, and released in 1990. Designed by Robert Slimbach, Minion combines the classic characteristics of old-style faces with the full complement of weights required for modern typesetting.

Typeset by Scribe, Philadelphia, Pennsylvania
Printed and bound by Berryville Graphics, Berryville, Virginia
Designed by Iris Weinstein